"HEY, WHA~~T~~
REGGI~~E~~

"Oh wow," Reggie added as he looked at the bottle his partner held in his hand, "I could've had a V8."

"Very funny," Blaze said, unamused, "I thought I told you to quit calling me that."

"You did and I'm sorry," he said in a voice that obviously wasn't. "It's just that it has such a nice ring."

"If you have to give me a stupid nickname, why couldn't you say Vampo private eye or Vampo PI or maybe Vampo gumshoe?"

"Listen, sweetheart," Reggie said in a deplorable Bogart imitation. "We're private dicks, see, and—"

"Okay, fine," Blaze interrupted, "I'm gonna have to start calling you Sammy Spade."

"Hey, hey," said the black man, "let's not get personal."

"So, no more Vampo Dick?"

Reggie held up three bent fingers, a reminder of the encounter with the vampire Rakz, "Scout's honor."

"You were never a Boy Scout."

"Okay, uh, asshole's honor."

Blaze smiled. "That one I believe."

HARVEST
OF BLOOD

VINCENT
COURTNEY

PINNACLE BOOKS
WINDSOR PUBLISHING CORP.

To Alice Alfonsi—
the world of horror fiction
would be a kinder and gentler place without you
and who the hell wants that?
Let's keep knocking them dead.

PINNACLE BOOKS

are published by

Windsor Publishing Corp.
475 Park Avenue South
New York, NY 10016

First Printing: November, 1992

Printed in the United States of America

Prologue

Maria Vargas floated in a vast sea of white. Her head throbbed as she tried to recall the events prior to her awakening into the brilliant light. Vague snatches of memory drifted in her mind, bobbing into focus then blurring. Men forcing her car to the side of the road. Strong hands grabbing. Pulling. Screams. The hot damp air choking her as she struggled with her assailants. A sharp pain in her arm. An injection that sent a black cloud rumbling through her body and into her brain. She watched the faces of her attackers smear together like a watercolor painting in a rainstorm, as the shroud of darkness swallowed her and later disgorged her into the white brilliance of the room.

Maria tried to sit up, but found that she couldn't move. Her arms and legs were frozen. She couldn't lift her head. Her legs felt like they were made of stone, and her arms felt heavy and thick.

As she struggled against the paralysis, panic swept over her like a horde of army ants crawling across her body; hot waves of tiny tingling feet marching on her ability to reason, their mandibles slashing, stingers stabbing.

She tried to get up. *Oh dear God, please let me move.*

Marie felt a hot tear roll down her cheek and slip off the side of her face. *Por favor, Madre de Dios. Don't let me be paralyzed.*

Maria lay back and tried to gather herself and beat down the panic that threatened her reason. *There is an explanation. Explanation. Think. Stop and think.*

Body frozen.

No?

Yes?

Paralyzed.

No. No. No! Dear God, help me. Help.

Her mind scrambled her thoughts together into a confusing mass of contradictions.

She couldn't move. Her body wouldn't respond.

She crooked a finger.

How?

Can't move.

Wiggled a toe.

She knew she could move. Again she tried to sit up.

No. Arms and legs locked. Trapped.

Got to move.

Just have to try. The drug had—

The drug had—

The drug—

Drug—

They'd given her a drug in Vergaza. *My God, it must have paralyzed me.* As the explanation for her inability to move hit her, she renewed her efforts to try to get up.

Got to get up!

Get up!

Up!

As she struggled to rise, Maria managed to turn her head just enough to see the straps that held her down; straps that meant she was bound, not paralyzed. A trace of relief stamped down the ants of panic, but with the recognition that she wasn't disabled came the

6

dampening effect of knowing that she was still a prisoner of her enemies.

The frightened woman took a deep breath to try to quell her fear. The powerful smell of stale alcohol permeated the air. The odor was strong and Maria felt a queasy sensation in her guts. She took another breath and realized that it wasn't the smell of the alcohol that made her feel sick. There was something else in the air, an odor beneath the alcohol. A sick ripening smell with almost a tangible warmth. Barely noticeable at first, this odor gradually began to overpower the alcohol, by swarming through it like a maggot through carrion. Once before, Maria had smelled such an aroma.

In San Riato.

After the massacre.

It was the foul stench of death.

What is this place?

The room around her was silent, but for a disjointed hissing like the sound of a bunch of old pumps. It was louder one moment, then softer the next, as if whatever was making the sound was moving around the room, or there were a number of them turning on and off. *Hissing pumps. Where could she be that would use a lot of pumps?*

She tried to gather her thoughts, but she could feel herself slipping back into the realm of darkness as the effects of the drug she'd been given began to manifest themselves again. Her eyelids felt heavy. She was unable to keep them open. The hissing sound grew louder and then faded as she struggled against the effects of the drug. *Have to stay awake. Find out where I am.*

She shook her head, trying to loosen the cobwebs that tried to trap her consciousness. She felt weak. Unable to hold on.

As she was about to fall back under the shroud of

forced sleep, she heard another sound that she recognized.

Clip-clop. clip-clop.

It was distant, but seemed to be moving closer.

Clip-clop. Clip-clop.

The sound wasn't menacing in any way, familiar in fact, and yet it was this familiarity, juxtaposed against her unfamiliar setting, that terrified Maria. Her skin crawled with goosebumps and her hair tingled as if tiny demons were tugging on every shaft.

Clip-clop. CLIP-CLOP.

Dear God.

It couldn't be what she thought it was and yet that was the sound. The sound of hooves approaching.

CLIP-CLOP. CLIP-CLOP.

Rotten air crawled into her nose and died as the footsteps continued to advance toward her. She choked back a throatful of bile and shivered with fear. Suddenly, the room around her went black as if some giant vampire had cast his cloak over it. In the darkness, she could still hear the sound coming closer.

CLIP-CLOP. CLIP-CLOP.

Maria opened her eyes and received a jolt of pain when the bright lights hit them. She blinked a few times and the room around her came into focus. She saw squares of white stippled with holes; the squares linked together by strips of white vinyl. A ceiling? Maria recognized the glowing white rectangle above her as being a fluorescent light. She also realized that the clip-clopping sound was gone. The only noise in the room was the bizarre hissing. It was as though the other sound had never been there. She must have been dreaming.

Relieved, she took a deep breath and almost gagged on a powerful stench.

In front of her, a beautiful woman appeared out of

nowhere. Suddenly she was just there. Long blonde hair flowed down her shoulders in a waterfall of shiny tresses. Her ivory skin was cast over delicate features, as if she were an exquisite marble sculpture. Luminous green eyes perfectly matched the glowing emerald gown that she was wearing. She stood in front of the imprisoned woman without saying a word.

Maria tried to speak, but found that her throat was dry, and she could only manage a creaky whisper.

"Where am I?" she asked.

The beautiful woman just stared at her with a peculiar power that made Maria feel uncomfortable. A penetrating stare, almost loving, and yet charged with feral intensity.

Maria wanted to look away, but felt strangely compelled to keep staring into those brilliant green eyes. So bright. Emeralds in white opals.

"Help me," Maria cried in a low raspy voice.

The woman gently brushed a lock of Maria's hair off her forehead, smiled and licked her red lips.

And Maria Vargas screamed.

And screamed.

And screamed.

Chapter One

1

The sun went down and they were open for business.

Christopher Blaze sat at his desk and opened the door to the small refrigerator beside it. He reached into the fridge and pulled out one of the bottles from Miami General. He took a drink from it, stilling the burning inside him, and looked out the big bay window of his office at the skyline of Miami.

Had it been a year ago today? The image of Batiste Legendre on that fateful night flashed in his mind. The incandescent electric-eye worms were crawling across his orbs. The blue light was slithering across the blade of the knife as it flew at Blaze, striking him, cursing him to a life of constant hunger. The words came back. Hateful, eerie, chilling words that had filled the warehouse with their power. *The death that is life. The life that is death. You will live on as one of the undead.* At the time, they were just words; words uttered by a madman. It was a month later that Blaze discovered their horrible truth.

It was a drug bust gone bad. Blown cover. He was trapped in an apartment with no escape, his partners

11

racing to his aid but too late. A trio of gunmen led by drug lord Tony Mancetti opened fire on Blaze, leaving him a pocked and shredded shell, oozing life. The darkness of death overwhelmed him. He remembered being cold, so cold. Then the heat. Hot breath scorching his lungs. A supernatural fire that belched up from the bowels of hell and filled him with life; only not life as he knew it. This new life was dominated by an insatiable thirst; a hunger that sank its fangs into your guts and ripped away at your humanity. The temptations of unspeakable power tainted this new existence. Supernatural abilities of deception and strength that could corrupt your soul and unleash the dark side of your nature. Primitive bloodlust. Murder without conscience. He had seen this dark side in the form of the vampire Yosekaat Rakz, the centuries-old killer he'd brought to justice with a stake through the heart. Through his struggles against the ancient vampire, Chris had seen what the insidious corruption of the soul could do to a man and he wanted no part of it. Every night, he fought a constant struggle against the dark temptations of power presented by his affliction. If he chose to give in to evil, he could rule the night— enslave others to do his bidding—drink fully and deeply from the living, and satiate his violent hunger. But to do so, he would lose all he loved: his wife, Sue; his friend and partner, Reggie Carver; his humanity. Those were prices too high to pay. So he lived his life as best he could; his life as a reluctant vampire.

The door to the office opened and his partner at their detective agency, Reggie Carver, came sauntering in. As usual, he was dressed to the nines in his black silk shirt, buttoned to the top, tan jacket, and pants a shade lighter than the jacket but perfectly matched. Soft leather loafers comfortably hugged his sockless feet. His new haircut was *au courant* among the brothers—

shaved on the sides and square on top. He was looking good.

"Hey, what's up, Vampo Dick?" the black man said smiling. "Oh wow," Carver added as he looked at the bottle Chris held in his hand, "I could've had a V8."

"Very funny," Blaze said, unamused, "I thought I told you to quit calling me that."

"You did and I'm sorry," he said in a voice that obviously wasn't. "It's just that it has such a nice ring."

"If you have to give me a stupid nickname, why couldn't you say Vampo private eye or Vampo PI or maybe Vampo gumshoe?"

"Listen, schweetheart," Reggie said in a deplorable Bogart imitation. "We're private dicks, see, and—"

"Okay fine," Chris interrupted him before Reggie got into his *schtick,* "I'm just gonna have to start calling you Sammy Spade."

"Hey, hey let's not get personal." Reggie said, with mock indignation.

"So no more Vampo Dick?"

Reggie held up three bent fingers, a reminder of the encounter with the vampire Rakz, "Scout's honor."

"You were never a Boy Scout."

"Okay, uh, asshole's honor."

Chris smiled. "That one I believe."

He set the bottle on the desk and leaned back in his plush leather chair. "So did you finish with the Meralda case today?"

"Yeah, she got the pictures and we got the check. Hope she likes the shot I got of her husband's ass sticking out of the closet when he tried to hide."

Reggie pulled a check from his pocket and tossed it on top of Chris's desk.

Chris scooped it up and thumbed it with a finger. "Good deal. I just hope . . ."

Without warning, the door to the office burst open.

13

Out of instinct, Chris whirled around in the swivel chair as Reggie reached for his pistol.

"What the hell?" Carver holstered his piece when he saw the disheveled man stumble in. The man's face was pallid, anemic. His dark moustache looked like a caterpillar frozen against the snowy white skin. His hair hung in sweaty clumps. The front of his shirt was soaked red with blood. He stepped unsteadily into the office and staggered toward Blaze and Carver.

Chris felt a pang of hunger when he saw the bloodstain. A low growl escaped from his lips. He turned away and fought the hunger with a sip of his dinner. He slipped the bottle of blood into his desk.

"Diego!" Reggie cried as he recognized the injured man.

"Reginald," the man whispered and then fell to the floor just in front of them.

Reggie rushed to his side and helped him sit up. Chris got up from his desk and joined his black partner. The man looked at Carver with blank brown eyes.

"Diego, what happened?" Reggie asked softly.

The man stared.

"Diego, what happened?" Carver asked again.

Diego's eyes focused. "I . . . I . . . traced her . . . here . . . to Miami . . ." The man gasped in a slight Spanish accent as he clawed at Reggie's arm. "Help me . . . find."

"Here. Let's get him on the couch," Chris said. He lifted the one-hundred-and-eighty-pound man as if he were a pillow, then carried him over and set him gently on the couch.

"I'll call Miami General and get an ambulance," the vampire detective said as he hurried over to the phone.

"Okay. Do it," Carver replied as he bent down to examine his friend's chest.

Chris dialed the hospital and ordered the ambulance.

"Let's see what happened to you," Reggie said as he opened his friend's shirt to check his wound. The man's chest was soaked with blood and Reggie couldn't see the wound clearly. He got up and went into the bathroom to get a wet towel and the first-aid kit. He came back out and started to swab the blood from the man's chest with the towel. As he wiped the blood away, Carver saw that there was an injury just under Diego's nipple near his heart. The round wound was about the size and shape of a nickel. The outside of the injury was stippled with tiny perforations. Reggie had never seen anything like it.

"Chris, check this out."

"An ambulance is on the way," Chris said as he bent down to look at the wound.

"What is it, aaah! . . ."

He turned away when he saw what was dangling from the injured man's neck. It was a golden crucifix.

"Please take it off of him," Chris said in a low, pained voice as he shielded his eyes with his hand.

"Sorry. Hold on," Reggie said as he slipped the necklace off. Reggie smiled grimly to himself as he tucked the cross into the man's pocket. A cross such as this one had once saved his life during the final confrontation with the vampire Rakz.

"Okay. Now check this out."

Chris bent over and looked at the wound closely, but did not know what to make of it. He touched it and felt the raised puncture wounds.

"Any ideas?"

"No, it looks like he was stabbed with a sharp pipe or something."

"Or something, yeah."

Reggie spread antibiotic ointment over the wound and covered it with a square of gauze. He taped the bandage down with white tape and slipped off the man's bloody shirt.

"Chris, could you get one of my spare shirts out of the closet?"

"Sure."

Chris came back moments later and helped his partner put the clean paisley shirt on the injured man.

"How do you know this guy, Reg?"

"I used to work with him when he was an assistant DA in Dade County. He was a good attorney. Real good. We used to hang out after work and suck down a few brews."

"So why haven't I ever met him?"

"Well, he went back to his native country to practice law a couple of years ago. I haven't seen him since then until tonight. Damn, I hope he's gonna be all right."

"The ambulance should be here soon."

"Cool."

Reggie turned to the injured man. "Did you hear that, Diego? We're getting you some help."

The man nodded feebly and tried to sit up.

"Whoa, man. Just be cool."

"Listen . . . to me," Diego whispered. "Must tell."

"Hold on," Reggie said quietly. He turned to his partner. "Chris." The black man acted as though he were writing a message in the air.

Chris nodded and hurried to his desk to get his pen and pad. He hustled back over the couch.

Diego's eyes were closed.

"Diego? What's this about?"

Painfully, the man on the couch opened his brown eyes. "She's here. She's here. I know it."

"Who?" Reggie said. "Who's here?"

"My . . . wife . . . Took her."

Chris started taking notes as Reggie questioned the injured man.

"Who took her? Who did this to you?" Reggie asked.

16

"Them . . ."

"Who?"

"Bob Handseth . . ."

Chris wrote down the man's name.

Diego tried to get up but was unable to raise himself. He fell back down on the sofa mumbling.

"Diego!" Reggie said, trying to snap the man back to attention. "Who is this Bob Handseth?"

"Real . . ." Diego gasped then continued. "My wife was—the village—Vergaza—must stop them . . ."

Reggie looked at his partner, Chris, with a mixture of concern and confusion.

Vargas drifted off again then opened his eyes. "You help?"

Reggie nodded and asked, "Diego, why did they take your wife?"

"She was going to visit her papa . . . in . . . the village—a meeting—they came . . ."

"Who came? This Handseth guy?"

"Men . . . the Scotchman . . . shouldn't have gone."

Chris looked at Reggie and shrugged. The story made little sense to them.

Diego looked up weakly and clasped Reggie's hand. "Do not go—police. Might be one . . . them . . ."

"One of who?"

Diego coughed up a spittle of blood. "You find her?"

"Yeah, Diego, we'll find her. Now one of who?"

"Take the money from—wallet—use it . . . Is five thousand dollars. Must—sleep."

"Wait."

The wounded man smiled then closed his eyes and passed out into a deep sleep. Reggie tried to rouse the man but Chris said, "Let him sleep."

Reggie nodded and covered Diego Vargas with a jacket that had been hung on the coat rack. He put his finger to his chin.

17

"Wonder what he meant about the police being one of them."

"I wonder what the whole damn thing means."

Reggie scratched his head. "Yeah, it is pretty screwed up."

"So are we going to unscrew it?"

"I am, but I can't ask you to help me. I'm not gonna take Diego's money, except for expenses, and I can't ask you to work for free."

"Hey, since when does a vampire need money. Besides, my wife's a doctor."

"I forgot you were a golddigger," Carver said, wisecracking, to cover his concern for his injured friend.

There was a knock on the door.

"That was quick," Carver said, as he and Chris walked over to the door.

"Come in," Chris said opening the door.

"You guys call for an ambulance?" a fat man in a blue uniform asked, as he gestured with open palm. The man, Raul Benteen, looked like he was not far from needing an ambulance himself. His face was pasty white and his eyes a runny yellow. He looked sick. The girl with him made up for her partner's appearance with a bright smile and pert little breasts that lifted her name tag, Missy Davis, in a pleasant angle.

"Yeah, over here." Reggie said, leading the two attendants into the office and over to the couch where Diego Vargas was lying. The man on the couch was paler than when he'd first arrived. For a moment Reggie thought he was dead, but then Vargas groaned.

"Was he able to tell you what happened to him?" Missy said, her smile fading into a look of concern.

"No. He didn't tell us how he got hurt," Reggie replied. "He has a weird wound on his chest and has lost a lot of blood. I cleaned it and put some antibiotics on it."

"Was he able to talk at all?" she asked as she felt Vargas's pulse.

"Yeah, he told us some things but they were all jumbled up."

"Hmmm," Missy said. "Well, we'll take it from here."

The two attendants wheeled in the stretcher and gingerly lifted Vargas onto it. One of them strapped a blood-pressure cuff on him as the other started securing him onto the mobile stretcher.

"He should be okay," Benteen said as he started to push the stretcher out of the room.

"Call a little later and check," Missy said, as she stood at the front of the stretcher and guided it out the door.

"We will."

Chris and Reggie followed the two attendants as they pushed the stretcher out the door, down the hallway and into the elevator. There was barely enough room in the elevator for the two EMT's and their patient. They squeezed in. Benteen was already puffing from the short trip down the hall.

"He'll be okay," Missy said as she pressed the button for the first floor. The detectives watched as the EMT's and Vargas disappeared behind the closing doors.

"I hope he's going to be okay," Reggie said as he and his partner walked over to the window that looked out on the front of the building and the street below. They could see the ambulance parked in the street in front of the door. "We need to talk to him, when he's more coherent, if we're going to make sense of what he said."

"No shit. He was rambling pretty bad."

The attendants and the stretcher with Vargas appeared as they loaded their patient in the back of the emergency vehicle. Missy got in with Diego while the fat man went to the driver's side. A moment later, they took off, red lights swirling.

"Let's go and look at my notes and see if we can make anything logical out of it," Chris said as he watched the flashing lights disappear into the darkness.

"Okay."

The two men walked back to their office and went inside. Chris sat down on the couch and Reggie joined him. They started going over what Vargas had told them, but had little success in making sense of it.

There was a knock on the door.

"I'll get it," Chris said as he got up and walked over to answer the door.

"Good, I've gotta take a leak."

Reggie went into the bathroom while his partner opened the front door and saw a man in the blue uniform of a paramedic.

"You call for an ambulance?" The tall man, Ronnie Rains, asked. His partner, Lee Conners, stood behind him. Rains was thin and resembled a humanized version of a flamigo, while Lee was stocky with a long nose and a double chin, a pelican in human guise.

Chris looked confused. "Yeah, we did. But somebody already came and got the man. You guys must have had some kind of a snafu."

The ambulance driver shook his head, slapping his long curly hair against his forehead. "I don't know how that could've happened. We're from Miami General and I think we're the only ones that got the call."

"Well, I'm telling you somebody else picked him up."

Reggie came out of the bathroom, saw the two men talking and walked over.

"What's up, Chris?" he asked, then saw that the man was a paramedic. "Hey, what are you guys doing here?"

"Wasting our time it looks like." Rains huffed, looking back at his partner. "I just can't see how it could've happened. You sure you called Miami General?"

"Positive. My wife works there. I know the number by heart."

"Hmm, well, I guess we'll just have to go back empty, Lee."

The stocky man in the back nodded. He had yet to utter a word.

"Sorry, guys," Chris said.

Rains scratched his head as he turned and started walking away, "Just don't see how it could've happened."

"Shitski," Lee said speaking the one and only word he would say.

Chris and Reggie looked at each other. Both were thinking the same thing. Something was wrong with this picture. Chris slowly shut the door.

Reggie spoke first. "That's really messed up. I mean how often does that happen?"

"Not too often, according to those guys."

"I saw a movie one time with Bill Cosby and Raquel Welch called *Mother, Jugs and Speed* that was about ambulance drivers ripping each other off. Maybe that's what happened," Reggie said hopefully although in the back of his mind he was worried about his friend, Diego.

"Maybe. If that's the case, how are we gonna know which hospital they took Vargas to?"

"I'll just have to check around tomorrow and see if I can find him." Reggie wiped his face in frustration, "Shit, why can't anything be easy?"

"It never is."

"I just hope those first guys were for real."

Chris nodded grimly and looked out the window at the city of Miami. "Yeah. Or we may never see your friend Diego Vargas again."

21

Chris got home a little after four in the morning. His wife, Sue, was sitting on their teal sofa in the living room watching an old movie on the television. She sipped a cup of warm milk as the black-and-white images on the screen cast her in shifting shadows. He watched her for a moment, enjoying her beautiful face as she enjoyed the film. She wore one of his oxford shirts that was short enough to expose just the right amount of thigh, and buttoned low enough to reveal just a hint of the firm roundness of her breasts. *You're a lucky man, Blaze,* thought Chris, as he stepped into the room.

"Hey, honey," he said as he came in and kissed his wife. "Whatcha watching?"

"Creepela's 'Late Night Creepers.'"

"And what's the movie for tonight?"

"Some awful thing called *Plan Nine from Outer Space*. God, is it terrible," she said eyes glued to the screen.

Chris unbuttoned his shirt. "Then why are you watching it if it's so bad?"

"Because, besides being one of the only things on, it's also so bad it's hilarious."

He sat down beside her and started to watch. "Hey, what happened? That girl just went from a road in the daylight to the woods at night."

"Oh, it's already done that about four times. Wait'll you see the guy in the Bela Lugosi cape."

As if on cue, a guy holding a cape in front of his face walked stiffly into the scene.

Chris laughed. "What is he supposed to be?"

"Well, at the first of the movie they showed the real Bela Lugosi walking around a suburban house dressed like Dracula. Then he died and became one of the living dead."

"That sounds familiar," Chris said as he thought about the curse that had transformed him. "But that guy isn't Bela Lugosi."

"I know," Sue said. "The host of the show, Creepela, said that Bela Lugosi made some test shots around his house with the director of this thing for a movie they were going to do called *Tomb of the Vampire*, but Bela really did die before they could start the movie. So this director put together footage of Bela and then added this guy with the cape to act as a double. I guess he figured that nobody would notice."

"Smart man," Chris said sarcastically, then changed the subject. "So how was work?"

"The same. Oh, hey, I got a response back from that new hospital that just opened. They said they were very interested in hiring me and asked me if I wanted an interview. I told them yes, so we're set for tomorrow. It's perfect too because they want someone to head up the emergency room night shift."

"That's great. I'm happy for you."

He kissed her.

"So how was your night."

"Not so good, I'm sorry to say."

Sue's brow knitted. "What happened?"

"It was really strange."

Chris started recounting the events of the evening. He told her about the injured Vargas stumbling into their office, the strange wound on his chest, his ramblings about his missing wife and the foul-up with the ambulances.

After he finished, Sue looked thoughtful for a moment and then asked, "And you don't know how the ambulances got mixed up?"

"No. Tomorrow Reggie is going to check the hospitals and see if he can locate Diego."

"It was probably just a mistake."

"Yeah, maybe. So anyway we're gonna check into it and we're also going to try to find his wife."

Sue shook her head. "This is some world we live in. God, I can't imagine what it would be like if you were kidnapped or missing."

Chris nodded. He knew what it was like to have a loved one taken away. "I'll never forget the sick feeling I got in my gut when I knew Rakz had you."

"God," Sue said shuddering, "I still get nervous about that night. Thank God, you were there."

"Yeah, well, I'm just glad my ruse worked. I don't think I could've beat him otherwise. He whipped me every time we . . ."

Sue interrupted him before he relived the anxiety of that night, "The point is that you did beat him. You used your powers to beat him just the way Rakz tricked Reggie. Now can we please change the subject?"

Chris smiled and snuggled up to his wife. "Sure, let's change the subject. What shall we talk about?"

He kissed her warmly on the lips.

"Oh, I don't know. What shall we talk about?"

"I've got it," Chris said as he pulled her close and gazed into her eyes with love, and kissed her softly. "Let's talk about making love."

Sue returned the kiss and said, "Do we have to just talk about it?"

Chris smiled, shook his head and carried her off into the bedroom. Their conversation ended and their passion began.

3

The end of a long night.

The sandman visited Reggie Carver by pitching sandy balls of sleep into the black man's eyes. Carver didn't want sleep to come and tried to fight it. He knew what sometimes happened when he fell asleep. He stared at the television screen across from his bed and tried to keep his eyes focused on the giant bird that flapped across the screen on its way to destroying Tokyo.

"Get 'em, Rodan," Carver mumbled, trying to stay awake.

But the sandman kept tossing strikes, hitting Carver dead in the sleep zone.

Bam! Sleep.

Bam! So heavy.

Tired.

Bam! Sleep.

Sleep.

His eyelids, loaded with sleep, soon drooped over his tired eyes. The sound of the television faded in and out as he tried desperately to remain awake. He sat up and flicked the channel to see what else was on, and saw *Plan Nine from Outer Space* and kept it on. He'd seen *Rodan* five times so he chose from the other "Le Bad Cinema" offering available that night; he'd only seen it four times. The detective adjusted his pillow. Lay back down. Sat back up. Lay down again. Anything to prevent sleep from taking him. But his efforts failed. His need for rest too great.

He fell asleep.

And soon it came, like a horrible slavering beast—the juggernaut that could not be stopped.

The dream.

The nightmare of his final confrontation with Rakz.

In the dream, as in the real life events of that night, Reggie opened the door to his apartment and invited his partner, Chris Blaze, into the house. The smiling Blaze entered, then shimmered and crackled, changing into Yosekaat Rakz. The vampire proceeded to attack

25

the black detective, snapping Reggie's arm, his leg and crushing his hand. But at this point, the dreams diverted from what really happened. In reality, Reggie had saved himself by pulling out the cross on the necklace around his neck and using its power against the vampire. But in the dream, Reggie reached for the cross and it wasn't there. A sense of overwhelming panic swept over him as he patted his chest searching for the crucifix that was supposed to save his life.

It was gone.

Laughing hideously, the vampire smiled and lifted Reggie by the throat.

"The blood is the life, Mr. Carver." Rakz said, mimicking the line from the movie, *Dracula*, then sinking his long teeth into the black man's neck, severing his jugular vein and drinking his blood.

As he was being drained, Reggie hovered over a dark pit where blood-soaked corpses reached up and started to pull him into their world. A bony hand grabbed his ankle and tugged on it. Another hand, rotten flesh, cold against his leg, slipped its taloned fingers around his calf and pulled. Then another hand grasped him. And another. Fingernails clicking. Flesh falling off in chunks as Reggie batted away at the horde of hands. The fetid smell from the pit gagged him as he struggled against the tide of clawed hands that slowly dragged him down into their world. The stench of death was overwhelming. A ripe putrid smell like being trapped in a sauna loaded with the two-day-old road kill. The odor was so strong that Reggie almost woke up, but didn't. He continued on his descent into Hell.

As the filthy hands pulled him down, he tried to grab the walls of the pit to stop his decline, but his hands slipped off the slick sides. Thick warm blood oozed from great open sores in the walls, making them slippery.

The hands swarmed over him, pulling him deeper and deeper into the cavity. He looked up at the opening above him as it began to form a tunnel and shrink into an impossibly small circle of light. A hideously huge eye appeared in the aperture staring at him as if he were a specimen under a microscope. Reggie knew that the bloodshot orb belonged to the vampire Rakz.

He was also at the bottom of the pit.

Reggie tried to scream, but as he did the blood on the walls splattered and poured into his mouth choking him. He couldn't breathe. The blood filled his mouth and ran over his cheeks.

Above him the staring eye narrowed at the corners and Reggie knew Rakz was smiling.

He couldn't breathe.

The pressure from his lungs pushed against his chest and esophagus and began to thump with the beat of his heart. The coppery taste of the blood sickened him.

Without warning, he landed with a thud on the floor. His breath whooshed back into his aching lungs. The blood had vanished. He was awake. The television screen hummed. Carver thought he still heard the thumping heart, but realized that the sound was coming from outside his apartment door—a sound like that of heavy-soled shoes creeping. The footsteps stopped abruptly. Reggie's first thought was of a prowler. He sat up on the couch and rubbed his bleary eyes. The dream had left him uneasy, as it always did. He stood up and walked over to the chair where his shoulder holster hung. He gingerly lifted the pistol from the holster. Slowly he walked toward the door to look out the peephole and see if anyone was out there. There had been a rash of burglaries in the area recently and Carver thought that he might catch one of the thieves in the act.

As he got to the door and peered out the peephole to

see if he could spot anyone, Reggie thought he saw someone standing in the shadows of the stairwell. It was just a hint of a shadow, but enough to arouse his policeman's instincts. He clicked on the outside light, but it didn't go on. Then Carver remembered that it had burned out two night ago. "Shit," he muttered.

Carefully, he opened the door and stepped out into the night air. He held the gun out in front of him.

"If somebody's there by the stairs, I suggest you come out and talk to me," Reggie said, trying to keep his voice steady. He pointed the gun and waited.

Nothing. No one moved from the shadows in the stairwell.

"Come on out," Reggie said, beginning to think that he'd let his imagination get the better of him. That damned dream always messed with his head.

There was still no movement at the stairs. No footsteps running off. No one stepping forward with hands raised. It was as if whoever was there was waiting for Reggie to make his move.

Waiting.

Nothing.

Carver stared into the shadows trying to see any movement. His eyes strained in the darkness and he made a mental note to change the bulb of the light outside his apartment. He took a step forward.

Still nothing but silence and inactivity from the shadows of the stairwell.

"Shit," Carver whispered as he considered his next move.

Abruptly, he heard a fluttering movement to his left. He turned and for a brief instant saw a pair of yellow-green eyes staring at him from the top of the big palm that fronted his apartment on the common grounds. With a great flapping, a bird rose up and vanished into the darkness.

"What the . . . ?" the startled Carver said, as he caught the smudged outline of a large shape swooping into the dark blue sky. He smiled when he saw that it was just a bird.

Suddenly, the outside light of the apartment next door came on, illuminating the stairwell and revealing the presence of no one.

"What's going on out here?" Mrs. Kowalski, Carver's neighbor, said in her creaky voice through a crack in the door. "Reginald, who are you talking to?"

"Nobody. Just thought I heard a prowler."

"A prowler. Oh my." She closed the door and Reggie heard an array of locks clicking as the old lady secured herself.

"There wasn't anybody, Mrs. K. I was hearing things," Carver said in a tired voice. "Mrs. K. Come on."

He hadn't meant to frighten the old lady. She was too paranoid as it was. The slightest noise would have her sticking her nose outside or provoking a late-night or early-morning call to Reggie, saying that she heard someone trying to get into her apartment.

"Mrs. K, I didn't see anyone," he said, trying to alleviate her anxiety.

He heard Mrs. Kowalski's muffled reply. "Maybe so, but I'm not taking chances."

"Okay, Mrs. K.," Reggie said giving up.

Shaking his head, Carver stepped back inside the apartment. He glanced at the clock on the wall and saw that it was almost five-thirty. Soon the sun would be coming up. He had to get some rest. Since he rarely had the dream more than once a night, he went into his bedroom and lay down on the bed. As he tried to sleep, he couldn't get that weird bird out of his mind. It was just a crow and yet he couldn't get rid of the feeling that the bird had been watching him. Those eyes staring at him from . . .

Ah come on, Reggie, Carver thought, *You're just being a chickenshit. A bird's eyes catch a little light and you think it's looking at you.*

He rolled over in the bed and tucked a pillow between his knobby knees. His concern over a bird tugged the corner of his lips into a smile.

"Man, that damn dream is really making me paranoid. Maybe I'll move in with Mrs. K. and we can sit around and imagine all kinds of things are after us," he said, annoyed at his self-perceived cowardice. He closed his eyes and forced himself to think about something else. The face of the vampire, Rakz, appeared, but was quickly erased from the slate of his mind with a swipe of his consciousness. He began to recall his recent dates with Janine and with Shasta and with Karen, and a smile slowly spread across his face. He remembered taking Janine to a little Cuban restaurant where they ate great food and drank sweet wine. Slowly he began to relax, and his conscious recollections drifted into the realm of the subconscious as sleep took him.

Chapter Two

1

After waking up feeling a little tired, Reggie went into the bathroom and turned on the shower. It creaked and shuddered as the water began to flow. Reggie slipped off his underwear and stepped into the hot water. He let the soothing heat pound the remnants of sleep out of his system. He lathered up with soap, cleaning the sweat off of his body, and he started to sing.

After he finished with the shower, Reggie got dressed, ate a bowl of cereal and some toast, then left for the first hospital on his list, Miami General, where Diego was supposed to have been taken for treatment.

As he drove down Biscayne Boulevard towards the hospital, he glanced in the rear-view mirror and saw a blue van that he recalled seeing parked across the street from his apartment. He remembered it because of a spider-web fracture in the right side of the windshield. A couple of cars in back of him sandwiched the van between them. Carver saw nothing suspicious about the van, but its presence gave him the sensation that he was being followed. He turned down a side road to see if the van would follow his car. The van slowed down, but passed, continuing along the street. Carver turned his car around, chalking up his paranoid feelings to fragments of the dream as he drove on to the hospital.

When he arrived at Miami General Hospital, Reggie parked the car and made the long walk from the parking lot to the lobby. Once inside, he went up to the registration desk to ask for help.

An old woman in pink stripes smiled up at him. "May I help you?"

"Yes, I'd like to check on a patient that should have been registered last night. His name is Vargas. Diego Vargas.

"I'll check and see."

Slipping on the horn-rimmed glasses that hung from a gold chain around her neck, she looked at the register and ran her bony finger down the long list. After completing her search, she took off the glasses, letting them slip down to the end of the necklace. She looked up at Carver and shook the tight curls of grey hair on her head. "No, there's no 'Varga Diegovargas' here."

"No ma'am," Reggie said holding back a laugh, "His last name is Vargas. First name Diego."

The pink lady pursed her withered pink lips in aggravation. "Well, why didn't you say so?"

Huffing, she put her glasses back on—with liver spotted hands—flipping her pages over and looked down the list again. She mumbled as she traced a line with her bony finger down the list of patients. When she came to the end of the last page, she took off her glasses and looked up at Reggie.

"No, There's no Vargas. There's a Marcos and a Verdos, but no Vargas."

"Are you sure? He came in last night."

Again the puckered lips appeared. "Sir, I have been a pink lady here for over ten years and I know if a patient is registered, but just to be sure I will check again."

She slipped on her glasses and began scanning the list of patients again. Her mumbling began to take on a coherent form. "Been here. Ten years. Oughta know if a patient's on the list. Damn fool youngsters."

"Excuse me, please," an oddly accented voice behind Reggie said.

Reggie recognized it immediately as the voice of the weirdo whom he'd met in this same hospital one year ago after he was injured in his fight with Charlie Burnson. Reggie had dubbed him Mahatma Goondick because of the strange pseudo-Indian accent. Reggie also remembered that the man had some strange philosophical notions about expression through bodily functions.

"Ah, do I not know you?" the man said, adjusting the turban on his head. He wore a weird gown that looked like a converted bathrobe. It barely covered the pot gut protruding from his thin brown frame.

Reggie smiled, "I don't think so."

"Yes," the man said shaking a long finger at Carver, "you are the man that hates paperwork."

"No, I love paperwork. Just love it." Reggie said, hoping that the man would go away.

But he didn't.

"Ah, then you have found the balance of expression. No longer do you like the trees from which the paper is made and hate your work creating a conflict that results in the blockage of your bowels. Are you regular in your movements?"

"Yeah, I spend most of my day in the bathroom, now if you would excuse me . . ."

"Oh joy! Great Vishnu, we have another happy minion."

He farted loudly and did a little dance.

"No, he's not here." The pink lady said with a finality

born of irritation.

"Huh," Reggie said, still trying to deal with the strange man's behavior. The man spun about, slapping his canvas sandals on the tile floor of the lobby.

The pink lady didn't seem to notice.

"Mr. Vargas is definitely not here at Miami General."

"What about a John Doe?"

"Doe. Doe. No. No Doe," she said, confident she would've remembered the name. "There's a Fred Dome, but there's no one named John Doe. Must be at another hospital."

"No, ma'am, a John Doe is an unidentified patient. Someone who came in without ID."

"Oh."

She gave the list a perfunctory search. "Sorry, no unidentified patients."

"Thank you," Reggie said then turned to leave.

The old lady snorted.

"Excuse me," he said as he stepped around the little dancing man. The man farted one last time and said, "Express yourself."

Reggie left and proceeded to go to all the other hospitals on his list. Each of which turned out to be a dead end. The answers were all similar.

"No sir, no patient named Diego Vargas."

"Sorry. No Vargas."

"Have you tried Miami General?"

"No, no one by that name."

"No, no unidentified patients."

"Sorry."

As he stood at the registration desk of his last possibility, Sisters of the Faith Hospital, the newest facility in the city, he hoped that he would have some luck finding his friend. If not, he was afraid that Diego Vargas had met with foul play.

34

"Afternoon," he said in a cheery voice, "I am looking for a patient. His name is Diego Vargas."

"One moment," the girl at the desk said as she checked her computer files. "I'm sorry, sir. We have no Vargas here."

"Damn! How about patients without IDs, listed as John Doe?"

She checked again, but found nothing.

"Reggie!"

Carver turned toward the sound of the woman's voice and saw Dr. Sue Blaze walking toward him. She was dressed in a smart navy blazer, red pin-striped shirt and white skirt. Blue leather pumps and diamond earrings completed the ensemble.

"Hey, Sue. New do?"

"Yeah, I just had it done. Maurice says it takes years off my face."

"What do you want to look like a teenager for? You looked good as a twenty-one-year-old."

"Thirty, but who's counting. Chris told me you were going to be checking around at the hospitals. Did you have any luck finding your friend?"

"No. None at all. It's like Diego just vanished into thin air. I'm starting to get the feeling that those guys last night weren't really ambulance drivers at all. God, I hope we didn't give Diego to his enemies on a silver stretcher."

"You didn't."

Reggie popped his fist in his palm. "Damn, this case is a bitch. We need to find Diego so we can talk to him and tie up some of these loose ends."

Sue put a warm hand on her friend's shoulder. "Well, I have faith that you and Chris will solve it."

"Yeah," Reggie said, perking up. "We will." He smiled. "So what are you doing here?"

"I have an interview for a job as the head of the

35

graveyard shift in the ER."

"ER. Emergency Room."

"Very good."

"Hey, I'm a detective."

"I hope I do well in the interview. Been awhile since I've done one of these."

"You'll kick ass."

"Thanks," Sue said glancing at her watch. "Well, I have to get going so I won't be late. Hope everything works out with your friend."

"I hope so too." Reggie said, but somewhere in the back of his mind he didn't think that it would.

"See you."

"Later."

Sue continued down the hall as Reggie walked out to his car and headed for home. He didn't see the blue van with the web windshield parked on the other side of the parking lot. The driver of the van cranked his engine and started to follow.

2

As Sue walked down the hallway toward the office of Dr. Gary Charles, the chief of staff at Sisters of the Faith Hospital, she noticed that there wasn't the usual throng of hospital personnel bustling down the hallways like there was at Miami General. The hallways were deserted, devoid of life. The quiet left Sue with a strange feeling of apprehension. She wondered why there was no one around. She followed the directionals to the Chief of Staff's office. On the way, she passed a couple of doctors and she began to feel a little better. Perhaps the deserted section wasn't open yet; after all, the hospital was brand new.

Beside the door she saw the placard indicating the

office of Dr. Charles, and she opened the door.

Once inside, the Chief of Staff's secretary, Myra Lee, greeted Sue. "You must be Dr. Blaze," she said in a thin reedy voice that set Sue's teeth on edge.

"Yes, I am."

"Have a seat. Can I get you something? Coffee? Tea?"

"No thank you, I'm fine."

The woman was oddly shaped, with a chunky frame set on long thin legs. She had a long nose tapered to a point. Her eyes were set rather far apart. She reminded Sue of a nervous bird as she got up from her desk and walked over to the coffee pot to pour herself a drink.

"You sure?" Myra said holding up her cup.

"Yes, I'm fine."

"Okay, just want you to feel comfortable."

Then stop talking, Sue thought, then felt guilty for being so mean. The woman seemed pleasant enough, but her voice gave Sue the yips like fingernails on a blackboard.

"Have a seat and I'll tell Dr. Charles you're here," Myra said, as she set her coffee cup down and walked toward the doctor's door.

Sue smiled politely and sat in the chair. "Thank you."

A moment later, Myra came back out. "Dr. Charles says to come right in."

Sue got up, straightened her skirt and went into the office.

The first thing Sue noticed about the office of Dr. Gary Charles was its immaculate condition. The walls were adorned with perfectly straight pictures in perfectly straight frames. His desk had perfect stacks of paper and a perfectly arranged phone. The desk looked like an advertisement for *Better Offices and Gardens*. The only aspect about the room that wasn't exactly right was the lighting, which was unusually subdued. In fact the only light in the whole room was that from a small lamp on the doctor's desk.

The chief of staff was as well kept as his office. Not a hair was out of place on his well-coiffed head. His clothes were pressed and impeccable—tailored to his broad shoulders and slim waist. Sue could tell that he kept his nails manicured—they had a healthy sheen and perfectly even shape. He had perfect even teeth that were movie-star white. All in all, Dr. Charles was an exceptionally handsome man except for a large mole with sprouting hair that glared at her from his forehead. The mole was so large that she could not help staring at it. She caught herself before he noticed her ogling and worked up a smile.

"Hello, Dr. Blaze," he said, his voice rich in tone and timbre. "I appreciate your interest in Sisters of the Faith. Have a seat."

"Thank you."

"Please excuse the low light, but I have a headache and this light helps soothe me." He smiled.

"Well, if you don't feel well, maybe, I should . . ."

"No, no, I'm fine. Please let's keep our appointment."

Sue smiled and sat in the plush chair in front of the desk.

"So," Charles said, as he looked at the file in front of him, "I see you've been working at Miami General for the past three years? A fine hospital."

"Yes, it is."

"So I guess my first question is why do you want to leave?"

Sue had anticipated his query and had prepared an answer for it. "Because Miami General is such a fine place."

A furrow of curiosity dug its way across the doctor's brow, causing the mole to dip down on his forehead.

"How do you mean?"

Sue ignored the mole and explained. "Well, Miami General has already been established. Everything is running well there and frankly I want to be part of something new, a part of starting another fine hospital."

"Hmmm, I see. And you think that would be Sisters?"

"I would hope that I could help it to accomplish that goal, yes."

Charles smiled and the mole danced on his forehead. He looked over her resume for a moment then spoke. "Your credentials are impeccable. I see you also do a lot of charity work."

"Yes, I like to donate at least ten hours a week to people less fortunate than myself."

"Hmm, I see no problem with that."

Charles leaned forward in his chair. "Dr. Blaze, I will be frank with you. I have already spoken to Dr. Marston at Miami General and he endorses you fully. I need not go through your career goals and all the other things that are asked in these tiresome interviews. I will offer you the position based on your past experience and Marston's recommendation."

Sue smiled. "I appreciate that."

"Your pay will be thirty percent more than it has been at Miami General, as we at Sisters of the Faith like to keep our employees for a long time."

"That's wonderful," Sue said smiling. "Thank you again." Thirty percent! She could hardly wait to tell Chris.

"I assume you will give your employers the customary two weeks?"

"Of course," Sue nodded careful to maintain her professionalism in the face of the exciting and unexpected news. She knew it was rare to be given a job

39

so quickly.

"Well, that's good, although unnecessary," Charles said waving his hand.

"How so?" Sue said knitting her brow.

"In my conversation with Dr. Marston, I informed him of the urgency in which we need help in the ER. I asked if we could have you a little early."

"How early?"

"Two days."

"Two?" Again the unexpected quickness of the job's arrival stunned her.

"Yes, we are in dire need. Our former head of the ER passed away suddenly. Needless to say, we were caught unawares."

"What did Dr. Marston say?"

"He said that they could work something out. Is that okay with you?"

"Fine," Sue said. She never did like the lame-duck tendencies of the final two weeks of a job.

"Good," Charles said as he got up from his leather chair. "Then we will see you in two days."

"You sure will."

Sue stood up and extended her hand. "Thank you very much Dr. Charles, and I know that I can be a great asset to your hospital."

"Yes, I'm sure you will be," the doctor said, as he started to usher Sue out. "Now Myra will give you the documents we'll need you to fill out for taxes and Social Security. I believe she'll also have some insurance forms for you to complete."

"Great."

The doctor stopped as he got to his door. He shook Sue's hand again. "I look forward to having you on staff."

"Thank you again."

Sue left the office and approached the secretary at

her desk.

"So," Myra said, "how'd you do?"

"Well, I need you to give me all the forms I need to fill out, like taxes and insurance."

"So you got the job?"

"Yes I did," Sue said excitedly.

"Great. You're gonna like working here. It's a great place."

"I hope so."

"Oh, you will."

The woman smiled.

For a moment, Sue felt unreasonably anxious. There was something about the woman's smile. It had a childlike quality as though she knew some awful secret.

"You'll just love it," Myra said emphasizing the word *love* in that high-pitched screech that sounded like a harpy's cry.

"I'm sure," Sue said politely.

The girl turned away and started getting the proper paperwork.

Sue dismissed her feelings about the strange smile as if they were a fancy created by her edginess when the woman spoke. There was nothing seditious in her grin.

Myra went to a file and pulled out several forms, then walked over and handed them to Sue. "You can take these home with you or fill them out here. Just get them back to me before you start, so I can get them to accounting."

"Okay."

Sue sat down and started to fill out the forms. She didn't want to put it off and have to make an extra trip.

After completing the forms, she gave them to Myra, who smiled and put them in the file box labelled outgoing.

"We'll see you in a couple of days, Dr. Blaze," she said in her reedy voice.

41

"Yes. Thanks for your help."

"It's my job."

Sue smiled and went down the hallway toward the exit. Suddenly something the girl said struck her as odd. *"See you in a couple of days, Dr. Blaze."* This Myra had definitely said a couple of days. Now how could Myra have known that Sue would be starting in two days instead of the customary two weeks? The answer was one of two things. Either Charles had told her beforehand of his decision to hire Sue, or else the Chief of Staff's secretary was an eavesdropper, who had been listening at his door. Sue figured that the latter was the case as Charles didn't seem to be the gabby type. Perhaps Myra's covertly obtained knowledge of Sue's impending employment was the reason for her knowing smile. Maybe Myra enjoyed her little secrets. She did strike Sue as bordering a little on the odd side. Oh well, she wouldn't have to deal with Myra too much, so let her have her little fun; she wasn't hurting anybody. Still she didn't like a snoop and would be on her toes when she was around the chirpy voiced birdwoman.

Sue continued walking down the hallway until she reached the lobby. When she stepped out into the orange glow of sunset, her apprehension melted in the sun's warmth. Dusk was her favorite time of the day because it signalled the approach of the night and the rebirth of her husband. She could hardly wait to get home and tell him the good news. She got in her car, headed out into the traffic and was on her way.

When she got to their home in the outskirts of the city, it was about fifteen minutes until sundown. She parked the car in the garage and made her way into the house. The minute she stepped inside, the phone rang. She hurried over and picked up the receiver.

"Blaze residence."

"Sue, this is Arn Marston. We're in a bit of trouble down here and were hoping that you could come in a little early."

She could hear shouting in the background.

"What happened?"

"There was an accident involving a busload of kids and we've got a shitload of injuries. We might lose a couple if we don't get to them right away. There was also a gang-fight downtown and some of the kids that were hurt there are also showing up. It's a fucking madhouse."

It sounded like a madhouse. She looked at her watch.

"I'll be there as fast as I can."

Marston sighed. "Great. See you in a bit."

"Right."

Sue hung up and quickly scribbled a note telling Chris that she had had to leave early. She tossed it on the coral carpet where he'd be sure to see it, and she left for Miami General. She would not see Chris again until morning.

3

The afternoon sun disappeared into the skyline of Miami. Chris Blaze awakened from his sleep and took his first breath of the night. His hunger growled at him and for a moment he felt the urge to sink his teeth into flesh and drink warm blood. He fought the feeling, as he always did, and got up. Slipping into his robe, he left the darkness of the room and stepped into the hallway leading to the kitchen. When he arrived at the kitchen, Blaze went to the refrigerator and took out his supply of nourishment for the night. Closing the fridge's door, he wondered if Sue would be able to continue to supply him with blood if she got the job at the new hospital. He was about to go and ask her when he saw the note she'd left him: "Dear Hubbie, Had to go into work early. I have a surprise for you when I get back. Love, Wifey."

"A surprise, huh?" Chris said to himself, then smiled.

He took a sip of blood from the bottle to quell his screaming gut and then poured the rest into his thermos. His hunger began to settle into the dull ache that was its constant state. Blaze would never fully satiate himself, for fear of losing his humanity to the dark side of his nature.

There was a knock on the door.

Blaze put the thermos down on the kitchen counter and went to answer the door. Peering out of the peephole, he was surprised to see Reggie standing outside. The black man was playing the drums on his chest and bobbing his head up and down to the rhythm. Blaze opened the door.

"Keith Moon, you ain't," Blaze said, commenting on Carver's impromptu drum session.

"I got more rhythm in my little finger than Keith Moon does in his entire body."

"What?" Blaze said raising the pitch of his voice at the incredible statement.

"Hey, the guy's dead."

Blaze shook his head at the morbid joke. "C'mon in."

"Damn critic."

Reggie stepped into the house and walked over to the sofa and sat. He enjoyed coming to the Blaze home. It possessed the flavor of Miami, with its flamingo, teal and white color scheme. The walls were a light, coral pink, the shade of the graceful birds with which Miami was identified. A huge abstract of flamingos flocking in a teal pond hung above the fireplace of white coral. Bright lights illuminated the entire house, creating almost a sunny climate. Since both Blazes worked at night and one of them would be burnt to a crisp if he came in contact with the real sun, the pseudo-sunlight was the closest thing that they could get to the real deal. The teal couch was comfortable, not like the lumpy old colonial couch that his mom and dad had given him. He hated the look of that couch but couldn't bear to part with it. It still had a couple of good years in it. The couch was a testament to Carver's frugal nature.

"So what are you doing here, Reg? I thought we were going to meet at the office."

"I was close by so here I is," Reggie said, motioning palms up with his hands.

"Want something to drink?" Chris asked, as he walked over to the kitchen counter and picked up his thermos.

"Uh, something a little less, uh, red than what you're having if you don't mind. You got Dr. Pepper?"

"No."

"Mr. Pibb."

"Negative."

Carver shook his head. "Mountain Dew?"

Blaze opened the refrigerator and listed the available choices.

"Orange juice. Apple juice. Grape juice. Gatorade. Water."

Carver shook his head. "Jeez, my body can't deal with it if it ain't got fizz and chemicals."

"How about Gatorade?" Chris suggested holding up the bottle while looking at the label. "That's got some chemicals in it."

"I guess I can do without my fizz. Gatorade then."

"How'd it go today?" Chris said, as he poured Carver a glass of Gatorade, dropping a couple of ice cubes into the glass. He picked up the glass and walked into the living room.

"Man, I have been all over this city to every hospital

45

and not one had Diego Vargas registered there."

"Shit. So those guys might have been phonies."

Chris handed the glass of the tangy lemon-lime drink to his partner.

"Thanks. That's what I figured, too."

Reggie took a sip of the drink. "Not bad. Hey, Chris, you think maybe those fake ambulance guys were the ones that hurt Vargas? Maybe he got away from them and they followed him to our place."

"Could be. But how the hell could they have access to an ambulance?"

"Hell, I dunno," Reggie shrugged, "I suppose they stole it."

"Hold on," Chris replied, "they stab this guy or whatever those marks were, and then they steal an ambulance to trick us, and take him away. That's supposing a lot."

"Yeah, it is."

"Are you sure somebody didn't make a mistake at the hospital?"

"I made them all check twice, some of them three times, but nobody had a Vargas checked in."

Chris suddenly had a thought.

"Wait a second," he said stabbing the air with a finger, "I hate to say this, but maybe he wouldn't be in a hospital."

"What do you mean?"

"Well, they wouldn't take him there if he was—dead."

"Shit, that's right," Reggie said as he stood up gulping down the rest of his drink and setting the empty glass on a coral coaster. "Let's go."

"Where to?"

"To the county morgue."

Chris nodded. "Just let me get a shower and put on some clothes."

46

"I wouldn't want you coming with me naked."

"You know what I meant."

Carver grinned as Chris got up and disappeared down the hallway that led to the bathroom. Reggie looked around and found a magazine to read while he waited. As he flipped through the pages of *Cosmopolitan*, Sue's favorite mag, he couldn't get out of his mind the chilling vision of his friend, Diego, lying on a slab amongst the dead of Miami. He set the magazine down and flicked on the television. The set popped and slowly a picture began to fade in. Reggie groaned when he saw that it was one of those manipulative pieces of trash television known as a thirty-minute commercial. The programs pretended to be talk shows or even science programs that seek to discover new and wondrous products, but in reality they were nothing but overlong commercials. The particular product being hawked on "Colossal Discoveries" was the Vac-U-Cut, a strange hair-cutting device that sucked up your hair while cutting it. Reggie watched for a moment as the phony host feigned astonishment at the rather mediocre haircut produced when the "inventor" rubbed the Vac-U-Cut over a willing sap's head. The shill then forced a smile when confronted with his newly styled hair and professed his everlasting gratitude to the inventor of this wonder device.

As Reggie clicked to another channel, he wished that whoever had started this particularly abhorrent strain of advertising would be sentenced to being covered in Didi Seven then slowly fileted with a Ginzu knife while listening to disco hits of the seventies.

"All right," Carver said when he saw the familiar face of Pat Buttram, Mr. Haney of the *Green Acres* show. *Green Acres* was one of his favorite shows. The irreverent humor was suited well to his tastes. Haney and the bumbling Mr. Hank Kimbell were his favorite

47

foils to the beleaguered Oliver Wendall Douglas, with Lisa Douglas and Eb the handyman, close seconds. He settled back and watched as Haney tried to sell Douglas a free trip to Pixley.

As the show ended, Chris came out from the bedroom. He was dressed in a plain blue oxford, jeans and deck shoes. His hair was slicked back with mousse, the easiest style to manage for a man who was unable to cast a reflection.

"You ready?" Chris said as he finished buckling his belt.

Reggie clicked off the television. "Let's ramble, bramble."

The two private detectives left the house and got into Reggie's car. Carver started the car which rumbled to life.

"I hope we're wrong about Diego," he said as he pushed the gear shift into reverse.

"We'll find out."

Reggie nodded grimly, backed out and headed down to the morgue.

4

"I'm sure they're sticking with the case. Carlos followed the black guy to every hospital in town today," the DTF agent said to his boss, whom he'd called long distance in Central America, to update him on the Vargas incident.

"They could interfere with the whole operation," the boss said in his thickly accented voice. "Are ye sure they are not giving up?"

"Yeah, we got a man on them right now," the drug agent said, glancing up from his desk and out of the office to see who was coming. He waited until the man passed.

"So what should we do?" he whispered into the phone.

"I wan' ye to keep on them and make sure that whoe'er they talk to does'na tell them too much."

"And if they do?"

"You know wha' needs to be done."

"The Children?"

"Aye, the Children."

5

The county morgue was not one of Carver's favorite places. It was always cold there and the smell was strictly *Eau de Stiff*. The bodies were tucked into drawers like flesh files. The vital information for their file: heartbeat, brain function, personality, was lost for good. The files simply waited to be tagged, burned or buried.

As they arrived at the morgue, they were greeted by their buddy, Ruther Pillman. Pillman was a rotund man with a broad laugh and a propensity for gallows humor that came with the job. Reggie called him the Stereotype Man, Stereo for short, because *all* medical examiners in the movies had a morbid sense of humor and the fat man fit the mold to perfection. Ruther munched on a tomato sandwich which he crushed between slightly buck teeth. He saw Blaze and Carver come into his office.

"Hello, gents, long time no see," Pillman said, as he got up from his desk and waddled over to shake the detectives' hands.

"Ruther."

"Chris."

"What's going down, Stereo Man?"

"Oh, about seventy-five of our guests. Six feet

down," Ruther said pointing a knockwurst-sized finger at the floor.

Reggie laughed and Chris managed a smile. Being one of them, the dead were not one of the vampire's favorite topics of humor.

"So, to what do I owe the honor of your presence?"

"We're looking for someone," Reggie said sitting on the corner of Pillman's desk.

"And this someone's name?" Pillman took a bite of the sandwich. A tomato seed clung to his chin.

"Diego Vargas," Reggie said staring at the seed and wiping his own chin hoping that Ruther would get the hint.

Pillman missed the subtle tip and took another bite of the sandwich. "And what happened to this someone named Diego Vargas?"

Chris explained the occurrences of the previous evening while Ruther took out a little pad of paper and a nub of a pencil and started to write down the information, pausing every so often to scratch his porcine nose. With his turned-up snoot, his rotund figure and round face, Ruther looked a little like the first version of Porky Pig.

After Chris finished the story, Ruther stopped writing and went over his notes. The tenacious tomato seed still clung to his chin, "So we may have a guest named Diego Vargas. Spanish guy. Checked in last night around seven o'clock."

"Probably. We don't really know. He may have made it to the hospital and then died later," Chris said.

"Okay, and we don't know which hospital picked him up."

"It was supposed to be Miami General but like I said we aren't sure because of the mix-up."

"Sounds funky."

"Yeah," Reggie said, "it does."

"So what's this cat look like?"

"He's about thirty-five," Reggie said as he flicked the seed off Pillman's chin. "Black hair. Dark eyes. He has a pencil-thin moustache. Six feet. Goes about one-eighty."

"And," Chris added, "he has a weird round mark on his chest."

"What kind of a mark?" Ruther said wiping his chin to make sure Carver had gotten whatever it was that he'd removed.

"Like a circle made by thick needles."

"That is weird."

"So can you check for us?"

Ruther took a bite of his tomato sandwich and said through a mouthful of food, "Give me some time to run this down. Say about an hour and come back."

"Okay," Chris said, "we'll be back in an hour."

"That'll work out." Reggie said, "I set up a meeting with Penny Ante to see if he knows anything."

"Good deal," Chris replied, "We've got a lotta things that we don't know and maybe he can help us."

He turned to the rotund Pillman. "We'll call you before we come back."

"Okay. Hey, do either of you want the rest of this?" Ruther asked as he held out the sandwich, which oozed a gelatinous mixture of tomato and mayonnaise.

"No thanks," Reggie said as his stomach churned, "I've had my quota of ptomaine for the year."

"Chris?"

"No, I'm trying to cut down."

"Seems a shame to waste," Ruther said as he inhaled the remains of the sandwich then turned and started back to the section of the morgue where they kept the corpses. "See you in a bit."

"See ya."

Chris and Reggie left for The Pig's Butt Inn, the bar

where they were going to meet James "Penny Ante" DeClick.

The Pig's Butt Inn was the kind of place that novelists always used as a setting for clandestine meetings between their heroes and shadowy characters. It was a dark and dingy place with holes in the carpet and dusty pool tables. A smell like musty age, dirty dishwater and ancient vomit permeated the air with its stench. The barest lighting kept the place and its customers shrouded in a murky ooze. That was the way they liked it. The bar was a cesspool; its customers the shit of society. But even the crap of the crop thought the Pig's Butt Inn was an awful place and they only frequented it because the Inn served the cheapest beer in town and provided shelter against the law. It was in this place that Blaze and Carver were to meet James "Penny Ante" DeClick.

Before his slide into the underbelly of the city, James DeClick had been a prominent penny stock broker. He had owned his own firm and hired only the best salesmen he could find, even if they had no knowledge of the stock market. He only wanted to sell product and would tell his men to say anything to further that end. His firm did well for quite some time until it was discovered that DeClick and Associates was lying to its clients about the stocks it sold them, and was bilking them out of hundreds of thousands of dollars. DeClick was arrested for fraud, convicted and served two and a half years in prison, where he was saddled with the nickname Penny Ante after the cons found out about his association with penny stocks.

When he got out of prison, he emerged with a ruined reputation and a vicious habit for ice—methamphetamine. In order to supplement this addiction, he'd formed a network of informants from men or friends of men with whom he had served time or from shady characters out of his past. He had snitches all around the city in the most unlikely places. One might be a stew bum on a street corner, the other a corrupt cop on the take. It didn't matter as long as they could provide information that he could sell. James DeClick was a money-grubbing, no-character, ice junky whose only redeeming quality to the detectives was that he had his finger on the pulse of the city.

Chris and Reggie sat in a booth with torn vinyl seats. Both were careful not to touch the underside of the table for fear of acquiring a wad of gum or the former contents of a biker's nose on their pants. The waitress, a huge fat woman nicknamed Toothpick, approached their table. She acquired the unusual moniker because of the huge gaps in her teeth between which she says she can slide a man's dork and pick her teeth while giving him a blowjob. It was a horrible vision but it suited the disgusting creature that inspired it. Toothpick had huge jiggling rolls of pockmarked blubber that were exposed by her short shirt and tight jeans as she waddled towards the table.

The men that had been following them for most of the night sat in the booth behind them.

"What do you two cops want?" Toothpick asked in a voice that sounded about as friendly as a pit bull's growl.

"Nothing, Pick," Reggie said. "And we're not cops anymore."

"Once a cop always a cop." She sniffed. "So what do you want?"

"We're waiting for somebody."

"Hey, the boss don't like people that take up space."

"Then why are you here? You take up three spaces," Reggie said.

Chris suppressed a laugh. He wanted to maintain peace. Toothpick just smiled at the jibe as if she was proud of her girth. She grabbed a handful of blue-veined blubber and squeezed it. "Suck on this, Carver."

"Jesus H. Christ," Reggie grimaced as he looked away from the flesh, marbled with blue. "Ugh."

Toothpick cackled, shaking her flab.

"Jesus."

Chris laughed at his partner's contorted face.

"Next time you'll keep your cracks to yourself. Now what'll you have?" she said.

Reggie shuddered one last time.

"A beer," he said adding hastily, "In a bottle. I'll open it at the table."

Carver didn't want to take any chances that the foam on top of his beer had been provided by the hefty waitress's mouth.

"How about you, blue eyes?"

"He'll have a bloody Mary," Reggie said, then smiled at Blaze, who grinned sarcastically in response to the in-joke.

"A beer and a Mary."

The fat woman waddled off in an obscene parody of a sexy wiggle.

"Why do we always have to meet DeClick in a place like this," Chris said.

"He says it has drama."

"The plague is more like it," Chris added as he looked around the bar at the assortment of rough-looking characters. One man caught his eye—a huge Oriental with a myraid of tattoos stippled on his body, and capped by a curly cow pie penned on top of his bald head. The Oriental looked grimly at Blaze, who turned away. The ex-cop knew that sometimes a stare was all that it took to start trouble in this kind of a place. Blaze could still feel the man's eyes on him when Reggie tapped him and pointed to the door from where DeClick emerged.

The informant spotted them and waved a hand in the air. He walked over to the table.

"Hello, gentlefolk, and what may I do for you this bright and cheery evening?"

"Have a seat, Penny."

"Thank you, kind sir."

Reggie rolled his eyes. He hated the false politeness that Penny always displayed—his phony attempts at projecting an air of respectability. Carver knew that Penny was a slimeball. Chris knew that Penny was a slimeball. And even Penny knew that he was a slimeball; so why the pretense?

Penny sat at the table. He pulled a hanky from his pocket and dusted the table off. He was a thin man with hollow eyes from overindulgence of ice. He was dressed in a worn blue suit, his tie was spotted with stains. He had scuffed loafers on his feet. He would have been truly pathetic if it had not been for the arrogance he displayed.

"Now what is it I can do for you, gentlemen?"

"A friend of ours and his wife are missing and we have a couple of names to check out," Chris said opening his notebook.

"And the names?"

"What do you know about a guy named Bob Handseth?"

"Bob Handseth?" DeClick said rubbing his chin, "Never heard of him."

"What about the Scotchman?"

DeClick's eyes lit up. "You mean the Scotsman?"

"Maybe," Chris said, "Who's he?"

"Ah, that is the hundred-dollar question."

Reggie reached into his pocket and took out a hundred-dollar bill. He handed it to Penny then pulled it away before the thin man had a chance to grab it. "Who's this Scotsman?"

DeClick smiled coyly and withdrew his hand. "Colin Macdow is his name. He's the man down in a Central American country called San Miguel. I think he owns some property in Miami, too. Puts on a front as a respectable businessman but he's a king snowman to be sure."

Chris looked over at Reggie who gave him a look that said they were onto something.

"So Macdow's bigtime into drugs?"

"Very perceptive, my friend. What else does San Miguel have to offer except a passel of peasants?"

"How did a Scotsman become 'the man' in a Spanish-speaking country?" Reggie asked.

Penny smiled. "That's all I know about the man. Asking questions about Colin Macdow can get you killed."

"Hmm," Reggie said turning to Chris, "I wonder what Macdow's connection is to Diego Vargas's disappearance."

"I don't know," Chris replied, "Was Diego a prosecutor over there?"

"I don't know. Could be."

DeClick interrupted. "Gentlemen, do you require my services any longer?"

"You know anything else about this Macdow? Telling us he's from San Miguel wasn't exactly worth a C-note."

"That's all I *want* to know about the Scotsman. Macdow maintains a very low profile and I don't think he likes prying eyes." Penny shrugged and then put on his phony smile. "However, I can check around about this Vargas fellow you mentioned, if you'd like. What happened to him?"

Reggie quickly explained the circumstances of the disappearance of his friend.

"I think I may be able to be of assistance." DeClick

paused, waiting for Carver to respond, which he did.

"How much?"

"A discount of two hundred."

Carver looked at his partner who gave him the go-ahead.

"Okay, but you better have something good or you don't get a penny."

"Will there be anything else?"

"No."

"Then," Penny extended his hand.

Reggie handed him the bill.

"Thank you. I'll be in touch."

As Penny Ante DcClick left the bar, he was followed out by one of the men who had been sitting behind Reggie and Chris.

"So the plot thickens," Reggie said. "We need to find out what Diego was investigating before his wife was kidnapped. Maybe they took her to stop his work."

"Maybe, but we're not going to find out by sitting around in this dump."

"Yeah," Reggie flipped a buck and a quarter out on the table. "This oughta buy Pick a couple of packs of twinkies."

Chris smiled and started to follow Reggie out. As they went to leave, Chris felt someone tap him on the shoulder. He turned around slowly.

"You eyebarrin' me at poorul taber, fuckface." the big Oriental said with a thick accent, "I don' rike you eyebarrin' me."

"Sorry, I was just looking around. No offense."

Chris started to leave, but the huge man grabbed him by the shoulder. "I not say you to reave, fuckface."

Reggie whispered to Chris. "Let me handle this."

Before Chris had a chance to stop him, Carver was talking to the tattooed giant. "He said he solly. Now we go chop chop."

Chris rolled his eyes at his partner's pidgin English. *This* was help?

The big giant stared at Carver who had his teeth sticking out in bucktooth fashion. Another man, a thin tall man with one tooth in his head, joined them. He looked like a weasel from Mr. Toad's Wild Ride at Disney World.

"Hey, Shithead," the man said to the Oriental man, who was obviously nicknamed for his tattooed pate. "These the dicks that were looking at us?"

"Look, guys, we don't want any trouble," Chris said trying to dampen the fiery situation, but receiving no help from his partner.

"That light," Reggie said still speaking pidgin English. "We want no tlouble."

"Knock it off, Re . . ."

Without warning, the big Oriental crashed his fist into Blaze's face flipping him over a table. Chris got up and saw the thin man with one tooth pull a slapjack from his pocket and narrowly miss Reggie, who ducked and crushed the man's balls with a vicious punch. The weasel crumpled like a stack of cards and lay moaning on the floor.

Unfortunately, Shithead was not such a bad aim. He hit Carver in the ribs with a side kick knocking the black man into the old jukebox, causing the song that was playing to skip with a loud skkkkt. Carver rolled over and got to his feet just as the big man drew back his fist to throw a punch.

Blaze was up and his eyes flashed red. He moved with lightning speed. Shithead threw his punch, but it was intercepted by a powerful hand. Chris pushed the big man back, slamming his butt into the pool table behind him.

"You pay for that, fuckface," the Oriental said, as he pulled out a large knife.

58

Blaze snatched the shiv as if he were a praying mantis and the knife was a fly. He bent the stainless steel blade into a U-shape, grabbed the shocked Oriental, and picked him up with one hand.

"Now, fuckface, let's see if shit can fly."

He tossed the two-hundred-and-fifty-pound man across the room and he landed with a crash on top of a thick table, which shattered. He didn't get up.

"Come, Leggie," Chris said, "Ret's bro this pop stand."

Carver smiled and dumped an ashtray on top of the still groaning thin man's head. "See you later, ash hole."

They left and headed for the morgue.

When they arrived they found Ruther Pillman eating a gooey cheese Danish while dissecting a bowel. Ruther motioned for them to come in. Neither Chris nor Reggie wanted to enter the examining room, but both hesitantly went in.

"You guys didn't call," Ruther said as he slit the bowel with the scalpel, unleashing a foul odor.

Reggie took a step back. "Jesus Christ," he said as he fanned the air in front of his scrunched-up face. The smell was horrible. He took a step away from the table. "We weren't too far away, so we decided to stop."

"Hmmm, could've saved you the trouble if you'd called."

Holding his nose, Reggie said, in a voice from Munchkin land, "So what's the scoop on Vargas?"

"There's no record of him down here. I checked it out and I don't think he made it."

"Hmmm, and there are no John Does that fit his description."

Ruther shook his head. "None that we've got. You know, he could have been registered as a John Doe at

59

the hospital or they could've fouled up his registration."

"We checked that," Chris said. "No luck."

"Hmmm, sounds like something ain't kosher," Ruther said, as he cut another section of intestine and plopped it into a pan. "Neither is this guy's bowel. Pee—fuckin'—ew."

"So you think you might have missed him?"

"No way. I checked everybody here. No Vargas."

"Damn. Those guys had to be phony."

"I'm afraid so, Reg. Your friend's gonna be damned hard to find."

"Well, boys," Ruther interrupted, "I have some entrails to get back to. If this guy Vargas checks in, I'll be sure to let you know."

"Thanks."

"See you later."

They left Ruther slicing into the bowel and chomping on the Danish.

"Man, I'll never have chitlins again." Reggie said as he recalled the panful of intestines. "Good thing I hate chitlins."

The two men walked down the chilly corridor.

"So I guess we should get back to the office and see if we have any messages. Maybe Diego called."

"I doubt it. I have a feeling we won't be seeing Diego again."

Chris nodded grimly and they headed back to their office.

6

Penny Ante popped the lock off the door of the gymnasium where he had been sleeping for the past week. He gingerly opened the door and slipped in, careful not to make any noise that might alert the night watchman. He closed the door just as quietly and walked across the gym floor to the stack of wrestling mats that made up his bed. From behind the stack he took his carefully secreted blanket. The gym was hot that night and he didn't need the blanket to cover him—instead he used it as a sheet. He spread it out on top of the mats, preferring the feel of the cotton blanket to the sticky rubber of the wrestling mats.

DeClick could've afforded an apartment if he'd wanted to rent one, but a known informant with a long list of enemies didn't need to be a target with an address. When you'd stepped on as many toes as James DeClick had, you didn't want a place where your enemies could easily find you and pop a cap in your head. That's why he stayed in the high-school gymnasium. It had soft mats to sleep on, showers, bathrooms, all the comforts of home, plus no rent and no way to trace him there. He was safe. All he had to do was avoid the night watchman and keep his things well hidden.

Penny lay down on the mat and patted his pockets. It had been a good night. A hundred dollars from Carver and Blaze, a hundred from Richie Carbon and fifty bucks from the Maggot. Two hundred and fifty smackers. A very good night indeed.

He settled down onto the soft rubber and bundled up his jacket to serve as a pillow. As he tried to fall asleep, he found that he couldn't. Something was troubling him. As he thought about it, he narrowed his consternation down to the conversation he had engaged in with Blaze and Carver. The conversation about the Scotsman and the missing man, Vargas. He remembered the time that Jilly Mannix had shot off his mouth about Colin Macdow, blabbing that he, Jilly, knew all about the Scotsman's operation and that he was going to blow the whistle unless he was compensated for keeping his mouth shut. One of Macdow's friends had heard about the informant's claims and informed the Scotsman that Jilly had a big mouth. A day later, Jilly Mannix was found with his head chopped off and his mouth sewn shut. As he thought about the fate of Mannix, Penny almost wished he had kept his mouth shut about offering information about the Vargas disappearance. If it had anything to do with Colin Macdow then he would have been better off to leave it alone and let the detectives assume the risk of incurring Macdow's wrath. But then again, two hundred bucks is two hundred bucks and it would buy a nice amount of methamphetamine crystals.

Just then he heard a creaking sound, faint, in the direction of the double doors. Alarmed that it may be the night watchman, he sat up and peered into the darkness but saw nothing. Penny kept staring into the inky shadows trying to see who or what was there but he was unable to see anything moving. Just my imagination, he thought as he lay back down. Penny adjusted his makeshift pillow and tried to get comfortable.

"Damn nerves," he whispered aloud. The cavernous gym made his voice seem louder.

As he tried to get to sleep, he tossed over on his side and then back again, but couldn't get comfortable, or rather his apprehension made him uncomfortable. A faint rotten odor tainted the artificial smell of the mats as if a rat or some other small animal had been trapped and died in the gym. He was surprised he hadn't noticed it before he laid down. He rolled over, punched his jacket a few times to make it the right shape, but couldn't rid himself of his anxiety. He sat up and once again stared into the darkness of the gym.

Nothing.

He lay back down and as he did, he heard the creaking again, a scraping sound that lasted a few seconds and then stopped. He sat up quickly and got to his feet. The frightened informant scooted back behind the folded bleachers and waited to see if he could hear or see anything else. Penny couldn't afford a B & E rap if the night watchman caught him inside the gym, so he was careful to remain hidden. The fetid odor was stronger under the bleachers and DeClick figured the dead creature was near.

At that moment, he heard a different sound. The sound of hard shoes on the wooden gym floor coming from the other side of the gym. Damn! The watchman! Penny quietly squeezed himself further into the narrow gap afforded by the folded seats.

The footsteps stopped.

Penny could see the gym floor through the slats of the seats, but saw no one there. The gym was pitch black save for the slivers of light that came through the gym doors from the security lights outside. He began to wonder if it was indeed the night watchman who'd come in. Surely a guard would be carrying a flashlight.

Penny froze as he heard the footsteps again. Slow. Methodical. Almost as though they were stalking. A wave of fear rumbled across his body, leaving ripples of gooseflesh in its wake. He was positive that someone was in the gym, but something was bizarre about it. The footsteps sounded odd. Different. Not shoes at all. More of a clip-clopping sound almost like . . .

The footsteps stopped again.

Penny could sense that whoever was out there was looking for him. He peered through the slats of the bleachers. What he saw there in the murky darkness made him gasp and fall back against the hard wall. Floating in the inky gloom, two green eyes glowed, catlike—the gleaming eyes of a predator. Fangs of fear traced a line up his spine biting him on the back of the neck. What the hell is that, Penny wondered as he silently slipped the .22 pistol from his pants pocket and held it down at his side. The handle of the gun felt slippery in his sweaty palm. This was no night watchman. The name Colin Macdow suddenly erupted in Penny's mind like a infected cyst. He should've kept his mouth shut.

Look out!

Quickly, he ducked away as the eyes moved in his direction. He waited for a moment then peered out through the slats again. The luminous eyes stared straight at him! He saw them turn up at the edges as if whoever was there had just smiled. Penny felt sick.

Clip-clop. Clip-clop.

Moving.

Closer.

Clip-clop. Clip-clop.

Damn!

Got to make a move.

Suddenly the intruder charged the bleachers, causing Penny to shriek. Heavy feet slammed against the wooden stands, shattering the silence with a loud bang.

Terrified, Penny fell back and tried to regain a semblance of composure. His knees felt weak.

Again the unknown assailant crashed into the bleachers, rattling them with a furious kick.

The informant hurried from his hiding place, almost dropping his pistol. He fiddled with the hammer of the gun until he cocked it. Running carefully along the top of the rolled-up mats, Penny stepped out onto the gym floor. He could see the interloper in the darkness, not ten feet away.

"Stay right there, y-you bastard. I've got a-a gun and it's pointed right at you," Penny said trying to keep his voice low and even, an attempt to sound menacing.

There was no response. The person just stood there, green eyes burning into Penny's. Smiling eyes. Utterly terrifying.

The informant's arms prickled with gooseflesh. He tried to suppress a shiver.

"I mean it," DeClick said. "G-Get the fuck out of here or I'm gonna start cranking with this thing."

A giggle escaped from the lips of the intruder in the darkness. A dry raspy laugh, the sound of which chilled Penny to the bone and echoed in the cavernous gym.

Clip-clop. Clip-clop.

The figure moved closer. Penny could not make out who or what it was, but the strange footsteps set his teeth on edge.

"Stay back or I'll blow your fucking head off!" DeClick shouted, pissed off that his threats meant nothing to his tormentor.

Suddenly, the intruder increased the pace.

Clipclop clipclop.

Instinctively, Penny took a step back and aimed the pistol. He started to fire at the shadowy figure that was suddenly before his face, but a vicious slap across the face stopped him. He rocked back and tried to recover his balance. Another crisp blow knocked the gun out of his hand. It landed with a clatter against the folded seats.

DeClick tasted the coppery salt of his own blood oozing from the cut in his mouth. He reached back into his pocket and pulled his other weapon, a switchblade, and flicked it open.

"You're dead, motherfucker," he growled.

He slashed with the knife but missed the intended target. Penny grunted as his shoulder felt like he'd torn it out of the socket from the ferocity of his offensive. He slashed again with the knife hoping to hold back his assailant.

The attacker leapt into the air and reared back. Penny tried to strike again, but a hard foot slammed into his forehead. His head snapped back and he fell hard against the concrete wall. Again the attacker struck with its feet catching the informant in the chest and cracking a rib. As Penny spun, the knife flew from his hand and stabbed into the soft rubber mats. His face was a crimson mask from the brutal blow that had struck him. He tried to get up, but was stilled by a crushing blow to the back of his head. His scrambled brain sucked him into a black pit of unconsciousness.

7

Chris and Reggie sat at the small conference table in their office, trying to put together the pieces of their puzzling case. Outside of the window, a black bird landed on the ledge and watched them with a lidless eye. Both Blaze and Carver were too intent on the case to notice the raven.

"So," Reggie said as he sipped a Coke, "for some reason, this Macdow character has Diego's wife kidnapped. Diego traces her to Miami and is attacked and then taken away by some fake ambulance workers to who knows where. He might be dead."

"They both might be dead."

"Could be. Dead or alive, I'm gonna find out who did it and pin them to a wall."

"With my help."

Reggie smiled, "Yeah, partner."

On the ledge, the black bird observed the two detectives. It hopped to the other side of the window as Reggie got up and started to pace. Chris sat in the chair and read from his notes. From below, a large tabby cat watched the bird with interest. Such a large bird would make a fine change from the usual *haute cuisine* of the garbage can.

"So let's go over what Diego told us again," Chris said, as he grabbed the notebook on the conference table.

"Okay."

Chris opened his notebook and flipped to the pages referring to the Vargas case. "Now, Diego said something about a village."

"Vergaza," Carver said remembering the name.

"Yeah, right. He said that his wife was visiting her dad and that they were having a meeting."

"A meeting between her and her dad? That's a funny way to put it," Reggie said rubbing his chin.

"Yeah it is. You don't have a 'meeting' with your dad."

"So she might have been meeting with someone else."

Chris nodded. "Sounds that way."

Reggie sat down and pulled his chair closer to Chris and pointed at a name in the notebook.

"And what about this other guy, Bob Handseth?"

"I don't know. Maybe that's who she was having a meeting with."

"No. Diego said that he was the one that had hurt him."

The raven danced across the ledge. It was time. It flew away and landed at the steps leading to the entrance of the offices. Watching the short flight, the big tabby licked its lip and crouched into a stalking position. The black bird hopped into the shadows as the cat made its move.

Chris slammed his hand down on the table. "Damn, we have to find out what Diego's relationship was to this Scotsman guy and who this Bob Handseth is."

Reggie looked at his partner and shrugged.

67

"So how are we gonna find the answers?"

"I guess one of us has to go to this Vergaza."

"And who might that be?" Reggie said knowing the answer.

"Well, since you're the one who can speak fluent Spanish and since I'm the one who will burn into ash if the sun hits me, I think that you would be a good candidate."

"You could take a night flight and a crash refresher course in Spanish," Reggie said smiling.

"Come on, Reggie, you know I wouldn't be able to function as well as you. You're better with the language and you can move around during the day. I can't."

The cat's claws sank deeply into the glossy black feathers of the big bird. The black bird cawed loudly as the feline's sharp fangs buried into its neck. The bird spun around in a circle, trying to shake the tenacious tabby, but the cat wasn't to be thwarted.

Reggie pumped his palm toward his partner to stop him. "Chill, bro. I was only kidding. *Yo voy a San Miguel.*"

"You'll go?" Chris said.

"That's what I just *hablo-ed.*"

"Great, while you're gone I'll check with some of my connections and see if I can get the official word on the Macdow guy."

The raven couldn't shake the cat off its back. The cat held onto its dinner with a tenacity born of near-starvation. Realizing that time was growing short, the black bird started to expand. Its feathers began to shrink as its body grew. Thin bones thickened. The hard beak softened and sucked inward. The changes were accompanied by a crackling sound as bone transformed and flesh enlarged.

"Cool. So when do I leave?" Carver asked.

"As soon as you can get ready."

"Okay, I guess I could be packed and leave tomorrow, on the first flight out. No sense in waiting."

"Hold on," Chris said urgently.

"What?" Reggie said concerned by the sudden change of expression on Chris's face.

"I don't know. I just felt . . . I dunno, a tingly feeling."

"Don't say that, Blaze," Reggie said, reminded of the vampire, Rakz, and his telepathy with Chris.

Chris stood up and concentrated, trying to figure out what was happening. He felt nothing. "No. It's gone. What time is it?"

"Almost six."

"Almost sunup. That must have been what I felt."

"Had to be," Reggie said, glad to have a reasonable explanation.

The cat lost its hold and fell to the ground. It looked up at what once had been an easy dinner and hissed, before a cloven foot crushed its head into pussy pulp.

"So tomorrow I'm heading for Central America. *Qué suerte.*"

"I hope we have some 'luck,' Reg," Chris said, walking over to his desk and slipping the pad in the drawer. He turned to his partner.

"I got a feeling about this whole thing."

"A good feeling?" Reggie said hopefully.

Chris shook his head. "No. A bad one. A very bad one. You better be careful when you hit San Miguel."

8

The early morning air was cool as the black bird flew back to its roost, its mission only somewhat successful. It had found out that Blaze and Carver were sticking with the Vargas case and that the two detectives had discovered the name of Maria Vargas's kidnapper; knowledge that dictated their capture. But because of the unexpected attack of the cat and the impending dawn, it had been unable to complete the second part of its mission. The Father would not be pleased about that. He had wanted Blaze and Carver to become the latest additions to the farm. Now their capture would have to wait until tomorrow.

9

An exhausted Dr. Susan Blaze arrived home just as the sun was peeking over the horizon. Sticking the key in the lock, she frowned, knowing that she would have to wait until nightfall to tell Chris the good news about her new appointment as the head of ER at Sisters of the Faith Hospital. She clicked open the dead bolt, then tucked the keys in her purse. Stepping into the house, the doctor went over to the kitchen drawer, removed the flashlight from it and walked to the door of Chris's sleeping quarters. Wanting to make sure Chris was safe, she stepped inside, careful not to let any sunlight enter, and then closed the door behind her. The room was pitch black from the heavy shades on the window that was also painted black; necessities in the resting place of a vampire. She flicked on the flashlight and pointed the beam of illumination at her husband. She saw him lying there on the bed, his face relaxed in repose, his chest motionless, his heart still. He didn't move at all, and that utter lack of movement always frightened Sue a little. She knew that at this time of the day, Chris Blaze, her husband, was clinically dead. He had no heartbeat. He didn't draw breath. She had never been able to measure his brain activity and someday wished to perform such a study, but she suspected that there was none. He was dead and yet at night he lived; the same kind man she had met and with whom she had fallen in love. It didn't matter what he was—his affliction, as she called it—because her love transcended all feelings of apprehension. He was her husband for better or worse.

She looked one last time at his inert form, smiled lovingly then clicked off the light and left the room as carefully as she had entered it. She put the flashlight away and proceeded to go back into her bedroom, reassured that Chris was all right. She was exhausted from the long busy night. As soon as she undressed and hit the bed, she was fast asleep and didn't wake until it was almost dusk.

Chapter Three

1

The flight out of Miami International to San Miguel left at two o'clock and arrived in Viera, the capital city, at five-thirty.

As Reggie Carver got off the plane, he was hit by the humid heat for which the country was noted in the airline's guide to San Miguel. The moist air was stifling. After the short walk to the terminal, Carver's shirt began to feel like a second skin. A thin sheen of perspiration dampened his brow. He walked through the terminal to the baggage-claim area. The airport terminal wasn't as shabby as he expected it to be. Certainly it couldn't be termed modern, but it was clean and well maintained. There were the standard gift shops touting souvenirs from San Miguel, such as straw hats, ponchos, postcards, the usual. A couple of shoeshine boys sat idle, engaged in a game of chess. A couple of security guards in ill-fitting uniforms swaggered by, swinging formidable nightsticks. One gave Reggie a yellow-eyed once-over before moving on.

Up ahead of him, Reggie saw the baggage-claim

area. He recognized a couple of fellow passengers standing around the rotating treadmill that carried the bags from their flight.

Upon arriving at the retrieval point, he found a gap in the passengers and waited for his bags to appear. A moment later, they popped through the slapping rubber slats and were on their way toward him. Reggie grabbed his two suitcases, then went out front where the cabbies waited like vultures.

"Geeve you a ride meester, cheap rate," a particularly violent-looking man with gold teeth said. The man looked like a bandito from the old Bogart classic, *The Treasure of the Sierra Madre*.

Before Reggie could answer, another cab driver, a thin man with greasy hair that looked like a flattened spider on top of his head picked up Carver's bag and started for his bruised Toyota Corolla. *Vaca, señor. Por favor."*

The other cabbie took exception to this maneuver and stepped in front of the thin man. *"Esto es mi hombre,"* he said, *"Yo veo primero."*

"Tengo las maletas," Spidertop said, holding up Reggie's bags.

"Wait a second, dudes," Reggie said then remembered he was in another country. *"Por favor, amigos, No necesito un taxi."*

The men ignored him and continued to argue. The volume of their voices rose in direct proportion to the speed of the sentences. A small crowd began to form and Reggie tried to ease the tensions.

"Mira, Señores, no necesito un taxi."

"I weel take you," the big man said as he grabbed the smaller man by the back of the neck and pulled him toward him. *"Dáme las maletas."*

Apparently seeing that he was outgunned, the small man with the arachnid haircut shrugged and handed the two bags to the smiling victor. He smiled, took a step back and then proceeded to punch the big man in his Fort Knox face, knocking him down and out. The little man picked up the bags. *"Vamos, señor, yo se toda la ciudad."*

Carver shrugged and got in the cab. After seeing the volatile nature of the driver, he decided that maybe he could use a cab after all. He had the cabby take him to the nearest rent-a-car place and drop him off.

"Gracias," Reggie said as he reached in his back pocket for his wallet. *"Cuánto cuesta?"*

"Diez dólares."

Reggie gave the cabby ten dollars and tucked his wallet back into his pocket.

"Esto es para usted," Reggie said as he tipped the guy a couple of dollars and got out of the car. The man smiled and drove off, happily bobbing to the rap song that was playing on the car's radio.

Reggie went inside and rented a semiintact Dodge Colt and put his bags into it. He asked the man behind the counter how to get to the Hotel Contado. The car-rental guy scrawled a map and Reggie was on his way.

The trip to the hotel gave Reggie a chance to see the countryside, and it was just as he expected—long stretches of jungle interrupted by occasional shacks and concrete-block houses in need of paint. Once in awhile, next to these hovels, he would see great stone walls or barbed wire fences with gates and dirt trails leading to haciendas set deeply in the woods—the homes of the country's wealthy. The juxtaposition of the mansions of the rich and the shacks of the poor was the perfect statement on the inequities of the country's economy and political system.

A couple of times on his trek to the hotel, he had to slow down and pass peasants driving wagons from

74

their homes to the city. Their burros were oblivious to his speeding vehicle as he drove by them.

Off in the distance he could see the hills where the country's crop of cocaine was grown and harvested. He thought how the mist that covered the mountainside looked like a gloomy shroud over a body bag. Reggie thought the shroud analogy appropriate as he considered how many lives had been lost or ruined because of those harvests.

When he got to the hotel, Reggie was pleasantly surprised by the condition of it. Judging from the countryside and its surroundings, he'd expected the Hotel Contado to be a run-down old building, but it wasn't. The hotel was of modern design, more Mediterranean than Central American. The walls were stucco, painted a light shade of umber. The clay-tile roof matched the exterior's color, only it was a couple of shades darker. Reggie parked the car under the *porte cochère* and was greeted by a bellman who took his bags out of the back seat. A valet drove the car into the parking garage.

Reggie liked the tropical foliage that decorated the exterior of the hotel. The big banana palms with their great leaves bursting with green, ripening bananas hanging from their branches. Dieffenbachia, with large oval leaves of green slashed with yellow, decorated both sides of the sliding electric doors. White and beige rocks created weaving trails between the plants. The landscaping gave the entry that tropical look you expected from a Central American hotel and yet it was tastefully done, without overkill.

The automatic doors slid open and Reggie followed the bellman inside. The interior maintained the Mediterranean motif of the hotel's architecture with its white-and-turquoise tiled floors, high ceilings and fountain ornamented with dolphins. There were large earthen pots flowing with silk flowers, colored in the bright hues of the tropical fish that swam in the Gulf. A sailfish leapt across the wall, its sleek body reflecting the light from the chandelier hanging in the middle of the lobby. *Someday I'd like to hook one of those,* Reggie thought as he walked to the marble desk and checked in.

"Room for Reggie Carver," he said to the clerk, who smiled and checked his reservations list. The clerk wore a bushy toupee that abruptly ended without quite covering the grey hair underneath it or matching his white eyebrows. He wore a too-tight shirt that had once fitted him, years ago when he was thinner, but had long since become a button popper. His pants hung low pushed down by his basketball gut. He self-consciously smoothed the back of his head as he went over to the box and got the key to Reggie's room.

"Cuarto veintesiete," he said, his corpulent double chin jiggling as he did. The turkey gobbler hung over the buttoned-up collar of his shirt, obscuring the knot in his tie. The man handed Reggie the dingy gold key.

"Twenty-seven. *Gracias.*"

Reggie took the key and reached down for his bags. They were gone! He felt a seizure of panic grip him until he saw the bellman holding his bags. He had a wide grin on his face and looked remarkably like the detective's cabby. He motioned to Reggie to follow him and Carver did.

A hungry Reggie asked the bellman if they had a restaurant in the hotel. *"Uh, tiene un comedor en Hotel Contado?"*

"Sí, La Cantina de La Rosa Blanco es muy delicioso."

"Donde está?"

The man pointed back towards the lobby and

76

Reggie saw the sign. *"Bueno."*

The two men got on the elevator, which took them to the second floor. Reggie followed the bellman out of the elevator and arrived at his room. The private eye opened the door with his key, took his bags from the bellman and set them on the floor. He reached into his pocket and gave the worker a tip. The man smiled and bowed a funny little nod, then left.

Reggie picked up his bags and stepped all the way into the room. He gave it the once-over. *Not bad. A little small, but not too shabby. Even has a balcony.* Reggie tossed his suitcases on the bed and began to unpack. After he was done unpacking, it would be into the shower, into some duds and into the dining room to chow down on some good Central American *cuisine*. Afterwards, he would see if he could find out where the village of Vergaza was, and make arrangements to go there in the morning. He needed to talk to Maria Vargas's father and see if he could find out the relationship between Maria, Diego and this Macdow goon.

Reggie put most of his clothes away, laying out his white linen suit to wear that evening. It was a little dressy, but that was his style. Look good. Feel good. Maybe even meet a cute *señorita* for a little cha-cha later on. But first, he had to wash the film of sweat off his body. He got undressed and went into the slightly cramped bathroom.

Getting into the shower, he turned it on. The water pipe groaned and a trickle of water sluiced out the end of the faucet. He got in and waited for the real spray to begin but found that the trickle was all that he was going to get. Later he would ask the waiter about it and be informed of a water shortage. With the hard bar of soap and drizzle of water, he tried his best to work up a lather, but the results were less than optimum. All he

77

managed to do was replace his sweaty film with a soapy one. He cupped his hands and splashed most of the soap off and then got out. He dried and then went into the bedroom to get dressed. Sitting on the bed as he put on his socks, Reggie saw the hotel's brochure on the bedstand. Curious, he picked it up and began to read. What he found was very interesting. The Hotel Contado was owned by a company called Sithco. The chairman of the board of that company was none other than Colin Macdow. Reggie was staying in the house of his enemy. He smiled at the irony of the situation and got dressed.

As he stepped out of the room into the hallway, he saw the bellman scurrying away as though he'd been doing something that he wasn't supposed to be doing. Reggie watched him disappear down the hallway and wondered if the man had been watching him. After considering the possibility for a moment, he decided that it was just a coincidence that he'd come out at a time when it looked as though the bellman was at his door. The man was probably just hurrying back to grab another guest's bags before they had a chance to do it themselves.

"You're getting paranoid, Reggie," the black man said as he started to walk down to the restaurant to satisfy his hunger.

2

"So that was the news I wanted to tell you. We got so damn busy last night that I couldn't get home before the sun came up," Sue Blaze beamed to her husband. She and Chris were in their bedroom getting ready to go out to work.

"That's great news, honey. Really great. I knew you

could do it," Chris said, pulling up his stone-washed jeans and buttoning them.

"I didn't, but hey, what do I know?"

"So when do you start?"

"Tomorrow night."

Sitting on the bed, Sue slipped on her bra and clasped the figure-eight-shaped clips together. She picked up her panty hose and stuck in one leg then the other, standing up as she pulled the undergarment up.

"That soon?" Chris asked. "Didn't you give Miami General two weeks?"

"Charles said he called Dr. Marston and asked him if I could start early. Marston said that it was okay with him. So I start work in, well, tomorrow night."

"And this is the night shift," Chris said making sure that his wife would be home during the day to ensure his safety from discovery.

"Of course. I told them that my husband was a vampire and they understood."

"I see." Chris said with a wry smile on his face.

"So how's your missing-persons case going?" Sue said, slipping on her yellow blouse.

"Well, Reggie left today for San Miguel to see if he can get some leads."

Chris took out his comb and started combing his hair straight back. Since he couldn't see his reflection in the mirror, it was a style of necessity, not preference.

"How's it look?"

"Fine. So what made you decide to go there?"

"We got some information that led to San Miguel for the answers. I just hope he finds something we can use."

Sue brushed her hair while she spoke. "You think you'll find this girl and her husband?"

"What kind of a question is that to ask the best detective agency in Miami?"

"So do you?" Sue said cutting through the false bluster.

"I don't know," Chris admitted. So far they hadn't done much.

"I think you will."

Chris smiled and kissed his wife. "Thanks for the faith."

"You've earned it," she said, meaning it.

"So what do you say we go out in the morning and celebrate your new job?"

"I'd like to stay home if you don't mind," Sue said provocatively. She pulled her husband close and kissed him—this time with more passion.

"Don't you think we could celebrate just as well here?" she said in a husky whisper.

"Here is nice." Chris said as his wife slipped her tongue into his ear. "Here is very nice."

"We have to go to work now, y'know," she whispered in his ear. Her warm breath sent a tingle through his stomach.

"I know."

"But we have tonight."

"Yeah."

"Until tonight." Sue licked his ear and bit his neck.

"Tease."

"Just a taste."

"Not enough."

"You'll get enough later."

She slipped away slowly, fingers lingering on the bulge in his jeans, and gently caressing him.

Chris shuddered and pulled her close, kissing her behind the ear and on the neck. He gripped her firm buttocks in his hands, disliking the texture of the hose. Skin was much softer.

"Work," she said.

"No. Pleasure."

Sue grinned and tried to pull away. "Time for work."

"Can't be late?" Chris asked, realizing that she would be, if they continued on their present course.

"Not for my last day," Sue said coming to the same realization. Her sense of duty wouldn't allow her to let down her co-workers for one day even if it was her last.

"Okay."

He reluctantly let her go.

She put on her blue dress that she'd laid out, and buttoned it. She slipped on the matching belt and tightened it around her slim waist.

"I love you, Sue," Chris said. "Even if you are a tease."

"I love you, Chris."

"Tonight I'll show you how much," he said provocatively.

"I can't wait."

3

Reggie had just finished eating the plate of *arroz bruta,* a rice dish featuring pork, chicken and whitefish, when he saw a commotion erupt at the entrance to the White Rose restaurant. The maître d' was falling over himself in his efforts to cater to the man who had just walked in. The subject of his attention was red-haired, tall and handsome. This obvious *jefe,* boss, was flanked by two hulking brutes and a gorgeous Spanish female. Reggie watched as the man and his entourage were led to a table with a wonderful view of the lush patio. Reggie motioned for the waiter to come over.

"Por favor, quién es el hombre con pelo rojo?"

81

"That ees Señor Macdow. *Un hombre muy impor-tante.*"

Reggie nodded, *"Gracias."*

Carver watched the Scotsman closely and saw how he commanded those around him. Macdow carried himself with confidence. His head held erect, shoulders back. He was well built, in that cowboy kind of way, all veins, tendons and taut muscles. His handsome face was ruddy, matching the curly red hair on top of his head. He could have been a model in an ad for Glenlivet scotch except for his eyes. There was something very dangerous about the man's green eyes. A feral look. A hunter's eyes. The eyes of a predator. Macdow even moved like a big cat—deliberate, graceful, but with a sense of coiled tension as if ready to pounce at any moment. Just from this brief first glimpse, Reggie got the feeling that this man could be very dangerous.

Macdow held up a fork and examined it. He motioned for the waiter to come over. The man did so and Macdow said something in a low voice to him then bent the fork in half and dropped it to the floor. The waiter bent down and picked it up and hurried to the kitchen to get another. The waiter buffed the new fork all the way from the kitchen to Macdow's table, holding it up to the light to make sure it was spotless. He set it gingerly on the mauve napkin. Behind him, another waiter was bringing out four trays of food. Reggie figured that Macdow's party had ordered before coming in.

Reggie ordered a piece of sweet cornbread for dessert and tried to size up Macdow without appearing too obvious. He glanced over to the table just as Macdow was gesturing toward him. The red-haired man turned to his companions and said something. One of the men got a vicious grin on his face, stabbed a bloody chunk of steak with his fork and devoured it. Reggie looked away and wondered if they were indeed talking about him or whether it was just his paranoia. He surreptitiously stole glances over at the table and tried to remember each and every face. He was a great believer in knowing his enemies.

The people at the table ate and left before Reggie had a chance to finish his dessert. He had spent too much time looking and not enough eating.

Carver signed his check and left to get a drink at the bar. Maybe there was someone there that knew something about the village of Vergaza. Perhaps he could even find someone willing to guide him to Marla Vargas's father. He could only hope.

As he stepped into the bar, which echoed the Mediterranean motif but was too dark for the décor to be noticed, he went up to the bartender and ordered a beer. *"Una cerveza. Sol."*

The bartender smiled, pulled a bottle of Sol out of the cooler and placed it in front of the detective.

Reggie took a sip and surveyed the bar. It was empty except for a man sitting at a table near Carver, and another couple, an older man and his wife who sat in a corner booth in the back. The couple were definitely tourists, with the shopping bags, bright flowered shirts and funny hats. Why did people insist on wearing outfits on vacation that they wouldn't be caught dead in at any other time?

"Tu hablas inglés?" Reggie asked the bartender, a muscular man who was replacing beer in the cooler.

"Yes, I speak English, Spanish, French and a little Swahili. What can I do for you?"

Reggie was surprised by the lack of a Spanish accent, although he shouldn't have been. The man didn't look of Spanish descent. With his blond hair and blue eyes, the man could've been Nordic in heritage or perhaps from the British Isles.

"So can I get you a drink?"

"You from the States?" Carver asked the man, whose intense blue eyes chilled him.

"Washington D.C."

"Washington, huh?"

The bartender added, "Yes. Came here to get away from it all. Now that you know my life story, what else can I do for you?"

Reggie pulled out his wallet and showed his PI license to the man behind the bar who was positively unimpressed. He shrugged his broad shoulders.

Carver tucked the wallet back into his pocket. "I'm investigating a missing-persons case."

"So?"

"So I was looking for information on a village called Vergaza. You ever hear of it?"

The bartender turned around and started drying glasses that Reggie noticed weren't wet. "Sorry, never heard of it."

"You sure? It's supposed to be near here."

"Nope. Sorry."

Reggie pulled out his wallet and took out a fifty. "Look, I just want to know how to get there. Is that too much to ask?"

The bartender saw the money, but made no move towards it. "In this bar it is."

The bartender went over and wiped off a clean counter. "Look, Mr. PI, you don't want to go there. Trust me, it's a hole. Nobody lives there except a bunch of peasants."

The bartender saw one of the men that had been with Colin Macdow come in. He waved. Turning his back on Carver, he started to make a drink for the big man.

Reggie realized that their conversation was over so he got up and sat at a table. Sipping his beer, he tried to figure out his next move.

He heard a man clear his throat.

Reggie turned toward the sound.

The man next to him looked at him and smiled. Reggie returned the smile and the man got up from the his table and came over.

"Hello, señor. *Cómo está?*"

"*Bien.*"

"*Tú eres americano?*"

"*Sí.*"

"That ees good. My name es Jaime. You?"

"Reggie."

"Ah, such a nice name."

"Thanks." Reggie said warily.

Jaime smiled again, exposing teeth that looked like cigarette butts. He reached out and patted Reggie on the arm with a clammy palm.

"Very nice."

Reggie kept smiling and slowly removed the man's hand from his arm. This guy was giving him the creeps. He looked about thirty-five, but was more likely in his twenties. The hard life was written all over his craggy face. His features at one time might have qualified him as cute, but now he had the look of an ancient teenager. His teeth could send a dentist on a round trip to Tahiti. Although the man's appearance was no bed of roses that wasn't what made Carver edgy. It was the fact that the man was so friendly so fast.

Too fast.

He thought that this guy might be putting the make on him.

"Look, bud, uh, Jaime," Reggie said as he started to stand up, "I have to be going . . ."

Jaime smiled his Pall Mall toothed grin again. "I hear you ask the bartender about Vergaza."

"Yeah." Reggie sat back down, his interest suddenly

85

piqued, "What do you know about it?"

"Vergaza is beautiful place. Not like what the man said. It is rich. I go there often."

"Do you know a woman there named Maria Vargas or her husband, Diego Vargas?"

The man put his finger to his stubbly cheek. "The name is familiar."

"He's an attorney and she's his wife. Her father lives in Vergaza."

"And what is his name?"

"Shit," Reggie said suddenly realizing that he didn't know Maria's maiden name. "I don't know."

"Hmm."

Reggie sighed. "Look, will you take me there tomorrow?"

"To Vergaza? *No sé.* I have to ask my boss and see if I could get off. Of course, you will pay?"

"*Sí,* I'll pay you a hundred dollars."

"Hokay, but I haf to talk to my boss. He only lives a short way from here. We could walk."

"Well, let's go. Maybe we can do business."

Reggie followed the man outside and across the street. The two of them went down a narrow alley. A dim streetlight provided the only illumination, a circle of light that died before reaching twenty feet from the light post. In the yellow glow, Carver could see that the alley was littered with trash.

"So, Reggie," the man said patting Carver on the back. "Do you have some money on you? You may have to give my boss *un poco* to make the way smooth."

"Yeah, I have some cash."

"How much?"

"Couple of hundred I guess. Enough."

"Good," Jaime said. He cupped the side of his hand to his mouth then shouted, "Leon! Guillermo!"

Reggie turned and saw two men came out of a doorway behind him; each carried a knife. The sick feeling that he'd been set up swept over Reggie. Instinctively he reached for his shoulder holster, but remembered that the gun was back in his room. The bedroom at his Miami apartment! He couldn't take it with him because of the strict restrictions San Miguel placed on possession of weapons. Carver's mind flipped to the bumper sticker that read: "If owning a gun is criminal then only criminals will have guns," to which he added. *"Or knives."*

"We will take your wallet, please, Reggie," Jaime said, still smiling, only his grin oozed with menace. He held out his hand. *"Por favor."*

If he only had his piece, he could plug a hole in this sleezeball who had tricked him.

"Now," Jaime said losing the smile and his patience.

Although he didn't have his gun, Reggie did have the slapjack strapped to his leg. Slowly, he bent down, ripping it from the velcro strap then brandishing it at his would-be attackers. "You got to take it, tamale breath."

The larger of the two men that had come out of the doorway, Leon, brandished his big knife. It reflected the light from the streetlamp in a sickly yellow flash. His partner, Guillermo, possessed an even bigger knife, the blade of which was too rusty to reflect any light.

"Then we will." Jaime said as he extracted a sharp blade from his pants pocket.

Carver darted to his left and swung the lead-packed leather strap at the smiling peg-toothed robber. Jaime dodged the blow and narrowly missed Reggie with the slashing blade. Carver backpedalled but saw that the big man, Leon, had moved around to stop him. The other man, Guillermo, had moved to Carver's right to prevent his escaping in that direction. The situation looked bleak. Three knives to one blackjack and he was outflanked. He swung the slapjack trying to catch Leon on the wrist and dislodge his weapon. Again he missed, but he heard a thump as if he had connected. Leon slumped to the ground. Guillermo lunged for Reggie but flew past him and landed in a crumpled heap beside a pile of crates. His flight was preceded by another dull crack of a shortened baseball bat crashing against his head. The third would-be mugger, Jaime, ducked the swinging club and took off running down the alley, leaving his two buddies laid out and on their own.

"Son of a bitch,"—Reggie managed to say.

"Follow me," the bartender from the hotel said, motioning for Reggie to hurry.

The black man did as he was told and followed the man back to the hotel. Once they got to the covered walk, Reggie slowed up and caught his breath. The bartender did the same, only he moved into the shadows where he couldn't be seen by prying eyes. Reggie joined him, sensing the man's apprehension about being seen with him. The man's anxiety didn't prevent the grateful Carver from extending his hand in thanks. "What's the name of the man that pulled my fat from the fire?"

The bartender hesitated, then answered as if the question pained him. "Richard . . . Richard Mixon." He shook Reggie's hand.

Reggie's face lit up with a smile at the unexpected moniker. "Damn, no wonder you left Washington. You must have been kidded out of town."

"No," Mixon replied shaking his head. "I left Washington because I killed a guy."

The smile froze on Reggie's face. He inadvertently took a step back.

Mixon saw the uneasiness in the black man's face and tried to set it to rest. "It was an accident. He was drunk, a teenager, and I hit him with my car, I wasn't charged or anything, but I couldn't get it out of my mind so I finally had to leave and get as far away as I could."

"That sucks, man."

"Yeah, big rocks."

"So what are you doing here saving my ass?" Reggie asked.

"I saw you go out with Jamie and knew what his game was. What'd he say to get you to go with him?"

"He told me he knew something about the village."

"He must have overheard you asking me about it."

"And since you didn't help me out . . ."

The bartender stopped. "Listen, this Vergaza is nothing special. It's like any other village in this place. Poor and dirty. Nobody in this country cares about it. The people who live there aren't even citizens according to the government because they don't contribute to the economy. They're mostly dirt farmers and I mean that literally."

"Well, thanks for the history lesson, but I need to go to Vergaza and talk to this missing lady's father. See if he knows a guy named Bob Handseth or Colin Macdow."

The bartender started to say something, but clammed up.

"What? What were you going to say?"

"Nothing."

"Come on. You were about to say something and then you shut up. What was it?"

"Look, uh . . ."

"Reggie."

"Look, Reggie, do yourself a big favor and get the hell out of San Miguel. This place is bad news. You go into one of those villages at the wrong time and they say

89

you won't come out."

That's what Diego said, Reggie thought. "What do you mean? Does somebody kidnap them for labor or for political reasons, what?"

"Listen, I only came out here to help save your money from those banditos as a favor from one American to another."

"Well, I thank you for that, but I still need somebody to take me to that village. I'll pay you a hundred dollars."

"I don't want your money."

"Then take me for free, I don't care. I just want to go to Vergaza. Now when do we leave?"

The bartender shook his head at Reggie's dogged persistence. "Man, you don't give up."

"No, I don't. A hundred bucks right now. Room 27. Come by at seven tomorrow morning and I'll pay you another hundred."

"I don't want your money. Just take my advice and stay out of Vergaza."

"So you're really not going to help me?"

"No."

"Thanks for nothing; man," Reggie huffed then turned and headed into the lobby. He was sure he could get someone there to take him.

He was wrong.

No one wanted to go to Vergaza.

4

The office of the Drug Task Force Chief, Leonard Singer, looked as if a paper bomb had exploded. There were stacks of paper on Singer's desk. Piles around the desk. Reams stuffed on top of every available surface. Paper everywhere. The walls were cluttered with maps

90

and photos of various drug lords speared with darts.

Chris Blaze had been leaving his house when he was approached by the two DTF agents and asked to come with them to their chief's office. Now as Chris sat in the chair opposite the chief's desk, he wondered what it was all about. In the chair next to Blaze sat deputy chief Mark McNally.

"What is it that I can do for you, Mr. Singer?" Chris said. "I have to tell you that your men took me a little by surprise."

Singer, a thin man with dark circles under his eyes and a weary expression on his face spoke. "Word is around town that you've been asking about Colin Macdow."

"So."

"So we were wondering why?"

"I'm a private investigator on a missing-persons case. We got a lead that Macdow might be involved in the kidnapping and I've been trying to find out how and why."

"And you're sure it was Macdow's name mentioned?"

"Yes."

"What's your client's name?" Deputy McNally said, speaking for the first time.

"His name is Vargas. Diego Vargas. His wife's Maria. They both have disappeared. Vargas's wife first, and then him, after he hired us."

Singer looked over at McNally, "This Vargas mean anything to you?"

McNally pursed his lips and shook his head, "Nope, never heard of him or his wife."

"So what's his connection to Macdow?" Singer asked turning back to Blaze. He pulled out a stick of gum and popped it in his mouth.

"Don't know for sure. The husband mentioned his

name when we spoke, as Macdow being the one responsible."

"Hmm, well, we're investigating Macdow heavily at the moment and your questions around town might put him on the alert."

"I don't think so."

"What you think doesn't matter," Singer said abruptly. "We have had this investigation going for the past six months and no missing-persons investigation is gonna botch it up."

"I used to work vice at Miami PD so I know a little about investigations, a couple of questions about Macdow isn't going to jeopardize your . . ."

The circles under Singer's eyes seemed to darken. "No, it's not, because you are going to lay off. If Macdow had anything to do with these people going bye-bye then there probably won't be anything left to find." He snapped the gum impatiently.

"So I should just give up?" Chris asked, his voice rising with anger.

"No. You should just stop asking questions about Macdow that might make him suspicious."

"Look, Mr. Singer, I'm trying to do my job. If that leads me to Macdow so be it. I can't worry whether your investigation will be affected, although I seriously doubt that it will."

Singer ran his fingers through his hair and sighed. He decided to try another tack. "Mr. Blaze, we have got a lot of man hours and a lot of money tied up in this thing. It's not just Macdow we're trying to nab. This investigation stretches into police organizations, political connections, the whole shooting match. We would really appreciate your cooperation on this. If there's anything we can do to help you we will. But I need to ask you to help me a little."

Chris saw that the chief was really weary and taut

over the situation. He remembered how much work was involved in a major bust and the dangers involved. He had been there before on many occasions. He decided to try and help out by maintaining a low profile. "Okay, I'll be careful. Now, I'm gonna take you up on your offer to help."

"Shoot."

"Okay. Our client also mentioned another name when he spoke to us. Does Macdow have anyone in his organization named Robert Handseth or Bob Handseth?"

Singer shook his head. "Not that I know of. What about you, Mark?"

"I never heard of him."

"Well, do you have any more questions?"

"Not at the moment." Chris smiled. "Thanks for all your help."

"Your welcome. The question is, can we count on *your* help?"

"I'll be careful and try not to get in your way."

"Good." Singer got up and shook Chris's hand. McNally followed his boss's lead and did the same.

"If you have any more questions be sure to call us," McNally said.

"I'll do that. Thanks."

As Chris left the building and walked down the street, he glanced at his watch and realized that he had to get back to his office in a hurry. Reggie would be calling soon with information on his investigation. Chris looked around and saw no one. He shimmered and popped. His arms lengthened. A flap of skin stretched from his sides and connected with the long tendonlike arms. His legs shrank and curled into clawed feet. His face hissed and pulled inward until he had changed from man to bat. He flew in the direction of his office.

When Chris got to the office, the phone was ringing. He started to change and picked up the handset.

"Skreek," he said, as his bat vocal cords struggled to catch up with his human transformation. He tried again, "Hello."

"What the hell was that all about? You letting your rubber ducky answer your calls?" Reggie said.

"Just had something caught in my throat. So how goes it?"

"Besides almost getting rolled and not finding someone to take me to Vergaza, it's going great. Damn place isn't even on a map. One thing though, I did meet Richard Mixon."

"Reggie, sometimes your sense of humor is bizarre. Nixon. Jeez."

"No, really, this bartender's name is Richard Mixon with an M. He stopped me from getting rolled, but wouldn't help me get to Vergaza. No one will. I tell you this place down here reminds me of one of those old towns in a vampire movie."

"How's that?"

"You know like when Van Helsing asks the villagers about the castle on the mountain, everybody just kinda clams up. Don't know anything. Start crossing themselves. I don't know what's up in Vergaza but I think I'm starting to catch your bad feeling. How's it going on your end?"

"Well, we managed to attract the attention of the Drug Task Force with our questions about Macdow."

"How did they find out about that?"

"Good question," Chris said, "I didn't even think about that until you just mentioned it."

"Some detective."

Chris ignored the quip and continued his train of thought, "It must've been Penny."

"Yeah, he'd sell us out in a heart beat. A guy like that

94

has no loyalty."

"I don't see how else they could've known."

"So what'd they want anyway?"

"They wanted us to lay off the case."

"Why?"

"They have a big sting investigation going and they're afraid we'll spook Macdow."

"Spook him? That's bullshit. Something smells like a whore's pussy after a good night."

"Jesus, that's crude."

Reggie laughed then got serious. "For real, I mean our questions aren't gonna mess up any drug sting. I think somebody's trying to get us to stop for another reason."

"Like what?"

"Don't know, but we need to find out."

"I guess if we keep trying we will."

"I guess."

"So what else did you find out in San Miguel?"

"Well, this Macdow is the Chairman of the Board of the company that owns the hotel where I'm staying. Weird coincidence. I even saw him earlier tonight at the restaurant. He had a couple of mean-looking goons with him. For a second I thought he might've recognized me."

"Recognized you? How?"

"I don't know. I was sitting in the restaurant and I looked over and he was staring at me."

"Could be coincidence."

"Maybe, but it got me thinking. What if Macdow's men tailed Vargas to our place?"

Chris ran his finger across his lip. "Then Macdow would know we were on the case or at least that we knew about Maria's disappearance."

"Yeah," Reggie replied. "Hey wait, say somebody at the DTF was funky then Macdow could turn them on

95

us to see if they could persuade us to stop our digging. Remember what Diego said about going to the police."

"Yeah. I guess it's possible."

"Possible, but on the other hand it sounds like a bad episode of 'Miami Vice.' But then again was there ever a good episode?"

Chris chuckled. "So what's your plan?"

"I'm gonna try to get to Vergaza in the morning."

"Okay. Keep on your toes."

"I'm already making like a ballerina."

"Call me tomorrow around this time and tell me what you found."

"Yeah, I will," Reggie said as he hung up.

As Chris put the phone down, he took a drink of blood and thought he saw a shadow pass in front of the glass pane of his office door. He got up and walked across the room. After he opened the door, events rattled off in quick succession.

Chris saw a shape coming toward him and was rattled by a powerful kick to his forehead, splitting the skin. The force of the blow drove him back and his attacker, whom he still hadn't seen, was at Chris's back. From behind, strong fingers wrapped around Chris's throat. The blood he had just ingested streamed down the gash in his forehead. Chris grabbed the assailant's wrists. He shifted his weight catching him off guard.

As he tossed his attacker into the big bay window, the invader let out a terrible scream that shattered Chris's eardrum. The force of the screech stunned Blaze. He staggered to the window and looked out. He saw the attacker crumpled in a heap on the concrete, then the person stood glaring up at him with fiery green eyes. It was a woman. She howled one last time and took off, running down the street. Blaze tried to follow, but the scream had damaged his equilibrium and he almost fell. He made it to the door and stumbled down the stairs as his vampiric power rapidly healed the damaged drum. He stepped outside the building and saw a rapidly moving form heading down the street. He started to follow.

"The end is near!" a voice behind Blaze shouted.

Chris turned and was rocked by what he saw. A wave of sickness swept over him as his eyes fell upon a stringy old man with no teeth shouting that the world was coming to an end and that the sinners should repent. The sight of the skinny, dirty street man was not what staggered Blaze; it was what the old man was carrying: a big wooden cross the sight of which slammed into Chris like a truck. He stumbled back from the cross as another wave of incredible nausea swept over him. He reeled over a trash can, spilling its contents, then fell to the pavement. The stench from the can slid across the pavement into his nostrils adding to his sickness. The man with the cross kept coming toward him as he lay in pain. Chris tried to scramble to his feet, but to no avail. The power of the cross held him in check.

The man kept coming.

"The end is near."

And Chris knew that it would be the end if the man got too much closer with the huge cross.

The old man kept coming closer, dragging the heavy cross. "Repent. Repent."

Relentless.

Oblivious.

Chris's guts felt as if he had stayed on a carnival ride for two weeks. His stomach was a frenzy of nausea and his skin began to feel warm.

A blister popped out on his arm.

Then another on his cheek.

He had to do something.

Looking away, Chris concentrated on changing his

appearance. His face crackled and snapped as it began to distort and mutate.

The old man with the deadly cross kept coming closer. "The end is near. Repent, you sinners. The end is near."

With his transformation complete, Chris turned toward the old man and hissed. His face was that of a vicious-looking monster bat, with eyes blood red and glowing in sockets of ebony. Nose pushed into his face. Growling lips pulled back to reveal long white fangs.

The old man's eyes widened. He took three steps backward before he even knew that he had. "Son of a whore's tit, the end is now!"

He spun around and took off running in the other direction: the cross dragging behind him scraping against the pavement.

Chris relaxed and his face changed back to normal. His stomach lost the overwhelming queasiness, although he felt his ever-present hunger clawing at his gut. The transformation into the bat had set it off as it always did when he used his vampiric powers. He was glad that he was close to his office. He got up from the ground and headed into the building to quench his craving.

5

In the veranda of a villa a few miles from the hotel, Colin Macdow sat in his wicker chair sipping on a rare unblended scotch whiskey. The moonlight shimmered off the blue water of his huge pool in splashes of white. The night air was warm and sticky, but a fan above Macdow's head helped keep him cool. The slowly rotating blades slashed the moonlight into shadows that played across the Scotsman's face as he toyed with the amulet around his neck. He was on the phone to his contact in Miami.

"So do ye thin it's safe enough to bring in a shipment?"

"No problem. Anytime."

"Good. What aboat this Blaze? Is he at the farm?"

"He should be by now."

"Good. The black one will be joining his partner right aboat this time and then we'll ha' no more problems from them."

"Is there anything else, Mr. Macdow?"

"No, that'll be all."

Macdow hung up the phone, smiling. Everything was going according to plan except for the interference of *El Frente* and that little group could have their stinking little country once he had made enough money to prepare for the Prophecy of the Second Genesis. This year was the first time that he had occasion to consider the possibility of its fruition, as the last of the Stephensons was dead. All that was left to do was to complete the farm and find the Mother Host.

He got up from the chair, left the veranda and headed into the villa. He cut through the dark living room that was decorated entirely in black and gray. The ambience of the room left visitors to the villa experiencing a sense of foreboding. A painting of the ritual of the Trinity of Consummation hung above a black leather couch with mahogany feet carved into hooves. The only splash of color in the painting showed three women in flowing green dresses as they danced around a blazing flame, their faces aglow with ecstasy. The shadowy figures that watched them were immersed in dark robes and blended into the night. Another woman lay on a slab of stone. Colin Macdow stood over her. Both were naked and gleaming with oil. The painting of the dance gave one feelings of exhilaration and of dread. Macdow had specially commmissioned the painting to reflect the Prophecy and what it represented. In the corner of the room, the family crest of Dow was carved into an immense slab of polished onyx and it stood perched on a grey-speckled block of marble. The strange crest had been created five centuries ago by Dow the Black at the time of the First Genesis. The carved lines formed a woman whose body gradually changed into a raven. The bird held a tablet in one claw and a sword dripping with blood in the other. The vague outline of another creature faded into the background behind the bird girl. The thing in back was just a notion of a shape, nothing definite, and yet when you saw it you couldn't help feeling that it was looking straight at you. The rest of the room was similarly in somber tone, which was the way Colin Macdow liked it. Visitors rarely returned.

He passed through the living room and went up the stairs to the second floor of the villa. The hallway down which he turned was stark, devoid of all decoration. He saw the flickering orange light coming from under the door and smiled.

He opened the door, stepped into the room, and in the dim light from the candle burning on the nightstand saw her lying on the soft mattress. Her firm breasts heaved as she sucked in the cool air and hissed like a cat. She was naked and waiting for him. The beautiful woman got up from the bed and started moving toward Macdow.

As she drew near, Macdow unbuttoned his shirt. He slipped it off, exposing his muscular chest and the amulet that hung around his neck.

She smiled and moved closer. Her skin smelled almost like a piece of chicken on the verge of spoiling. Macdow didn't notice.

"Soon, Dru," he said taking her into his arms.

"Miami will be our new home and the babes will have all they'll need."

She smiled and kissed his breast. Her lips moved slowly over his flesh, tasting the sweat. Macdow watched her, and stroked her blond tresses. He closed his eyes and readied for the penetration.

It happened quickly. The sharp needles piercing the flesh. A trickle of blood slid down his chest. Her darting tongue caught it and followed the trail back to the small wound just under his nipple that she had inflicted.

Macdow gasped with pleasure as she began to suckle, moaning gently as she did. The intense sucking traced a line of pleasure from his chest to his crotch. He was hard.

She sucked harder; a drop of blood spilled from the corner of her mouth. It slid down his chest until it submerged in the sea of red pubic hair. Macdow felt his member start to tingle as it always did when he nourished his children. They needed his love.

As she took the vital fluid from him, Macdow shuddered and came with such force that he blanked out for a moment.

He came to and realized that she had taken enough. Macdow gently pushed her away. He still had to feed Mary when she came back from the hunt.

She was reluctant, but she didn't wish to incur the wrath of the Father. Besides she knew he was right. She could already feel his blood begin to revitalize her.

Macdow met her green eyes with his own and smiled, showing his even white teeth. His canines seemed to lengthen as he spoke. "I need ye to do something for me."

Dru looked up and returned the grin, knowing what it meant. Her eyes shone with the lust of the hunter.

101

Now all she needed to know was who her prey would be.

The long day had made it easy for the intruder to take Reggie. He was so tired that he couldn't prevent the Sandman from taking him into the land of dreams. Carver tossed in his sleep as "the dream" menaced him once again, only this time the dream was out of sequence. He was home, not in his apartment awaiting the arrival of the vampire, Rakz. It was the house he'd lived in as a child, growing up in the suburbs. He recognized the wooden floors polished to a fine lustre; the landscapes—painted by his little brother, Ronald —that hung on the walls of the living room; the fake brick wallpaper, his father's favorite chair—everything as it was when he was a child, only the perspective was out of kilter. The walls leaned back and stretched endlessly into the black void above. The chair quivered and heaved as if alive. When he looked closely at the landscapes, Reggie could see slavering, stooped creatures scurrying about the palmettos and cypress trees. Beady red eyes stared out at him. Faint laughter, like rasping files cutting metal, set his teeth on edge. To his horror, he saw that the fanged hellspawn were chasing Ronald, who was just a toddler. The three-year-old ran, chubby legs churning, as he fled from the monsters. His screams for help were distant, proportional to his size in the painting, but nonetheless terrifying to hear. Reggie stared helplessly at the painting and the tiny demons as they caught the three-year-old and began tearing him apart. A creature with four horns and a mouthful of jagged teeth gnawed on Ronald's head, grinding the sharp teeth on the boy's skull. Another thing with the head of a bird and the body of an ape pulled the boy's arms from his socket and cleaned them of flesh with its uneven beak. Reggie knew that his little brother was twenty-five years old, alive and working as a commercial artist in Orlando, but the vision of his death mortified the black detective. He had to look away. He stood up and tried to get away from the painting.

The wooden floor beneath him heaved and shook as he tried to run. The planks popped up, sending nails flying like deadly projectiles. Reggie could feel them pierce his flesh, but saw no blood. He stumbled on the throbbing floor as he tried to escape the tiny screams of his brother, while the creatures continued to eat his flesh. A wicked stench slipped through the cracks in the floor. A smell like dead fish and wet musty clothes.

Reggie heard a clip-clopping sound in the dream that had never been there before this time. Clip-clop. Clip-clop. The footsteps were faint. The sleeping detective didn't know that the sound was coming from the hallway outside the hotel room and his mind was forcing it into the perspective of the dream.

Suddenly a voice called out from behind the black man. "Reggie Carver, as I live and breathe."

At once, the floor stopped moving and returned to normal; the torn planks were replaced by fresh shiny ones; the cries of his brother were gone. Reggie turned around and saw his old friend, Burly Fayer, sitting in his father's favorite chair. On his ample gut rested the big plastic bowl that Carver's father used to load with goodies to eat while he watched television. Burly also enjoyed a repast from the green tupperware bowl as he popped a brown chip into his mouth. Reggie moved closer to the big man and saw the bullet holes that riddled his body. Half of his face was shot off and Reggie could see the big Georgian's teeth as they

103

crunched down on whatever the giant man was eating. His father's chair looked strange, as if infected with huge boils. Great rounded lumps bulged from the brown-and-tan tweed fabric. Reggie saw a blank eye socket staring at him from a tear in the fabric. Another rip revealed yellowed teeth and white bone and Carver realized that the chair was stuffed with human skulls. He heard the footsteps again and the dream shifted quickly to a closeup of Burley's feet. They were hooves that danced on the wooden floor. The cloven feet were another new addition to the dream. He could hear them rapping on the floor.

"Burley, you're dead," Reggie said, his voice sounding hollow. "Charlie Burnson shot you."

"How about a chip?" Fayer said as he held up a dark burnt chip and ate it. Reggie could see Fayer's teeth crunch the chip and watched Burley's Adam's apple bob when he swallowed the treat. A moment later, Reggie stared in horror as the chip crawled out of one of the bullet holes in Fayer's stomach and went back into the bowl to be eaten again. Fayer's feet danced.

Clip-clop. Clip-clop.

"Sure you don't want one?" Burly asked as he extended the bowl out for Reggie.

Carver stepped back in horror as he saw that the inside of the bowl was swarming with roaches. Hundreds of them. Their brown bodies slithered together creating a whispering that sounded like "kill kill kill."

Burley took one out and crunched it merrily in his mouth. He stopped dancing.

"Hey, nigger."

Reggie turned toward the source of the racist comment and saw Charlie Burnson sitting on the rocking chair that Reggie's grandma used to sit in when she visited. Reggie couldn't see his grandmother anywhere. The rest of the room was now a hazy blur, but he knew she was there. He knew she'd been murdered by the thing sitting in her favorite chair. Reggie's dead ex-boss smiled as he rocked back and forth in the oak rocker. There was a huge hole in his chest from the shotgun blast that had killed the servant of Yosekaat Rakz. Reggie saw his lungs moving and his shattered heart pumping blood out onto the dead man's stomach.

"Want a little pussy?" The former police lieutenant laughed as he reached down and picked up a small calico kitten. He stroked the little furball lovingly and then ripped it open with his ragged teeth. He took the screeching kitten and put it against his greedy lips sucking the tiny creature dry. His mouth was huge and hideous as he chugged down his grisly repast, blood spurting out and running down his cheeks. He tossed the spent body away, wiping his bloody maw on his sleeve.

"Sure you don't want some pussy?" Burnson hissed in a menacing voice as he picked up another kitten and bit its head off. Reggie was ten feet away and he could still smell the rank breath of the deceased lieutenant. Rotten.

In the dream, Carver heard a rattling sound that clicked on the warning light of reality in his head. Immediately, he woke up from the dream, lurching to a sitting position while he sucked in air. Confused with terror, he stared wide-eyed around the room. With his eyes peering into the darkness, he caught a thin stream of light to his right, as the door to his room started to open very slowly. Unprepared for intruders, Carver didn't wait to see who came in. He got up and hustled over to the glass doors leading to the small balcony. Luckily he had opened it to let in some fresh air. He slid through the opening and then climbed down the outside of the balcony and hung there on the railing. His actions reeked of cowardice, but he didn't know what else to do. He didn't have a gun and there might be more than one of them. Looking through the crack to see who was there, he saw the silhouette of a woman step into the room. He felt a little foolish hanging there and almost pulled himself up, but wanted to see what she was doing.

As the woman approached his bed and found it empty, he heard an angry hiss and a ripping sound of such intensity that he felt his balls dive for cover as his scrotum did an imitation of a prune. Reggie started to feel less foolish and more afraid, as the ferocity of the intruder became apparent. He watched her as she walked away from the bed and began her search.

The woman looked around and he saw green eyes floating in the darkness of the room. The fear that had touched him slapped him in the face with a cold palm as he stared at the glowering eyes of the interloper. This shit was getting serious.

The woman walked over to the closet and tore it open. She stuck her head inside to check it out. Reggie could hear her scrape her fingers on the wall in anger as she found nothing. Fear placed a clammy palm against the nape of his neck. His balls burrowed for his Adam's apple. His shoulders ached from gravity's relentless pull. Carver's palms had started to sweat and his handhold was beginning to loosen. He tightened his grip and watched.

The woman went into the bathroom and seconds later came back out, green eyes flaring. She slashed the air with sharp fingernails.

Reggie wished that the strange woman would leave so that he could climb up before his grip weakened or before she found his ass hanging out to dry. He wondered what it must look like to someone below him; a black man in his underwear hanging from a balcony. The consideration was a quick dash of humor in a tense situation—the tension stretched into terror as the woman turned and looked in the direction of the balcony. Reggie could almost sense a smile come over her face and he knew that he wouldn't be climbing up soon. Maybe never. He heard the dull thump of her footsteps on the carpet and oddly thought of the old childhood taunt, "Yo' mama wears Army boots." He would've laughed if fear hadn't paralyzed his face. He looked up and saw that the woman was coming toward him. Her eyes gleamed with unearthly light. Her face emerged from the room, only Reggie didn't see it. He had slipped down to the end of the railing and was trying his best to hide.

She stepped onto the patio . . .

Clip-clop. Clip-clop.

. . . And she started walking toward the edge of the balcony.

7

Chris had arrived back at his office and was waiting as the phone at the Hotel Contado rang for the seventh time. A drained bottle of blood sat empty on the desk, his third of the night. The vampire detective had returned from his attempts to find the woman who had attacked him. Her trail was too cold to follow. He had found no trace of her. No one had seen anything, either, or if they had, they weren't talking. He'd asked a few people that were hanging out on the corner, but no one had seen a woman. It was as though she had been sucked into the pavement. It was unfortunate that he'd been "assaulted" by the man with the cross and been forced to transform because he could've followed her and maybe, just maybe, solved the damned case. It if hadn't been for that incident, he wouldn't have had to go back up to the offices, wasting precious time to quench his insatiable thirst and then go out to find an icy trail of nothing. When he had returned to the office, he had dialed the number of the hotel where Reggie was staying in order to inform Carver of the attack and warn his partner that he might also be in peril.

The phone rang for the eighth time, but no one at the hotel was answering. Chris knew that it was late, but he had to let Reggie know that someone might be after him. If the attack on Chris did have something to do with the Vargas case, and he suspected that it did, then Reggie might also be in danger. At the time, he didn't know just how right he was.

8

Reggie hung from the rail, trying to hold himself so that he wasn't visible from the balcony. A drop of sweat slithered down the side of his face, veering into his ear. He heard the woman's footsteps change from dull thumps into a hard knocking as her feet hit the concrete of the balcony. Carver's left hand slipped and he strugged to regain his grip. Any moment he expected to look up into those fierce green eyes and feel her fingernails gouge his flesh. Carver looked down and to his relief saw that there was grass below him. At least he hoped that was all that was down there.

The woman stopped in the middle of the balcony and Reggie breathed a short sigh. He was suddenly aware that he hadn't been breathing. The detective hoped that she would turn around and head back into the hotel room; a hope crushed under a heavy foot slowly stepping forward toward him. She was coming.

Clip-clop. Clip-clop.

What to do?

He glanced down, judging the distance to be about twenty feet to the ground—soft grassy ground, he hoped.

Clip-clop.

What if there was a sprinkler head down there waiting to irrigate his asshole? he thought grimly.

Clip-clop.

Closer.

Shit.

With a silent prayer, the detective let go and fell the twenty feet, landing on his feet and rolling with the force. Quickly he scampered into the bushes and looked up.

A moment later, he saw the woman peer over the ledge, or rather he saw her eyes—twin beacons of emerald hate. He ducked back into the hedge, afraid that she would see him. He wondered if she could see in the dark, a thought that never would have crossed his mind if it were not for the fact that he had a vampire for a business partner.

Seconds felt like minutes as he waited. His shins ached from the impact with the ground. He rubbed them, thankful that sore shins was all that he had incurred from the fall.

From above, he heard an angry growl and its savageness sent a snake of fear winding up his spine. Instinctively, he pressed closer to the wall of the hotel, trying to hide from the brutality of that snarl. He heard distant steps as she walked across the balcony and into the room. The footsteps faded, and all was quiet. Reggie didn't dare move, for fear that the girl would detect his presence and attack him. He pictured those demonic eyes smiling, and he shivered. Just then, out of the corner of his eye he saw movement to his left. He

109

scrunched deeper into the bushes and looked over. He saw the woman from the room disappear into the jungle that bordered the back of the hotel property. She seemed to float into the dark shadows and reminded Reggie of the vampire women in the movie, *Dracula*. She was even wearing a long gown of some kind. Weird. A wave of relief swept over the frightened man, only to be replaced by a sense of foreboding. Who, or more appropriately, what the hell was that bitch?

Carver waited for an hour in the brush. Occasionally he dozed, then awakened in a panic as he thought he sensed a presence near him. But it was just his imagination.

After he was sure the woman wasn't coming back, he got up, brushed the leaves and brown grass clippings from his body, then hurried back into the hotel.

She was there.

He ran straight into her.

"Oh my word," the woman shrieked as she saw the black man in his underwear. Never before had Mrs. Gladys Perriman seen a black man so close to total nudity except in the *National Geographic,* to which she subscribed in her native Iowa.

For the first time, Carver became aware of his unclad condition and covered up. He worked up a smile for the old lady. "Pardon me, ma'am, I, uh, lost my pants in a poker game." It was lame, but all he could think of at that moment.

Mrs. Perriman stared at him and then nodded her head. She understood losing, as she had dropped two hundred dollars at the Casino Grande Rojo next door to the hotel. She brushed past Reggie and went to her room. She hoped her husband was asleep so that she could win the money back before he found out.

Reggie quickly glanced around the deserted lobby

for any possible surveillance, but found no one. A man behind the counter held the phone in his hand and shouted at Carver to get out of the lobby. Hurriedly, he went back to his room. Once inside, he secured the door with a chair. He closed the balcony doors and slid the metal bar between the jamb and the door frame. Satisfied with his security measures, he went over to the bed and climbed into it.

As he pulled the sheets over him, he saw that the sheet had four long jagged rips in it. Reggie poked his fingers through them and shuddered. The sheet was brand-new and made of sturdy cotton. The woman's nails had shredded it as if it were cheap toilet paper. He got up and went back over and checked the door again and then the glass doors. Once again satisfied, he got into bed and fell asleep without further incident.

9

It was an hour before sunup. An hour earlier, Chris Blaze had finally gotten someone to answer the phone at the hotel. A bleary, heavily accented voice had croaked *¡Hola!* into the phone and Chris requested the connection to Carver's room. After a tangle of tongues, the man finally realized what Chris wanted, and connected his call to room 27. As the phone in his partner's room rang and rang, Chris began to get a sick feeling in his gut that something had happened to the black man. It was too late for him not to be there unless he had a lead on the case and had pursued it. That was definitely a possibility, a probability in fact, because Carver was like a bulldog once he got a lead in a case. Still, Chris's uneasiness remained. The phone switched back to the lobby desk and the man picked up the call. Chris had been about to ask him a question when the

111

man shouted in Spanish. Chris translated the words, "get out" and "no clothes," but that was all. When the man spoke to Chris he muttered something about a *loco americano negro* and hung up before Chris had a chance to stop him. He dialed the hotel again, but the man had gone back to the office to catch up on his sleep. He let the phone ring and ring. Finally Chris had given up, knowing the crazy black American had been his partner. Carver was safe, somehow without clothes, but safe. Chris could hardly wait to hear Reggie's story the next night. Satisfied that Reggie was all right, Chris had decided to go home.

When he arrived home, still wondering what could have happened to Reggie, he was surprised to see his wife sitting seductively on the couch. She was clad in a red teddy—that was the full extent of her attire. Her smooth legs shimmered in the light of a candle sitting on the coffee table. Chris could see the light brown areolas of her nipples through the sheer fabric of the teddy. A dark brown triangle of hair peeked out from the lace fringe of the teddy that barely covered her thighs. She motioned for him to come over, and all thoughts of Carver's escapades were overrun by his stampeding libido. He smiled and walked over to the couch and picked his wife up in his arms. She kissed him with passion and he returned her ardor. Sue broke the kiss and started to unbutton his shirt. Slowly she slid the buttons through the stitched slits in the cotton cloth, pausing to kiss his nipple as she did. She slipped the shirt off his well-muscled shoulders and tossed it over the top of the couch. She began to unbutton his jeans with the same deliberate pace she had used with the shirt. Once she unbuttoned them, she slid the jeans down his legs until she dropped them into a crumpled heap onto the carpet. She slid her fingers under the band of his briefs and lifted them over his hard penis.

Her hot skin radiated through the silk teddy as she dropped the underwear and climbed onto his chest guiding him inside her. She gasped at the same moment he did as they joined in love. Slowly, they began to rock in exquisite unity. Two as one. Husband and wife. Man and woman. The most basic relationship of humanity combined with its most noble attainment; pure unadulterated love.

After they satisfied each other, Sue walked her fingers across Chris's chest. "Still think I'm a tease?" she said, softly reminding her husband of his comments that evening.

"The best kind," Chris smiled as he pulled her close and kissed her lips, tasting their sweetness.

"Love me?" she said.

"Nah, but I think I'll keep you around for the sex."

"Bastard," Sue grinned.

"Beautiful," he said gazing lovingly into her eyes.

Chris took her in his arms. He glanced at the clock and saw that there was fifteen minutes before the sun rose. It was more than enough time. He cupped the back of her head in his hand and drew her lips to his. Their lips met, and the passion they felt signalled the beginning of the second coming.

Chapter Four

1

It was morning, and Reggie was surprised to see Richard Mixon standing at his door. The bartender was dressed in a blue T-shirt and jeans. He wore a tired-looking pair of boots. In his hand, he carried a canvas bag. "You still want to go to Vergaza?"

"Bet your ass I do," Carver replied. "Why the change of heart?"

"I started thinking about how you didn't know the country and about how you almost got ripped off and I decided to help you." He didn't tell Carver the real reason for his sudden change of heart.

"Well, help is what I need," Reggie replied, refusing to look a gift horse in the ass. No sense in risking a load of shit in the eye. "Just let me get a shirt on and we'll hit the trail."

"Okay, One thing though. I want to be out of there before nightfall."

"Why's that?"

"That's when people start disappearing."

Reggie looked grim. "Like Maria Vargas."

"Maybe." Mixon said. "Just so we're on the road

114

before the sun goes down. That's when the death squads come."

"Okay. Come on in," Reggie said, as he opened the door for Mix and let him in. He went into the drawer of the dresser and pulled out a light cotton polo shirt then slipped it on. He slid a pair of socks on his feet and then his Air Jordans. He wanted to be able to fly if he had to.

"Let's go."

Reggie followed Mix out the door and down the hallway to the stairs. He could tell by the way Mixon walked that he was athletic. The man walked with a confidence of step that spoke of power and grace like a champion guard dog. Reggie remembered that Colin Macdow had walked with the same confidence, only his poise was feline in nature. Two coins from the same mint only pressed from different molds. Natural enemies.

As Mix opened the door to the car, Reggie turned over the engine of the battered Colt. It coughed to life, exhaling a black plume of smoke. Next to the black private eye, Mix sat smoking a particularly foul cheroot.

"Hey, Mix, you smoking a loaf of shit?" Reggie said fanning his face with a rapidly moving hand. "Do me a favor and toss that stinky thing out the window."

"Hey, it relaxes me to have a good smoke in the morning."

"Well, if that's a good one I'd hate to smell a bad."

He rolled down his window then pulled out of the hotel parking lot and onto the main drag of the town. "Where to?"

"Turn up here onto Calle Azul and follow it all the way down to end of town. Then we'll hit a fairly big highway, by San Miguel's standards anyway, called La Oche. We'll take that for a couple of hours and then we take another road to Vergaza."

115

"So what are we looking at?"

"Three hours. Give or take thirty minutes."

"Damn," Reggie said, as another cloud of the noxious smoke floated into his nostrils. "Mix, you sure that's tobacco and not somebody's shredded underwear?"

"If you're gonna complain the whole time, I guess I'll have to put it out."

"Thank you."

Mix ground the butt in the ashtray and leaned back in his seat. He took a magazine out of his canvas bag and started to read. Reggie glanced over occasionally when he discovered that the magazine had pictures of some rather gorgeous ladies in the buff.

"Hey, keep your eyes on the road," Mix said, when he noticed Reggie's glances becoming more frequent, "There are potholes in this road you wouldn't believe."

"I haven't seen any."

"That's because you've been too busy looking at the magazine."

"Chill. I'll keep my eyes on the road and my hands at ten and two if it will make you happy."

Mix smiled and went back to reading the article. "You can look at the women later."

Reggie looked out to the highway ahead and smiled when he saw a gash in the road that could've been topped by a man hole cover. He almost said something to Mix, but decided that he wasn't going to give him the satisfaction of being right. Reggie liked the bartender turned guide, and felt as though they were hitting it off rather well. He also had an indistinct feeling that the two of them might be heading into trouble.

"See that," Mix said pointing to the barely visible top of a large mansion.

"Yeah?"

"That belongs to Colin Macdow."

116

"Some place. Man must be making some serious jack."

"Yeah," Mix nodded.

"You know anything about Macdow?"

"Not much. Only that he's gonna fall one day." Mix stared at the clay-tile roof of the manse as if willing the structure to collapse.

"You sound sure," Reggie said, noting the conviction in Mix's voice.

"They all do. Somebody will catch up with him."

"Let's just hope he doesn't catch up with us in the meantime," Reggie said.

After driving for a couple of hours, they came upon the road that led to Vergaza. It was little more than a cart path.

"Turn here," Mix said, startling Reggie, who had been daydreaming about fighting women with emerald eyes and talons of steel.

"Hold on," Carver said as he whipped the car onto the dirt road. He thumped his head on the roof of the car as they hit a bump in the road.

"Shit, this is worse than the highway," Reggie said rubbing the top of his head.

"Don't worry, we're only on it for an hour or so."

"Great," Reggie said sarcastically. "Now I know what a can of paint feels like when it's on the mixer."

Mix smiled. "Want me to drive a little while?"

"Sure, but I don't see how that will help my kidneys."

"It won't but at least you can look at some hot women." He held up the magazine.

Reggie pulled over and they switched places.

"Hey, Mix, ask you a question?"

Mix turned his head toward Carver. "Sure."

"Why the change of heart? I mean last night you weren't exactly the friendly neighborhood scout."

"I have my reasons," Mixon said meeting Carver's

eyes with a gaze that requested trusting acceptance. "Just let it go at that."

Carver didn't want to press, since Mix was helping him. Still he wondered why the sudden offer.

An hour later, Reggie and Mix were on the outskirts of the village. Mix parked the car on a dirt enclave and got out.

Reggie popped the creaky door open and stepped out of the car. Stretching his arms, he groaned, "Man, those last roads were as lumpy as a fat chick's ass. Jesus, my back is killing me."

"Hey, I told you this is a poor country, they don't build roads."

"I heard that."

"Well, there it is," Mix said waving his arm at the squalid little shantytown that sat in the middle of nowhere. The village consisted of about ten or fifteen shacks, and a couple of larger buildings that must have been the poverty-row equivalent of a shopping center. In the middle of the town square, was a large well—a community watering hole.

"Jeez, what a place."

A thin dog barked and came running up to Reggie. Carver bent down to pet it and the skinny mutt growled then scampered off. "Hmm, some welcoming committee," Reggie said.

"I'm going over to the cantina, Mix suggested. "The post office, such as it is, is located over there in that building. They could tell you where this chick's father lives."

"So you're not coming with me?"

Mix shook his head. "No. I said I'd get you here and I have. I'll be over there." He pointed to a wooden building at the end of the village. The cantina looked like a saloon in a western movie, or more appropriately a saloon in a ghost town. All that was missing was a dusty breeze and a couple of tumblin' tumbleweeds.

"Okay. I'll come get you when I'm done." Reggie bent down and tied a deviant shoelace then stood up.

"Just remember, we're out of here by nightfall," Mixon reminded the black man.

"I remember."

Reggie headed for the post office while Mix went to the bar to find a phone. He had to call in and report to the boss.

2

Reggie sat outside the squalid shack that was the home of Tomas Montoya and waited for the old man to come back. He had gotten the address from the postmaster after much explaining and a twenty dollar "research fee." He had been waiting about fifteen minutes when the old man appeared. At first glance, Montoya appeared to be a small man, but upon further examination, was really quite large. It was the way he carried himself that gave him the shrunken appearance. It was as though the weight of the world rested upon his shoulders and the burden was too heavy to carry. His shoulders were slumped inward, caving in his chest. His eyes had the weary look of a man who had seen too much in his lifetime and was unable to look anymore. He was clad in threadbare clothes that at one time had been the best money could buy. Age and lack of cleaning had robbed them of their lustre. Montoya went to the front door and was about to enter when he was interrupted by Reggie.

"*¿Señor Montoya?*"

The old man turned wearily. "*Sí.*"

"*Señor Montoya, Me llamo* Reggie Carver and I'm looking, oh, uh, I mean, *yo soy mirando . . .*"

119

"You may speak English if you want," the old man said, realizing that Carver was American.

Reggie smiled, relieved. "Thanks, Mr. Montoya . . ."

"Please come in. It is too hot to be out in the sun."

Again Reggie smiled. "Thank you."

The two of them went into the house and Montoya motioned for Reggie to sit down. The interior of the shack was well kept. The furnishings had the same look of faded wealth as the old man's clothes. The oak dining room table was scratched in numerous places, as if it had been on many journeys. The china cabinet had one of its glass doors broken and the other had a thin hairline crack in it. It was obvious to the black detective that at some point in his life Montoya had been a man of wealth and means.

"So, Mr. Carver, what brings you to such a place as Vergaza?"

"Mr. Montoya, a few nights ago, your son-in-law, Diego Vargas, came into my office in Miami. I knew Diego when he worked in Miami. We were friends. When he came in, he was injured, and told us that his wife had been kidnapped when she was visiting you in Vergaza. I'm here to investigate."

In seconds, Montoya looked several years older and seemed to shrink even further into himself. He shuffled over and sat down in a torn chair. "Mr. Carver, are you familiar with the politics of San Miguel?"

"Somewhat."

"This is a dictatorship and it's run by a man named Colin Macdow. He's not the leader in the eyes of the world, we have the puppet Pedroza for that, but in this country Macdow's power is absolute."

"I've heard about him."

"So you know the story of his rise to power?"

"Not really."

"Macdow met and married the daughter of General-

120

issimo Francisco Mendolina when she was on vacation in Europe. She fell very hard for him and insisted that they live in San Miguel. It was what Macdow wanted all the time."

"So he married into power."

"Yes. Two months after they married, Generalissimo Mendolina was killed in a car-bomb explosion. His daughter was distraught and Macdow had her committed to the state hospital. He engineered his man, Armando Pedroza, into the position of ruler, which made Macdow the de facto leader of the country."

"So Macdow had planned it all along."

"*Sí.* Once he had the power he began to escalate the drug trade and steal from the treasury. Anyone that stood in his way disappeared."

"How do your daughter and Diego fit in?"

Montoya sighed as if he was wasting his time telling the story, but he told it anyway. "As you might be able to see, at one time I was a man of slightly more importance than the peasant you see before you. A lawyer, in fact. But there is no need for lawyers in a government with no justice. Diego and my daughter were trying to change that."

"How?"

"A revolution."

Reggie sat up in his chair and leaned forward as Montoya continued.

"They have become clichés, our little revolutions, but it is the only way that we can take back our government. My daughter and Diego were involved with *El Frente,* a revolutionary group. Diego was one of the leaders. That is why Maria disappeared. I believe they took my daughter in an effort to blackmail Diego into stopping the resistance movement."

"I hate to ask, but why didn't Macdow just have Diego and your daughter killed?"

121

"Diego had been forced to go underground and Macdow couldn't locate him. My daughter came to Vergaza to tell me goodbye, since they wouldn't be able to surface until they had formed the core of the resistance and started the overthrow."

"So how did . . ."

He shook his white-haired head. "One of her best friends was forced to talk. She told Macdow of the visit and he had someone waiting outside of town. I never did get to talk to her."

His eyes misted over and he wiped them with his forearm. "Diego and the others found out who the informant was and through her discovered where they had taken Maria."

"Miami."

"That is what the woman said."

"So Diego went to us for help and we let him fall right into their hands. God, I'm sorry."

"What do you mean?"

Reggie looked concerned. "After he talked to my partner and me, Diego was taken away in an ambulance and we haven't been able to find him. We think someone may have intercepted the message and somehow faked the call. Damn! If I had only known."

"But you could not have known."

"I guess, but still I should have done something. Now Diego and Maria . . ."

Montoya finished Reggie's sentence for him. ". . . are both probably dead."

He paused. "Unless . . ."

"Unless what?"

"Unless you believe in fairy tales."

Reggie got a cold feeling in his stomach as if he had just swallowed a block of ice. He thought back to the woman with the glowing green eyes. "What do you mean fairy tales?"

122

"There is a story that the enemies of Macdow are taken so as to serve the Baobhan Sith."

"Diego mentioned him. Who is this guy Handseth?"

"I do not mean a person, The Baobhan Sith are supposed to be things, evil things."

Reggie looked at him with fearful eyes.

"What kind of things?" he asked apprehensively, afraid of the answer.

Montoya waved his brown leathery hand in front of his face as if to dismiss the notion of evil monsters.

"They are childish superstitions, Mr. Carver. Fantasy to frighten the villagers, who speak of them in hushed tones. A story spread by agents of Macdow to keep the ignorant peasants afraid."

"So you don't believe?"

"Señor Carver, my daughter was a very brave girl and she probably died for what she believed in. Diego loved her very much and lost his life trying to find her. I loved them both, but they were not taken by any evil supernatural creatures. The only evil creature in this country is Colin Macdow."

"So you don't think . . ."

"No. I don't. The only thing I know is that Macdow took my family from me and for that he will be punished."

Montoya's eyes clouded again. He wiped them and his expression grew fierce. "I will dance on the grave of Colin Macdow one day, Mr. Carver, I assure you."

Reggie nodded.

"Mr. Montoya, could you tell me the names of any of the people in *El Frente* so that I can talk to them?"

Montoya involuntarily drew away from Reggie.

"I don't know their names."

Reggie noticed the sudden distress and figured out what was wrong immediately. "Mr. Montoya, I'm not one of Macdow's goons."

"Then you will understand why I cannot give you the names. If you know their names and someone finds out you know—I cannot have your torture and death on my conscience. Already it is too heavy."

He paused to wipe his brow. "If you are one of Macdow's men then my keeping the names from you will save the lives of my countrymen. If it is any consolation, I do not think that you are."

"Thanks and I get your point. Well, I have enough to go on anyway. Just for kicks, who's the resident authority on these Baobhan Sith things?"

"Bernado Cilon. He owns the cantina. You cannot miss him. He has a small scar the shape of a quarter-moon on his cheek."

"Bernardo Cilon. Scar on cheek." Reggie jotted the notes down on his pad. "Thanks."

Montoya lifted himself up out of the chair and stood up, a signal to Reggie that their conversation was at an end. Reggie got up and headed for the door.

"Thanks for all your help. I'll be in touch with you when we find out what happened."

"Be careful, Señor Carver. Macdow has many friends."

Reggie stepped out of the screen door and into the dusty street. He turned and faced the weary man. *"Gracias, Señor Montoya. Yo creo que su hija está viva."*

Montoya smiled sadly. "I hope she is alive, too."

He turned and went back into the house.

"Adiós."

"Vaya con dios."

Going with God is the only way to go, Reggie thought. He made his way down to the cantina.

When he arrived and went inside, Reggie saw Mix sitting on a rickety stool at the bar talking to the bartender, an older guy dressed in a simple white

124

cotton shirt and pants. Probably comparing notes on how to make a fuzzy navel. The black man went and sat beside his guide.

"Hey," Mix said between sips of a beer, "Did you find what you were looking for?"

"Some."

"Hey, Reg. This is Bernardo, a fellow bartender."

"Hello."

Reggie smiled when he saw the crescent-shaped scar on the man's cheek. This was the man with whom he wanted to talk. "Bernardo, it's a pleasure."

"The pleasure ees me, señor," the skinny man said.

"Can you get me a beer?"

"Jess, of course."

The man deftly pulled a bottle out of the cooler and decapitated it in one motion, setting the cool beer in front of the black man.

"Thanks," Reggie said as he drained a third of the bottle. "Hot day."

"Jess, Vergaza ees very hot."

"So Tomas Montoya says you are the smart one in this place."

"I no smarter than most," Bernardo shrugged his angular shoulders almost touching his oversized ears. Reggie figured that with such large ears Cilon stayed inside during a windstorm.

"Bernardo, did you know Maria Montoya Vargas?"

"Only to see her."

"I'm looking into her disappearance. The last place she was seen was in Vergaza."

He shuffled a bit as if the conversation was making him feel uncomfortable. "Maria was headstrong girl. She make trouble for Scotsman."

"Yeah. So Montoya said. He also told me about something else."

"And what ees that?"

125

Reggie leaned over and stared into Cilon's eyes. "Bernardo, what do you know about the Baobhan Sith?"

A look of fear quickly swept over the bartender's thin pockmarked face. He turned away and started wiping down the glasses. "As I tole your friend, I know nothing of such things."

Reggie looked at Mix, who stared into the end of his bottle and said nothing. Carver looked back at Cilon. "That's not what Montoya told me."

"He is an old fool who is not afraid of death or worse."

"What do you mean or worse. What could be worse than death?"

The man turned around and whispered to Carver, "There are many things worse than death. Now *por favor,* I am very busy."

The cantina was empty except for Reggie and Mix.

"I need your help."

"I need my life."

A man came in to the cantina and sat down at a battered table near the door. He leaned back in the rattan chair and watched Carver, Mix and Cilon. Bernardo didn't see him.

"Come on, Reg. Let's go," Mix said, looking at his watch, "It's getting late."

"Just a second," Carver said, waving Mix off, then turning to Cilon. "Please, Bernardo, help me."

"I will give you this advice," Bernardo whispered, "do not stray from the roads."

Reggie's brow knitted with confusion at the strange admonition.

At that moment, the bartender saw the man sitting in the back. Their eyes met. The man shook his head slightly. Bernardo got a frightened look on his face and looked away.

126

"I have to get back to work," he said, then disappeared into the storeroom in the back of the bar.

Reggie turned to Mix. "Don't stray from the roads he says. No shit. And why did you clam up when he said you were asking about the Sith?"

Mix ignored the question. "Let's go. It's getting late."

"Wait a sec," Reggie said.

"Come on. You got all you're going to get out of that guy. Let's hit the road. Remember our deal."

"Coming."

Reggie got up and walked slowly out of the bar. His eyes met the eyes of the man who had frightened the bartender. The two men stared at each other for a moment. The man at the table smiled. Reggie nodded and kept going out the door. The warning of Bernardo Cilon played in his head like a broken phonograph. *Don't stray from the road. Don't stray from the road.*

Mix interrupted the litany inside Reggie's head. "To answer your question, I was asking about that guy you mentioned, Bob Handseth."

"Oh," Reggie said, accepting the comment. He had mentioned the now-misinterpreted name on the way to Vergaza. "Well, let's take Scarface's advice and 'get the fock out of her, mang'."

Mix grinned at Reggie's imitation of Al Pacino's Tony Montana in the movie, *Scarface,* and stepped up his pace a bit.

They walked in silence the rest of the way to the car. Mix considered what his next move would be, while Reggie thought about two things: the warning from Cilon and the torn sheet on his bed; the four slashes in the heavy cotton fabric. He felt a tingle creep up his back as he imagined those claws ripping into him. He shuddered.

The sun was just dipping into the horizon as Mix got

127

into the car with the thoughtful black man. Carver looked concerned. Mix then realized that it was not a look of concern that Reggie had on his face, it was the unmistakable mask of fear.

3

Chris Blaze woke up worried about his partner. His concern hinged on the fact that Reggie didn't know about the attack on Blaze last night. If that damned idiot at the hotel desk had answered the phone the second time, Chris would've been able to tell his partner what had happened. The vampire detective had to get through to Carver tonight. He knew that Reggie would be unprepared for the kind of powerful assault that Chris had repelled the night before at the office. The woman's strength was supernatural, of that Chris was sure. He had barely been able to use his own strength and leverage to get her off him. Chris still wondered what had caused the sudden pain that she seemed to experience, but he knew from the scream that it had been agonizing. Perhaps he had snapped her arm or dislocated a shoulder when he'd thrown her out the window. He wished he knew.

Chris picked up the phone and started to dial the hotel room. To his amazement someone answered on the first ring. It was a woman.

"¡Hola!"

"Yes, I need to speak to Reggie Carver please."

"Wung moment."

Chris heard a click and then the phone ringing. After the fourth ring he knew Reggie wasn't there. He waited for the operator to pick up. She did on the sixth ring.

"He ees not in. May I take a message?"

"Yes, have him call Chris at the office as soon as he

128

gets in, please."

"Grits?"

"Chris, C-h-r-i-s."

"Oh, Chrees," she said.

"Yes."

"I weel give him the message."

"Thank you."

Chris hung up, sat back in his chair and waited for the call, so that he could warn his partner that there might be supernatural beings involved in the case. He just knew that Reggie would be thrilled.

4

When the car hit the gash in the road, Carver knew immediately that the Colt had blown a tire by the unmistakable sound, a pop like a gunshot and the sudden lurch to the right. He slowed up and pulled the car into a clearing so that they would at least have the light of the full moon to see what they were doing. Mix had amazingly slept through the explosion but was awakened by the silence when the car stopped.

"What's up?" he asked, stifling a yawn.

"Damn flat tire." Reggie grumbled as he opened the squeaky door and stepped into the grass. He was immediately set upon by a flurry of mosquitoes.

"You little bloodsuckin' bastards," he said as he swatted the pesky insects. He went to the back of the car and opened the trunk. Getting out the jack and the spare, he rolled the tire to the front of the car. Inserting the jack underneath, he started to crank the car off of the ground.

A shadow flew across the hood of the car. A suggestion of something quickly appeared then vanished. Carver looked up but saw nothing. A twist of fear stabbed him in the gut.

"Don't stray from the road," Mix said, in a deep ghoulish voice, then laughed.

Reggie jumped at the sound of the man's voice. The strange warning had spooked him and he was in no mood for levity. "Cut the jokes and help me get these lug nuts off."

Still chuckling, Mix grabbed the lug wrench and started twisting the nuts off the wheel. They came off as easily as if an infant had screwed them on with a toy wrench. "Where the hell'd you rent this thing? This tire's barely on here."

"Some rental place, I don't know. Just hurry up. This place gives me the willies."

The night was silent save for the buzz of mosquitoes and an occasional cricket. A bird cawed in the night air.

"Damn, cheap-assed country ain't even got street-lights" Carver said staring up into the treetops.

"Hold these, will you?"

"Yeah."

Mix handed the nuts to Reggie, who put them on the hood of the car.

The bird cawed again, only louder this time.

Closer.

Reggie realized that the sound was just a bird and yet it frightened him. There was something different about it that Reggie couldn't place. It had an almost human quality.

"Did you hear that?"

"Yeah."

"Are there crows down here?" Reggie said looking in the direction of the sound of the bird.

"I guess. You heard one, didn't you?"

"Yeah."

"Gimme that spare."

Reggie handed the bartender the bald tire.

"Nice," Mix said when he saw the lousy condition of the spare.

"Yeah, Telly Savalas designed it. Will you hurry up?"

Lining up the holes in the rim with the bolts of the tire drum, Mix slid the tire on.

"Nuts," Mix said.

Reggie turned to him and said in an urgent voice, "What's wrong?"

"The nuts," Mix said, pointing to the nuts on the hood. "Gimme them."

"Oh."

Reggie scooped up the nuts and handed them to his friend. Mix affixed them to their respective bolts and started screwing them on by hand.

Just then, Carver saw the shadow dance across the hood of the car again. He looked up to try to see what had just flown by, but saw only the bright moon. He heard the crow again. Its cry sounded almost like a laugh. A shiver of fear ran up his spine and pinched his neck.

"Hurry up, Mix."

"Be done in a jiffy."

The shadow flew over again and Reggie heard the flapping of large wings. Again he looked up and tried to spot the flying creature, but saw nothing. A drop of sweat rolled down the side of his cheek.

"Hurry," he said in an almost inaudible whisper.

Mix used the wrench to crank the nuts on tighter.

Reggie rubbed a drop of sweat out of his ear. A creeping sense of dread began to crawl over him as the words of the bartender Bernardo Cilon came back to him, *Don't stray from the road.*

Reggie looked over in the direction of the cawing bird and shuddered.

"There," Mix said, tightening the last bolt. "All done."

131

"Let's get the hell out of here."

"Hold on. I want to tighten the bolts on the other tires. If they were like the last one I'm sure they could use it."

Reggie sighed. "Go ahead."

Mix began to pop off the hubcaps and tighten the lug nuts of the other tires.

The crow chattered noisily.

"Shut up," Reggie said as he picked up a rock and hurled it in the direction of the bird's call. Once again, he heard the flapping of wings as the bird took off.

"Son-of-a-bitch bird."

Mix was finishing up with the last tire when Reggie heard something land in a nearby thicket of trees. He peered into the clump of woods trying to see if he could find the bird. The trees were a mass of shadows that moved with the slight breeze. They looked almost like a living thing—a malevolent shadow beast that sucked you into its dark maw. For a moment, he thought he saw green eyes staring at him, but decided that it was just the moonlight reflecting off the shiny leaves of a bush. He turned away and started for the driver's seat.

Then he heard it.

A strange crackling sound that chilled him to the marrow. The sound was exactly the same as the noise that Chris made when he transformed from a bat into a man. A popping, stretching sound of bone and flesh reshaping. Reggie knew that something was out there in the woods changing shape—something horrible—and he wasn't about to wait and find out what it was.

"Let's go," Reggie whispered.

Mix stood there as if he was waiting for whatever was approaching. "Wait a minute . . ."

Reggie heard branches snapping and footsteps in the soft earth. Footsteps coming towards them. Heavy footsteps.

"Now!" he shouted again almost in a panic. "Get in the fuckin' car!" He pushed Mix towards the door.

"Hold on, Reggie . . ." Mix said, struggling to break free of the panicked black man.

The footsteps picked up their pace.

Carver opened the door and shoved Mix in then ran around the front of the car and jumped behind the wheel and cranked the engine. Without checking to see if there was any traffic in the road, he gunned it and took off, leaving behind whatever was there.

"What the hell was that all about?" Mix said, seemingly bewildered by the black man's actions.

"I thought I heard something in the woods."

Mix looked at Carver.

"I didn't hear anything," he lied.

"Well, I did and I wasn't about to stay and find out what it was."

"You're letting that Bernardo guy get to you. I didn't even finish the back tire."

"It got us here. It'll get us back," Reggie said. His face was a mask of sweat. He wiped his brow with the short sleeve of his shirt. He turned to Mix. "Look, let's just forget it. Maybe I did panic."

Mix nodded and sat back in the seat, as Reggie stared at the road ahead, careful to avoid potholes.

When Reggie wasn't looking, Mix slipped his weapon back into his pocket and settled back into the seat.

"You don't believe in monsters, do you, Reggie?" Mix asked.

"No," Reggie said not wanting to be made the butt of a joke. "Why, you know of some I should?"

Mix paused for a moment and then shook his head. "Let's get back to Viera."

As they drove back to the town, Reggie wondered why Mix seemed to be upset because of the quick departure from where they'd pulled over to fix the flat. Carver remembered how he had struggled to stay, almost as if . . . no. If Mix had wanted to set Reggie up, he could've pulled a gun and shot him anytime. On the deserted roads that they were travelling, Reggie wouldn't have been found for days. Besides, Mix did save Reggie from the three banditos last night and why would he have done that if he meant to kill him? Carver looked over at the man next to him and decided that Richard Mixon was not his enemy.

Mix turned and smiled as if he'd read Carver's mind.

5

Reggie pulled up to the outside of Mix's apartment building. A two-story affair, rectangular, functional, stucco walls.

"Well, here we are," Reggie said, glad to be back in town and away from whatever the hell that was in the woods.

Mix got out and walked around to the window on the driver's side.

"You look beat," he said, pulling his shirttail out. "Whew, hot night."

Groggily, Reggie stuck out his hand. "I am beat. Thanks for helping me get to Vergaza, Mix."

"Hey, forget about it. Besides you did pay me, remember?"

"Yeah."

"So are you gonna be leaving San Miguel now?"

"Not yet. I want to see if I can find out anything more about this Macdow, his background and stuff."

"A man can get killed asking questions about him."

"Yeah, well. A man's gotta do . . ."

". . . what a man's gotta do." Mix said, finishing

Reggie's sentence. "Man, you must be either a movie buff or else you just like clichés."

Reggie ignored the remark, "I'll see you later."

"Hey, Reg, be careful."

Reggie worked up a smile and then drove back to the hotel. He parked in the hotel lot. Wearily, the tired detective got out of the car and dragged himself into the hotel. The tension of the near confrontation had sapped him of his energy.

When he got up to his room, Reggie opened the door and was startled by the sight of a man about to leave. He reached for the blackjack strapped to his leg, but stopped when he saw that the skinny man's eyes were wide with fright.

"What the hell are you doing in here so damn late?" Carver asked, his voice laced with anger.

"Perdón a me, señor. I wass making the bed. The maid no show up today. We jess find out."

"Boy, news travels slow around here," Carver said, looking at his watch. He didn't believe the bellman, but didn't press the issue. This was a poor country and the man was probably looking for something to "borrow."

"I replace the sheet that got torn."

"Good," Reggie said wondering why the man was so nonchalant about it.

"Buenas noches, señor," the bellman said as he backed out of the doorway into the hall.

"Night."

Reggie checked his belongings and found nothing missing. The man must have just arrived and not had time to see what was available. Carver made a mental note to check the bellman's story with the manager, but that was for the morning. For now he had a phone call to make. He went over to the phone and dialed his partner's number. After a couple of rings, Chris picked up.

135

"Blaze, Carver and Fayer. May I help you?"

"Yeah, get me the hell outta here."

"Reg." Chris said relieved to hear his partner's voice.

"Yeah, what's up?"

"Well, other than getting jumped by someone or something last night after I got off the phone with you not much."

"Shit! What do you mean someone or something?"

Chris told Reggie about the sudden attack. The kick to the head. The powerful fingers around his throat. His countermove and the deafening scream that followed it. He also told his partner about the fierce green eyes. "I tell you, Reg, she was as strong as me and got up from the fall like it was nothing but an inconvenience."

There was a pause at the end of the line.

"Reggie?"

No answer.

"Reg? Did you hear what I said?"

"Fuck a duck. Another vampire? Jesus Christ, how many of you suckers are there?"

"Wait a sec, I didn't say she was a vampire, I don't know what she was, but she was damn sure powerful. I don't know why she didn't come back up either."

"Well, a bitch just like you described came into my room last night, green eyes and everything. She ripped my sheet into shreds with her fingernails."

"Let me guess. You were in bed, heard a noise at the door, got up and went out on the porch."

"Balcony," Carver corrected, enjoying Chris's Sherlock Holmes imitation.

"Balcony," Chris corrected himself then continued, "And you waited to see who came in. After you heard her ripping things up."

"And saw those mean eyes."

"Let me tell you," Chris said.

"Go on."

"So when you saw that there was something not quite right about her, you made a quick exit by jumping to the ground, only you didn't have time to put on any clothes."

"Just undies, but that's pretty good. How'd you know? And if you say, 'Elementary, my dear Carver,' I'll slide through the phone lines and kick your ass."

Chris told Reggie about his call and how he overheard the clerk call out to Carver before hanging up the phone.

"And that lazy son of a bitch never answered again?"

"No. But I guess my warning was unnecessary anyway. You found out for yourself."

"Yeah, twice. I think someone or something was after me tonight, too. And I might know what."

"What do you mean you might know what?"

"Well, when I went to Vergaza, I talked to Maria's father."

"And what did he say?"

Reggie related the conversation with Montoya to his partner, including the part about the Baobhan Sith. He also told Chris about the discussion with Bernardo and what he had said about the Sith.

"So we mistook Diego's message as meaning a man's name, not a thing?"

"We sure as hell did."

"You think these Baobhan Sith are what you saw and what I fought with?"

"Well, if you had asked me a year ago, before I met a vampire cop, I would have laughed in your face, but now I'm not so sure."

"Same here," Chris said. "So what happened tonight?"

"When we were driving back from Vergaza we got a flat. Me and Mix got out to change it. While we were

137

fixing the tire, a bird kept flying over. Damn," Reggie said, suddenly remembering something that had happened the night Diego had disappeared.

"What's the matter?"

"The night Diego got taken when I got home I remember hearing someone outside my apartment. I got up and went outside, but didn't see anybody. Just a big black bird. It looked like it was watching me."

"You sure?"

"It struck me as weird at the time, but I chalked it up to my usual paranoia. Now, I don't know."

Chris frowned at this bit of news. The case was slipping further and further into the twilight zone.

"So, finish what happened on the road?"

"Well, I heard this bird land in the woods close by and then I heard something that about made me shit a brick."

"What was that?"

"It was the same sound you make when you're changing. Y'know that weird crackly shit. When I heard that, I thought my ass was shredded meat. Mix said he didn't hear anything, but I know I did."

"So what happened?"

"I hauled ass. I wasn't about to hang out and find out I was right and Mix was wrong. I got in the car and drove back to the hotel without stopping."

"We need to find out what these things are."

"That's a no-shit statement. I'm going to try and see if I can find out a little more about them and what their connection might be with Colin Macdow."

"Okay, but be careful."

"I will, dad. Send Sue my love."

"Sure," Chris said, then added in a stern tone of voice, "Watch your ass, Carver."

"I got my head glued on backwards, checking it out."

Chris smiled. "I'll see you."

"You bet your vampire ass you will."

Reggie hung up the phone. He was tired, but the call to Chris had provoked him to action. First he'd catch a couple of hours sleep and then head out to Macdow's villa for a look-see. Maybe the villa was where these Sith things lived.

He set his alarm clock and lay down. The bed was so soft he felt as though he melted into it. So comfortable. He closed his weary eyes and drifted . . .

"Shit!" He said as he sat up quickly.

The door!

Carver jumped up from the bed and hurried over to the front door. He reinforced it with a heavy chair then went over and checked the sliding glass doors to the balcony. The bar was firmly entrenched in the slot. He smiled and went back to the comfort of the bed. Sleep snatched him in a couple of minutes.

The alarm buzzed right on time and a refreshed Reggie got up. He grabbed his binoculars and his cross and made his way out the door. He got down into the lobby and continued straight through to the door leading to the parking lot. He got in the rented car and pulled out of the parking lot. In his haste, he didn't see the man start to follow him from a safe distance.

6

Humidity clung to the detective's skin like graveclothes. An oily coat of perfumed bug spray kept the mosquitoes at bay. They hovered around Reggie like vultures waiting for an animal to die. Carver crouched on top of a hill overlooking Macdow's villa. He'd parked the car in a gap in the dense foliage of the jungle and had made his way up to this vantage point.

From the top of the hill, he could hear a whining

sound that set his teeth on edge. The noise appeared to be coming from the direction of the villa. Carver put the binoculars up to his eyes and surveyed the area near the house. The squealing sound changed and music began to play, a high-pitched whining melody. He looked over and saw a faint light shimmering through the gaps in the bushes that blocked his view. He got up and shifted his vantage point so he could see more clearly.

When he improved his view, Reggie saw two women dancing around a fire in a brazier in the courtyard. Each one wore a long green dress that swirled in hypnotic fashion as they spun around the flame. Both had flowing tresses of blond hair that glinted as they caught the shimmering flame in their lustrous shine. He watched the spectable below him with a mixture of curiosity and fear, heavy on the fear. He recognized one of the women as being the one who had invaded his hotel room last night. There were two men watching the dance and clapping in rhythm to the music, which was not Latin as one would expect in a Spanish-speaking land. The music had a distinctly British flavor, almost like an Irish jig, but not quite. Reggie moved again so that he could see better. When he saw the red hair of Colin Macdow glowing in the light of the flames, he recognized that the tune was Scottish and the whining instrument the bagpipes. Macdow clapped and seemed to be enjoying himself. Reggie couldn't see the face of the other man that sat with Macdow, as his countenance was obscured by a palm tree.

The tempo of the music increased as did the speed of the women's dance as they spun around the fire. The music seemed to be building to a climax.

Dancing. Whirling. Clapping.

The music. Squealing. Swelling.

The girls twirling faster in time with the music.

Faster.

140

Building.

Fiery hair shimmering.

Colin and the other man were stomping their feet, clapping their hands.

In the din, Reggie thought he heard the wail of a baby. A squeal of fear.

No.

Bagpipes.

God, he hoped it was the bagpipes.

Reggie watched the bizarre scene that was being played out in the courtyard and fear bubbled in his gut.

The music changed pitch and picked up the tempo as the girls began to blend together in a swirling blur of golden hair and fabric. A glint from the hand of Colin Macdow caught Reggie's attention and then he saw the knife.

The bagpipes cried.

One of the girls tossed her head back laughing as she spun around.

Reggie wanted to get closer. He took a step and slipped on a slick patch of slimy soil. He slid, grasping a large dead branch to stop his descent. The branch snapped loudly. Instinctively, the detective ducked into a thick clump of palmettoes to avoid being seen, although there was little chance of that. They couldn't have heard him over the din . . .

Abruptly, the music stopped.

Dead.

Nothing.

Carver hid in the bushes as he waited for something to happen. His mouth felt dry as he smacked his lips together. There was no way they could have heard him.

Slowly, he put the binoculars back to his eyes, bringing the courtyard into his field of vision. In the circular view through the binoculars, he saw the two women staring at him from below. Wild-eyed. Vicious.

141

The feral expressions on their faces reminded Reggie of tigers set for the kill. His heart jumped. They pointed in Carver's direction. One of them smiled and took off running toward him.

7

Chris and Sue arrived at the house at the same time. "Hey, honey, how was your first day at work?"

"It was good. I had a lot to do, paperwork, and things like that, but overall I think I like being in charge."

"That's great. I'm proud of you."

Chris stuck the key in the lock and opened the door. He held the door for his wife and she went in. He followed.

Sue went into the kitchen and poured a glass of water. "How's your case going?"

"Slowly," Chris said, leaving out any reference to the attack on him. He didn't want Sue to worry. "Reggie's in San Miguel following some leads. I think we're making progress."

"You sound funny. Is something wrong?"

Damn, Chris thought, *she sure is perceptive.* "I'm just frustrated."

Sue went over and put her arm around him and gave him a big hug. "You'll find them."

Chris smiled and nodded. But he thought not of the Vargases but of the creatures that Reggie had mentioned, the Baobhan Sith. *Yeah,* he thought grimly, *we'll find them or they'll find us.*

8

Carver's eyes widened when he saw the speed at

142

which the woman travelled. She would be on him in no time at the pace she was running. He spun around and started down the hill, taking it in skidding leaps. He tried to maintain his balance as his momentum began to cause him to lose control. A low-hanging branch thick with heavy thorns tore a flap of skin from his cheek. Quickly, blood began to flow.

"Fuck," he hissed as pain lanced his face.

Carver hit a root and almost fell but maintained his pace. As he stumbled in the darkness of the woods, he held the flap of skin tightly to his face, trying to stop the flow of blood, but the slippery flesh kept sliding from his grasp. He could hear the crashing branches behind him on the other side of the hill as he fled deeper into the woods. His stomach flipped over when he heard the malevolent laughter. A demonic giggling, like that of a little girl at a slumber party in Hell.

Suddenly, the laughter stopped, as did the crashing of the brush. Carver had reached the bottom of the hill at the edge of the clearing where his car was parked, when he saw the silhouette of a man standing beside his car. He skidded to a halt and hid inside a patch of heavy foliage. He couldn't see who the man was, but reasoned that it was one of Macdow's men who had found his car and was waiting for him.

"Damn," he whispered as his source of escape was thwarted. He waited to see what the man would do before he formed a plan.

The woods were silent save for a tit-tit sound, like water dripping on paper. Reggie wondered where the sound was coming from, then realized that it was drops of blood falling from his face onto the leaves on which he lay. He pulled out the tail of his shirt and pressed it against his assaulted flesh.

"Fucking monsters," Reggie whispered as he clasped the cross tightly in his hand.

143

He hid in the bushes as quietly as he could. As the initial rush of adrenaline wore off, Carver began to feel the pain from the gash in the side of his face. It burned as if it was on fire. God, he wished he had something to numb the pain. Anything.

He heard a low moan. The desolate sound frightened him as he looked around for its source before realizing that it had come from his own tortured mouth. *It was me! No. No*. The man must have heard him. He looked up and saw the man move away from the car. Carver hunkered down in the brush, wondering whether to make a run for it or not. A sudden chill swept over him as he waited for his assailants to strike.

Nothing.

He waited.

The woods were quiet. Cemetery quiet.

His face screamed at him for relief from its anguish. He stifled another moan.

A horsefly landed on the bloody cheek for a free and easy meal. Reggie didn't dare slap it away, for fear of making a sound. He winced as its sharp proboscis pierced his flesh and the insect started to dine.

Suddenly, there was a crackle of leaves in the shrubs a few yards away from him. Reggie tried to pull himself into the ground as he peered into the darkness that engulfed him, but in the inky gloom he could see nothing. Whatever was out there was obscured in the shadowy woods. He could only wait and hope that Macdow's man or the weird woman didn't find him.

A twig snapped.

His heart hammered in his chest and he could have sworn that anyone within fifty feet could hear it. It banged against his chest driving more of his blood out of the wound in the side of his face. He heard the crackle again, only closer this time. Much closer. He knew in his heart that they were going to find him.

The satiated horsefly buzzed away.

Reggie's blood spattered the ground.

The crunch of dead leaves filled his ears.

Closer.

Crunch. Crackle.

Drip.

Closer.

Crackle.

Drip. Drip.

Almost on top of him.

Visions of his body being torn apart ripped his mind.

Closer.

Death was coming for him.

Reggie tensed and prepared to bolt.

Suddenly, he heard a flapping sound above him. Big wings displaced the humid air. He looked up as a huge black bird dove upon him stabbing his wounded cheek with its sharp beak. He screamed from the sudden and intense pain. The raven stabbed at the wound again and flew up into the night. The opossum in the brush, where it had been foraging, scurried away when it heard the frantic screams of the doomed Reggie Carver.

9

Macdow heard the distant screams of the black man and smiled. He pulled Mary close and kissed her. "Your sister seems to ha' found our little Peeping Tom."

"Is she ginna bring him back so that I can ha' a taste."

"Aye, we'll all ha' a taste of his red life before we take him to the farm."

He turned to the man with the bagpipes. "Play us a song, Seamus. Make it a happy one."

The bird swooped down on Carver again, hitting him on the shoulder with its sharp beak. He didn't know whether it broke the skin but he wasn't hanging around to find out. He scampered to his feet and made it three feet before the beak found its mark on his temple. Pain jolted him again. It felt like the time he was hit with a baseball when he was a kid playing Little League. He went to his knees and then to his face. Darkness started to cover him with a black sheet as if anticipating his death. In the distance, he could hear the bagpipes playing and thought grimly how he had always wanted an Al Hibbler tune to be played at his funeral.

The last thing Carver heard was the crackling and snapping of transforming flesh. He didn't hear the screams that followed.

11

Drucinda smiled as she stared at the unconscious black man. She almost picked him up and carried him back to the villa to share him with her sister before they took him to the farm, but she wanted the first sip. She crouched down and ripped the front of Carver's shirt. Her tongue danced around her lips as she bent over to attach the needlelike teeth of that tongue to the black man's chest. A thin trail of spittle traced a line from the corner of her mouth to her chin. Fresh blood was always the best. Her tongue made contact with Reggie's skin when all of a sudden she felt indescribable pain rip through her gut. As she stood up and stared at the sharp end of the oak spear that protruded from her abdomen, she knew that it had pierced her abnormally located heart. She screamed as she felt the spirit of the Earth Mother spread from the wound and start to destroy each cell in her body. Her upper torso started to collapse onto itself as she quickly shrank from the power of the wood. She turned her head just before the cancer spread and saw the man who had killed her standing behind her. He smiled as she groaned the word, "Stephenson," then collapsed into a gooey mess of flesh. The earth sucked the ichor into the ground, and the grass within ten feet around the spot died. A moth flew over the patch of ground and immediately fell to the ground dead. The man who had killed the Sith lifted Carver and carried him back to Reggie's rent-a-car. He put Carver in the passenger seat, put an herbal remedy on the wound on the black man's cheek and then bandaged it. He hurried back to the death site and picked up the oak spear that had done the deed then went back to his vehicle. As he got into the car, the last of the Stephensons was happy. *One down two to go,* he thought, as he started the car and took Reggie back to his room.

12

Where was she? Colin Macdow wondered as he waited for Drucinda to come back with the black detective. Sunup was fast approaching and she couldn't withstand the power of the Eye of the Sky Father.

"Michael. Paulo." Macdow called to two of his bodyguards. "Come wi' me. We must find Dru before the sun rises."

"Let me go wi' ye, Father," Mary said. The thought of drinking from the detective had made her hungry and she wanted his blood.

147

"Na, you canna go. It is too close to sunrise."

"I thirst terrible."

"There's nourishment inside."

"I want it fresh na from some half-dead . . ."

"Dinna argue wi' me. Go inside."

She glared at him, but did as she was told.

Macdow turned to the two men. "Come on, lads."

The trio went out into the woods to find her.

When they got to the spot where Dru had captured Reggie, Colin saw the dead grass and the pile of insects and small creatures of the night that had ventured over the tainted area and died. He knew that Drucinda was dead. The Earth Mother had swallowed her and left the ground lifeless.

He fell to his knees and howled the cry of the dead to warn the Dark Mother that a child was coming. The sound tore through the brush and trees reaching the villa, and Mary knew that her sister was gone. The men with the Scotsman turned away from their leader's anguish. They knew of their boss's unpredictable nature and didn't want to risk incurring his anger by watching him in his grief.

Macdow howled one last time and got up, brushing the dirt from his knees.

"Let's git back to the villa," he said in a voice so cold you could swear you could see his icy breath.

Paulo and Michael followed Macdow, neither daring to speak. They could see that their leader was deep in thought.

Colin knew that somehow this Reggie Carver had gotten lucky and killed his Dru. Carver couldn't know about the Blessed Red Life or even have access to it so he must have stabbed her through the heart with a wooden stake or spear. That had to be how she died. The Scotsman pictured the scenario. Dru had attacked Carver. He'd picked up a sharp stick and stabbed her in

148

the abdomen, luckily piercing her heart. There was no other explanation. If the last of the Stephenson clan wasn't dead, Colin would suspect that the Destroyer was behind it. But Macdow had chopped off his head personally and knew that he was gone from this earth. There was a slim chance that perhaps they'd made a mistake in their assumption that Stuart Stephenson was the last of his line, but that was merely speculation. Macdow had to know the truth about what had happened to Drucinda and there was only one man who knew that fact, a very lucky black man. Macdow scowled evilly. But your luck just ran out, me bonny lad. It just ran out.

Chapter Five

1

Groggily, Reggie got up out of bed and then with a start realized that he was alive.

"Hey," he said as he looked at himself in the mirror. "Not too bad for a dead guy." He gingerly touched his bandaged face and wondered who had saved him and why. He knew who had attacked him, the Baobhan Sith, but he had no clue as to who his savior had been. Perhaps the man beside his car had been an ally not an enemy.

He went into his luggage and pulled out the bottle of aspirin and shook three out of it. His head ached, especially his temple where the bird had struck him. He went into the bathroom, poured a glass of slow moving water, and took the medicine. A yawn stretched his mouth open. He was still tired, but at the moment, sleep was a luxury that he couldn't afford. He had to get up and get to work. His flight out to Miami took off at five that afternoon and he wanted to gather as much information as possible in the time he had remaining.

After relieving himself, the weary detective reached into the shower and turned on the water for his morning "trickle." After he was through taking the drizzly shower, making sure not to wet his bandages, he got dressed, brushed his teeth and packed. He wanted to be ready to go when the time came to leave.

Carver went down to the restaurant and had a breakfast of *chorizo con huevos,* sausage and eggs. He decided that he would go and talk to Mix and see if he might know someone who would be able to help him find out more about the Scotsman and the Sith.

After he finished eating, he got up, paid his bill and went down toward the street that led to Mix's apartment house.

On the way, the streets were quiet. A few vendors prepared for the day's business. One swept the sidewalk in front of his shop, pushing the dirt out into the street. Another arranged his wares in a pleasant manner on a large table outside of his small store. One store owner motioned for Reggie to come over. The vendor was holding up a purse made out of a dried frog, and he was calling Carver to come over and inspect it. There were many things that Reggie might like to purchase as a souvenir of his trip to San Miguel; however, a preserved amphibian purse was not among them. If the man had a book on how to kill a Baobhan Sith, he would have a customer. The man waved the dead frog at Carver who smiled politely and shook his head, then continued down the street until he arrived at Mix's apartment building. Walking up the short flight of stairs, Carver made his way to Mix's apartment. He knocked on the door and waited.

There was no answer.

He knocked again.

Still no answer.

Reggie rapped a little harder. The door was solid wood and hurt his knuckles.

"Damn hard-assed thing."

There was still no answer.

"Come on, Mix, answer the door," Reggie said to

151

himself as he rapped one more time on the door.

Still the bartender didn't come to the door.

Reggie had a bad feeling about the situation. Sensing trouble, he took out his skeleton key and quickly jimmied open the lock on Mix's door. Stepping into the apartment, he scanned the living room. There were clothes strewn about and the cushions on the sofa were askew. It looked as though there had been a struggle. Reggie could see pictures in his mind of the woman with the fiery eyes ripping into Mix with the sharp nails and dripping fangs. Perhaps the dance had been a celebration of the kill.

Just then, Reggie heard a sound coming from the room off to the right. It was a low moan.

Mix was in trouble.

Reggie hurried to the door and was about to open it when he heard the unmistakable sound of squeaking springs and human passion. The relieved, embarrassed detective realized that Mix was in the middle of a lovemaking session.

"Whoops," Carver whispered as he took his hand off the doorknob. The only trouble that Mix was in was that his condom might spring a leak.

Quietly, Reggie turned around, making his way back to the front door. In a half hour or so, he'd come back and ply the bartender for more information. That'd give the man more than enough time to wet his wick.

After locking the door, he walked outside into the stifling heat. Already the morning sun had evaporated the dew, thickening the air into a hot choking mist. Reggie wiped his brow on his sleeve and sat on the sidewalk for a moment to rest. His face ached where the thorn had ripped his skin. He gingerly touched the bandage and felt a wet spot. The gauze needed changing. He saw a storefront sign. *Farmacia,* and went in to get some bandages to change his dressing.

Colin Macdow sat next to the sleeping Mary and stroked her long blond hair. He glanced over at the empty bed next to her and anger swelled in his breast. Drucinda had been his favorite, and now she was gone. Killed by a damned lucky black man after living for centuries, surviving the battle of Glenscary and the constant hounding attacks of the Stephensons. Such a pity. She wouldn't live to see the second Genesis. Oh, how things were going to change when that happened. Macdow bent over and kissed Mary, then got up to get some rest himself. He was about to lie down when his man, Paulo, knocked on the door.

"Wha' is it?" Macdow said angrily.

"Miami on the phone."

"It's about time. I could use some good news."

He went into his den and picked up the phone.

Colin Macdow was puzzled and angry after he received the news about the failed attempt to capture Blaze in Miami. From the description given to him by his connection in the city, the Scotsman knew that somehow this Blaze and Carver had discovered what they were dealing with and had somehow obtained the knowledge of the Book of the Banished Ones. It seemed impossible, as Macdow possessed the only copy of that ancient sacred tome, but how else could they know how to kill or prevent capture by the Sith if not through the unholy relic?

That morning he'd believed Carver to be lucky when he'd killed Dru, but with this new development he knew that luck had nothing to do with it. The black man knew what he was doing or else he had help. The only possible solutions were that these two detectives had learned the ways of destruction or that another Stephenson was alive and in league with the two private investigators. He picked up the phone and started to dial. He had to have some answers.

3

After finishing his first-person aid, Reggie bought a couple of candy bars and left the store. He glanced in the direction of Mix's apartment, but decided to give him a little more time. Reggie elected to do a little browsing. As he walked along the dusty sidewalk, the vision of the dancing women from last night's early morning party flashed in his mind. The shrill music of the bagpipes. The fervor of the dance. Reggie shuddered when he recalled the fierce intensity of the two women when they'd discovered his presence in the jungle. The wild savagery in their eyes sent a chill spinning up his spine, pinching off at his neck. Goosebumps danced across his arms. He could almost feel those deadly green eyes and this feeling began to be a palpable awareness, as if he was being watched.

Sensing a presence, Carver turned around and thought he saw someone duck into the alley behind him. The black detective stood for a moment, waiting to see if the person would be revealed. A dog barked, and Reggie heard its padded footfalls as it ran away. That must have been what he'd seen.

Shaking his head at his foolish anxiety, he turned back toward the road in front of him and started to walk in the direction of the hotel.

"A dog. I let a damn dog scare me," Reggie said trying to work up a disgusted tone of voice. "Damn chicken shit afraid of a dog."

He picked up his pace and started walking toward the hotel again. Carver hummed the old Platters song, "The Great Pretender," as he tried to maintain his cool. As much as he wanted to believe that it was the dog that he'd seen run into the alley, the feeling of a foreboding

154

presence didn't leave him. It hung there in his gut like a cold slab of beef.

As he walked along the street, he heard a sound come from the alley in front of him—an erratic clip-clopping that started, then stopped. The noise came from deep in the alley but sounded as though whatever was making it was approaching the exit to the street where Carver stood.

For some reason the sound made Reggie uneasy. Perhaps it was the strangeness of it in the still of the morning or its erratic nature. Maybe his anxiety was a manifestation of the sense of being watched. Whatever the cause, Reggie stopped for a moment and waited.

The sound started again, only to stop after a few halting steps. Reggie recognized it as being the sound of hooves on the stone road. *Yes. That was the sound. Hooves.* Then he remembered the dream the night the girl came into his room. The strange footfalls he'd heard and then the girl appeared. He put two and two together and got scared.

But it couldn't be the Baobhan Sith. After all, it was broad daylight and monsters don't come out during the day. *At least not any that you've ever heard of,* another voice in his head said, warning him not to assume anything. He reached up to his neck and took out the cross that hung from the gold chain. He pulled it out and let it drop down the front of his sweat-stained shirt.

The sound of the hooves got louder. Closer.

Reggie decided to wait until whatever was in the alley came out. He didn't want to pass the alley and let the thing get behind him. He waited.

A trickle of sweat traced a path down the side of his cheek and disappeared into the fabric of his shirt.

Clip-clop. Clip-clop.

The sound of the approaching hooves filled Reggie with dread. There was no reason why such a sound should frighten him and yet it did. He thought about

155

running back to Mix's apartment, but decided to stay. Maybe he could solve part of the case if he stayed. Maybe he would die, too.

Clip-clip-clop.

The creature paused—perhaps sizing Carver up for the kill.

Reggie decided to forget about the case and haul ass back to Mix's apartment and wait for him. He could wait to see whatever was there some other time . . . like in the next century. He was about to turn around when it emerged from the alley.

The creature that came out from the alley caused Reggie to laugh when he saw what had caused his alarm. A pudgy man was trying to get his stubborn donkey to come with him. The burro carried a sack of goods on his back.

Relieved, Reggie shook his head at his own foolishness. *A donkey made an ass out of me,* he thought, laughing at the sorry pun.

Suddenly, he was grabbed by the arm. He turned, expecting to see Mix, when another man grabbed his other arm. The men were of swarthy complexion, obviously Latinos. One of them was a big man dressed in a guayaberra shirt and jeans. Older. Probably in his forties. Black hair. Brown eyes. Ugly. The other was a younger man. Twenties. Thin. Scar on his left cheek. Looked like he could star in an episode of "America's Most Wanted."

"Hey! What the hell . . ."

"Come with us, Señor Carver," the older man said.

"Who . . . ?"

The two men ushered Reggie into a waiting car. The driver, another Latino, looked furtively around to see if anyone had seen the abduction, then drove off.

In the car, the befuddled Carver wanted answers. "Look, who the hell are you guys and where are you taking me?"

156

"We are friends of Maria Vargas, I am Julio," the old man shook Reggie's hand. "This is Miguel and Ricardo."

Carver nodded to the two men. *"El Frente?"* Carver said hopefully.

"Sí."

"So how do you know me?"

"Montoya called us."

"I didn't think he was part of the group."

"He only wanted us to help you. What happened to your face?"

"I had a little scrape last night."

"Ah, what happened?"

"Where are we going?"

"To a safe place," Julio said as he adjusted his coat. Carver noticed a bulge there and figured it was a gun. "So who did you fight with?"

Reggie wondered why the man was so interested in the events of last night, but answered the question. "Nobody. I was on a stakeout, got spotted and ran into a thorny branch. Not very cool, but that's the story."

"You said you had a fight. Who with?"

The man's interest began to worry Carver. This Julio would not let it go. "I said a scrape not a fight. I guess it lost something in the translation."

"You did not fight with a woman?"

"What?" Carver said, alarmed that the man knew about the woman that had been chasing him.

"A woman. One of our men was following you last night and said he saw a woman attack you."

So that was who I saw by my car, Reggie thought. But it wasn't a woman that had attacked him, it was a bird. And who saved him if not the man by the car? Something was not right.

"Look, dudes, I need to get back to town. I'm meeting a friend of mine."

"But town is not safe."

157

"I'll take my chances."

"But we cannot take you back."

"Why's that?"

"Because Macdow's men are all over. They know about the woman."

"What the hell are you talking about?"

"Meester Carver, you need to tell us everything that happened last night so that we can help you."

Reggie tried to decide whether to trust the men. Their man might have seen him attacked, but why no mention of the bird and why no mention of the rescue? He made his decision. "Look. Just take me back. I'm meeting a friend and I have a plane to catch in the afternoon."

"We cannot."

"Look. Julio . . ."

"Please, Señor Carver, we must know about the woman."

"Why?"

"It is important."

"I don't know anything about her. I was knocked out by a bird." Reggie realized how damned silly that sounded, but it was the truth. Only the men weren't buying it.

"Please, the truth or we will have to find out the truth."

"How do you think you're gonna do that?"

The man casually scratched his head. "I'm afraid we'll have to torture you."

"Goddamn it. You ain't gonna torture me."

Reggie tossed a punch that missed the man and glanced off of the window. The man, Miguel, quickly withdrew a pistol. "We will have no more of that."

"Man," Reggie heaved a frustrated gush of breath.

The driver turned down a dusty side road. The car rumbled down the bumpy trail as Reggie tried to come up with a plan that would get him out of his fix, but nothing concrete came to mind. *A plan. I need a plan. What was the plan?* He tried to come up with anything. A wisp of a notion. A trace of an idea. A smidgen of a suggestion. Anything.

His mind was a blank and if he didn't think of something soon, it would be torture time.

4

After his girlfriend left, Mix got dressed and walked down to the hotel. As he arrived and went into the lobby, he looked around for Carver but didn't see him. The only one in the lobby was an old man who sat in a coral-colored chair, reading a magazine. The man was dressed in a guayaberra shirt and Bermuda shorts. Sandals with black socks. Mix walked over to him. *"Perdón a me, tú ves un hombre negro que espérame?"*

The old man looked up, cupped a hand to his ear and said in a very loud midwestern voice, "What's that?"

Mix smiled. He should've figured the man was a tourist. "I said excuse me, but did you see a black man that was waiting for me."

"That's not what you said. You said something else. Two's a number of negro kids sprayed me or something." The man scratched his bald, sun-splotched head.

"Yes, sir, it was Spanish."

The old man appeared bewildered, "But I'm not Spanish, I'm Ted Perriman from Iowa."

"I didn't know that. Sorry."

"What are you sorry about? You couldn't have known that."

Mix forced another smile. "Yes, sir. So have you seen a black man waiting in the lobby?"

"How could you know? I might look Spanish to you and you thought I was. After all this is a country that speaks Spanish."

"That's true. So . . ."

"Honest mistake."

Mix sighed, "So have you seen a black man?"

"No. Haven't seen anybody since I sat down here. Damn place is deserted. The brochure said Viera was the fun capital of San Miguel. Some fun. My wife, Gladys, stays up all night in the Casino next door and then stays in bed till noon while I sit around reading magazines. Some fun."

"Thanks for your help."

"But I didn't really help, I . . ."

The man's voice trailed off as Mix walked over to the restaurant and looked in there, but there was no sign of Carver. The waiters were finishing with the breakfast crowd. One of them recognized Mix and waved.

"Tito, Tú ves un hombre negro?"

"No," the portly waiter replied as he stuck a plate and silverware into the bus tray.

"Gracias."

Mix walked out of the restaurant and out the hotel.

"Where the hell is he?" Mix whispered to himself.

He hurried back to his apartment and got on the phone. He dialed the long distance operator and made the connection.

"Hello."

"Hello, this is Mixon. Our boy is gone."

"What happened?"

"I was supposed to meet him at the hotel lobby, but he's not here."

"Damn it, I told you to keep an eye on him."

"Yeah, I know."

"Well, find him."

"Yes, sir."

Mixon hung up the phone and started for the door. He had to find Reggie Carver.

160

A side of beef. That's what he felt like. A side of beef hanging in a slaughterhouse waiting to be carved. Reggie hung from a rope tied to a beam in an old warehouse in the middle of nowhere. The strain on his joints sent a steady stream of pain shooting through him. He watched as one of the men, the young one, Miguel, rolled in a device that looked like one of those computer car-testers, but Reggie knew that it wasn't. The device had two electric probes sticking out of it like jumper cables except the ends had what looked like cotton pads or mops attached to them. Reggie had seen something similar in the movie, *Lethal Weapon,* when a vicious-looking Oriental guy used such a machine on the hero, Mel Gibson. Although Reggie knew that old Mel wasn't really being shocked and that his screams were just an act, he also knew that his own electrocution and the accompanying screams would be the real deal.

Miguel clicked on the machine and tested it. Sparks arched between the two pads, a blue bolt of lightning. Reggie struggled with his bonds but to no avail. The beef was ready to be cooked.

"I am sorry, we have to do this in this way," Julio said as he helped wheel the machine closer to Reggie and wet the pads in a bucket of water.

"So don't . . ."

"But I am afraid I must."

Julio, the older man, splashed water on Reggie while Miguel started to put the ends of the electrodes against his wet flesh. Reggie squirmed as the humming electrodes drew closer to his wet bare flesh.

"How did Drucinda die?" Julio said.

Miguel stabbed Carver with the electrodes. The black man screamed.

"I don't know," Reggie gasped.

"How?" the old man shouted.

Suddenly there was a loud burst that sounded like a string of firecrackers and Miguel was no longer there. He was spinning around trailing red splashes of blood. He thumped into an old crate and fell to the ground a dead man.

Hearing the shots, Julio whirled around pulling his pistol, but did the machine-gun boogie before falling down in a heap of torn flesh and blood.

Two men and a girl, all carrying automatic weapons and wearing bandannas over their noses and mouths to obscure their features, came into the small shack. The girl ran over to a relieved yet confused Reggie and cut him down.

"Who the hell are you guys?"

"We are friends," she said, her voice slightly muffled by the bandanna.

"Friends? Look this shit is . . . look out!"

Ricardo, the driver who helped kidnap Reggie, stepped out from behind a stack of crates and fired his pistol. The girl went down spinning and firing her machine pistol as she did. Her burst peppered the man's chest as he fired the rest of his ammunition clip into the roof then slumped to the dirty floor.

"Come we must go," she said urgently as she pulled Carver along.

"Who are you?"

One of the men approached him. "We are with *El Frente*. I am David."

"*El Frente?* I knew those fucks were lying."

"I imagine they were going to torture you for a long time and then let you go. After such treatment, you would not seek the help of *El Frente* in your search for Maria and Diego Vargas. In fact, you would become a hater of *El Frente.*"

Reggie grimly shook his head. "Good plan."

"It is an old propaganda trick that Macdow uses.

162

Rather than kill an enemy, he makes them an enemy of their own organization. One infected cow can spread disease among the entire herd and sometimes kill it."

"That may be true in some cases, but I don't think they were going to let me live. How'd you know they had me?"

"We've been following you. Tomas Montoya contacted us and asked us to keep an eye on you. Now he has disappeared and we believe that Macdow has taken him."

"Shit. That red-headed asshole's got this place by the nads."

"But he cannot stop us. Even now our people are getting stronger and we have recruited a great number of the army. It's only a matter of time before we strike and take our land back."

One of Reggie's saviors approached them. *"David, apúrate."*

"Sí," he shouted, then turned to Reggie. "Come. We must go where it is safe."

The four of them ran out of the barn, got into a small dusty station wagon then drove off quickly.

"Señor Carver, we must thank you for trying to find Maria," David said, pulling the bandanna down. He was a good-looking young man about twenty-five. His eyes were dark brown with long lashes that lent an air of sincerity to his comments.

"Hey, Diego and I were good friends when he was in Miami. I owe it to him to try and help."

"You are a good man to attempt such a task. There are many dangers."

"I only hope I can find out what happened to them," Reggie said, rubbing his ribs where the electrodes had touched him. His face ached where the thorn had torn the flesh.

"Are you all right?"

"Not really."

"Take this," David said, handing Carver a couple of pills and a canteen of water.

Reggie took the medicine and relaxed. In a few minutes, he was asleep.

6

Mix was convinced that something had happened to Carver. No one in the hotel had seen him except the cleaning woman, who said she saw him step out an hour ago while she was vacuuming the lobby. She said she remembered him because of the pretty gold cross he had dangling from his necklace, and she'd thought how lucky he was to have such a crucifix.

Mixon went back to his apartment to see if the private detective had gone there, but found no one. He glanced at his watch. Reggie was officially one hour late. Mixon didn't know what to do. His orders were to keep tabs on the black man and now he had no idea where he was. Perhaps Reggie had decided to leave early and give up his search for information on Colin Macdow. The PI didn't seem the type, but he had been awfully scared last night.

Mix kicked himself for not checking to see if Carver had checked out. He had only asked the woman behind the check-in counter if she'd seen a black man and the reply had been in the negative. Maybe Carver had checked out before her shift. He grabbed a beer and headed back to the hotel. The morning heat had already given him a powerful thirst and beer was the one thing he knew of that wouldn't give him the diarrhea. Drinking the water in San Miguel was a sure-fire way to get the blatz. He drank half the bottle before he left the hallway of his apartment building, and the rest on his way to Hotel Contado.

When he got there, he checked with the front desk. The woman at the station told Mix that Carver's bags had been taken and his bill paid. She said that the bellman had taken care of it. *So he did get the hell out of Dodge,* Mix thought, then thanked the clerk. He went back to his apartment.

In a way, Mixon was glad that Carver was gone. It would save him the trouble of dealing with the detective. He had developed a fondness for the wise-cracking Reggie, and hated the duplicitous role he had assumed so as to protect himself from discovery. But he had a job to do and he would do it no matter how two-faced it made him feel. He picked up the phone and dialed his boss in Miami to tell him Carver was coming back to the city.

7

"We are here, David," The driver of the car, Sebastian, said, as he steered the vehicle into the dirt driveway of an old wooden house fronted by a dilapidated fence. The yard was red clay and dust. A single scrawny palm tree slumped in the middle of it.

"Where's here?" Reggie asked rubbing the sleep out of his eyes. He had awakened when the car had taken a turn onto the bumpy road leading to the house and the interior suddenly became a miniature version of an earthquake.

"A safe haven," David answered. He patted Carver on the shoulder. "How are you feeling now?"

"Better. Not great, but better."

"Good."

David opened the door and let Reggie out of the car. He led the private eye and the others into the shack house. Inside, the home appeared to be abandoned, as there was no furniture except an old couch that seemed to be the home of a colony of spiders. The wooden floor and the couch were covered with a layer of dust. A pungent rotten odor permeated the hot air in the shack as if a small animal had died and made the house its mausoleum. In the middle of the room, Reggie saw his suitcase and garment bag.

"Hey, that's my stuff."

"Yes," David said. "Francisco brought them here."

"Who's he?"

"The bellman at the hotel. He is one of us."

Suddenly, the strange activities of the bellman made sense. He was sent to spy on him. "So that's why he was in my room? Checking me out."

"Yes, we also have our 'eyes and ears,' as you say. We wanted to make sure that you were who you said you were. We heard of your arrival from Tomas and you fit the description of the man in Miami, whom Diego said he was going to see. Francisco checked the things in your room to make sure."

"I don't like people getting into my stuff, but I guess if I were in your shoes I would do the same thing."

"We are fighting for our freedom."

"And mine, too, it turns out. Thanks for getting me out of that jam."

"You are welcome, Mr. Carver, but I am afraid that after our shoot-out, San Miguel is no longer safe for you. You must go back to Miami."

"I'm booked on a flight this afternoon."

"Yes, we know. Francisco told us you were checking out. Have you found what you need to know in San Miguel?"

"Some," Reggie said. "Question. What do you know about the Baobhan Sith?"

David appeared nonplussed. "Only what we hear from the peasants. It is silly superstition."

166

"Yeah, well, indulge me and tell me what you hear about them?"

"Very well. They say they are monsters that snatch you in the night and take you to the place of evil."

"Place of evil?"

"Yes. As I said the whole story is superstitious nonsense made up by Macdow to frighten the poor and keep them from fighting him."

"What does he tell them about this place of evil?"

"We must hurry, Señor Carver, the airport is some distance from here and the other car will be here soon. Surely you don't believe in . . ."

"Let's say I'm a superstitious kinda guy," Reggie knew from their attitude that they would never believe him about the bird's attack on him or the strange things that he had seen, so he didn't mention them.

David sighed at the silly American. "It is said that if you are taken by the Sith, you will go to the place of evil and become one with the *vacas*."

"*Vacas?* I'm not familiar with that. What's *vacas?*"

"It is Spanish for cattle."

"Cattle? What the hell is that supposed to mean?"

"I do not really know. We think it means you will become a prisoner in the work camps they run."

"Yeah, but why not just say that?"

"Most of the peasants here are farmers. Cattle are familiar to them. Macdow knows that, and uses it to illustrate his threat."

Carver still found the term odd, but didn't pursue it. It was obvious that David didn't believe in the supernatural and no matter what Carver told him, his disbelief would probably remain.

"Does anyone know where this place of evil is?"

"It is said to be far away."

"Like in Miami?"

"Perhaps."

167

"Let's say you're right about these work camps. If Diego and Maria were taken there then they're probably still alive. Tomas Montoya might be alive too."

"Yes. We have always believed that to be true."

"Then why haven't you gone to find them?"

"Our troubles here are many and we need everyone to fight. We must stay and continue with the plans that Diego and Maria have laid out if we are ever to be free from Colin Macdow's evil. They knew the risks if they were captured."

David's face brightened and he clasped a firm hand on Reggie's shoulder. "But you, Señor Carver, you can find them. Diego had faith in you and so shall we."

"I'll try not to let you down. At least now I have the belief that they're alive and still in Miami."

"Oh shit," Reggie said suddenly remembering his meeting with Mix.

"What is wrong?"

"I was supposed to meet someone back at the hotel."

"I am afraid you will have to miss the meeting."

"But the guy will think something happened to me."

"Who is this man?"

"His name's Mixon. He works in the bar."

"Francisco will get a message to him."

"Thanks."

"El otro automóvil está aquí," the girl with the machine pistol and the unerring aim said, as she stepped away from the cracked window at the front of the house.

"Good. Come. The other car is here."

Reggie picked up his bags and followed the group out to a yellow sedan. He got in and they drove to the airport.

168

Chapter Six

1

The evening air was cool as Chris and Sue sat on the dock and watched the waves lap against the sides of the sea wall. Sue didn't have to be at work until ten o'clock and she wanted to spend some time with her husband. They had been there for the better part of two hours, just sitting and talking, enjoying each other's company. It was almost time for her to get ready for her shift. She glanced over at the handsome man she'd married and saw that he was deep in thought.

"Whatcha thinking about?"

"Huh," Chris said, suddenly aware that she was talking to him.

"Why are you so quiet?"

"Oh, it's just this damn case. I can't seem to get anywhere with it."

"Isn't Reggie supposed to be back tonight?"

"Yeah at eight."

"Well, he should have something that will help."

Chris nodded but wasn't so sure.

Sue put her arm around her husband. "Don't worry

169

so much. You guys have solved tougher cases."

Blaze almost mentioned the Baobhan Sith to his wife, but decided to wait. As long as he was with her, she didn't need to know about the supernatural beings. He could protect her. If they did attack, she would find out soon enough about them. While she was at work, he would tell her to stay around other people at the hospital. If the Baobhan Sith, like him, craved secrecy, he didn't think that they would reveal themselves in front of others. Although he suspected that the Sith were nightstalkers, he couldn't be sure, so during the day he would hire the Brand Agency to watch over his place. Ryan Brand was a good man and would keep a low profile. In the back of his mind, he knew that he should tell Sue about the weird women, but he just didn't want her to have to go through the kind of terror she'd experienced when the vampire, Rakz, had been chasing her.

"Chris, I asked you what you needed," Sue said impatiently. It was the third time she'd asked him the question.

"Oh, uh, we need information about some aspects of the case. If I could only get to one of Macdow's men, I could use my mind control to get into his thoughts and find out some answers."

Sue thought for a moment. "Well, can't you find somebody you can use your powers on to get that information?"

Chris's face lit up. He pressed his palms against Sue's cheeks and kissed her full on the lips. "Honey, you are a genius."

"Well, I know that," Sue said feigning conceit. "So you have anybody in mind?"

"Yeah, I've got just the guy."

They got up and headed for home to get ready.

"You back again?" Len Singer asked as Chris Blaze stepped into his office. He was surprised to see the private detective, after their little talk the other night. "I thought I made it clear that we didn't want you or your partner interfering with our investigation.

"Yeah, well," Chris said, as he stared intently into Singer's eyes. "I wanted to see if you could help me with the names of some of Macdow's operatives in Miami."

Singer looked at him incredulously, "You don't hear so good, I said that we don't want you to interfere."

"Just one name," Chris said in a low whisper as he began to stare into Singer's eyes using his vampiric powers of suggestion to control Singer's will and get him to help Chris get the name of one of Macdow's men. He stared deeply into the Task Force chief's eyes focusing on capturing his will.

"No. I can't do it."

"Just one." The stare deepened and Singer was unable to look away. There was a vast world inside those icy blue eyes. A world that sucked Singer into it. A world tinged in a red haze. Floating in the haze were faces. A black man. A woman. White coat. Stethoscope hanging from her neck. A doctor. Friendly faces. Singer began to feel like a part of that world. He felt safe, comfortable.

"Just one."

"One." Singer repeated as he shook his head trying to shake Blaze's world out of it. In his mind, he was flying. Dancing on a red cloud.

"One name is all I need."

Singer started to speak, but was interrupted when Deputy Chief McNally burst into the room. "We've got a break, Len."

Chris looked up, breaking contact with Singer. He didn't want McNally to think something was wrong with his superior.

"Damn!" Chris muttered in frustration as Singer blinked and snapped back from the trance.

"What was that, Mark?"

"The Macdow case. I might have a good lead on a major buy."

"Great," Singer said, as though nothing had happened. "Mr. Blaze was just leaving."

"Please, I need one of the names of Macdow's men."

"Mr. Blaze, I already told you we can't do it. Now please."

Chris got up and started walking out of the office. He knew that he had failed and saw no sense in hanging around.

"Let me make sure he goes to his car, Chief."

"Go ahead and then come back here and tell me what you got."

"Okay."

Chris was halfway down the hallway when he heard a voice call out behind him.

"Hold up, Blaze."

Chris turned around and saw the second-in-command, Mark McNally, smiling—a friendly smile revealing straight even teeth. McNally was Chris Blaze's size, about six feet, a hundred and eighty pounds. A handsome man, McNally had dark features that were the opposite of Blaze's light complexion. McNally had thick black hair cropped short with a spiky line of hair around his part. Dark brown eyes. Full lips. His nose was slightly bent, but just enough to give it character. With his taut build and features, McNally looked like a prize fighter who'd quit after breaking his nose in his first fight, but kept in fighting shape anyway.

"Come to make sure I'm a good boy?" Chris asked sarcastically.

"I want to talk to you about Macdow. Meet me at this address." He handed Blaze a card with an address written on the back.

Chris took the card from the DTF agent. "You're gonna help me?"

"Yeah."

"Why the heave-ho of Singer's orders?"

"Let's just say I want to get Macdow any way I can. It's personal."

"What do you mean?"

"Look," McNally said with impatience, "do you want my help or not?"

"Not without an explanation of why."

"Fine, then forget it."

McNally turned around and started walking back to his office.

Chris had to make a decision. Trust McNally or try and find out about Macdow from his informants. He decided to take a chance.

"Hold on, McNally."

The DTF agent stopped and turned around. "You willing to listen?"

"Yeah."

"And with no explanation?"

"Okay. We'll say that . . . for the moment."

McNally walked back to where Blaze was waiting for him. He put his hand on the vampire's shoulder. "Meet me in about three hours. Do you know where the Casa Del Mar condos are?"

"On the beach."

"Right. Meet me there in the parking lot and we'll talk."

"Okay, See you then."

McNally turned and went back into Singer's office to

tell him about the drug deal. Chris took the hallway to the door, exited and drove back to his office to make a few calls and wait.

As he drove, he noticed a car trailing him about five cars back. He remembered it from the parking lot of the Drug Task Force Building. A tan LTD. He wondered if the man was a member of Macdow's group. He slowed up and let the car get right behind him so that he could see the driver. He recognized him from the DTF offices. It was the black man who had just been leaving Singer's office when Chris had come in to hypnotize the DTF Chief. He recognized his broad flat face. The man was a DTF agent.

When he parked his car in the parking lot of his office building, Chris got out and watched the tail pull into a parking space across the street. The man parked the car and Chris saw a match flare and the dull glow of a cigarette.

Not wanting the DTF man following him to his rendezvous with McNally, Chris raced quickly to the trees that lined the sidewalk next to the section of the road where the man's car was parked. Snakelike, he slid across the darkened walk until he was next to the car. With his powerful fingers, he tore off the valve stem of the front tire then did the same to the back one. The hissing sound filled the dead night air. He slithered back into the bushes and darted back to the parking lot, then walked up to his office as if nothing had happened.

3

Name: Unknown
Approximate age: Twelve years old.
Hair: Black.

Eyes: Dark Brown
Race: Black
Cause of Death: Cocaine overdose.

As Dr. Sue Blaze filled out the report on the little black boy that had died on the stretcher while the attendants wheeled him toward the operating room, she felt a profound sorrow. Such waste. A young boy who should be home playing video games or camping out with his buddies in the backyard was now lying on a metal drawer in a chest of corpses. A statistic in the losing war on drugs. Dead at twelve years old, his heart unable to deal with the intruder in his system. Sue wished that the bastard that had given such a young boy the dangerous drug would die the same horrible way that the boy did, gasping and gurgling for breath. She knew, as a physician, that such thoughts were against the Hippocratic oath, but at the moment she didn't care. She had seen too much of the death and pain caused by the white powder from South America. She was sick to death of it. The time had come for the government to wage real war on the drug lords and their minions, not just pay lip service to it.

Trying to get her mind off of the boy's senseless death, Sue picked up a memo that had been left on her desk that afternoon. The memo was written on the chief of staff's stationery.

To: All Employees
From: Dr. Gary Charles
This is a reminder to all employees that the sixth floor is off limits to personnel unless written permission is obtained from my office. Those violating this request will be subject to immediate termination.

That was all that it said. There was no explanation as

175

to why the sixth floor was off limits or why such stern measures were being used to enforce the edict. Sue wondered what could be so important and secret that dismissal was the appropriate response to employees venturing to the floor without permission. When she got the chance, she would ask somebody what was so special about the sixth floor and what the reasons were for such security and stringent punishment.

She set the memo aside and picked up the report on the boy. She finished filling it out and slid it into the out file on top of her desk.

Picking up the memo again, she read it, shrugged and got up from her plush office chair. She needed a cup of coffee and an aspirin. Slipping on her white lab coat, Sue walked out of the office and down the hall toward the cafeteria.

4

The night sky around the city was clear, with no cloud cover to reflect the lights of Miami in their tiny condensed water droplets. There was no moon. The stars seemed lost in the inky darkness. The black night was foreboding, as if nature was in league with an evil that had come into town and provided it with shelter from the light of discovery. Ahead of him, the lights from the beach stretched into the sky only to be swallowed by the vast darkness. The three hours had gone quickly. Chris drove his car to the site of his meeting with the deputy chief. He chuckled as he recalled the angry reaction of the man tailing him when the guy discovered the flat tires.

When Chris arrived at Casa Del Mar, the condominium complex where McNally had said to meet him, Chris marvelled at the impressive architecture of

176

the structure, which stretched eleven floors up from the beach. The surf rolled softly in the background. He pulled into the parking lot and wondered why McNally had chosen this place to meet. Chris doubted that a deputy chief with the Drug Task Force could afford such fancy digs. Just then, he saw a car pull up and park. Chris got out of his car when he saw McNally exit his vehicle and sit on the hood. He walked over and joined him.

"So what's up, Mark," Chris said, then added, "Mark, right?"

"Yeah."

"Nice place."

"Yeah, Chief Singer lives here. That's why I asked you to meet me here."

"Why's that?"

"I heard you in there talking to our chief and knew you wouldn't get anywhere with him."

"Why's that?"

"Well, on top of being an A-one prick. I think he's on the take."

"From?"

"Macdow, of course. How do you think he lives in such a fancy place. He doesn't even use his own name. Uses a phony." He pointed to a painted sign over one of the covered garages. It read. Reserved for Dr. Argyll.

"Why tell me?"

"It feels good to tell somebody. I don't know who to trust. I checked up on you through Miami PD and you got all A's."

Chris smiled. "Glad I'm still on the honor roll. Still doesn't tell me why you told me."

"I want you to help me."

"Help you what?"

"I want to hire you."

"Hire me?"

177

"Yes, to find somebody for me. I think Macdow has taken a woman to the same place as this Vargas couple you're investigating. I believe they tie in. But there's more to it than that. This girl is . . ."

McNally stopped in midsentence as if he was about to reveal something he didn't want Blaze to know. He waved his hand. "Well, it's a fucked-up scene."

"Wait, you were going to say something. What was it?"

"Nothing. So let's forget it."

"No, we won't forget it. There's something you're not telling me and I want to know what it is. It's got something to do with this girl."

"I said no questions."

"That was for *your* help not mine. I need to know everything if you want me to help you."

Mark looked at Chris trying to decide if he should tell him the reason. He turned away and stared at the front windshield.

Blaze wouldn't let it go. "Come on, tell me. It might do you good to get it off your chest."

Mark sighed and turned back toward Chris. "All right, I'll tell you, but you gotta promise not to tell anybody."

"You got it."

"The night after you came into our office asking for information, my girlfriend, Peggy, left town without a clue as to where she was going. We hadn't had a fight or anything. As a matter of fact, we were getting along better than we ever had before. Anyway she just disappeared and I haven't heard word one from her. Then I got a call from someone telling me the girl was alive, but wouldn't stay that way if I didn't lay off the Macdow investigation. They knew from Singer that I was the one leading the push against the Scotsman."

178

"So why don't you go to the FBI or the police?"

Mark looked out the window. "I, I can't tell you."

"Why?"

"I can't."

"You mean you won't. Why?" Chris said. He had to know what was wrong with this picture. Why couldn't McNally go to the FBI or the police department?

"I have my reasons for not telling you."

"Then I guess we won't be working together. I'm keeping what I find to myself," Chris said coldly, hoping the rebuke would prod Mark into revealing the truth.

"You bastard! I gave you . . ."

"Look," Chris said interrupting McNally, "I want to know why you can't go to the FBI . . ."

"She's a fugitive!" Mark blurted out. "All right? Satisfied? My girlfriend's wanted in Kentucky for forgery. She told me all about it and I happen to believe her when she says she's innocent."

"Then why won't a judge and jury believe her."

"Not after she ran. She got scared and jumped bail. It was a federal rap so the FBI is after her."

"And you knew all this and still went out with her," a skeptical Chris said.

"No. At first, I didn't know. We met in San Miguel when I was there on assignment. We went out for about ten months. She didn't tell me about the crime until I started talking about marriage, then she broke down and confessed everything. Peggy was in San Miguel to hide out. At first I was shocked and angry, but then I realized how much she meant to me."

Mark turned away and wiped a sleeve over his eyes, "I love her, Chris. I swear if we find her I'll convince her to turn herself in."

Chris saw the earnest expression on the face of McNally and decided that he would be good to have along—a man that is searching for a loved one is dedicated to the point of fanaticism. Chris thought he might need a fanatic when he was dealing with someone as dangerous as Colin Macdow seemed to be. "Okay. We'll keep working together. Now what have you got on Macdow?"

"Well, that's the second part of it. It's pretty weird. I mean really weird. Bizarre. I don't know exactly how to say it."

"Is it about the Baobhan Sith?" Chris asked taking a shot.

McNally's mouth dropped open. "Yeah. You've heard of it?" McNally said raising his eyebrows in astonishment.

"Yeah, it's been mentioned to us in our investigation." Chris said it in a casual manner. He was reluctant to tell McNally any more until he knew where the DTF agent stood on the issue of the supernatural. He might think that Chris was a candidate for the Planter's Palace of nuts if he told him about the women that had attacked him and Reggie.

"Have people told you any weird things about them?" McNally said, leaving Chris an opening to broach the subject.

"Like they're some kind of supernatural being?"

"Yeah. Do you believe it?"

"I don't know. Do you?"

McNally hesitated, then answered. "Something took my Peggy out of a fifth-story window without using the front door. I found her bracelet in the grass below the window and strange round marks deep in the grass beside it like, I don't know, like somebody jumped with her from the window and landed in the grass. Crazy, huh?"

Chris shook his head, remembering the Sith's fall from his window. He decided to tell McNally most of what he knew, "Not so crazy. I had a fight with one of them."

"What?" McNally said.

"The other night at my office. I was jumped by this woman and I got lucky with a toss and she went out the window of my office. She landed in the street and got up like it was nothing."

"You didn't do anything else to her?"

"No, why?"

"I don't know. It seems like a thing like that wouldn't be so easily handled. I mean you've gotta be some kind of strong to take a fall like that. Why didn't she come back up and continue the fight?"

"Well," Chris said. "I don't know." It was the truth and Chris didn't see any need to delve further into it for fear of revealing his vampirism. He didn't want McNally to know that he possessed supernatural strength.

"Do you know a man named Stephenson?" McNally asked.

"Stephenson? Why?"

"It's a name that's been mentioned to our informant in San Miguel."

"What's this Stephenson's part in this?"

"I don't know. I was hoping you'd tell me."

Chris shrugged his shoulders. "Don't know him. So what do we do next?"

McNally paused as if he was going to ask another question then answered Chris. "There's gonna be a drug buy. Big one. Macdow's boys."

"Where's it gonna be at?"

"My man doesn't know yet. Said he'd find out soon."

"So what's this drug buy got to do with the Vargas case?" Chris asked, not seeing the connection.

"My informant says that they're gonna cross the buyer, a rich kid from Coral Gables, and hold him for

181

ransom. His dad's damned near a billionaire and loves the kid even though he's big-time trouble for the family. I figure we let the deal go down and follow them when they take him. Chances are they'll go to the same place they have the others."

"What's this kid's name?"

"Jimmy Baines. Dad owns a huge chain of video stores. I should know by tomorrow when the deal's going down. I told Singer something completely different so that he wouldn't tell Macdow I knew what was happening."

"Sounds like a good move. But I heard you say, 'we.' Does that mean you're going with me?"

"Absolutely."

"Good," Chris said, welcoming the help.

"I'll call you tomorrow. By then I'll know where it's gonna be at."

"Call me in the early evening. I sleep during the day."

"Okay," McNally said, as a twinge of curiosity nipped at his mind. "I'll be in touch." He got off the hood of the car and started for the door.

"Chris," McNally said, leaning over on the seat, "can I trust you to keep my secret about Peggy safe?"

Chris smiled. "Yeah, Mark, you can trust me," the vampire said, "I can definitely keep a secret."

5

Sue sat down at a table where a young M.D. sat sipping a cup of hot cocoa. The doctor, Don Argyll, was a second-year resident whom Sue had met during her first night at Sisters of the Faith. Argyll was handsome, with the slender build of a tennis player. He reminded Sue of Jonathan Wadsworth, her ex-fiancé, who had died so brutally at the hands of the vampire

182

Rakz. Sue felt a tinge of grief when she thought about the grisly circumstances of Jonathan's death. A shudder rumbled through her body, then she shut out the powerful images of the vampire's demolition of Wadsworth. The memory was too shocking.

"You all right, Dr. Blaze?"

Sue looked up from her reverie, thankful for the interruption from the frightening memory.

"You were shivering," Argyll said. "Are you feeling okay?"

She nodded as she focused her attention on the blue eyes of the man in front of her. "Oh, yes, Don. Just a chill. And please call me Sue."

"Sure."

Sue took a sip of the coffee that had cooled to just the right temperature. "Good coffee."

"I prefer tea, but I hear that the coffee *is* good."

Sue pointed to the cup. "Take my word, this stuff is great."

Argyll smiled, revealing the only flaw in his handsome features, a set of teeth that were best described as having the tint of rancid butter. They were so discolored that Sue immediately wondered why he didn't have them bonded white. It was an easy procedure and would add immeasurably to his appearance. But there was also something else about his smile that Sue didn't like. It reminded her of someone, but she couldn't place her finger on who it was. She just knew that it was someone for whom she didn't care.

He cradled his cup of tea in his delicate hands. "So Sue," he said, "how do you like Sisters of the Faith so far?"

"Well after only two days I can't make a good judgment, but so far I like it."

Who was it the smile reminded her of?

Argyll continued talking, the smile still plastered on his face, "It's a great place. Lots of exciting things going on."

"I noticed. Speaking of that, I read a memo a few minutes ago about the sixth floor being off limits to unauthorized personnel. Do you know what they're doing up there?"

Argyll's smile wavered for a moment, then propped itself up. "Yes, we're doing research on highly contagious diseases including the HIV virus and a strain of the Asian flu. Security has to be strong so that no one will go in, catch something and spread it around the hospital. I'm in charge of the night shift."

"I see. Interesting. I didn't know that Sisters of the Faith was actively involved in research."

"Oh, yes, the whole sixth floor is dedicated to it. Maybe some night I'll give you a tour."

"That'd be great," Sue said, as she sipped coffee from her mug. "I've always had an interest in research. Just haven't had the time. Always been in emergency care."

Don nodded, then the smile slipped from his face. "So, I heard we had a little boy die of a drug overdose."

"Yes, twelve years old. Died before we had a chance to work on him."

Sue stared into the bottom of the mug as she remembered his contorted face.

"That's terrible," Argyll said as he took her hand, "When the hell are kids going to understand the dangers of drugs?"

"I don't know," Sue said, casually slipping her hand out from under his. She didn't know whether he was being kind or making a move on her. Better safe than sorry.

Argyll seemed nonplussed by the subtle rebuff. He simply smiled and said, "So, Sue, are you going to services after your shift?"

The return of the smile reminded Sue of her inability to identify the resemblance it suggested. "Services?" she asked, remembering the question.

"Yes, we have a chapel on the second floor. Almost everyone attends."

"So early in the morning?"

"God is awake at all hours," Argyll said, taking a dainty sip of tea, and looking up at her as he did. "So will you come?"

"Oh, well, I, uh, have to get home. My husband works late too and we have so little time together. Maybe some other time." Sue smiled and took the last drink of coffee.

"Yes, maybe some other time. One trip and you'll always want to go." Argyll smiled again.

Then it came to her. The smile didn't remind her of a specific person, it reminded her of a television evangelist. The smile was too broad for the occasion and present most of the time. It was the kind of vapid grin that adorned a mannequin. It wasn't that his smile wasn't pleasant, it was just that it was too pleasant. Too phony. Something about such a smile made her uneasy—so did being pushed on the subject of religion.

In college, members of the congregation of the Crossroads Church were always trying to enlist students like Sue to come over and attend Bible studies. They would smile at her with the same kind of insipid grin as Don Argyll's and talk about how God and the Bible could help you get an A in life. She would politely decline their requests for her to attend Bible studies, and she would never hear from them again. It wasn't that Sue was against religion. Far from it. It was just that she preferred to worship in her own way. God was very important in her life, but a flock of Bible-thumping, self-righteous hypocrites was not. She only hoped that she hadn't stumbled into a nest of born-

185

again Christians who would be on her case to convert her from beginning to end of her shift.

She ended the conversation by getting up from the table, cup in hand. Argyll stood when she did. "Well, I guess I better get back to the ER."

Argyll looked at her with the smile still stuck on his face. "We'll see you at the chapel sometime?" he said. "Very soon." His smile shifted just a fraction, so as to almost seem menacing.

"Maybe," Sue said as she smiled and turned away, her expression shifting to one of consternation. This guy didn't quit. She made a mental note to stay away from Dr. Donald Argyll unless on hospital business. She walked back toward her office. Before she had a chance to get there, she got a page from the emergency room and had to rush back to take care of the victim of a traffic accident.

6

Reggie had already been waiting for Chris for an hour when the vampire private eye came into the office. Sitting at the desk with his feet propped up, Carver sipped his second can of Mountain Dew, hoping the caffeine would keep him awake after the long day and the plane flight back to Miami. When he saw his partner come in, he stood up and met him halfway across the floor.

"Hey, man. How you doing?" Reggie said, as he shook Chris's hand.

"Hold on." Chris went over to the refrigerator and pulled out a bottle of blood. His hunger was ravenous. At the end of the ride back to the office it had come on him hard and the bestial part of his nature reared its ugly head. He could barely control the urge to slash open a pedestrian outside the parking lot and gorge himself on the warm blood. When he left the car, he rushed like the wind up the stairs to the office, swirling by the bewildered janitor, who tucked his bottle of whiskey back into his pocket and swore off drinking— at least for the night. Chris tilted the bottle back, emptying half of it into his screaming body.

Reggie had to look away as the sight of the blood made him feel queasy. "So," he said as he gulped down a throatful of bile, "Aren't you gonna ask me what happened to my face?"

Before Chris answered, he started to drink again. His hunger was greedy that night, and it had to be satiated. He finished his second helping.

"Hey, could you put that in a mug or something, it's, uh, y'know . . ."

"Sorry," Chris replied. He took the remaining contents of the bottle and poured it into a tall thermos, then walked over and sat down at the desk.

"Thanks," Reggie said as he sat in the chair at the front of the desk.

"So what happened to your face?"

"Tell me what you've been doing first."

Chris sighed. "Why?"

"Because I want to keep you in suspense."

"Sometimes you are a royal pain in the ass."

Carver grinned. "That's me. So where've you been?"

"Making friends with the DTF."

"DTF? I thought those dudes gave you the bum's rush?"

"They did or at least their chief did. Turns out he's on the dole from Macdow."

"No shit. Your new buddy tell you this?"

"Yeah. Deputy Chief Mark McNally."

"So why's he making nice?"

Chris explained McNally's interest in the case,

187

leaving out the part about the girl being a fugitive.

Reggie suspected that Chris was holding something back, but held his comments. If Chris had a good reason for not telling him something, he wasn't going to pry. In fact, the last secret Blaze told him was that Chris was a vampire. That was enough of a revelation to last a lifetime.

"So this McNally believes in these Sith things?"

Chris took another drink from the thermos. His hunger had dulled to a low roar, the state that it was always in. Chris never satisfied it completely, for fear of giving in to the dark side of his nature.

"I think he does, to a certain extent, because of the nature of the girl's disappearance."

"Man, I hate all this monster shit."

Reggie got up and paced the floor in front of the desk. The jolt of caffeine was beginning to make him antsy.

"So what happened to you?" Chris asked, pointing to the white bandage taped to his partner's face.

"Oh nothing special. Just dancing girls, killer birds, places of evil, kidnapping, rescue. The usual."

Chris stood up and went around his desk to sit on the corner. "Okay, Uncle Remus, tell me your story."

"You got it. Once upon a time, there was this good-looking black detective . . ."

Reggie recounted the entire story that had taken place since the last time they talked. About how he went to observe Macdow's place and saw the dancing girls and how they saw him. Reggie shivered as he recalled their fierce expressions and deadly eyes and the struggle for his life. He told his partner about the timely rescue by the mystery man and how he woke up in his bed, bandaged and safe.

"And you have no idea who this guy was?"

"No. I don't even know if it was a guy."

"So what do we do now?"

"Wait, there's more."

Reggie continued telling Chris about the morning after, when he was grabbed on the street by Macdow's men, impersonating members of *El Frente*. He told Chris about the close call with San Miguel Power and Light via the shock machine and the timely rescue by the real members of *El Frente*. He told Blaze all of the information—it was not much—that he'd picked up from them about the Baobhan Sith. He finished up in the style of Reggie Carver: "So the moral of the story is that private-detective work can suck huge donkey dongs."

Chris laughed. "So they said that Macdow's enemies are supposed to work in 'the place of evil' in Miami."

"Yeah, that was the rumor, but none of them believed it. They said it was just superstitious bullshit."

"And what do you think?"

"I think I want to go on a long vacation."

Chris smiled. "What do you really think?"

"I think we better find out what these Sith things are and how to deal with them before they end up killing the one of us that isn't already dead."

"I agree."

"So they didn't know where this place of evil is?"

"No."

"Well, if things go well tomorrow night we might be able to find out where it is. This is all starting to make sense in a screwed-up kind of way."

"Well, I'm going to go to Rasta's tomorrow afternoon and see what I can find out about these Sith things. Maybe I can come up with something that will help us. At the very least, I hope we can learn just what the hell those bitches are."

"So you think you might have that info by tomorrow night?"

"No can tell. I hope so."

"Well, we could use it. After the kidnapping, McNally and I are going to try to follow Macdow's men to the location of that place of evil."

"I know that wherever that place is, it's also gonna be where we find Diego and Maria."

"I think so, too."

"You know what else I think?"

"No, what?"

"I think that when we do find this place, we're gonna be walking right into Death's door."

Chris nodded solemnly. "Let's just hope that when we do, we can find the exit."

7

Chris and Reggie were walking toward their respective vehicles when two men got out of their car and came toward them. Chris recognized DTF chief Len Singer immediately. He also recognized Joe Dustin, the man that had been tailing him. Instinctively he looked down at the men's hands to see if they were carrying weapons. They were not. Chris decided to take the initiative.

"What can we do for you, Mr. Singer?"

"Where were you tonight?" Singer said gruffly.

"Around town."

"Where around town?"

"A lot of places."

Dustin pulled the chief to the side and spoke to him in a low voice.

"Hey, Chris, who is this guy?" Reggie asked.

Singer stepped back over to the two men. "I'm trouble if you boys don't get your noses out of our business."

"And what business is that, Mr. Trouble?"

"The investigation of the drug trade in this city, smart ass."

"Ah, you must be the amenable Mr. Singer that my partner here has told me so much about. I haven't had a chance to thank you for all your help."

"Knock it off, Mr. Smart Ass," Singer said, aping Carver's sarcastic "Mister" comment. "Blaze, I told you to lay off this case. It's our business."

"Well," Reggie interrupted, "we are in business, too, and we are employed to find out where a certain woman and her husband are and if that conflicts with your work then so be it."

"Who the hell are you anyway?"

"Reggie Carver if you gotta know."

"Well, Reggie Carver, I've heard all this bullshit before and I'm sick to fucking death of it. I told your buddy here to lay off and you just can't seem to get it straight in your heads." Singer sighed and ran a hand through his hair. "Look, I'm asking you as one law enforcement officer to another. Get off this case."

"I'm sorry. We can't," Chris said.

"You're gonna have no license if you keep it up."

"We haven't done anything to justify pulling our license."

"Well, maybe I can make something up."

"Look, Singer . . . ," Reggie said.

"No, you look, you smug son of a bitch. I know for a fact that Macdow has got men out after you guys and he's not gonna make any moves until he either snuffs you or you lay off."

"And how do you know that—inside information?" Chris replied.

"Just what the hell is that supposed to mean?" Singer said, his brow dipping into the bridge of his nose.

"Just what it sounds like."

Singer ignored the comment. "I'm telling you for the last time to lay off this case. We don't need you spooking possible witnesses or messing with our informants with all your poking around. Now stay out of it. If and when we bust Macdow, we'll find your missing people . . . if they're still alive."

"We think we'll just keep our fingers in the pie," Reggie said. "If you don't mind."

"And if I do."

"Tough titty as they say."

"Okay, if that's the way you wanna play it. But I'm gonna check you boys out and see if there's anything about you I should know," Singer said insinuating that he would try to use that information against them.

"Find away, Mr. Trouble," Reggie said. "We got nothing to hide."

Yeah, right, Chris thought.

"Come on, Joe," Singer said.

Singer walked toward his car with Agent Dustin tagging behind him.

"Damn, that asshole's going to make it hard," Reggie said as soon as the DTF agents were out of earshot.

"Yeah, I guess. That guy with him was the one that was following me."

"Until you poached his tires."

"Yeah," Chris smiled, then grew pensive. "But if Singer's in with Macdow then why does he keep telling us to get off the case? I mean it doesn't make sense. One second Macdow's goons are trying to dust us, the next second he's having Singer trying to get us to cooperate with the law."

"Well, they've tried once to nail you and three times to get me. Maybe they figure they can use the law to make us stop our digging."

"That might be."

"Or maybe whoever helped me that night put the fear

of God in them," Reggie said, shaking his finger as if that was the correct answer. "Yeah, those guys that tried to fry my ass wanted to know how Dru or Lou or somebody died. Whoever helped me must have wasted the bitch."

"Maybe."

"I know I'm right."

"You *think* you are."

"Okay, I think I am." Reggie said, conceding the point, "So what do we do with the rest of the night?"

"I suggest that you go home and get some rest. You've just had a helluva day."

"An understatement. So what are you gonna do?"

"I'm going back to the office and reread every damn note I've got on this case and hope for divine intervention."

"You hear that?" Reggie said, looking up into the dark sky. "Cut us some slack and send us a sign."

"You can get in trouble for messing with the Big Guy, Carver."

"Yeah, well, I don't guess I could get us into any more than we're in now."

"No. I guess not."

8

Night had settled down on Macdow's villa in San Miguel. Howler monkeys screeched in the nearby jungle. Crickets chirruped and then quieted when Macdow came out onto the veranda. Colin reread the note taunting him about the rescue of the detective, Carver. It was signed *"El Frente."* The postscript warned him to get out of San Miguel. He smiled, crumpled the note into a tiny ball and tossed it onto the tiled floor.

193

"I'll be leavin' soon enough," he whispered. His smile twisted into a frown as he stared at the wadded paper. He couldn't believe his men had botched the interrogation of the black detective. Now he would have to wait to find out what happened to Drucinda. Damn *El Frente* for butting their noses into his business. He ground the note into the tile with the heel of his boot. He had yet to hear a progress report from Miami. Time was growing short.

He called Mary into the room. "I want ye to meet your sister, Glynda, in Miami. I'll have Manolo get the plane ready for tomorrow night."

"What'll I be dune?"

"Taking care of business," Macdow said, a wicked gleam in his eye.

She smiled and licked her lips.

9

The night air was cool on Sue's skin as a thin mist of dew settled. A row of streetlights illuminated her path in the parking lot as she trudged wearily out to her car. She had just finished her shift at the hospital. Her calves ached from standing all night and she could feel every throbbing muscle in her lower back. Things had picked up in the early morning hours and she had spent the last part of her shift taking glass out of a would-be terrorist who'd constructed a homemade bomb that went off at exactly the wrong time. The man's body looked like a Jackson Pollack painting as she tried to put him back together. She had done the best that she could to patch the man up, but he lost his right arm, and his face suffered severe burns, resulting in blindness. It was a miracle he wasn't dead. The operation took the better part of three hours and Sue

194

was bushed.

As she stopped in the middle of the lot to get the keys out of her purse, she glanced back at the hospital. An orange glow came from one of the curtained windows on the second floor. *That's strange. I wonder what the heck is going on.*

Curious, she turned around and watched the window for a moment. The orange glow seemed to flicker, but Sue figured that it was just her tired eyes playing tricks on her. Just then, a shadow passed across the lighted square of glass then another and another. A procession.

Then she remembered. *Oh yeah, the church services. The chapel's probably on the second floor. That must be what it is.*

The people kept moving past the window until one of the shadows stopped in front of the curtain. Whoever was there pulled back the curtain and looked out into the parking lot. Sue felt like a kid with her hand caught in the cookie jar. In the dim light, she could see that it was Dr. Don Argyll. He looked right at her and a false smile spread across his face like butter yellow fungus. The smile sent shivers up Sue's spine. Sue gave Argyll a halfhearted wave and turned around to face her car. She fished for her keys in her purse, found them and started toward the vehicle again. She could feel Argyll staring at her from the second-story window and another shiver of fear danced up her spine. Why was she letting him get to her? It was probably just a coincidence that he looked out the window at the same time that she was in the parking lot looking up. Besides, when he saw her he gave her a friendly smile. There was no menace intended. A friendly smile at a coincidence. That was all.

She turned around and Argyll was gone. The orange light burned no more. The window was as black as the

Devil's heart. The abrupt disappearance of the doctor and the light didn't help alleviate Sue's apprehension. Her heart was thumping in her ribs like a caged rhinoceros. Sue stopped for a moment to calm herself.

Got to chill, Doc, as her young patients would say. *Be calm.*

You're just letting your imagination run away with you.

Just then, she heard a dull thump behind her as if something had landed in the grass. A quiver of fear pinched her neck, sprouting a crop of goose pimples. She heard the slow crackle of leaves as if someone had taken a cautious step toward her. She started quickly for her car, causing her calves to cry out from the exertion.

The soft rubber soles of her shoes thudded against the pavement as she hurried toward her car. Her purse was jinging as she did. She didn't dare glance back, for fear that she would see her assailant come out of the brush and she'd be unable to move.

As she stopped at her car, she heard another snap and then a footstep on the asphalt.

Then another.

They were coming for her!

Fear dried her mouth.

She fumbled in her purse for the can of mace that Chris had given her for protection, then she remembered that she had left it on the dresser in her bedroom. In her mind's eye, she could see the orange and silver label of the small can.

She heard the steps coming closer. Her heart thumped in her chest as she let out a tiny moan. She wanted desperately to spin around and scream, but feared that if she did and saw Argyll there, her vocal cords wouldn't respond. Argyll! Why did she think it was him? He couldn't possibly have gotten down to the

196

parking lot so fast unless . . .

Hurry!

She jammed the key into the door's lock just as a hand grabbed her. Sue sucked in a rush of air and spun around swinging her purse at the assailant.

"Hey, honey, take it easy," Chris said as he blocked the purse with a quick easy movement.

Sue's brow dipped into the bridge of her nose as a wave of anger replaced her fear. "What the hell are you doing sneaking up on me like that?"

"Sorry, I thought you heard me back there when you took off running and were kidding . . ,"

Sue interrupted him. "I did hear something, but how the hell was I supposed to know that it was you?"

"Don't you remember me telling you that I'd take you home?"

"No. Well, maybe, but that's still no reason to sneak up on me."

Sue was hot and Chris couldn't blame her.

"I'm really sorry, hon. I guess I'm just a boneskull." He hugged her close. "Forgive me?"

The anger melted from her face replaced with a reluctant smile. "Boneskull? That sounds like a Reginald Carver moniker."

"Yeah, it does, but it's one of mine. So do you forgive this boneskull?"

"Just don't do it again," Sue said turning the key in the lock.

"Promise."

"So why are you taking me home? Not that I'm complaining." His wife asked as she opened the door.

"I just wanted to see you. I thought we could take a walk through the park before we went home."

"Sounds great, but I am b-e-a-t."

"No problem. I'll just carry you in my arms. Remember I have a little more strength than the next guy."

197

"Could we make it another time?" Sue said with a combination of apology and regret, "I'm really tired."

Chris couldn't mask his disappointment. He wanted to be with his wife. Other than this evening, they'd done nothing other than see each other at home in between work. He missed not sharing special time with her, but understood that starting a new job could be taxing.

"Okay. Maybe tomorrow."

"Maybe."

"Let's go then. Since you're so tired, I'll drive."

"Good, I hope I can keep my eyes open until we can get to the house."

When they got the house, Chris lifted his sleeping wife out of the passenger seat and carried her into their home like a babe in arms. He laid her down in her bed and gently undressed her, trying not to wake her. He had changed his mind about telling her the danger of the Baobhan Sith. After talking to Reggie, he decided that it was better that she know about the threat so that she could take precautions. The attacks on Carver had convinced Chris that anyone related to the case might be a potential target. Tomorrow night he would tell her all about the case. He didn't want anything bad to happen to the woman he loved.

Chapter Seven

1

The shrunken head greeted Reggie as he stepped out
of the rising midday heat of the street and into the cool
air inside of Rasta's House of the Occult and Deli. The
smell of salami and dust mingled together amongst the
strange and wondrous items that cluttered the shelves
of the odd store. The first thing that caught the
detective's eye was a stuffed two-headed goat that
stood perched on a rock. The goat stared at him with
four glass eyes.

"Is it true what they say about two heads being better
than one," Carver mused, for his own enjoyment.

He continued down the narrow aisle. The store was
so crammed full of items that Reggie got a sense of
claustrophobia as he walked further into it. He passed
a suit of armor, complete with a helmet from which a
rubber mask of Barnabas Collins, the vampire from the
old soap opera, "Dark Shadows" peered out. Stacks of
old books and monster magazines were stuffed onto
shelves in crusty boxes. A rubber bat was dangling
from a string suspended from the ceiling, and Reggie
flicked it out of his way. It flew up and then hit him on

the back of the head. He heard a laugh and saw a teenager standing behind the counter of the deli section of the store. Carver ignored the teen as he looked up at the menu posted above the kid's head and read the names of the sandwiches you could order. There was the Real Finger sandwich, a hot dog with an onion-slice fingernail and a dollop of ketchup at the other end for that nice, hacked-off appearance. There was the Fried Eyeballs in a Sliced Forearm which was really a meatball sub. The Cow in a Blender, a hamburger. Burnt Bird, a blackened, Cajun chicken sandwich. All the menu items had gruesome names, in keeping with the mood of the store, but, surprisingly, the deli's aroma was quite appetizing.

"Can I help you?" A voice said.

Reggie looked at the boy behind the counter and wondered if he was a ventriloquist since his lips hadn't moved. The boy looked back at him and grinned as he remembered the bat hitting the back of the detective's head.

"I said can I help you?"

Carver was looking right at the teen when he heard the second offer of aid and was sure that the boy hadn't spoken. He turned around and looked for the person who had. A few feet away, he saw an upside-down pair of legs, looked down and saw the face of a thin black man who was suspended about two feet off the ground. His dreadlocks almost touched the floor. Reggie recognized the inverted man as the owner of the store, Matha Rastas. The old man, wearing a pair of gravity inversion boots, was hanging upsidedown like a bat. Rastas's perch was an aluminum sculpture that looked vaguely as if it were a butcher holding Rastas like a dead chicken.

"Good for de back," Rastas said in a heavily accented reply to the strange look on Reggie's face.

"Yeah, I bet," Carver said, trying to be nonchalant. "I don't know if you remember me but, uh, I was in here about a year ago."

"Ah, the vampire man. Of course, I remember. You bought every known repellent of de undead."

He swung up and pulled the hooks of the boots off the sculpture and spun off his perch. He landed softly on the hardwood floor. He pulled an errant lock of matted hair out of his green bloodshot eyes that sharply contrasted with his dark brown skin.

"What can I do for you today, mon?"

"Well, I was kinda looking for information."

Rastas straightened the front of his brightly colored Hawaiian shirt. "And what is de topic you wish to check out?"

"Well," Reggie said, unsure how to phrase it, "These, I don't know, creatures, I guess you could call them, are called Baobhan Sith. I have no idea what it is or what it relates to."

"Baobhan Sith. Hmmm, sounds Indian or perhaps maybe, yes. Let me check something."

Rastas disappeared into the back of the store and came out carrying a large volume that appeared to be very old. He held it up with a wiry arm. *"Le Demonitrium.* A book of the myths, monsters and legends. Very informative."

Reggie nodded as if he knew what Rastas was talking about.

"Now let's see," Matha said opening the book, "Baobhan Sith. Do you know how to spell it?"

"Not really. I'll guess, B-o-b-a-n S-i-t-h."

"I will try that."

He opened the book and started flipping through the pages. The yellowish tan pages of the book looked brittle, as if ready to tear at any moment.

"Ah, look at this, mon."

"What?" Carver said, surprised that Rastas had found the information so quickly. He came around to the old man's side and looked over his shoulder.

Rastas held up a withered flat flower with a piece of ribbon hanging from it like green gristle. "Dis is my first boutonniere from prom. I wondered where dat got to."

Reggie faked a smile. "Great."

"Could you put it over dere on de counter for me? I want to show it to my wife."

"Sure," Reggie said, taking the dried carnation over to the counter where Rastas had pointed. He started walking back to where Matha was reading when he stopped to examine a couple of strange items that looked like monkey's paws.

The old man went back to looking for the Baobhan Sith. He checked Reggie's spelling, but found nothing. "It is not under dat spelling. Hold, let me check."

He flipped back the pages humming softly as he did. He went back to the beginning of the letter *B*.

While he waited, Reggie unconsciously twisted his finger around the long hair of a shrunken head until he saw what he was doing and pulled away quickly.

"Ah hah," Rastas said, shooting an index finger straight into the air. "Now we gettin' somewhere."

"What did you find?" Reggie said sarcastically. "Your first love letter?"

"No," Rastas said with a wicked gleam in his yellow green eyes. "I found . . ."—he paused for dramatic effect—". . . Baobhan Sith."

"What does it say?" Reggie asked excitedly, as he hurried to look over the old man's shoulder.

"The Baobhan Sith. A Scottish legend sometimes known as 'glaistigs.' De Baobhan Sith were a group of beautiful women dat came upon unwary travelers and sucked their blood. Dey would dance like a whirling

202

dervish, hypnotizing their victims, and afterwards drain them of their blood."

"That's all it says?"

"Dis book is only an overview. I can find more detail in de writings of Grimaldi Carabucci, *Il Demonis y Monstrueros.*"

"Do you have a copy of that?"

"No."

"Shit."

Rastas smiled. "But I know where I can get one."

"Really?" Reggie's eyes brightened. "Where?"

"A man named Kargosi. He is a collector of de occult and has one of de only copics of Carabucci's work in existence."

"So can you have him send it here?"

"No, I'm afraid de book is not for sale. It is priceless."

"I don't want to buy it, I just need the information."

"You must go to California . . ."

"Go to California? Why can't the guy just read it to me over the phone."

"Mr. Kargosi doesn't speak over the phone."

"What?"

"He's a bit on de eccentric side of life. Lives on a mountain. They only way to get him is by fax."

"Fax?"

"Yes, he says by using the fax he can respond when he wants, not when someone calls him. He will also charge you."

"Charge me? For looking at a book?"

"It is not just any book. It must be translated from Latin and other ancient languages. Very time-consuming."

"Jesus, sounds like a real nut."

"A very wealthy nut."

"So have you got a fax?"

"A business would not be complete in dis day and age wit out one. But I am afraid dey are the same as a long distance call."

"I'll pay whatever it costs."

"Then it is done. Please."

Rastas motioned for a piece of paper so he could write down the message. Reggie handed it to him. Rastas wrote out a quick note asking Kargosi if Reggie could come see him. He explained Carver's interest in the work of Grimaldi Carabucci and asked what would be a good day to see him.

"Hey, Mr. Rastas. Why don't you just ask this dude to fax me the information on the Sith?"

"Oh no, he needs you to pay him in cash in person. It is the only way he'll do business."

"Shit, damn kook. Okay. Looks like I'm going to California."

Rastas finished the note and then went in the back to send it. He came back out a couple of minutes later.

"Why don't you have a seat and a sandwich, Mr. Carver? We have a special on the Cow in a Blender. I told Kargosi that you were waiting."

"Sure, why not. Only I'd like to try the sliced pig with pocked skin on rye."

"Billy, make dis man a ham and swiss on rye."

"With mustard," Reggie added.

"Wit mustard."

Billy gave his boss the okay sign and grabbed the ham from the glass display case. He started the slicer and began to make the sandwich.

After a couple of minutes, the kid behind the counter rang a bell, signalling that Carver's sandwich was ready. The detective went to the counter and paid for the sandwich. The ham was stacked high, topped by two slabs of swiss cheese, all between two slices of fresh-baked bread. A firm dill pickle accompanied the sandwich, in addition to kettle-fried potato chips. Reggie took the platter and sat on a stool at the counter.

Before he had a chance to take a bite, he heard a beeping sound, signalling the arrival of a fax. The beep was followed by a sound like a hive of angry bees with little typewriters. A moment later Rastas came out holding a piece of paper.

"He says he will see you Thursday."

"Great," Reggie said, setting down the sandwich.

"Here is de address and directions," Rastas said, handing Carver the fax with a scribbled map on the back. "I have been to Kargosi's house once, I am sure you will find it most interesting."

"Fine. Thanks a lot," Reggie said as he handed Rastas a five, expecting change but receiving none.

"Thank you," Matha said, tucking the five-spot into the pocket of his black polyester pants. "If I may be of assistance in any other way, do not hesitate to call, mon."

"I won't."

"I hope you find what you're looking for."

"So do I," Reggie said.

"Well, I will let you finish your lunch. I have to order some more hemlock. You never know when a customer is going to need some."

"Thanks again." Carver took a healthy bite of his sandwich. He held it up and said, around a mouthful of tasty meat and cheese, "Good stuff."

Rastas smiled and vanished into the back room.

A few minutes later, Carver finished his meal and headed for the door. As he stepped outside into the summer heat, Carver decided to head for the office and make some phone calls. He needed to book a flight and a hotel room. In the back of his mind, his fear scurried about like a rat searching for a place to feast—nipping at him whenever the words that Rastas had read came back to him. *Beautiful women that drank blood.*

"Shit," he said aloud, "more goddamned vampires."

A woman walking next to him looked at him as though he had just pulled down his pants.

Reggie smiled weakly and quickly put some distance between himself and the lady, a move that was no doubt a relief to the woman.

"Damn." Reggie said, unable to stifle another expletive, as the thought of tangling with more vampires scampered around in his mind. The last time he'd picked a fight with one of the undead it had nearly cost him his life. He wondered if this time he would be so lucky.

2

The afternoon sun slipped further into the skyline of the city as Sue got ready for work. She wanted to head in early to catch up on a little administrative paperwork. She had slept till about two o'clock and spent the rest of the afternoon watching television. At about six o'clock, she got a call.

"Hello."

"Sue, this is Dr. Charles."

"Oh, hi, Doctor. What's up? You need me in early? I was already planning . . ."

"No. Oh no. It's nothing like that. I just wanted to chat and see how you were enjoying your work at Sisters of the Faith. I get very little chance to see you."

Sue's curiosity stitched a crease in her brow. "That's nice of you and I'm enjoying it very much," she said slowly, trying to figure in which direction the conversation was heading.

"That's good. Good." Charles hesitated then continued. "One of my concerns with all my staff is that we should get to know each other better. I like people to meet and relate on a personal level. I think its important. Don't you?"

"Yes," Sue said, still wondering where the doctor was headed with this line of thought.

"Yes, well, I talked to Don Argyll today and he told me that he invited you to the services last night and you said you were tired, but you might be able to make it some other night."

So that was it. Sue got a creepy feeling in the pit of her stomach. "Listen, Dr. Charles, I have to be honest with you. I don't go in much for church services," she said, adding in her mind, *especially at five in the morning.* "I choose to worship God in my own way."

"Fully understandable," Charles said, in a cheerful but determined voice, "I just thought that it might be a good way to meet some of the staff on a, you know, personal basis. Would it be too much to ask you to attend tonight's service? Quite a bit of our staff attends, and I think it would be a good way to meet some of them. Many of them, like you, were reluctant to go, but once they did they found it very rewarding."

"I'm sure it's nice, but . . ."

"Then you'll go."

"Well . . ."

"Just this once. Just to meet everyone. See if you like it. It can help you—after a long night of watching death and pain—to relax. The services help you unwind."

"Okay, I guess I could make it," Sue said, feeling boxed in. Charles sounded so sincere that she couldn't refuse his request without feeling like an ass. What harm could it do to go one night?

"Very good," Charles said with a smile in his voice. "I hope you'll find it beneficial."

"Me too."

"Good-bye, Sue."

"Bye-bye, Doctor."

As Sue hung up the phone, she felt just as she had the time her cousin, Zoey, had invited herself along with Sue and her friends on a night out on the town. The cousin was a real weirdo, a certified loony binner, but Sue didn't have the nerve to say she couldn't go. In addition to being a strangeoid, Zoey had a fragile ego and would cry for hours if her feelings were hurt. So instead of telling Zoey that she could go with them if they could drop her off at Chattahoochee, the state mental institution, Sue said, "Sure it might be fun." The curse of politeness wouldn't allow her to say anything else. So they went out and Zoey made a real fool out of herself and almost got them thrown in jail. Back then she knew that taking Zoey with them was a mistake, and yet, she let her go in order to spare herself the guilt from rejecting her cousin and hurting her feelings.

Now it was the same thing. She didn't want to go to the stupid services, but her inability to refuse a sincere invitation forced her to agree. She glanced up at the clock and saw that it was getting to be time to go. She got up off the bed and went into her closet to get her outfit for the night.

Sue slipped on a mauve blouse, tucking it into her grey slacks. Chris came into the room and greeted her with a kiss.

"Evening," he said, hugging her close.

"Hey, honey."

She kissed him and continued getting dressed.

"I'm really sorry I scared you last night," Chris said.

"Oh, that's all right. I shouldn't have been so edgy. Just had a long night is all." She pulled a dark grey belt through the loops of the slacks.

"So how about we make that little sojourn in the

park after work tonight?" Chris said smiling.

"Oh, I'd love to," Sue smiled, then added, "but . . ."

The smile slid off Chris's face. "But what?" he said curtly.

"This afternoon Dr. Charles called and invited me to attend services that they have at the hospital chapel and I thought it might be good PR to attend one."

"Services? Church services at five in the morning?"

"I know it sounds strange, but the chief of staff said it would be a good time to meet people." Embarrassed by her lack of willpower, she turned away unable to face her husband and started brushing her hair.

"Five in the morning?" Chris repeated, to show Sue the folly of her acquiescence to the request, and to drive home the oddity of it.

"He was so sincere, I couldn't say 'no' and besides . . ."

Chris interrupted. "In other words, he sapped you into it."

"No, I just thought," she stopped and nodded her head. "Yeah, he sapped me into it." A sigh whistled from her lips. She slipped on her shoes and headed into the living room.

"What the hell kind of services do they have at a hospital?" Chris said, following her.

"I don't know. They say it helps them unwind. They have a chapel and everything." She flapped her hands in frustration. Sue went to the refrigerator and pulled out some ham, cheese and bread.

"You haven't stumbled into a nest of born-agains, have you?"

"Cut it out. No. I mean, I hope not." Sue hadn't considered the possibility, and the thought of it filled her with anxiety. She started making a sandwich for her dinner.

"I wish you'd learn to can that politeness and just say

209

'no thank you.' I don't think we spend enough time together." Chris said flatly.

"It's just one night," she said, slapping a slice of cheese on top of the ham slice on the bread. "It might help me make new friends at the hospital and it never hurts to have friends when it comes time for a promotion. I promise we'll go out tomorrow after work and do something fun."

She put both hands on his shoulders and kissed him.

Chris sighed still peeved. "Just try not to make it a habit."

Sue kissed Chris again. "Thanks, honey, I won't."

The lady doctor opened the refrigerator and took out a jar of brown mustard. She spread it on the sandwich and then took a bite. She put the sandwich on a plate, sprinkled some potato chips on an open spot and took the light meal into the family room to eat it.

Chris reached into the fridge and grabbed a bottle of blood. He poured it into his thermos and then went into the family room to join his wife. "Sue, I want to talk to you about something very important."

The doorbell rang.

"I'll get it," Sue stood up to answer it.

"That would be my partner," Chris said finishing off his liquid supper and following Sue.

"Get out the cheese puffs and Coke," Sue said loudly as she went to get the door. She opened it and there was Carver smiling. In his hand he held a flower that he'd pulled from Sue's garden.

"I don't know whether I should give you this, after you just slammed my eating habits," he said as he held the Gerbera daisy in front of him. The flower was a deep red purple.

"She's sorry, Reg," Chris chimed in. "Give her the flower. After all, it is from her garden."

Reggie got indignant. "Hey, I resent that remark."

He handed Sue the daisy.

"Thanks, Reg. My husband doesn't give me flowers—even from my own garden."

"Nightshade doesn't bloom in Miami," Reggie cracked.

"Funny," Chris said, then turned to Sue. "My wife's never around to get flowers. She's too busy."

Sue frowned. "Drop it, Chris. I thought we settled it."

"Yeah, you did," Chris replied with a barbed tone in his voice, then turned to his partner and motioned for him to go into the living room. Reggie nodded, walked over and sat on the couch. Chris followed and sat in the chair opposite Carver. Sue closed the door and went into the living room as well.

"Is there something else you want to say about us, Chris?" Sue asked.

"No," Chris said bluntly.

"Sooo," Reggie said interrupting the fight that seemed to be brewing. "I'm going to Californ-eye-ay."

"What?" Chris said.

"Some guy's got a book there that will tell us about the Baobhan Sith."

"The what?" Sue said her face registering puzzlement.

Reggie looked at Chris. "You haven't told her?"

"Not yet," Chris said sharply. He had wanted to tell his wife in his own way, but now he couldn't because his blabbermouthed partner had let the monster out of the castle.

"Well?" Sue said impatiently.

Chris sighed and explained to Sue what he knew about the Baobhan Sith, conveniently deleting the parts where he and Reggie were attacked.

Surprisingly, Sue was not shocked. In fact, she laughed.

"Are we characters in a novel or what? I mean, it isn't everybody that runs into monsters on a yearly basis. How many supernatural beings are there in the real world?"

"Too got-damn many," Reggie answered for all of them. "But that ain't all. I found some things out today from Matha." Reggie explained what he had learned at Rastas's House of the Occult and Deli and the existence of the book that might contain the key to fighting the Baobhan Sith. "So that's why I have to go to California."

"And this Kargosi, jeez, what a name, this guy has the book we need?" Chris asked.

"Yeah, hopefully he's gonna tell us about the Sith in detail."

Reggie took a hazelnut from the bowl on the coffee table and cracked it with the heavy metal nutcracker. He popped the tasty nut into his mouth.

"Good," Chris replied. "I've got a meeting with Mark tonight to find out where this drug-buy kidnapping thing is going down. By the way, have a nut."

Reggie grinned and took another. "Good for you," he replied holding up the reddish brown nut. He cracked it and ate the meat.

"Once I meet with this Kargosi dude, maybe I'll be able to tell you something over the phone to help you deal with those bitches," Reggie replied hopefully.

"Sounds like we're finally making progress."

"We better be. All these shitty attempts to get rid of us are beginning to get on my nerves."

"What attempts?" Sue cried, and looked harshly at her husband for sugarcoating the truth. "Chris!"

Chris glared at his partner then turned to his wife. "We've had some trouble with these things already."

"What kind of trouble?"

"The details aren't important. We're both okay."

"Oh great," she said sarcastically. "And what about the next time?"

"That's why Reg is going out to see this guy in California. Sue, now that we know about these things we'll be on guard. Remember they don't know what I am and that gives me an advantage."

"And if they find out?"

"I'll worry about that if it happens. Now I want you to stay around people at the hospital at all times. Make sure you're never alone," Chris said. "I'll take you to and from work."

"Okay, but what about during the day?"

"I've got Ryan Brand keeping his eye on the place. He's good."

"Who's he?"

"Got his own PI agency. We work together sometimes."

"Brand's a real tough cookie," Reggie added.

Sue looked worried. The seriousness of the situation was apparent. She remembered the huge Burly Fayer and how he had been hired to protect her from Rakz and his servant, Charlie Burnson. The big Georgian had fought bravely, but Sue had still been abducted by Burnson. She didn't relish facing such prospects again.

"Sue, everything will be cool. I promise." Chris said, putting his strong arm around her waist.

"Yeah, Doc, if we can kick Rakz's ass then these bitches will fall like Dominoes pizzas."

Sue smiled weakly.

"So, Reg, when's your flight leave?"

"Tonight at seven-thirty."

"You better get in gear."

"I got my stuff in my car," Reggie said, hiking a thumb toward the outside. "Got time to give me a ride? I hate to waste money on parking."

Chris got up and chided his partner, "Did anybody ever tell you you're cheap?"

"Only the women I date."

Chris laughed. "Let's go. We can drop you off on the way, hon."

"Let me get my purse."

"I'm not cheap, anyway, I'm thrifty," Reggie said as he grabbed a couple of nuts and cracked them, sticking the meat into his shirt pocket.

"Cheap."

"Thrifty."

"I'm glad you two are able to kid around," Sue said sarcastically. She was frightened.

Chris turned around and rested his hands on the muscles on the sides of her neck. "Honey, chances are that these Sith don't know I'm married and like I told you we're going to find out about them from this guy in California. As long as we're on the alert, we should be fine."

Sue nodded, but she was still uneasy. The three of them went out to Reggie's car and got in. Chris was in the driver's seat, with Sue in the middle and Reggie beside her in the front. They drove to the hospital to drop off Sue.

When they arrived, Chris pulled to the back entrance near the emergency-room exit and parked the car.

"Remember to stay around crowds, Sue," Chris reminded her before she got out of the car. "Don't go off by yourself."

"Believe me, I won't," Sue said as she kissed Chris. "See you."

"I love you, honey. And don't worry."

Reggie opened the door and got out so that Sue could get out of the car.

"Do I get a kiss?" Reggie said, sticking out his cheek and pointing to it.

"Sure, I think there's some Hersheys left over from Halloween in the glove box."

"She's getting to be quite a wise ass, Chris," Reggie

said, pointing to Blaze's wife.

Sue smiled and gave Reggie a peck on the cheek. "Bye."

"Bye."

"See you."

Sue waved to Chris. Carver got in the car and the two watched Sue to make sure she made it without incident. She arrived at the door, turned around, waved and then stepped inside.

Chris sat for a moment before putting the car in gear. Not being around to protect his wife left him feeling uneasy.

"She'll be okay, Chris," Reggie said, noticing the concern etched on his partner's face.

"Yeah. Let's go," Chris replied, pulling the gearshift into drive. He was anxious to take Carver to the airport so that he could begin his fact-finding mission.

3

As Sue walked down a hallway that she thought led to her office, she noticed that there was no noise. The corridor was absolutely silent. There wasn't the usual moaning of patients in pain or the PA system that she remembered as the constant background at Miami General. Just total silence.

She turned the corner and realized that somewhere along the line she had taken the wrong turn and ventured into this section of Sisters of the Faith Hospital by mistake. The silence left her with a disturbing sense of apprehension. It was the second time she had felt that way about the hospital, echoing her first trip to Sisters of the Faith. Couple that bit of *déjà vu* with the news of the supernatural beings that Chris and Reggie had told her about, and it was enough to jangle her nerves. To top it off, in three minutes, she

215

had already violated Chris's edict to remain in the company of others. She was alone. She picked up her pace and turned the corner.

"Aaah," she shouted as she ran into someone. Strong hands grabbed her arms.

"Sue!" Dr. Don Argyll said, letting go of her arms. "I'm sorry. I didn't mean to scare you." A slight smile slid across his face. "I was just on my way to a patient."

"That's okay," Sue said gathering her composure. "I got lost and was trying to hurry up to get to my office."

"It can happen. The directionals aren't up in this section yet."

"I did notice how quiet it was. Is this section operational?"

"Not yet, there are still some minor adjustments," Argyll replied, tweaking his fingers. "I find the silence very pleasant, don't you think?"

"Yes, I guess it is," Sue replied, trying to keep the fear out of her voice. "I'm just not used to it, coming from Miami General, which can be quite a madhouse."

"I suppose. I've only worked here at Sisters of the Faith."

"Really?"

"Yes," he said, almost bursting with pride, "and I doubt if I'll ever leave."

"You really must like it."

"I love Sisters of the Faith," he said looking around him with what seemed to be genuine love in his eyes.

"That's great." Sue replied then thought, *I've got to stay away from this character*.

Argyll turned his smile up a couple of degrees. The overhead lights died against his butter teeth. "So Dr. Charles said that you would be joining us tonight."

"Yes," Sue replied, trying to smile, "I told him I'd try to make it." *Why was Charles gabbing to Argyll about her?* The question made her feel uneasy.

"Good, look forward to seeing you there."

216

He touched her forearm and smiled. Sue tried to contain a shiver.

"Well," Argyll said, "I have rounds to make. Services begin at quarter after five."

"I'll try to be there."

"Just keep going on this corridor and you'll find the elevators."

Argyll smiled and walked back down the hallway from the same direction that he'd come. Sue wondered why he was going that way since he had just said that he was going to see a patient and that this section of the hospital was not operational; two statements that contradicted each other. Sue scratched her head and shrugged. The strange behavior reinforced her conviction to stay away from the odd Dr. Argyll. She continued down the corridor to the elevator.

When she got to her office, Sue began to wonder if coming to Sisters of the Faith Hospital hadn't been a big mistake. Things were so different here. The strangely silent halls. The odd Dr. Argyll. The request by the Chief of Staff to attend church services. It was so totally unlike Miami General that the change frightened her. She'd never worked at a private hospital, so she didn't know what to expect, but it certainly wasn't anything like this.

She picked up her stapler and squeezed a couple of crimped staples onto the top of the desk. She set the stapler down and picked up one of the bent staples. Twisting the metal in half, Sue tried to rationalize her decision.

Maybe she was making a fuss over nothing. After all, every workplace has its weirdos. At Miami General, there had been a doctor, Dr. K. B. Sims, who was always trying to get her to go nude skydiving with him. What an oily creep he was. And the chief of staff was an avid football fan that tried to get his personnel to attend the Dolphins' games to support the team. Dr.

217

Daniel Shear was so rabid about the Dolphins that he had a life-sized portrait of Don Shula in his office. Was there that much difference between a chief of staff who worshipped Don Shula and one who worshipped God? Sue smiled and wondered if maybe Dr. Charles didn't have an edge in the normal department.

She thought about the reasons why she had come to the new hospital. Sisters of the Faith hospital was equipped with the latest technology and well staffed. Her ER crew was first-rate. She was in charge of the whole department and the responsibility was something she relished at this point in her career. These factors weighed in favor of the hospital.

To be fair, the news that Chris had given her this evening had frightened her, and perhaps that fear had added to her uneasiness about the hospital. When she was alone and lost, her imagination may have exaggerated her trepidations about Sisters of the Faith.

She brushed the staples into the trashcan and made up her mind to stay with it—with a couple of exceptions. The first was already a given: stay away from Dr. Donald Argyll. The second was attend the services and if she was pressured in any way to join the church, she would tell them to back off. If they continued to press, she would try to get her old job back at Miami General and chalk this one up to experience. She pulled her pen out of her desk and started to write her letter of resignation. Just in case.

4

A jet roared overhead. People kissed. Taxis pulled in and out. A man in a blue uniform carried two suitcases fifty feet and received a three-dollar tip. Chris pulled up to the curb at the entrance to the terminal.

"Well, this is as close as I can get," he said, sticking his hand out in friendship. "Good luck, Reg."

The black man took his hand. "Thanks, partner. I hope I won't need any."

Reggie got out and opened the door to the back seat. He grabbed the handle of his suitcase and pulled the heavy bag off the seat and onto the pavement. He reached in and retrieved his briefcase.

"Get those for you, sir?" a porter said, with a rehearsed smile. He was a small thin man, whose uniform fit like a glove on a three-fingered man.

"I can handle them," Reggie replied, with an equally false smile.

The phony smile remained on the porter's face, but didn't reach the man's eyes. "Suit y'self."

Reggie leaned into the car. "I hate those guys bugging me."

"Makes you feel like a cheapskate, doesn't it?"

"Don't start that again," Carver warned, clenching his fist.

Chris laughed, then got serious. "Now you stay on your toes out there. We don't know what to expect from this Macdow or the Baobhan Sith."

"I expect the worst."

"Just find out what you can from this Kargosi and get back here, so we can try to end this thing."

Carver stepped back and clicked his heels, tossing Chris a salute. "Yes sir."

Chris shook his head. "Be careful, you asshole."

Reggie smiled. "Bet on it."

Carver bent over and picked up his bag and waved good-bye. He started walking toward the automatic doors leading to the terminal.

As Chris watched his buddy enter the doors that opened and shut with a hiss, he noticed that the confident cocky bounce in Carver's step was missing.

The lack of confidence boded ill. Suddenly, the vampire detective had the feeling that he would never see Reggie Carver alive again.

5

After checking his bag, Reggie needed a fix for his habit. It had been too long. With all the long nights and the investigation, he hadn't had time. He sat down in the chair and pulled the change out of his pocket. He dumped a tarnished quarter into the machine and the screen started to hum and come into focus. He clicked through the dial and found a rerun of the "Beverly Hillbillies." It was the episode in which Granny thinks that Mrs. Drysdale has hired a man to kill the Clampetts when in fact he is a gardener who is planting tulips in their honor. It was the perfect fix for a television junkie. A couple and their small child sat across from him in the regular seats waiting for their flight to board. The little girl cooed and laughed as the father made faces at her and tickled her sides.

"Mookie mookie mookie," the man said as he ballooned his cheeks out and bulged his eyes.

Reggie looked up from the television set, met the man's bulging eyes and smiled.

The man lost the goofy baby face and looked a little embarrassed.

"Pretty little girl," Reggie said trying to get the man off the hook.

"Thanks," the father said rubbing the little girl's hair.

Reggie went back to watching the show. He laughed as Granny told Jed what Mrs. Drysdale was up to and heard Jed's stoic response. The show broke for a commercial. Then a news break came on. Reggie sat up when he heard the commentator begin to talk about an

220

attempted coup in the small country of San Miguel.

The television screen flashed, then shrank into a tiny circle of blue light as time ran out.

"Shit!" Carver said as he fished in his pocket for another quarter. All he could find was a dime. The break would be over before he could get change. He would have to try to find out about the coup from somebody on the plane or wait until he got to California.

"Flight 109 boarding for San Francisco."

Reggie looked up and saw that passengers were boarding his flight. Uttering a disgusted hiss, he got up and picked up his briefcase. He walked over to the gate and handed the stewardess his ticket. She took out the necessary forms and perused his boarding pass. "Have a nice trip, sir," she said.

"I'll try."

He walked down the tunnel and was greeted by another flight attendant, who smiled and pointed to where the seats were. Reggie always thought it was funny that they did this, since it was the only place the seats could be located unless he was the pilot. Reggie went down the aisle and found his seat. He started to put the briefcase in the compartment above, when he felt a sharp pain in his right shin.

"Oww," he said looking down at his leg. A small boy was standing there with a mean look on his face.

"Get outta de way, Mister," the little hellion said as he drew his foot back and launched another kick at Carver's leg.

"Now stop that, Tyler, the man is trying to put his luggage away," a woman's soft voice said.

The boy kicked Reggie again. "I wanna sit down."

"Just a second, kid," Reggie said trying to control the urge to dropkick the little shit across the cabin.

"Wanna sit!" The boy punched Reggie in the thigh

almost striking paydirt in the family jewels.

His mother bent down and softened her features to match the tone of her voice. "Now, Tyler, I'm very disappointed in you. I feel that you are letting me down when you act this way," the mother said, trying to reason with her four-year-old boy as if he were an adult.

Reggie quickly shoved his briefcase into the compartment and sat down before Buster Brat had another shot at him. To his horror, he saw that Tyler and his mother were to be his companions on the voyage.

"I'm very sorry about Tyler, he's just a little high-spirited," the woman said, patting her son on the head as he pulled out an air-sickness bag and spit into it. "Tyler, people have to pay for those things. You shouldn't waste it."

Reggie smiled and nodded.

"Hey, mister, are you made o' chocolate?" Tyler asked, touching Reggie's cheek then tasting his finger.

"No, Tyler," the woman said. She later told Reggie her name was Butterfly World, "He's an African-American."

"You gotta elephant?"

Reggie smiled in spite of himself. He was trying not to like the little tyke.

"You gotta elephant?" The boy asked again.

"Yeah, a big purple one," Reggie answered.

The little boy's pale blue eyes lit up and he barked a laugh.

"Excuse me, sir," the mother interrupted, "but please don't put such notions in the boy's head." She turned to her son. "Tyler, there are no such things as purple elephants."

The smile fell off the little boy's face and Reggie suddenly felt sorry for the little brat who moments before had used Reggie's shin as a soccer ball. It was

222

obvious what was wrong with him. His mother was treating him like an adult instead of as a four-year-old kid. Reggie hated to see a child being robbed of the one thing that makes him or her special—the ability to see the world through innocent eyes; to imagine and pretend. Reggie winked at him and the boy smiled.

After a while, the mother dozed off and Reggie amused Tyler by making his hand into a creature by extending his middle finger and walking around on the remaining four. The hand beast amused the little boy and Reggie had him giggling so loud that his mother woke up and put a stop to the fun. Tyler fell asleep soon after that. His mother pulled out a book, *Childcare for the Nineties. Dealing with Children as People,* and started to read. Reggie turned away, knowing that the book was an accessory to the murder of the boy's childhood. Damned fool books. *His* mother hadn't needed any book to raise him and his siblings, and they had come out just fine. He shrugged.

"Can I get you anything to drink, sir," the flight attendant, Jane Smiley, asked Reggie as she pushed a cart filled with sodas, beers, fruit juices and bottles of water. A tub of little liquor bottles was attached to the cart for passengers that wanted a little bite to their drink.

"I'll have a Coke," Reggie said.

The flight attendant smiled and handed Reggie a plastic cup filled with ice, and a can of soda. "Here you go."

"Thanks. Hey, have you heard anything on the news about a revolt in San Miguel?" Reggie asked, remembering the interrupted broadcast he'd heard earlier.

"A little. I think their dictator was overthrown, but I'm not positive. It's funny, I just flew there two months ago and everything seemed fine."

"Really," he said as he smiled. Maybe the overthrow

would keep Colin Macdow busy, giving Reggie and Chris the chance to get the nitty and the gritty on the Baobhan Sith. Surely the overthrow created a bad situation for the de facto leader of that country.

"Peanuts?" Jane asked.

"Sure," Reggie said, taking the metallic blue bag of nuts.

Jane continued down the aisle as Reggie struggled with the top of the bag. He finally tore it open but spilled the majority of his nuts out onto his lap.

"Shit," he hissed, drawing a disapproving glare from Butterfly World, Tyler's mom.

"I mean shoot." He corrected himself, but too late for absolution from the "by the book" mother.

She continued to express her disapproval with pursed lips and shaking head.

Smiling sheepishly, Reggie picked the salty peanuts out of his lap and ate them.

Butterfly went back to her book.

As Reggie sat back in the chair and closed his eyes, his mind wandered to the Vargas case and his assignment in California. He shuddered as he contemplated finding the answers to his questions about the Baobhan Sith. His trepidation was predicated on the fact that he knew he wasn't going to like those answers. He wasn't going to like them one damned bit.

6

The Miami Beach surf rolled in the background as Chris sat in his car waiting for McNally to show up for their meeting. It was past nine and the meeting had been set for eight forty-five. The salt air floated gently down onto the windshield leaving a foggy film that diffused the light from the streetlamp overhead. The light sifted through the glass in a blur of yellow, staining Chris in amber hues. The vampire detective began to suspect that McNally had lied to him, but could think of no reason to confirm that suspicion.

Just as Chris prepared to leave, he saw the grey sedan that belonged to the DTF agent pull up and park next to him. Chris got out of his vehicle and met McNally midway between the two cars.

"What's up, Chris?" McNally said, shaking the private eye's hand.

A seagull chattered overhead and disappeared into the night sky.

Chris shook his head. "Nothing. Reggie's gone to California to check up on information about the Baobhan Sith. You find out anything?"

"Where'd he go in California?" McNally asked, curious to know where such information could be obtained.

"Some place on Mt. Tam. A guy named Kargosi lives there. Reggie gets into San Francisco late tonight and meets with this guy tomorrow."

"Good. I hope he finds something out that will help us."

"Me, too. We don't know jack about these things."

McNally sat on the hood of a parked car and fired up a smoke. He took a deep drag and exhaled a bluish grey plume of polluted air.

"I found out the deal's going down in two nights at Monkey Jungle," he said, taking another puff.

"A drug deal at Monkey Jungle?" Chris said.

"I know it's sounds weird, but that's one of the reasons they do business there. Nobody would think that they would use a zoo as a front. My informant told me that one of the workers there is a dealer. In two days, he and the rich kid are meeting there at eleven."

"Does Singer know about it?"

225

McNally shrugged and a trail of smoke escaped as he said, "I don't know. He probably knows about it from inside Macdow's camp, but as far as his official knowledge as head of the DTF, no, he's pretending not to know. He's acting like he believes my story."

"So how many guys did your man say would be there?"

"Let's see. The Baines kid. A couple of Macdow guys and the worker. So, four."

"If we get there early and corner the guy that works at the place before his buddies arrive, I could probably get him to talk," Chris said, confident of his mental powers.

"How you gonna do that?" McNally asked, dropping the butt and grinding it out with the ball of his loafer-clad foot.

Chris smiled. "Trust me. I can do it."

McNally didn't press.

"So let's say nine o'clock we get there," McNally said. "That means we meet at about what on Wednesday?"

"Do you want to meet at my office at about seven?"

"Okay, that should work. We can make some plans and then go scope the place out and find this guy."

"So seven's about right?"

"Yeah. Good," Mark said, scribbling the time into his notepad. He took another cigarette out of his pack. "Hey, Chris, what are we gonna do if these Sith things are there?"

"We'll deal with that if it happens."

McNally nodded and wiped a bead of sweat from his brow.

"Well," Chris said, "I have to go back to the office and check my messages."

"I have some stuff to catch up on outside the office, so I should be able to steer clear of Singer. I really think he's beginning to suspect I'm onto his connection with Macdow. I can't afford to lose access to the DTF's info bank. If he finds out I'm working with you . . ."

"He won't if we're careful. The main thing is we find the Vargas's and your lady."

"Yeah," McNally said grimly with just a touch of sorrow. "That's the main thing."

"So I'll see you in two nights."

"Seven o'clock."

As Chris watched McNally pull away, he caught a set of headlights turning on. A car pulled out and started to follow McNally. Chris got a sick feeling in his stomach and it wasn't the usual hunger pangs. If the tail was put on McNally by Macdow through Singer then it was only a matter of his reporting back to the DTF Chief about Chris and Mark's meeting. Singer would know McNally was helping Chris and that might jeopardize the whole plan. He started to jump into his car and head out after the tail, but decided he could make better time in the air. He looked around to make sure that he was alone. Satisfied of his isolation, the vampire concentrated and soon the transformation from man to bat was complete. Flapping his wings, he set out after the tail.

7

DTF agent Joe Dustin was once again assigned to surveillance, only tonight's target was Deputy Chief McNally, not the Miami private eye. Dustin didn't know why Chief Singer had requested that he follow his second-in-command, but he wasn't about to question his orders, with his annual review coming up next month. He needed to make brownie points after last night's foul-up in the Blaze tail. How he could've missed someone cutting the valve stems on his tires was something he would never figure. But tonight's little discovery of the partnership between McNally and Blaze would more than make up for the blunder. He slowed as McNally made a left turn ahead of Dustin's car. Dustin took the corner and got behind another car in the right lane.

Joe heard a thump on top of his car. The sudden burst of sound startled him. He stepped on the gas to keep pace with McNally's vehicle when all of a sudden a face appeared in front of him. He yelled and slammed on the brakes. It was *his own* face that was staring at him upsidedown through the windshield. His flat nose and brown skin. His curly hair. His scar under his left eye from a well-aimed elbow in a pickup basketball game. His face didn't move. Agent Dustin stared at his doppelganger and slowly reached for his pistol. The face vanished. The front door opened and a powerful hand reached in and grabbed Dustin before he could get his .38. With a great tug, the pseudo-Dustin pulled the agent from his vehicle.

"Hello, Joe," he said to himself.

The real Dustin just stared into the reddening eyes of his likeness. The glowing eyes sucked him inside their sanguine orbs. His fear melted. He began to feel warm. Words began to enter his head.

"You will forget seeing Mark McNally. You will forget seeing Chris Blaze. You will only remember seeing yourself. That is what you will tell the chief. You only saw yourself."

Dustin felt himself nodding. Smiling in the comfort of those eyes. "Only saw myself."

"Get in your car and go back to your office," Blaze commanded.

Dustin nodded and got behind the wheel of the car. He put the vehicle into gear and drove off.

228

Chris watched the taillights shrink in the distance, looked around and changed back into himself. He started to feel woozy from the rapid transformations from himself to bat to Dustin back to himself. The changes had used up most of the life force, the blood, in Chris's system. All of a sudden, he was starving.

8

Pam Dumas was running late for her job doing late-night inventory at the local all-night drug store and she wanted to get there before her boss arrived. Matt Killarney was a nasty son of a bitch who loved to rant when one of his employees was late, and she didn't feel like hearing him. Matt knew that she was his best worker and yet he spared no one if they violated a rule. She stepped up her pace, paying no attention to the man bent over in front of her. She kept walking, drawing closer.

Blaze's rampant hunger hit him with unexpected force. A surge of pain clawed its way from his guts to his mind. Visions of throats spurting blood strobed in his brain. Torrents of blood. Delicious.

Pam slowed her pace when she saw the expression on the man's face a few feet ahead of her. He looked crazy. She started to turn around when he made his move.

Chris snarled and lost control as he grabbed the woman and pulled her close to him. The veins in her neck seemed to bulge with blood as he craved the warm life force.

She gasped, too frightened to scream.

"Marjory!" Blaze said quickly, as he subdued the urge to bite deep into her throat. He released her arms.

"What?" the woman said still startled by his actions.

"Oh, I'm sorry," Blaze said trying to act as though he

229

had made a mistake. "I thought you were a friend of mine."

"No problem," the woman said, rubbing her arms where he'd grabbed her—her face a mixture of relief and confusion as she hurried away from the lunatic with the weird eyes.

Chris groaned as the hunger tore into him with razor-sharp talons and he regretted his little joke on the DTF agent. He should never have used his power of transformation to confuse agent Dustin. The energy expenditure was too great and took him to the brink of his darker side; the side of his nature that he constantly battled so as to maintain his humanity. But his vampirism needed to be addressed and in a hurry. He needed blood!

Seeing no one, Chris took off at super speed and ran toward his office. When he got to the outside of the building, he ran into an impenetrable wall and fell to the ground.

Chris sat outside the front of his office, unable to enter because of the accident. A produce truck had collided with another vehicle, scattering the contents of the vehicle all over the street in front of Chris's office. Celery, carrots, lettuce and ginger root were strewn about the sidewalk from the overturned truck. Also included in the load were hundreds of bulbs of garlic, crushed by the heavy crates of carrots. Their pungent aroma filled the air. The sickening smell repulsed the vampire. He couldn't go near the building until the mess was cleaned up, which from the looks of things might be hours. He would have to go home and retrieve a bottle from the refrigerator.

But did he have time?

The hunger inside him was a vicious ravenous beast slashing his guts and his brain with pain. His thoughts twisted from the cold bottles at home to the warm blood coursing through the veins of the bystanders that crowded around the crash site. It would taste so good.

"No! I won't give in," Chris said in a tortured whisper as he clenched his fists and hurried away from the crowd. The dark side did a little whispering of its own.

"Take them all. Drink till you're bloated like a tick. Drink."

Chris looked back and saw the people. He could almost see their veins flowing with what he needed. His stomach screamed. He started heading back when he heard a nasty voice slice through the night air.

"Gimme the fuckin' money, ya old bitch, fo' I cut yo' ass."

The voice came from a dark corner of the parking garage behind him. He turned and saw with his extraordinary night vision a husky black man holding a knife on an elderly black woman. Chris could smell her fear. His hunger banged inside his gut like a starving tiger. His legs carried him into the garage as if the hunger had taken control of them. Chris needed blood.

"Please don't hurt me, ain't got but a few dollars," the old lady cried. The wet lines of tears on her brown cheeks reflected the light from a single bulb on the ceiling of the roof.

"Shut yo' ass up, bitch, and gimme that money."

Shabazz El Akim wanted to gut the old bitch, even if she did give him her money—stupid bitch, carrying on like his grandma used to do when he beat her up for a few dollars.

"Hurry up fo' I git real mad."

"I ain't got but a few dolla."

"Fuck that. I know you got mo' than that. I know when you old bitches git yo' social 'curity. You better cut that . . ."

231

Suddenly, Shabbaz felt a cold hand grab him by the back of the neck and he was no longer on the ground. His short flight ended when he slammed against the concrete wall. The startled mugger let out a little yelp before recovering his cool and readying his blade to cut the fucker that had grabbed him.

The old woman ran faster than Blaze thought possible as he watched her take off in the direction of her car.

"Hey, mother-fuckin' hero."

Chris turned his attention to the big man with the shiny knife.

"You is a dumb mother fucker fo' helping that old bitch, Homes. Now I'm gonna cut yo dick off."

Blaze smiled, exposing his fangs to frighten the swaggering black man, but the sight of them did nothing to erode the bravado of the defiant mugger.

"So whut, you got some fuckin' long teeth. Supposed to scare somebody?"

Blaze couldn't resist the temptation. He leapt at the black man and plucked the knife from his hand. Holding the knife out, Blaze plunged it into his own stomach. Akim's eyes bulged as he backed away. Blaze pulled the knife from his gut and tossed it back to the now-terrified man. Chris smiled, exposing his fangs, and grabbed the black man by the throat and launched him into the air again. The black man screamed and fell into Blaze's waiting arms.

"Please, man," the mugger pleaded.

Blaze smiled with such malevolent glee that Shabazz whimpered like a puppy.

Again, the vampire tossed the mugger fifteen feet into the air and caught him. He enjoyed Shabazz El Akim's torment and toyed with him like a cat with a mouse. Blaze was losing control. His evil side was beginning to take over. He laughed as he snatched

232

Akim out of the air and pulled him close.

"Gimme yo' blood, bitch," he said mocking Akim's words to the old woman.

"Please, man," Shabazz said crying.

Chris laughed and then quenched his thirst.

As the blood began to cool the burning in his gut, Chris began to recover his senses. Suddenly he realized that he intended to completely drain the man.

Quickly, he withdrew his fangs and stopped drinking, leaving enough blood to keep the man alive. As he saw the blood on the man's neck he almost started to feast again, but held back. He let Shabazz slide to the ground. He doubted if the bold mugger would continue in his line of work after tonight's little episode.

Blaze positioned the dazed Akim against the wall and started for home. He swore that he would never let himself become that low on blood again because he knew that if he did, someone would die.

9

The rest of the night went by quickly for Sue Blaze. There was a spurt of activity in the emergency room in the latter part of the early morning. The cases were all treated with success and now the morning shift had arrived.

As the tired doctor started for the exit, she saw Dr. Argyll coming up the corridor and she remembered the services. In the tumult of cases, her promise to attend had completely slipped her mind—with her subconscious providing the grease. Since he was in research on the sixth floor, she wondered what Argyll was doing in her section of the hospital. She suspected that he'd been waiting for her. Damned zealot. He approached with a big smile on his face.

233

"Hello, Sue."

"Hi."

"I heard things got pretty busy in there tonight."

"For a little while."

"So," Argyll began the question that the tired Sue was dreading, "are you coming to the services this morning as you said you would?"

Sue was tired, and the last thing that she wanted to do was attend church services at five in the morning. What she really wanted to do was to go home and get into a hot bath and relax. She hesitated before answering.

Argyll got a look of disappointment on his face. "Don't tell me you changed your mind, Dr. Charles assumes you'll be going." His expression shifted into a self-assured smugness.

Sue understood the underlying meaning of the statement. It would not do to upset the applecart when she was planning on talking to Dr. Charles about using the hospital's research facility for her own personal project. Earlier that night, before the rush, she had come up with the idea that maybe her husband's vampirism was a disease and through research she could possibly find a cure. It was worth a shot and the research facility at the hospital might be just the place. With the strong security, she'd be able to work in private. With this in mind, she decided that one more hour of her life could be sacrificed in the interest of hospital politics and her husband's well-being. She only hoped that she could stay awake. "Oh, I'm going, Don, just have to finish up one of my reports."

"Fine. I'll see you there."

Sue went back into her office and sat at her desk. She would go to the services and hope her attendance would placate them. Surely after this morning's participation, she wouldn't be pressured to go to any

234

more of the services. She had shown her good faith and would simply say that she chose to worship in her own way. If not . . .

She glanced at the drawer containing the resignation letter. For a moment, she stared at it thinking about a quick termination. *No, I can't,* she thought. She opened the drawer and took out the letter. She thought of her husband and tore it up. If this place's research facility could help him, then she would just have to suffer through the services. Who knows? She might even enjoy them.

Yeah, right.

She got up from her desk, left her office and walked down to the nearest elevator and pushed the up-button. After a moment's wait, the elevator hissed open and she got in, pressing the second floor button as she did.

The elevator arrived at the second floor seconds later and Sue got off. She followed the signs to the chapel area. A few people entered through the wooden double doors. Sue did the same, pausing to study the layout. The chapel was dimly lit, with none of the usual icons that one associates with Christianity. The walls were barren except for a strange crest above the pulpit. It was finely polished metal that reflected the dim light in the chapel. The pews were lined up in a V pattern forming a funnel effect toward the front of the church. The amazing thing was that the chapel was full of people. She saw most, no, all of the emergency staff from her shift sitting in various places around the room. She knitted her brow and the sick feeling in the pit of her stomach returned. *My God, was the whole staff of the hospital involved in this religion?* Anxiously, she licked her lips and walked down the aisle to find an inconspicuous seat.

Dr. Argyll saw her and motioned for her to sit down next to him. Feeling trapped, Sue smiled and went to

235

sit next to the man she couldn't seem to avoid. Damn her inability to be anything but polite.

"I'm glad you decided you could make it," Argyll said smiling. "I think you're going to find it quite rewarding."

"I hope so," Sue said, still doubting that she would. She was glad she was in the aisle seat so that she could make her exit quickly.

"Hello, Don," A pretty blond girl said as she sat in front of Argyll.

"Sally."

Suddenly all the lights in the chapel went off and Sue felt a slither of fear snake up her spine. *What the hell kind of a service was this?* she asked herself again.

An orange glow followed by a shadowy face moved across the front of the pulpit, stopping in the center. Another orange glow followed then another. Soon there were four people standing behind the pulpit. The light from their candelabras filled the room with an eerie glow. Sue recognized one of the people as Myra Lee, Dr. Charles's assistant. She smiled and looked straight at Sue.

The people in the congregation stood as Dr. Charles came in wearing a heavy fabric robe that seemed to be made of rough wool or cotton. The black robe didn't look like any religious garment Sue had ever seen. She was stunned to see that the chief of staff was going to be conducting the services, and once again she felt the sick feeling in the pit of her stomach return. The situation was getting stranger by the moment. Charles walked up to the pulpit and stood for a moment with his arms outstretched, and gazed out into the congregation. His eyes met Sue's and he smiled. Her stomach dropped to her toes and a heat wave swept over her.

"Please be seated," he said, lowering his arms.

The congregation sat.

"Before we begin the services, I would like to welcome a new member to the church and to the hospital, Dr. Susan Blaze. Sue, would you please stand up?"

Embarrassed by the attention, Sue stood and waved halfheartedly to the crowd. For some reason the sea of beaming smiles around her was frightening. Everyone in the entire church smiled with the same vapid grin as if they were toys constructed by the same unimaginative toymaker. She sat.

Argyll leaned over and whispered in her ear. His breath smelled like fish. "They like you."

Sue worked up a smile. God, did she want to get the hell out of there. It was too weird for words. Time to get the resumes flying thick and fast. In her mind, she was already recalling the contents of her resignation letter when Charles began to speak again. Her fear erased any notion of vampire research. She could find somewhere else to accomplish that goal.

Charles cleared his throat and opened his arms. "In the beginning there was Dow."

The congregation finished the sentence. "And He was the Father."

What the hell was this all about? Was this Taoism? Sue wondered as she recalled her resume. *Let's see, graduated from University of Florida medical school . . ."*

Charles's loud voice cut into her thoughts. "He called upon the Dark Mother . . ."

The crowd answered. "For She was the Uniter."

Oh God, I have got to get out of here. Started working at Miami General . . .

"And Maureen opened for him."

"For she was the Mother Host."

Charles smiled and clasped his hands together. "Join hands."

Argyll reached over and took Sue's hand in his. Sue instinctively shivered at his cold touch. She thought about shaking loose and bolting out of there, but figured she would wait and suffer through it. She was definitely out of Sisters of the Faith the next day.

Charles continued in that deep stentorian voice, "The Dark Mother used her womb and the Children were born threefold."

"To rule the flock of the world."

Now Sue's urge to flee these proceedings and never come back to the hospital manifested itself into action. She tried to get up and leave, but Argyll held her hand clamped in his. He squeezed it painfully. She glanced over at him. He turned and smiled at her. A smile that was so benign it was frightening.

Charles's eyes rolled back in his head exposing the whites and Sue felt her legs grow weak. She had to get out of there. She had stumbled into a nightmare. The moment that Argyll released her hand she would get the hell out of Dodge. If he didn't let go soon, she would jam her fingernail file into the top of his hand and make him let go. She reached for her purse with her free hand.

Charles continued to speak, his voice suddenly an octave lower and more resonant. "Give yourself to the Dark Mother and serve her Children for they are the power and the glory . . ."

". . . for ever and ever."

"Destroy those who would oppose us . . ."

". . . for they are the descendants of the Destroyer."

Sue tried to get her purse, but Argyll squeezed her hand painfully. A woman, paramedic Missy Davis, got up and squeezed in next to her, grabbing Sue's hand as she did. Sue's knuckles ground together. She could almost hear them crack as the woman constricted her hand. Argyll smiled again as did the woman. Sue was trapped.

238

"Bring us another to the flock . . ."

". . . for the Mother needs our love."

"Come to us, Sue Blaze. Become one."

The room went silent for a moment. Sue felt as though the eyes of the world were upon her. She had stumbled into a nightmare and there seemed to be no escape. The congregation began to chant.

"Become one with Baobhan Sith."

Baobhan Sith! Where had Sue heard that before?

"Become one with Baobhan Sith."

Sith? Where?

Oh my God.

"Become one with Baobhan Sith."

Chris's investigation.

"Become one with Baobhan Sith."

They were the things . . .

"Become one with Baobhan Sith."

Sue started to feel an energy begin to swell in the room. It was a force, a mental force, that started to put pressure on her mind. The pressure increased as if something or someone was forcing themselves into her mind, causing her thoughts about her husband and the investigation to be pushed out. The pressure was like what you might experience on a plane, only more powerful. Images began to flood into her. Green eyes, luminous. Faces of people. Rocky lands. Fog-shrouded lakes. Naked girls and boys. People dressed in robes and men in dresses. Visions of the past. A pagan world where human sacrifice was performed. Sue saw blood spurting from small children's chests. Awful sights of death. She tried to expel these visions from her mind, but they would not vanish. Instead they continued to streak rapidly, becoming blurred, merging into one thought. Two words. Words she had heard before but did not understand. Two words with meaning she would come to learn. Just two words tumbling over and over in her mind as she became a part of them.

Baobhan Sith.

Baobhan Sith.

Baobhan Sith.

10

The ride home with her husband, Chris, had been a vague blur. She barely remembered leaving the hospital at six and had no recollection of the services that she knew she'd attended. Her memory of the early morning event was a great blank slate that had been written on and then erased. The last thing that she recalled was seeing Chris waiting for her in the lobby. Moments later they were in their car on their way home.

"Hey honey," her husband said glancing over at his wife who stared blankly out the window. "You okay?"

She looked up and smiled. She shook her head. "Not great. A little tired."

"So you didn't tell me how the services you got sapped into were?"

"To tell you the truth, I fell asleep," she said, not remembering the services and coming to the conclusion that she slept through them.

Chris chuckled. "So I guess your PR campaign was a flop."

"Oh, I talked to a few people before the services got started so it wasn't that bad." Sue vaguely remembered a conversation with Don Argyll and a woman that sat next to her. And didn't Dr. Charles speak with her? She couldn't be sure and desperately tried to recall.

"I hope you didn't snore," Chris said.

"Huh?" Sue said not listening, as her mind sought to recollect the morning's events.

240

"I said I hope you didn't snore during the services."

"Oh, right," Sue said trying to work up a smile, but creating a kind of half-grin, half-grimace. "I don't think so. I tried to sit in the back just in case I did fall asleep." *Didn't she find an inconspicuous seat before the services began or did she just try to find one?* She couldn't recollect.

"I bet you're glad you did."

"What?" Sue said trying to pay attention but having a hard time.

Chris smiled and closed his wife's tired eyes. "You need to go back to sleep. You're like a zombie."

Sue blinked her eyes open. "I told you I'm tired. What time is it?"

Chris pressed the gas pedal and looked at his watch. "Six-ten."

Sue nodded and closed her eyes. A quick spark of orange light burned and she saw a worm with needle-sharp teeth. She opened her eyes. Nothing was there.

Chris popped the button to the garage door, and the metal door yawned. He pulled the car into the garage and parked.

Before he could say another word, Chris felt his body tingling, which meant only one thing; the sun was coming up. He had to get into the safety of the dark room.

"Well, time for me to hit it," he said, as he opened the door to the house. "Old Sol doesn't wait for anyone. I'll see you tonight." He kissed Sue again.

"Okay. G'night."

"Call this number," Chris said as he got a piece of paper and a pencil. "Tell Ryan to forget daylight surveillance on the house and come inside to protect you. Okay?"

"Sure."

"Love you."

Chris hurried into the darkened room and made it to his bed just before he collapsed into the sleep of the dead.

Sue remained in the living room, and fell asleep on the couch. She dreamed of rocky land and slaughtered children.

11

Chaos! Screaming servants ran about the house covering their heads. Bullets shattered the mirrored walls of the dining room. Paulo Singuelo aimed his ouzi machine pistol, but a bullet burrowed into his temple. He fell forward, smashing his nose on the corner of a marble coffee table. Shots rang out all around the villa as Macdow's bodyguards tried to keep the invading troops away from the helicopter. Their boss had boarded and was cranking off rounds from a modified AK47 as the pilot started the engine and the props began to whirl. The money-gathering stage of Macdow's plan was over. The coup had happened sooner than expected, but Colin Macdow had been prepared. He had taken almost 50 million dollars from the state treasury along with another 250 million in ill-gotten drug money. The money was resting safely in a number of Swiss bank accounts and offshore banks throughout the islands of the Caribbean and off the coast of Florida in the Atlantic Ocean. It would be used to finance the beginning of the Second Genesis.

A bullet slammed into the bodyguard next to Macdow. Miguel Silvera cursed, grabbing his side. He held up his blood-stained palm and stared at it, before slumping onto his benefactor. The bullet had torn up his insides. Macdow pushed the dead man off him, returned fire and then shouted at the pilot. "Tommy,

242

git this bloody thin' off the ground."

The pilot pushed the throttle and the copter began to lurch hesitantly off the ground. As the rotor whirled the propellers faster, the chopper rose quickly into the air. Macdow grabbed the dead guard and heaved him out the side. The body flew loosely to the ground, landing with a cracking thump. Macdow fired the last of the clip and watched with satisfaction as one of the invading forces went down from the sleet of lead.

"Y' bastards," he said, as he leaned back in his seat and breathed a sigh of relief.

"Take us to the airport. The jet's waiting."

The pilot of the chopper gave Macdow the thumbs up and steered the helicopter in the direction of the private airfield where Macdow's jet was stationed.

The Scotsman was glad that Mary was safe in Miami with her sister, Glynda. His sending her there had been fortunate, in that the coup might have presented a danger to her. Since the troops of *El Frente,* after executing Pedroza at the nation's capital, had arrived at Macdow's estate that morning, she would have been helpless. They could have dragged her into the sun. He couldn't bear to lose another one of the children in so short a span of time. The thought of the dead Drucinda pushed his mind away from the coup and toward the two detectives that seemed to trigger events against him. Things had been so hectic that he hadn't had a chance to check with Miami on their progress. He didn't know if the detectives knew the old ways, had gotten lucky, or if a member of the clan Stephenson was alive. But he would find out once he arrived in Miami. And if he found out that the two detectives had merely gotten lucky, they would either be captured for the farm or they'd be dead by morning.

Chapter Eight

1

The damaged fingers on Reggie's hand ached as he clutched the wheel driving up the narrow mountain road that led to the home of Kargosi. The road was barely wide enough for two vehicles. Since there were no barriers to prevent him from dropping the one thousand feet to the bottom of the mountain, the going was slow. Reggie strained to maintain his concentration as he drove higher and higher up the mountain road that narrowed ahead of him. He felt a peculiar lightheadedness from the fear that was running rampant in his body. He had lived in the flatlands of Florida his whole life and had never before driven in the mountains. Trepidation numbed him. The car crept along at about fifteen miles per hour and he still felt like he was going too fast. Visions of his car plummeting over the cliff and crashing on the ground below would not leave him. A sensation of dropping lurched in his gut. His legs felt heavy, as he tried to keep them from pushing too hard on the gas pedal. His entire body ached from the tension. He had never concentrated so hard in his life.

Up and up he drove.

Reggie had left after obtaining directions to Mt. Tam from the hotel manager. He had been less than enthused about the prospects of driving up a mountain since he was a virgin to that particular experience. The reality of that prospect heightened the dreadful anxiety he felt as he lost his cherry on the forbidding mountain road.

The wide-open spaces yawned in front of him as the road took a sharp turn. He swallowed dry air and turned the wheel. His arms ached.

He made it around the curve, only to be confronted by another vast space that stretched out in front of him, and a twist that was even more treacherous.

One false move and . . .

He quickly wiped a drop of sweat from his brow; his hand was a blur as he didn't trust himself to take a hand off the wheel for more than a second.

"I'd like to meet the son of a bitch that built this piece of shit road," Reggie mumbled to himself. Visions of murder filled his head as he pictured pushing the architect of such a dreadful road over one of the cliffs that dropped steeply off the side of the road.

Carefully, he negotiated the curve and saw the narrow path that led to a house on the side of the mountain. Reggie figured that this Kargosi guy must be a real lunatic. Anyone that lived in a place like this would surely have to be out of his everloving gourd.

Reggie breathed a sigh of relief as he finally reached the driveway and parked his rental car. He stepped out of the car on weak legs. The energy seemed to have been sucked out of him by the incredibly tense journey up the mountain.

Reggie sat on the hood of the car for a moment in an attempt to recover some of his strength. A man called out from the house.

"Mr. Carver?"

"Yeah, that's me," Reggie said, amazed that he had the strength to shout.

"Please come up."

"Just a second."

Reggie heard a door open, and saw an obese giant coming towards him. Kargosi looked like a demented version of the Sta-puf marshmallow man. His hair was a crewcut that veered into a widow's peak. He had a goatee and was dressed in a silken black robe. It took Carver a moment, but he recognized the outfit from the 1930's movie, *The Black Cat*. It was the same as the one Boris Karloff wore in his role as the mad architect and Satan worshipper.

"You didn't enjoy your drive up I take it," Kargosi said, wheezing slightly from the short walk to Reggie's rental car.

"Let's just say I'd rather wear a honey suit and be staked to an anthill than drive up another mountain."

"That could be arranged," Kargosi said in his high-pitched voice that in no way matched his physical appearance.

Startled, Reggie took a step back.

Kargosi waved his hand broadly. "A joke, Mr. Carver. A joke."

Reggie forced a laugh, "Funny."

"Won't you come in?" Kargosi swept a plump hand toward the entrance to his home, the blubber under his arm swinging back and forth as he did.

"Thanks." Reggie said, as he followed the behemoth into the house.

The living room looked as if Kargosi had hired the Addams family as his interior decorators. There were stuffed animals in combination. A rat with the body of a snake. A goat standing upright like a man with arms that seemed to be those of a monkey. A glass cabinet housed skulls of all types and sizes. The home looked much like Matha Rastas's place of business, which Reggie had never thought of as being creepy, but somehow seeing such oddities in the setting of someone's home definitely gave Reggie a case of the heebie-jeebies.

"So you wish to see *Il Demonis y Monstrueros?*"

"If I could. See I'm trying to find out all I can about a legend called the Baobhan Sith."

"Hmm, Baobhan Sith."

"Yeah. They're sorta like vampires I think." Reggie was annoyed that the man hadn't already looked up the information, but held his tongue. He didn't want to get on this whacko's shit list.

"Well," Kargosi said, picking up an aged-looking book from a table with gargoyle legs, "I have the volume right here so let's take a look."

Kargosi opened the book up and started carefully to thumb through the ancient pages. The yellowed paper crackled and sounded as if it would break off in brittle chunks as the fat man turned the pages.

"How old is that thing?" Reggie asked.

"Centuries." Kargosi said without looking up. He continued to scan the pages of the ancient tome as Reggie returned to checking out the interior of the house. In the corner of the room, he saw a coffin that looked remarkably like the black coffin of Yosekaat Rakz the vampire. Afraid he would see the demon rise out and attack him, Reggie shivered and turned his eyes away from it. Instead, he focused his attention on the painting of the hermaphrodite that hung over the cavelike fireplace. The man/woman was reaching for an apple in what appeared to be the Garden of Eden. A serpent smiled from the branch of the apple tree. Reggie shook his head at the weird work of art, unwilling to attempt to comprehend what the artist was trying to say. Probably some BS about the duality of man's nature in the masculine and feminine aspects or some such crapola. He turned to Kargosi.

"Man, you sure gotta creep- . . . uh, unusual house."

"Thank you."

Kargosi continued to look through the book as Reggie settled back in his chair and started to read a magazine called *Fangoria* that was also sitting on the medieval-looking table.

Reggie had just finished an article on a new book by William J. Ronat called *Bone* when Kargosi found the passage for which he was looking. "Ah, here it is. The Baobhan Sith."

Reggie set the magazine down and leaned forward, elbows on his knees. "What does it say?" he said urgently.

"Patience. This book is written in the tongue of the ancients. It will take time for me to translate."

Reggie silently cursed. He didn't want to spend any more time in this dungeon than he had to, but he decided to make the best of it. "How long do you think it will take you?"

"Oh, the rest of the day perhaps."

"A day!" Reggie exclaimed, and then toned his reaction down when he saw Kargosi's raised eyebrows and expression, "I mean, a day, that's okay."

"Good. In the meantime, would you like something to eat?"

"No, I'm not hungry," Reggie lied. He was starving, but he didn't feel like any eye of newt or henbane soup.

"Hmm, I have a couple of filets in there that are just waiting to be grilled."

"Filet of what?" Reggie asked.

"Mr. Carver," Kargosi said in a tired voice, as though he had confronted the black man's attitude from others in the past.

"Reggie."

"Reggie, just because I enjoy the mysterious doesn't mean that I am a monster. I eat regular foods and enjoy them a great deal, as you can tell." He patted his great girth. "I just happen to be fond of the occult and its many secrets."

"Okay," Reggie said, embarrassed at his silly fears, "I will have that steak then."

"Good. And would you like any bat intestines with that?"

Reggie laughed. "Maybe a little."

"Good, the steaks are in the refrigerator. I could cook them but I know that you are in a hurry."

"Okay," Reggie said catching the fat man's drift, "I can do it."

"Good."

"Mr. Ca- . . . I mean Reggie. If you don't mind my asking, why do you want this information?"

"It's just a curiosity."

"I see, you fly from Florida to California for a curiosity."

"Let's just say that I'm a little eccentric myself."

Kargosi smiled. "Very well, we will say that—for the moment. Now why don't you get those steaks on the grill?"

As Reggie started preparing the lunch, the men that had followed Carver up the mountain took up a position across from Kargosi's home and watched the house with great interest.

2

Sue woke up feeling rested. She got out of bed and went into the kitchen. Hunger nipped at her stomach. She opened the freezer and grabbed her lunch, putting

249

it in the oven. She had a feeling that there was something she should do, something Chris had said, but she couldn't remember what.

She made herself a glass of chocolate milk and grabbed a couple of pretzels. She sat at the kitchen table and munched sullenly on the hard sourdough pretzel. She took a drink of the milk, then sighed.

She looked over at the door to Chris's bedroom and wished that her husband was awake so that she could talk to him. She felt bored. Anxious to do something.

Unexpectedly, a flash of Dr. Don Argyll's face erupted into her consciousness. He was grinning. Sue's hand ached. The vision disappeared and Sue couldn't recall what it was. Unconsciously, she rubbed her hand. *Damn it, I must be working too hard.* She drained the milk, got up and rinsed the glass then put it in the dishwasher.

The alarm on the stove went off, startling Sue, who went over and shut it off. She wondered how the alarm could have been set and then she smelled pizza. A wave of heat assaulted Sue as she opened the oven door and discovered a well-cooked pizza.

"What the hell?" Sue said, rubbing her chin. She went over to the drawer and pulled out the spatula. She took the pizza from the oven and put it on a plate. She closed the door to the oven and opened the drawer to the garbage bin where she saw the frozen-pizza box. The sight of the opened box reminded her that she had put the pie in the oven when she'd come into the kitchen. The aroma of the pizza sitting on the plate filled the kitchen. Despite the pretzel snack, she was still hungry.

After eating half the pizza and putting the rest in the fridge, Sue busied herself with straightening the house. Maybe that would alleviate her boredom. She set about the tasks with the fury of a fastidious housewife out of the nineteen-fifties. Sweeping, vacuuming, scrubbing, dusting. She wanted the house spotless.

After completing her cleaning tasks, she decided to go the grocery store to get some things she needed. She had just gone to the supermarket two days ago, but felt that she'd forgotten a couple of things that they needed.

When she got home from the grocery store, she put the food away and got ready for work. She didn't have to leave for another three hours, but she felt compelled to go. There was nothing left to do around the house and she didn't want to sit idle.

As she put on her makeup and fixed her hair, she felt almost giddy. She was excited to be going to work. She felt the way she had felt at the time of her first day as an intern at Miami General. Butterflies danced in her stomach to the tune of "Anticipation."

Dressed and ready, Sue grabbed her purse and keys and went out to the garage. She hummed as she got in her car and turned the key. The engine rumbled and she was soon on her way. She had completely forgotten Chris's orders to have him take her.

3

Kargosi continued to translate the book's passage until the steaks were sizzling on a plate.

"Come and eat." Reggie said.

The big man hefted his considerable girth out of the chair and waddled over to the table.

"I found some lettuce and stuff in there and made a couple of salads," Reggie said, "I hope you don't mind."

"No. Excellent."

Kargosi sat down at the table as did Reggie. They both began to enjoy their meal.

After they ate the steaks, Kargosi went back to translating the book's passage on the Sith, as Reggie kicked back and fell asleep in his chair. The dream

251

came almost immediately. In it, he and Chris were in a dark house. Pitch black. He couldn't see his partner, but knew that he was there. They were walking toward an eerie chanting, a power that drew the two men to it. The dirge was almost soothing. Reggie felt at peace.

Suddenly he and Chris were in the middle of the Freedomtown riot again. The jarring contrast between the chaos and the calming refrain caused him to stir in the chair. But he didn't awaken. Reggie saw the fierce faces of his black brothers and sisters as they tossed bottles at him and his fellow officers. Fires burned around him. Cars aflame. Angry shouts stung his ears. The black men and women started flying in the air like ragdolls. At first Reggie thought that explosions were causing such damage, grenades tossed by overzealous cops, but then he saw the force that was sending these people into the air. Sickness swelled inside his gut. This force was Yosekaat Rakz, the vampire. He walked toward Reggie, who turned and saw that he was suddenly all alone. The rioters flew into the air, landing in bloody heaps as Rakz tore through them. Behind the vampire, hordes of rats and cockroaches swarmed over the screaming bodies of the rioters. The sounds of the roaches' spiked legs, and of the tiny shredding of flesh, swelled a thousandfold as the rats and the roaches feasted on the howling mass of people. Rakz kept coming toward Reggie. His face twisted with rage—a hideous countenance. His nose was pushed back into dark black nostrils. His eyes blazed red. Huge fanged teeth jutted out of his mouth. He kept coming.

Reggie reached into his bag to pull out his cross, but as he did, he screamed. He withdrew his hand and a brightly colored coral snake clung to the meaty portion of his palm. He felt the hot poison seeping into his veins.

Rakz exploded with laughter and the snake changed into a tiny fetus of a vampire. It scrabbled across the

252

black man's hand and suckled on his finger like it was a teat. Reggie screamed and tried to shake the miniature monster loose. He brought it up to eye level and saw that the creature had the face of Chris Blaze. Reggie's partner reached out and hooked the black man's cheek with a tiny clawed hand. The monstrous little version of Blaze swung onto his face and hung there for a moment before sinking its fangs into Reggie's eye.

Carver screamed.

"What's wrong, Reggie?" Rakz said, suddenly appearing before Reggie in gargantuan size.

Reggie tried to reply, but when he opened his mouth, the vampire fetus clambered inside and started chewing on his teeth. The scraping was worse than a thousand fingernails on a thousand blackboards.

"What's wrong? Wake up."

Reggie heard Rakz say those words, but it wasn't the deep chilling voice of the vampire. Reggie felt a strange presence hovering over him. He wanted to open his eyes, but the eyelids were too heavy. He knew that he was awake, but he could not force his eyes open. He tried and tried, but they were tightly shut, held together by some kind of psychic glue. Reggie was frightened— he felt out of control. Something was very wrong.

Suddenly his eyes burst open and Kargosi loomed in front of him, a giant wall of flesh. Reggie sat up abruptly and caught his breath.

"Are you all right?"

"Yeah, I'm fine. Just a damned dream." Reggie wiped his face and then swept his sweaty palm across the front of his jeans. "I'm cool."

"Good," Kargosi said, as he stepped back to let Carver get up, "because I have something very interesting to show you."

"About the Baobhan Sith?"

"Oh, better than that," Kargosi said as he burped a laugh. His eyebrows skittered off his forehead as his face began to suck in.

Reggie gasped.

Kargosi started to change. His corpulent frame began to implode inward. The flesh seeming to collapse onto itself at a rapid rate. Fat cells popped and deflated. The flattop haircut squirmed in rapid motion like a thousand maggots on a griddle. With each wiggle it grew and changed color to blond. The fat man's legs lengthened and stretched. His fingers also elongated into talons.

Reggie felt his stomach turn over as he began to recognize who Kargosi was becoming. The shapely frame. The yellow-green eyes that had frightened him. The sharp white fangs.

It was the woman from the hotel in Viera. She had come to kill him.

4

The window to the upstairs bedroom of the Kargosi house was open as Carl Kleegle slid the frame up and stepped inside. He looked around the bedroom, shaking his head at the strange decor. He checked the pistol in his pocket and screwed the silencer onto the barrel. Silently he crept over to the door and opened it, hoping that it wouldn't creak. To his relief, it didn't. He stepped lightly across the hall and jumped back when he heard a scream.

5

"What's the matter, Reggie? Never seen a transformation before?"

"Holy shit." Reggie whispered.

"Such language."

The woman's face twisted with rage and she was upon Reggie before the black man drew another breath.

"You should've stayed off the case, like Singer said," the vampiress said as she picked Reggie up by the throat and hurled him across the room. Reggie thumped against the wall and she was on him in seconds. She picked him up and tossed him again. Only this time his journey was a short one, as he collided with a strange sculpture of a demon and impaled his heart on the sharp horns of the creature. Shouting, Reggie woke up with a pain in his chest.

"Are you all right, Reggie?" Kargosi asked, startled by the shout.

"Yeah, bad dream."

Reggie shook his head and got up off the couch. The dream had frightened him, but his relief at realizing that it was just a dream overcame his fear.

"I'm glad you're awake," Kargosi said shifting his bulk in his chair. "I've found what you're looking for. It's here in *Il Demonis y Monstrueros*."

"Oh, great." Reggie got up and walked over to the desk where Kargosi was sitting. "So lay it on me."

Kargosi began to read from his translated notes. "The Baobhan Sith are Scottish in origin. They, uh, roam the night and drink the blood of the living. This next part was difficult to translate. I believe that they were born when someone named Dow deliberately or inadvertently dabbled in the black arts. According to Carrabucci, this Dow summoned the Dark Mother and had sex with her through a surrogate mother that played host to this dark mother's spirit. Interesting, eh?"

"Yeah, great," Reggie replied with little enthusiasm. The bizarre circumstances were about what he had expected. *Monsters! Shit!*

Kargosi continued. "I'm not sure, but I believe it says

255

that the woman or women had given themselves freely to the night or something like that before they had relations with Dow. After the intercourse, they gave birth to what became the creatures of legend known as the Baobhan Sith."

Carver just shook his head.

"I couldn't get the rest too clearly, but I think these Sith can change into other creatures."

"Like birds?"

"Yes, how did you know?"

Carver shrugged. "Lucky guess." He changed the subject. "Does it tell you how to kill one of them?"

"Yes, but well, I'm afraid the translation is of little help."

"Why? What does it say?"

"It says to kill the Sith one needs the arm of the Earth Mother or the Father's eye."

"Now what the hell does that shit mean?" Reggie rolled his eyes in frustration.

Kargosi offered an explanation. "Well, in some ancient cults similar to that of the Druids, the Earth Mother was represented by an oak. That would fit in with other vampire legends—a wooden stake through the heart. The Father was said to be the earth's opposite."

"The sky. The eye in the sky." Reggie put a finger thoughtfully against his cheek. "Yeah, the sun. The sun will kill them. Yeah, that's like Chri—uh, a vampire, too."

"There's also a sentence about protection."

"What does that say?"

"Open the vein of the dam and protection will flow. Bless this red life and the Sith will die."

"Jesus, what the hell does *that* mean?"

"I don't know. Maybe it has to do with running water. Some legends say that vampires can't cross a flowing body of water."

"Yeah, I read that, but I don't know. There's lots of flowing waters all over the place. I can't see how that could work."

"Hey, I don't write the legends I only translate, besides it's only legend."

"Man, why don't these people write like normal folks. All this cryptic crap gives me a headache. Is that all it says?"

"That's about it. There's some other things that I couldn't translate, but I think that's the gist of it."

Reggie scratched his chin and took the paper on which Kargosi had written the translation. "So how much do I owe you?"

"Well, you've got my curiosity piqued. Tell you what, there's no charge if you give me an explanation as to why you need all this."

"Like I said I'm an eccentric nut, Mr. Kargosi."

"My ass. You're no eccentric. Now what's the real reason?"

Reggie forced a laugh. "That is the reason. What do I look like, a liar?"

"No, you look frightened, Reggie. That's what you look like."

Reggie tried to maintain his smile. "I am. I'm scared to drive back down the mountain."

Kargosi just shook his head. "I might surprise you if you told me the truth. I might even be able to help."

Reggie looked into Kargosi's eyes. "Okay, I guess I can tell you."

After Reggie finished telling Kargosi about the strange things that had happened to him in San Miguel, and to Chris in Miami, Reggie sat back in his chair and studied the fat man's face for a reaction.

Kargosi started to smile. "You know, Reggie, I think you might need help."

"Good. I can use some. What do you have in mind?"

"I have a doctor in mind."

"A doctor?"

"Are you kidding me with this stuff? Come on. I might collect these things as a hobby, but I surely don't believe it."

"You don't believe me?"

"No, I'm sorry. I don't."

Reggie was confused. "Then why did you say all that stuff about helping?"

"I can help. I know a doctor in San Francisco and . . ."

"A doctor?"

"Yes, he's helped a lot of people who take this stuff too seriously. That's why I wanted to see how far you were into this, uh, fantasy."

"I wish it was, Kargosi, believe me."

"I know it is fantasy and I do believe that you think it's true. You don't know how many people come to me with stories."

Reggie just shook his head. "Well, I appreciate your help, but I have to hit the road."

Kargosi got up from his chair and started toward Reggie. "Please think about what I said, Reggie. A doctor would be the best thing for you."

"Maybe I will call somebody." Reggie lied.

"Let me give you the number."

"I know somebody in Miami."

"I want to help you, Reggie," the big man put his hand on Reggie's shoulder.

"I have to get back to my hotel."

"You could stay here?" Kargosi said, then smiled. "I could call my doctor friend and have him meet you here."

"I appreciate the offer but I have to catch a plane later tonight."

258

"Couldn't you catch a later flight?"

This guy was persistent, Reggie thought, but no amount of coercion would get him to stay. He had to get back and catch the next plane to Miami. He had the info that he and Chris needed to combat the Sith.

"Thanks for your help," he said as he made his way to the front door and opened it. He looked out and a shiver of fear slid across his body. The sun had gone down. He looked at his watch. It was only six o'clock and already it was dark. A feeling of dread came over him as he thought about having to drive all the way down the side of the mountain in the darkness. It had been hard enough in the middle of the day. He almost thought about accepting Kargosi's offer to stay the night, but time was of the essence. His flight left at 11:45 and he wanted to catch some zzz's at the hotel before he had to leave. He decided to suck it up and brave the journey down.

"Thanks again."

"If you're not going to stay, at least think about what I told you."

"I will."

Reggie walked slowly to his car. Kargosi watched him for a moment and then turned and went back into his house. He watched from the window as the black man got into his car and cranked the engine.

Reggie turned the car around in the narrow driveway and crept out onto the mountain road.

A set of headlights came on behind Reggie and they started to follow him. The man upstairs at the Kargosi home started to creep down the stairs.

6

Macdow's private jet had landed at Miami International Airport at around nine o'clock. He had managed to escape San Miguel without incident and was now en route to Sisters of the Faith Hospital, the site of his new home. He needed to talk to Dr. Charles about the progress being made at the hospital. His last message said that the staffing was now completed. It was time to focus on the creation of the Mother Host and the fulfillment of the prophecy as written in the book of the Banished Ones. The only thorns in his side were the two detectives and the possibility of another kin of Stephenson being alive. But he knew that the wheels had been set in motion to solve those problems and he was confident that his orders would be carried out.

The limousine arrived at Sisters of the Faith and pulled around to the back entrance. After telling his chauffeur to park the limo and meet him on the sixth floor, Macdow got out and entered the hospital. The lean Scotsman walked briskly down the corridor toward the elevator that would take him to the sixth floor, where Dr. Charles waited for him. He made it to the elevator just as Dr. Sue Blaze turned the corner of the hallway.

Sue wondered who the handsome red-haired man standing in front of the elevator was, but the question floated away as quickly as it had come; an occurrence that had happened earlier when she'd seen Dr. Charles and experienced a flashback vision of the chief of staff in a strange robe, conducting some kind of seminar. It was just a brief spark and then it vanished and she couldn't recall it.

The man with the red hair turned and smiled. He was ruggedly handsome and Sue felt an instant attraction to him. She needed to meet him. As she walked over to introduce herself, the shiny metal doors of the elevator opened and he stepped inside. The doors shut, leaving

Sue feeling strangely empty. It was as if she'd missed out on a wonderful opportunity to meet someone special. She knew that the red-haired man was touched by greatness. She wanted to know him. But in that brief moment of wanting, Sue felt as though she had betrayed her husband in some way and was racked with guilt. *What was happening to her?* She gathered her composure and went to her office.

Before she could even sit down, Don Argyll popped his head inside the open door space. "Enjoy the services this morning?"

"Yes," Sue said before she was even aware that she had spoken.

"Good, good. We enjoyed your attendance."

"I did, too," Sue replied, realizing that she hadn't enjoyed them, but unable to remember why.

"So you'll be joining us tonight then?"

No, she thought. "Yes," she said.

"Good, we'll be looking for you."

Dr. Argyll smiled and left. As Sue sat down in her chair, a feeling of confusion and helplessness began to take hold of her. In the back of her mind, she knew that something very strange had happened last night at the hospital services and yet she didn't feel the slightest inclination to investigate.

Sue sat in her chair and focused on breaking through the mental force clouding her thoughts. Rubbing her temples, eyes closed, she tried to crash through the barrier with the sheer force of will. But as she did, her mind automatically shifted away to something else: a trip she needed to make to the store; Chris's birthday; Reggie telling a funny story; all sorts of unrelated concerns would pop up as she tried to figure out what was happening to her as a result of her employment at Sisters of the Faith.

After a few minutes of this intense concentration, she

stopped and noticed that she was drenched with sweat. It was almost as if someone had poured a bucket of water over her head. She got up and went to the restroom, where she washed her face and towelled off as much of the sweat as she could. She was thankful that she kept a spare blouse in her office closet in case of emergency. She went back into her office and put it on.

When she sat down at her desk again, she had forgotten what had caused her to sweat so profusely. The only thing that was now on her mind was the upcoming service at the chapel. She couldn't wait to go.

7

"Don't move, blubber gut!" Carl Kleegle shouted as he pointed the gun at the startled Kargosi, then completed his journey down the stairs. "Back up and sit your fat ass down on the couch."

Too stunned to speak, Kargosi did as he was told. While he was backing up, his left calf hit the coffee table and he almost went crashing to the floor. Barely maintaining his balance, he corrected himself and sat on the leather sofa. He found his voice.

"Who are you?" He gasped.

"Shut up, blubber gut." The man pointed the gun. It hissed and a hole appeared in the couch, next to Kargosi's arm. The corpulent man clamped a fat palm over his mouth.

"What did you tell the black guy?" Kleegle said as he sat in the chair across from Kargosi.

"He was a client who wanted information."

"On what?"

"I have money in my safe, I'll give it to you . . ."

The gun hissed and a bullet cut a path through a

layer of fat under Kargosi's arm and exited into the couch. The obese giant howled like a baby. He started to cry.

"Look, blubber gut, I want to know what the hell that black dude wanted."

"Information," Kargosi sobbed. "About a legend called the Baobhan Sith."

The man smiled. "He didn't know anything about them?"

"Not much. Please help me, I'm bleeding."

"In a minute. What'd he know?"

"Oh, it hurts."

"You want another, you fat fuck!" Kleegle screamed. "Now tell me what he knew!"

Kargosi wiped his face with the back of his fat hand. "I think he knew that they could transform into birds and maybe that they were like vampires." His mind whirled as the bizarre situation assaulted him. Could the black man have been telling the truth?

"Did he know how to kill them?" Karl asked jerking the gun barrel at Kargosi.

"Only what I translated."

"He didn't know before?"

"No. I don't think so."

"What book did you translate from?"

"That one there on the desk."

The man got up and grabbed the volume. He tossed it on the floor and looked around the room. Seeing the bottle of 151-proof rum on the bar decorated with carvings of gargoyles, Kleegle walked over and grabbed it. He poured the contents of the bottle onto the book, causing Kargosi to shriek louder than when he'd been shot.

"No! That book is worth a fortune. Please; I have money."

"I told you," Kleegle said, as he pointed the pistol at

Kargosi. "I don't need your money." He pulled the trigger and the fat man's head rocked back, a hole neatly centered in his forehead. The hit man pulled his lighter out of his pocket, lit a piece of newspaper that was on the desk and tossed it onto the rum-laden book. The fire lapped at the liquor and then started to consume it rapidly. The book began to crinkle in the heat.

Kleegle unclipped the shortwave radio from his belt and called his partner, Kerry Balpine, who was following Reggie down the mountain.

"Well?" the driver of the car answered in a raspy growl.

"The black dude didn't know shit about the Sith. Try to take him so we can find out what happened to Drucinda."

"If I can't? I kill him."

"Just get him to pull over and then pull a piece on him," Kleegle said. "We need to talk to him. Macdow says we'll get paid double if we bring him in alive."

"That sucks."

Kleegle rolled his eyes. His partner liked killing more than money. "Just do it."

8

Reggie clicked off the radio and drove in silence. He needed every ounce of concentration as he weaved down the narrow mountain road. His palms had already started to sweat profusely, and he had only gone a quarter of a mile. The headlights faded into the vast space in front of him as he looked out over the edge of the cliff. In his mind, he pictured what would happen if he pressed the accelerator down to the floor and took off like a great steel bird over the precipice. He could almost feel his leg willing him to push his foot down. He let it off the pedal and tried to concentrate. His ears were clogged from the altitude and he wanted to reach into his pocket for his pack of gum, but he couldn't seem to get his hands to release the wheel. They were locked in place. His mouth was dry, as his tongue touched the roof of it.

The headlights of another car appeared behind him in the rearview mirror. "Another unlucky bastard," Reggie whispered as he tried to remain calm.

Reggie steered the car around a winding curve in the road and breathed a sigh of relief when he saw a fairly long stretch of straight road. When he got to the end of the stretch, there was another bend.

The car behind him was just coming onto the straightaway and seemed to be picking up speed. It disappeared from Reggie's view as he turned the corner and saw another series of curves and twists. Again there were no guard rails to prevent his falling over if he somehow made a mistake.

"Damn, this sucks."

The headlights from the other car came into view again and in seconds filled Carver's mirrors with their bright light.

"Turn off your brights, you son of a bitch," Reggie cursed, as he steered the car around another bend.

The car behind him appeared quickly.

"Get off my ass!" Reggie shouted trying to remain calm. The road yawned in front of him.

The driver in back of Reggie flashed his brights and honked his horn, as though he wanted Carver to pull over.

"Hey, you dumb fuck, where do you think I can go?" Reggie said angrily. His nerves stretched tautly.

Again the driver flashed his brights and honked.

"I can't go anywhere," the frustrated and terrified

Carver shouted. He would gladly pull over if he could, but there was nowhere.

Suddenly, the headlights of the car sped toward him, filling the rearview mirrors with their brilliance.

"Shit!" Reggie shouted in disbelief as the car behind him slammed into the back of his vehicle. He struggled to control the vehicle as the car slammed into him again. The precipice loomed in front of Carver, who knew he would be flying over it very soon.

9

Kerry Balpine had beeped his horn for the last damned time. If this stupid home boy wasn't going to pull over, then Kerry was going to fulfil his contract with the other option. It was a lot less money but a lot more fun. He picked up the radio and called his partner.

"Karl, I can't grab him," Kerry said. "There's no room for him to pull over and I don't think he would anyway. I think he's onto us." Balpine made up the last bit because he was in the mood for mayhem. He didn't like the idea of just capturing the black man and then letting someone else have the fun of torturing him.

Kleegle sighed. "Look, I just got word that we've got people at the hotel. So just follow him. Macdow needs to talk to him."

Balpine frowned. "What was that? You were breaking up."

"You heard me, you sadistic bastard," Karl growled. He knew he shouldn't have given his partner, Balpine, the task of capturing the black man. The psychopathic son of a bitch liked to kill. Damn! He looked over at the stiffening wall of blubber and wished that his partner's bullet had been the one that killed the fat man. "Kerry,

266

do not hit Carver!"

Balpine's frown changed to a grin. "What? I can't hear you."

"Macdow's not gonna like it if you toast the black man!"

"I can't stand all this static. I'm shutting down the radio and the black dude."

"Balpine, you fuck!" Kleegle would have to make up a lie to cover his partner's actions.

Balpine smiled. "Listen, I'll let you hear the action," he said, then set the phone on the dash so that his partner could hear him kill Carver. He pressed down the gas and surged forward.

10

"What the fuck!" Carver shouted as he felt the impact of the vehicle behind him.

CRUNNNCH. The car hit again and the tires of Reggie's car skittered towards the edge of the mountain road.

Reggie pulled the wheel away and the car barely held the road.

CRUNNNCH.

The car hit again.

"You goddamn bastard!" Reggie hissed as he struggled to keep the car on the road. He could hear the car behind him revving its engine preparing another strike. Reggie pushed down his accelerator and the car lurched forward. The vast maw of open space yawned in front of him like a giant mouth waiting to swallow him and grind him against the molars of the mountain. He drove as fast as he could, trying to avoid another collision. Reggie knew full well that one false move and it would be car-condensing time.

The car behind him suddenly caught up and hit him again. Reggie banged his head on the headrest and saw stars. When his vision cleared, he saw the turn. He spun the wheel to the left, but it was too late. His car skittered and the right back tire hung over the edge of the cliff.

"Shit!" Carver shouted as he looked into the rearview mirror to see where his attacker was. To his amazement, the car was gone!

Then he saw a faint red outline of a chrome bumper. The car's headlights were shattered. It was the reflection of Reggie's one remaining brake light that he saw shining in the bumper.

The car behind him slowed up as Balpine tried to determine which brake light was working on Carver's vehicle. He wanted to be sure to hit the car squarely in the middle so that there would be no chance of escape.

Amazed that the car hadn't slammed him over the edge yet, Reggie floored the accelerator and by a complete stroke of luck found that the car had front-wheel drive. The tires bit into the asphalt and with a squeal the car took off.

Kerry Balpine made out the location of his target's car and floored his vehicle in an effort to send Reggie's car over the edge. But Carver's vehicle roared away just at the point of impact. The black sedan tried to stop, brakes squealing burnt rubber stench, but it was already committed. The front tires went over.

Kerry shouted into the radio now lying on the floor of the car. "Karl, shit, I'm hung up. The goddamn bastard got lucky. Shit. I'm . . ."

The car hung precariously for a moment and then dove over, tumbling down, leaving pieces of its shattered hulk lying every ten feet on its journey down. Balpine, except for his left arm, which was severed and was left hanging from a scrubby root a hundred feet up from the mountain floor, made it all the way to the bottom.

In the rearview mirror, Reggie saw Balpine's taillights go over the edge and knew that his erstwhile assassin was now a traffic statistic. The adrenaline-pumped detective paused to catch his breath. "Jesus, are these dudes all over the place?"

He sat in his car for about fifteen minutes to settle his nerves then carefully drove the rest of the way down the mountain and made it back to his hotel. They were waiting for him when he got there.

11

When Chris had awakened and discovered that Sue had gone to the hospital without him, he was pissed. He had told her explicitly to allow him to escort her to work and yet she had apparently gone without him. And where was Brand? He looked in the ashtrays around the house for cigar butts, as he knew that Brand never worked without puffing on a stogie. He found no trace of the filthy habit. He picked up the phone and dialed the number of the Brand Detective Agency. The phone rang ten times before the answering machine picked up. Chris left Ryan Brand a message to call him, then hung up and looked up Brand's home number. He dialed the seven digits and waited. Brand answered on the fifth ring.

"Brand speaking."

"Why the hell weren't you here today?"

Brand paused. "Who the hell is this?"

"Chris Blaze. I thought my wife told you I wanted you to stay with her inside the house."

"Hold on a minute, Chris. She never called me. My man followed her to work at about three, but she didn't

269

call about bodyguarding."

Chris's mouth popped open in disbelief. "What? She never called?"

"No. You know I would be there if she had, man. Didn't hear word one."

Chris couldn't believe that Sue could've forgotten, especially after his telling her about the Baobhan Sith.

"What's going on, Chris?" Brand asked.

Chris realized that he was still on the phone with Ryan. "Oh, that case of ours I told you about, it's getting a little dirty. I need you to move inside to make sure nobody messes with my wife during the day."

"Who'd want to do that?"

"A man named Colin Macdow. He's involved in a missing-persons case that looks like a kidnapping, with him as the kidnapper. This Macdow plays ultra-hardball and wants us off the case."

"So you think he might take Sue to keep you off the scent?"

"Exactly, so I, uh, need to work the case during the day to try and put an end to it." He paused. "I can't believe she didn't call you."

"She didn't. But I'll be at your house tomorrow morning."

"Good. Thanks, Ryan."

"Save your thanks until after you get my bill."

Chris smiled. "See you."

He hung up. The vampire couldn't understand why Sue hadn't called Brand or why she hadn't waited for him before leaving for work. He looked up the new hospital's phone number, picked up the phone and dialed.

A pleasant voice answered. "Sisters of the Faith. May I help you?"

"Yes, Dr. Susan Blaze, please."

"Please hold."

There was a momentary pause and then the woman

came back on the line. "I'm sorry, sir, she's in surgery. May I take a message?"

"Yes, have her call her husband at the office."

"She knows the number?"

"Yes."

"Very good." the woman hung up as did Blaze. Picking up his car keys, Chris left for his office.

12

Reggie stepped into his hotel room, relieved to be staying on the first floor. No more heights for him, thank you. He'd had enough high places to last a lifetime. Carver kicked off his shoes, took off his shirt and tossed it onto the bed. He went to unbuckle his pants when he heard something move behind him. Quickly, he drew his pistol and whirled. He saw a man smiling at him. Suddenly, another man appeared from behind Carver and clubbed him with a slapjack. Reggie staggered for a moment, almost pulling the trigger before the gun fell out of his hand. He toppled to the ground. The detective tried to struggle to his feet, but the smiling man was on top of him injecting him with a syringe filled with some kind of drug. Soon the world started to drop out of focus and blur. The walls of the hotel room seemed to expand and stretch out into the vast emptiness of space. The room looked like the inside of the Vehicle Assembly Building at Kennedy Space Center. The television set seemed to be miles away. Reggie reached out for his gun that lay in front of him and saw his arm stretch out like Plastic Man's in the comic books Reggie used to read in his youth. It stretched and stretched and yet never seemed to get any closer to the gun. He felt himself being lifted up and carried out of the room.

271

The phone sat on the desk like a dead soldier. Unmoving. Silent. It had been four hours since Chris had arrived at the office. Four hours of waiting for Reggie's call that would help Chris fight the Baobhan Sith. Four hours of staring at the dead soldier.

The vampire looked at his watch and saw that it was past midnight. Reggie's flight left San Francisco at 11:45, so if the black man was going to call it would've already happened. Now he would have to wait until tomorrow night before he could speak to his partner. He tried to think of a reason why Carver wouldn't have called, but could come up with nothing but dismal scenarios. He called the airline to see if Carver had made his flight, but the reservation clerk told him that it was company policy not to give out that information. He would just have to wait and hope that Reggie made it home all right.

Chris called Sue at the hospital again, but was told that she was still in surgery and unavailable. He had tried on and off to reach her, but each time was told that she was busy.

As he hung up after trying to call her for the fifth time that night, he wheeled around in his swivel chair and stared out the bay window of his office and into the black sky. *This is turning out to be quite a shitty night,* he thought, then added, *I just hope it doesn't get any worse.*

14

Sue had not been able to keep her mind on her work all night. She had almost blown a diagnosis in the emergency room because of her preoccupation with the time. The clock, ticking away on the wall, loomed large and ominous as the hands spun around, drawing her nearer to the service that she couldn't wait to attend. For brief interludes, she would remember bits and pieces of her first service, but the recollections would disappear and she would be unable to recall them. They would vanish, leaving behind a vague notion of apprehension that shifted into anticipation of that morning's service.

The second hand of the clock spun around, clicking off another minute. Soon it would be time to attend. The thought of the services would fill Sue with exhilaration one moment and with dread the next—a seesaw battle between her conscious and subconscious mind. It was as if she wasn't in control and yet seemed to be able to function. The feeling was alternately calming and frightening, depending on which side of her mind was in control.

All night in the ER, her co-workers smiled at her and at each other as if they all had some awful secret between them. Sue knew that something had happened to her at the services and yet she couldn't conclusively say what it was. The lack of understanding was frustrating.

After finishing up with a car-accident victim, she went into her office and left the lights off in case anyone came looking for her. In fact, she had seen Dr. Argyll pass by twice in the past fifteen minutes. Each time she had stayed hidden behind her desk as if she was looking for something on the floor that she had dropped.

She glanced up at the clock in her office for the fourth time in the past five minutes. It was five after five. The service would be starting soon. She smiled, got up from the desk, grabbed her purse and started out the door. She could hardly wait to join the congregation.

Once outside the office, a voice in her head told her to leave the hospital and skip the service. Something very wrong happened at the services. She walked quickly down the hallway, avoiding the eyes of the nurses and the aides as she did. She could feel their stares boring holes through her mind, unleashing her traitorous thoughts. A strange feeling started in her brain. A tingling sensation. She picked up her pace as the feeling began to spread across the front of her skull. It felt like the scratchy feet of a thousand ants walking across her forehead. She began to lose her concentration as the feeling shifted into a numbness that started to spread across her mind.

"Got to keep going," she told herself in a weak voice. The numb feeling started to spread down her neck when the voices began to sound in her mind. At first there was only one voice. Low almost inaudible. A voice that she couldn't understand, until another joined in.

And another.

And another.

Soon a chorus of voices was in her head shouting for her to stay. To keep going down the hallway past the lobby . . .

To the elevator . . .

To the second floor . . .

To the chapel!

She tried to fight the roar in her head, but her mind's voice was overcome by the sheer volume and intensity of the other voices that boomed in her head.

She saw the lobby ahead of her, and the exit. They seemed to stretch away for miles and miles, while the distance to the elevators looked as though she could reach out and touch the up-button with one delicate finger.

"The Dark Mother awaits," the voices in her head said.

"Got to go home," Sue said aloud, as if the tangible sound of her voice would drive the people out of her head.

274

She walked into the vast chasm that the lobby had become. An immense wasteland was separating her from the exit door, the parking lot, her car, and what surely was her freedom.

"Go to the chapel!" the chorus in her mind commanded. *"The chapel. The Dark Mother awaits."*

Sue felt her feet twist and her legs follow, as she turned away from the exit and started staggering towards the elevator.

"Go to the chapel, Sue."

"The chapel, Sue."

"Chapel, Sue."

"Sue!"

A single voice above the din. A voice she recognized.

"Sue, where you going?"

A concerned voice. Real.

"Chapel, Sue."

"Sue, hold up."

Chris.

Sue stopped and turned. The voices in her head faded into what Sue perceived to be an undercurrent of anger. She shivered at the intensity of it.

"Chris, what are you doing here?"

"I came to take you home and find out why you didn't call Ryan Brand like I asked you to."

"Oh Chris, I . . ."

Sue was about to tell Chris about the strange occurrences that had been happening to her, when a collective shout as loud as anything she had ever heard slammed into her mind, driving the thoughts from it. She instinctively grabbed her ears, trying to shut out the obscene noise.

"What's wrong?" Chris said, alarmed by Sue's behavior.

"My head," Sue felt herself say, "I have a monster headache."

"Can I get you anything?"

"No, I just took a couple of aspirins. I just need to get home and into bed." She smiled weakly. "I'm sorry about not calling your friend. I lay down for a minute and didn't wake up till late in the afternoon—so instead of calling I just went straight to work."

Sue could still feel the seething anger inside her mind, but it was growing weaker. It felt as though the people inside her head were straining to hear her conversation with Chris, but were unable to understand. She didn't know how she could feel that, but she did.

"Honey, you've got to be careful. I talked to Ryan tonight and he'll be your shadow starting tomorrow."

"Good," she said, as the rage inside her simmered to a low heat. She continued to feel as though the mind-people were unsuccessfully eavesdropping.

Chris's face grew grim. "I'm afraid something might've happened to Reggie. He didn't answer the phone at his hotel."

"Oh no," Sue said putting her hand to her mouth. She could barely perceive a change in her mood, from anger to satisfaction. She suppressed a smile.

"When we get home, I'll give him another call and maybe he'll be there," Chris said.

"I hope so."

Sue turned away from Chris and smiled.

Chris took his wife by the arm and led her out of the hospital. She felt the voices leave her. Suddenly she wanted desperately to tell her husband what was happening to her, but her mind began to cloud the issue. She couldn't put the words together. They slipped from her conscious efforts like greasy avocado slices. She tried to grasp them and wrest them into her mouth to speak the thoughts, but she simply couldn't. It was as though someone or something was sliding them back into the subconscious crevices of her mind where she couldn't reach them.

276

"Sue, what's wrong with us lately. I mean, ever since you started at this new job, we haven't seen each other or done much of anything together. Today you left for work without waiting for me, even after I told you about what we're dealing with. Have I done something?"

"No, I've just been really busy at work and I've been tired."

"Are you sure that's all it is?"

"Yes, I'm sorry if you took it the wrong way. It's just taking me a little time to get used to this new job. I have a lot more responsibility than I did before and it's gonna take a little more adjusting." Sue felt the lies flow out of her as if she was tapped into the psyche of a con artist. Only they didn't feel like fabrications. They felt good; so good that she almost wanted to believe them herself. The real truth, tucked away deep in corners of her mind, was too awful to face.

She touched his cheek.

"You know I would never intentionally hurt you. I love you too much."

Chris smiled. "I know. I just feel like we don't see enough of each other. And then you take a chance by leaving for work alone. You could've been kidnapped."

"I'm sorry. I swear, just give me a little more time to adjust to this new job. It won't be much longer," she said, as she reached over and pulled him close, kissing him fully on the lips.

"So how about a quick walk in . . . no, never mind, let's go home," Chris said, remembering that his wife was tired and had a headache.

"Thanks, honey, and I swear that things are going to get better."

She smiled and the voices in her head appeared again for a brief whispered message. *"Yes. Things are going to get much better."*

15

What seemed to be moments later, Reggie woke up in the seat of a small plane. He could hear the men talking, but their words were distorted and unreasonably loud. They faded in and out.

"Macdow wyull be rappy too rear tha we got him."

"Reah, too bad arout Balpeen."

"He rus a dun bastar."

"The back guya make a good ow forra faarm. Huh, Karl."

The voices ceased and Reggie felt himself floating above his own body. He knew that he was dead, but still felt conscious. It was frightening looking down at himself. He stared at the black man slumped there as if he were a stranger or a character in a movie. A thin trail of drool slid down the side of his chin. Every so often, a twitch convulsed his body. Death throes. He'd seen it before in accident victims. He looked for the telltale signs of urine on the front of his pants, but couldn't see, in the darkness of the plane. Reggie wondered where he would go next on Death's journey.

He never found out, as the next moment, a man was picking him up and dragging him into the blinding sunlight. Carver didn't know it, but seven hours had elapsed since he had been drugged. The men, Daniel Dorek, a pharmacist at Sisters of the Faith, and Karl Kleegle laid the dazed black man onto the stretcher and rolled him upstairs to the sixth floor. When Carver became conscious, he would solve the case of the missing Vargas family.

Chapter Nine

1

"Are you sure McNally knows about the deal?" Chief Len Singer asked his operative, who'd just arrived from San Miguel. The two men sat on a bench in the park so that they wouldn't be seen by Deputy Chief Mark McNally who was at the office. Singer had told McNally that the man was still in San Miguel, so as to throw him off the trail.

"Yes, he knew."

"So tonight we take him?"

"I think it would be the best move. We have enough."

"I think so too." Singer nodded grimly.

"Does anyone know I'm back in Miami?" The man said through a cloud of smoke.

"No, I made sure of that."

"Good, let's keep it that way. So what about the detectives?"

"I had a chat with them last night, but I don't think I did much good." The DTF chief's face clouded with anger. He wished Blaze and Carver could have been more cooperative. They were screwing up his deal.

"Well, we'll have to take them in when the time comes."

"Yeah, I guess you're right." Singer rubbed a tired hand through his hair. "We'll do it tonight then."

"Okay."

"Now will you do me a favor?" Singer said, pointing to the object pinched between the man's finger and thumb.

"What's that?"

"Put that stinking cheroot out."

2

Reggie felt weak. Helpless. He lay strapped down in a bed. He turned his head and looked around the room. The sheer starkness of the white walls pained his eyes. He blinked once, twice. A man lay in another bed two beds down from Reggie. As Carver's eyes adjusted to the pallid surroundings, he saw that this man was Diego Vargas. He was alive, but looked as pale as a ghost—a perfect match with the ivory walls. Reggie tried to sit up, but found that he was bound tightly to the bed. He could see an IV needle piercing his arm. He believed he was in a hospital, but didn't know where or why. The fluorescent lights above him gave the room a surrealistic appearance. A nurse approached his bed. In her ivory uniform, against the white background, she seemed to be a disembodied head, looming in white space. She smiled. Reggie tried to speak but found that he was too weak to utter more than a cracked whisper. He felt as though someone had drained him of all his energy. The nurse checked his pulse and took the glass bottle that led from the IV. Reggie figured that it was some kind of medicine or something.

He was wrong.

In the next moment, he saw what the nurse had in her

hand. It was a bottle of blood. And the horrid realization hit him that the blood was his. Immediately the significance of the words told to him by David of *El Frente* hit him like a bolt of lightning. *"You will go to the place of evil and became one of the vacas."* Yeah, *vacas:* cattle. With grim deduction, he knew that the place of evil was a dairy and he was one of the cattle to be milked of blood. Reggie Carver, cattleman. He grinned weakly at the ironic accuracy of the phrase and then passed out.

3

Sue stood amidst a circle of people. Men and women dressed in robes and gowns of rough wool were gathered around a small boy lying on a slab of cold rock, tears streamed down his cheeks. A man dressed in an ornate ceremonial robe stood over the boy. The robe looked similar to the one that Dr. Charles had worn on the morning of her first chapel service, but the man wasn't Charles. It was the red-haired man she'd seen at the hospital. Sue couldn't understand what the man was saying, as it was in a language that she had never heard before in her life. Yet somehow she understood the meaning of the words. The land around her swirled with mist, blurring the faces of the people who surrounded her. Sue saw one of the women lick her lips and thought how peculiar the woman's tongue looked. The red-haired man in the robe raised his hand above his head and then brought it down quickly. The little boy cried once and then was still. Sue watched the man raise his hand again and saw the blood-drenched stone knife that he held. The man inserted a hollow tube into the bloody gash and then sipped from it. The tube looked strangely like the woman's tongue. The man beckoned others to come up and join him.

Sue felt herself being compelled to move toward the man and the ghastly straw. She started slowly walking in the direction of the stone altar. The others in the congregation were doing the same. As Sue approached the boy on the slab, she felt a smile crease her face.

Suddenly a howling band of men carrying heavy wooden spears and swords swooped down upon the group. The bearded men were dressed in great fur bodices and heavy leather boots. Their long hair flowed behind their heads as they ran. Sue hid behind the stone slab, afraid of the rough-looking attackers. The men and women's faces curled into snarling masks of hate as the invaders descended upon them. One of the girls screamed as a spear pierced her gut. The man who had struck her slashed her head off with a gleaming sword. He grabbed the head by the hair and wiped the bloody stem that was once her neck across his body. He tossed the bloody thing to another man who also spread the gore across his body. This warrior dropped the head, as it began to bubble and deteriorate. The woman's flesh quickly collapsed into a sickening yellowish grey pus as it was absorbed into the earth. Sue felt an unbridled hatred for these intruders and wanted to kill them. They were the Destroyers.

A blonde woman shimmered and crackled as she transformed into a huge black bird and flew off. Another woman tried to fight but was slaughtered by the howling band. Three spears ripped into her guts before she had a chance to strike her first blow. The attackers took jugs and filled them with the blood of the dead, a ghoulish trophy of the slaughter. They hurried away with their grisly collection, before the corpses collapsed into revolting sludge that sank into the ground.

The boy who had been sacrificed rolled over and said to Sue, "Kill them. They are the enemy of the Sith."

Sue grabbed the knife from the stone slab and charged into the men slashing and hacking. Suddenly she found herself thrashing about in her bed. She sat up, the sheets sticking to her back from fear-induced sweat. For a moment, she thought she saw a giant in a sheepskin loincloth and smelly robe as he brandished an axe, but it was only a lingering vision in her mind's eye.

Sue got up from the bed, ran into the bathroom and threw up, as the memory of the carnage in the dream triggered a wave of nausea. It was as if she had witnessed the slaughter of her family. Wiping her brow with a cool towel, she went back into the bedroom and sat on the corner of the bed. Glancing at the clock on the nightstand, she saw that it was two o'clock. She got up and went back into the bathroom. She turned the knobs on the shower and the water began to stream against the tile. Sue stripped and stepped into the torrent of hot water.

When she finished washing away the remnants of the dream, she put on her makeup and dressed. Hungry, she went into the kitchen to get a bite to eat.

Opening the refrigerator door, she saw Chris's blood supply and her mind flashed back to the bloody sacrifice in the dream.

A compulsion to leave the house and head for the hospital overcame Sue, as she closed the refrigerator and started for the door. She grabbed her purse and was about to open the door when she heard a voice call out behind her.

"Dr. Blaze?"

Startled, Sue turned and saw a short stocky man who looked as though he'd left his neck at home. He packed a .357 magnum in a shoulder holster strapped across his broad chest. Ryan Brand was completely bald and possessed a pug nose that split two dark brown eyes set deep in his face. He clenched a fat unlit cigar between his teeth. "Dr. Blaze, I'm Brand. Chris hired me to protect you."

Sue smiled and extended her hand. "Oh right. Brand. You're the detective."

Ryan nodded and adjusted the holster. "Yeah. Goin' on fourteen years, Dr. Blaze."

"Call me Sue."

The two shook hands. Sue's fingers barely made it around Brand's meaty paw.

"You going out?" Ryan said, nodding at her purse.

Sue glanced at the clock and saw that it was only three o'clock. Her shift at work didn't begin until ten. She covered up quickly. "Oh, uh, I was just going to Mickie D's to get some lunch."

"Chris told me to stay with you at all times."

Sue smiled, feigning forgetfulness. "Yes. I, uh, I'm just not used to having someone watch me."

Brand grinned, revealing large, even teeth. "Yeah, takes some getting used to. Lemme get my windbreaker. People get nervous when somebody comes into a fast-food restaurant with one of these." He lifted the gun then slid it back into the leather holster.

Sue smiled, but inwardly her anger bubbled. She wanted to get to the Sisters of the Faith, and this stump of a man prevented her.

"We'll take my car. If you don't mind," Brand said, assured by the weapons he had stashed in his vehicle.

Sue smiled, gesturing with her hand toward the door. "Lead the way."

Brand slipped on his jacket and went out the door. Sue followed.

4

The afternoon dragged like a twenty-pound tail on a chihuahua. The lunch at noon seemed like days ago.

284

Sue had gotten dressed for work at about five o'clock and now she stared at the television set while she waited for another half hour to crawl by. She thought about the hospital for what seemed to be the hundredth time since awakening and going to get lunch. She got up, went to the window and looked out at the darkening sky. Soon Chris would awaken and she would be able to get to work.

"When's Chris get home?" Brand said, distracting Sue. He had spent most of the day reading one of those true-life murder stories and had finally finished it.

"Oh, any minute . . ."

As if on cue, the door opened and Chris stepped into the foyer. He'd slipped out the back passage that he'd had specially built for those circumstances when he couldn't enter or exit the front door, and he'd gone around the house to make it look as though he was just getting back from a day of investigation. He didn't want Brand to know about his inability to protect Sue during the day, as it was something that was not easily explained, or rather, not easily accepted.

"Hey, honey," he said kissing his wife. "Brand, how you doin'?" He shook the stocky detective's hand.

"Good, Chris. How's the case going?"

Chris shook his head. "Not so good. Any trouble today?"

"Not peep one."

Chris turned to his wife. "How are you, hon, that headache gone?"

"Yep," she smiled. "Just needed to get a little sleep."

"Well, I'm taking off," Ryan said as he got up from the couch. "Same time tomorrow?"

"Yeah. Same time."

Brand put a hand on Chris's shoulder. "See you tomorrow night." He smiled at Sue. "I'll see you in the morning."

"Bye, Brand."

Chris opened the door for his friend. "Later."

Brand nodded and went to his car.

Chris shut the door just as the phone rang. He hurried to answer it, thinking that it was Reggie calling to tell him what happened.

"Hello."

"Chris, it's me Mark."

"Damn!" Chris said, expecting to hear a smart-ass comment from his partner. His concern for Carver heightened.

"What's wrong?" McNally said.

"I thought you were my partner, Reggie."

"You haven't heard from him?"

"No, he hasn't called," Chris replied, as he glanced over at his wife, who looked concerned.

"And he was supposed to be there when?"

"Early this morning. I'm gonna call his hotel and see if he checked out." Chris ran his fingers through his hair and sighed.

"I'll hang up so you can call him," Mark said.

"Thanks."

"Call me back."

Chris and Mark hung up their phones at the same time.

Chris opened his phone directory and looked up the number of the hotel where Reggie was staying. He punched in the eleven-digit number. The phone at the other end rang twice and was picked up.

"Day's End."

"Yes, I'd like to speak to a Mr. Reggie Carver, please."

"So would we," the clerk said in a huffy tone of voice, lisping on the *s* in "so."

"What do you mean?"

"Mr. Carver left and didn't pay his bills. He skipped out." The man's lisp made him sound like an angry snake.

286

Chris got a sick feeling in the pit of his stomach. There was no way that Reggie would have skipped out on a hotel bill unless he was in trouble.

The guy went on, "Sir, do you know where we can get ahold of Mr. Carver?"

"Here let me give you a credit-card number and clear up the bill." Chris gave the man the number, waited until he got authorization and then hung up.

He called Mark. The phone rang once then McNally answered it.

"So what's the scoop?" the DTF agent asked.

"He's gone from the hotel and he didn't check out or pay his bill."

"Damn. That sounds bad."

"I'm leaving for the airport to see if Carver was on that flight."

"You still making our meeting at seven?"

"I might be late," Chris said. "We'll still have time to be there before the deal goes down."

"Yeah," McNally said with a trace of disappointment. He had hoped to get there early and start things rolling.

"I'll be there as soon as I can," Chris said with determination as he hung up. He turned to his wife.

"Sue, can you go into work early tonight? I really need to get to work on this thing. Reggie's in trouble."

"Oh my God, what happened?"

"That's the trouble. I have no idea."

"Sure, hon, I can go in early." Sue said, then added gleefully in her mind, *I'd love to go in early.*

"Thanks, babe." Chris said as he got his car keys. "I've got to find out what the hell is going on."

"Let me get my purse."

Sue hurried to the kitchen counter and grabbed her purse. Chris held the door for her as they left the house.

When Reggie woke up again he had no idea of the time. He tried to get up and his bonds reminded him that he was a prisoner. He struggled against the nylon straps for a moment and then gave up, realizing the futility of his efforts. One of the fluorescent lights above him flickered. He could hear the other people in the beds around him breathing and it reminded him of leaking gas lines. The reek of alcohol confirmed his suspicion that he was in a hospital.

Suddenly, a thought popped into his head and he checked to see if he had dreamed it. He looked over and confirmed that what he had seen was true. Diego Vargas was two beds down from him.

"Diego!" Reggie whispered.

The man didn't react.

Reggie noticed that Diego was still white as a sheet and looked very anemic. *Another cow at the farm,* he thought grimly. *What the hell was he going to do?* He called out again, "Diego."

A glimmer of life crept into the eyes of the man in the bed. He turned his head and saw Reggie. A smile tugged at his lips, but didn't form. It took too much energy. Diego's face fell back into a listless stare. He was too drained to speak.

"Diego, are you all right? Where the hell are we?"

The stricken man just looked at Carver and blinked.

"What hospital is this?"

Again the blank stare.

Reggie thought that maybe Vargas could communicate by blinking. Carver remembered it from a movie, but couldn't place its name. The drug they'd given him still clouded his mind. He shook his head to clear the cobwebs and then spoke to his friend. "Diego, can you blink once for yes, two for no?"

Vargas blinked once.

"Do you know where we are?"

Blink. Blink.

"No. Is your wife here?"

Blink.

"Is she alive?"

Blink.

"Are you . . ."

Suddenly, a nurse appeared, injecting a needle into Reggie's arm. He tried to make it difficult for her to find the vein, but the needle found its mark, and he reeled from the effects of the tranquilizer. He tried to remain conscious, but the prospect was doubtful. He stared as Diego began to shrink and in moments was the size of a GI Joe doll. The alcohol smell was rich almost cloying. The white light above him seared into his mind and he closed his eyes. An extreme blackness came over him as if he'd just taken a negative picture of the intense brightness on the inside of his eyelids. He tried to open his eyes, but they felt like they were lined with lead. He struggled to remain conscious, but the fight was rigged and Carver took a dive into the black world of the unconscious.

The nurse hooked up another IV and began to take another pint of his blood.

6

Chris's efforts to locate his partner had been a complete failure. He had gone to the airport and with a little hypnosis of one of the reservation clerks found that Carver had not been on the flight from San Francisco last night. There was no record of him checking himself or his bags. At the terminal, Chris called Rastas's House of the Occult and Deli to get the number of the man that Carver had gone to see, but the shop was closed and there was no listing for Matha

Rastas in the phone book. Realizing that there wasn't much else he could do without blowing off the important deal at Monkey Jungle, Chris had resigned himself to that unfortunate fact and gone to the office to meet with McNally.

Once the vampire detective got there, he and McNally swiftly mapped out a plan, most of which had been worked out beforehand by the deputy chief of the DTF. They went over the plan a couple of times to be sure that they knew it would work, and then they left for the zoo.

As they stood at the gate of the park, McNally pulled out a key and inserted it into the lock. The lock popped and the DTF agent pushed open the gate in the chain link fence.

"How did you manage to get that?" Chris said, as the two of them slipped inside the metal gate.

"I got it from the curator of the zoo this afternoon. I explained to him the situation and he complied."

"Good. So which way?"

"The guy works feeding the monkeys and the food shed is over in that direction." Mark pointed toward a darkened building about fifty yards ahead of them. Chris nodded and they started for the building.

Sensing the presence of something unnatural among them, monkeys chattered as the two men stealthily moved past the cages. A howler monkey screamed, startling Chris, who turned and saw the black ape clinging to the top of its cage. It looked at him with wide, frightened eyes. The warm air was tainted with the odor of monkey crap and urine. Chris's heightened senses picked up the scent of their blood over the odor of the excrement. His stomach growled. The monkeys bounded around their cages screeching. Chris turned to his partner. "Are you sure this is where that guy is going to be?"

"Yeah, he'll be here."

They continued moving toward the building, making sure to stay in the heavy shadows cast by the bright tungsten lights that illuminated the park. McNally led the way.

Chris followed, anxious to get the man and find out where this place of evil was located. He had a feeling that Carver was alive and had been taken there.

"Hey, here he comes," McNally whispered turning to Chris.

The sudden interjection interrupted Blaze's train of thought and focused him back on the situation. He felt a quiver of anticipation.

"Get back behind that cage," McNally said, pushing Blaze back, then standing beside him. The capuchin monkeys in the cage cowered in a corner. As Blaze tried to get a look at the guy who was coming out of the shed, a sudden premonition that something was wrong tapped the vampire detective on the shoulder.

The man walked toward the hidden men apparently unaware of their presence. With his night vision, Chris could see that the man was beefy. Thin cotton undershirt clinging to a thick barrel chest. Muscular thighs bulging from dirty jeans. Black hair. Mean narrow eyes separated by a broad flat nose.

As the man came closer to the bushes, Chris readied himself to grab him. He heard a click beside him and thought McNally was cocking his pistol, but the sound didn't match that action. Curious, he looked down and saw a knife in McNally's hand. Chris thought the switchblade unusual for a drug-enforcement agent, but even more unusual was the fact that the blade of the knife was touching Chris's ribs.

7

The ambience of the hospital felt like a heavy fur

coat. It was warm and reassuring against the cold realities of the outside world. Sue felt it the moment she had arrived that night and continued to feel it as she worked on her staff's progress report. It was a cozy feeling, and she felt no need to worry about what she perceived to be happening to her. There was no point. With each night's stay at the hospital, she felt more and more at ease. She felt like she had found a home.

Don Argyll stepped into Sue's office. He pulled a pipe from his coat pocket and lit it. Blue smoke swirled around his head as he spoke to Sue. "We missed you last night."

Caught off guard, Sue stammered to explain her absence, "I, uh, my husband . . ."

"Yes, we know. We know all about it," the smiling Argyll said, as he puffed on the pipe, firing the embers in the bowl. The rich aroma of cherry rum saturated the air. "You did the right thing by going with him."

Dr. Argyll's words soothed Sue. His tone of voice was melodic. She felt safe.

"You will be coming to the service in the morning." He stated it as an order, not a request. He pointed at her with the end of his pipe. "We want you to be part of the family."

Sue smiled. A warm feeling came over her. To be part of the family sounded wonderful.

"See you in the morning," the doctor said, tamping his pipe out in Sue's empty wastebasket. Argyll tucked the pipe into his coat pocket, smiled and left the office.

Sue sat at her desk and wondered why she felt so good.

8

"Manolo, come here." McNally said to the approaching man, as if he would know that they were

292

there. He jabbed Blaze in the side with the point of the knife. "Get up, Chris."

Blaze did as he was told. Although Chris knew that he could easily get out of his situation, he wanted to see if he could learn anything before the two men attempted to end his life.

"So, it was you, not Singer," he said.

"Don't you feel like a sucker?" McNally replied grinning.

Chris shook his head. "You sure had me fooled."

McNally snapped his fingers. "Piece of cake. That little bit about my girl being a fugitive had a nice ring to it." He paused to admire his cleverness. "Y'know, Chris, you should have done like old Lenny said and dropped that Vargas case. Nothing you could do for them anyway."

McNally put the knife away and motioned to Manolo who trained a pistol on Blaze as Mark continued.

"You don't know how much trouble you caused for me with the Father? One more mistake and I would've been a statistic. Why couldn't you have given me a straight answer when I asked you how you got away from Glynda? That worried the Father for a long time. He didn't know how you could've known about the red life. We had to find out the truth from your buddy, Carver. By the way, thanks for the tip about his visit to the guy in the mountains. Our guys had no trouble finding him."

Chris felt his anger bubble in his gut. "Is Carver all right?"

"He's a little drained," McNally said laughing at the self-directed in-joke. "But he's fine. You'll be joining him shortly."

Chris acted angry, but inside he was smiling. McNally was going to take him to wherever Reggie was. He couldn't have hoped for a better turn of events.

McNally smiled and slipped a gun from his shoulder holster. He pointed it at Blaze. "Since you and your friend don't know squat about the Children, we want to know who's helping you."

Before Chris had a chance to consider the question, a voice cried out, "Hold it right there, McNally!"

Chris cursed silently as he recognized the voice of DTF chief Leonard Singer. What else could go wrong? Just as was he about to find out where his friends had been taken, the Drug Task Force shows up. Now there was little chance of him being taken to where Reggie was held hostage.

"Drop the gun, asshole," another voice called out. Chris didn't recognize the man's voice, but figured it was another agent. They must have known that McNally was corrupt and been following him. That would explain the DTF tail on Mark the other night.

"Do it now!" Singer boomed.

Events snapped in rapid succession.

Manolo grabbed Blaze and pulled him in front of him to use as a shield. McNally pulled his pistol and spun around the corner of the monkey cage. He pointed the silencer and fired several rounds in the direction of the chief's voice. The shots were quiet, just a hiss; the agents didn't even know that he had fired them, since all had missed their intended targets.

Seeing that someone could get killed, Blaze drove his elbow deep into Manolo's guts and then grabbed him and hurled him ten feet against the shed. Manolo crumpled and lay still.

McNally whirled and pointed his pistol at the quick-moving detective. "Dumb fuck," he said as he squeezed the trigger.

"Hit it," Singer shouted seeing Blaze make his move. Chris took the bullet squarely in the throat as he lunged for McNally with both hands hammering the gunman's chest. Mark flew back, his face twisted with

294

rage. He recovered his balance, aimed his gun and tried to fire again. Suddenly he pitched forward. Chris prepared to defend himself again, but the DTF agent just fell to the ground. When Blaze saw the pulpy condition of McNally's skull, he knew that their fight was over. Instinctively, he stepped back and prepared for a new opponent.

The DTF agents approached en masse. A whirligig of guns, shouts, thudding feet and curses.

"Move it."

"Freeze. Freeze. Freeze."

"DTF. Bastards, don't move."

Prepared to fight but seeing no opponent, Chris heard screaming in the direction of the cage of howler monkeys. Only this was no monkey. It was Manolo, screaming terribly as something grabbed him and pulled him into the darkness.

"What the hell is going on?" Singer said, as he slowed up and heard Manolo's screams silenced by several horrendous thumps.

"Look out," Chris shouted as he saw something burst from the shadows and attack one of Singer's men. The man, special agent Dale Cross, was killed before he had a chance to fire his riot gun. A flashing hoof caved in his face driving bits of bone into his brain. Two other men, Fortismo and Cahill, saw the woman kill their partner and they opened fire with their 9mm pistols. The bullets found their mark as the girl spun from their force. But the Sith, Glynda, did not fall.

Suddenly, there was a great whinnying scream from behind the two agents. Cahill was kicked in the back of the head with such force that his face touched his chest, snapping his neck killing him instantly. Mary landed on cloven feet and hissed at Fortismo.

"What the hell . . ." Singer said, as he tried to comprehend the situation, then realized that there were two of these creatures.

The second Sith, Mary, screamed as Fortismo cranked off the rest of his clip into her breast. The bullets found their mark, burying into her flesh with dull splats. The DTF agent started to reload, when Mary's sister, Glynda, fully recovered from the slugs in her body, charged.

Chris saw the Sith hurtling toward the hapless DTF man. He warded off the attack on the agent by using his exceptional speed. He grabbed the woman by one of her powerful legs and flipped the Baobhan Sith to the ground. Glynda's face lit up in the halogen lights and Chris saw that her features were twisted with an expression of total surprise. Blaze leapt for her, but with preternatural agility, she sprang to her cloven feet and fled into the night.

Seeing her sister leave, Mary followed, disappearing into the shadows of the night.

One of Singer's men followed the two creatures' trail, only to discover that they had vanished into the night. Agent Richard Mixon walked back to the scene of the disastrous encounter, while Singer tried to restore order.

"All right, everybody stay where you are," Singer said, trying to keep the situation cool. Two of his men were dead. "Jesus Christ. Fortismo, go call Miami PD for backup. Hurry! Shit."

"You okay, Singer?" Chris asked the DTF chief, who looked like an albino who'd seen a ghost. A sheen of sweat covered his pallid face.

"Shit, man, what the hell were those fuckin' things? I know my guys hit them." He stared at the dead men and wiped his face with the sleeve of his shirt. His stomach churned as he tried to contain the hot dog he'd eaten for dinner. He burped mustard, digested meat and relish. "What the hell were they?"

"I don't know if you'd believe me if I told you," Chris replied.

"Christ, I don't know if I wanna know. Damn. Lucky for Fortismo you stopped that one before it got to him. Thanks."

Chris nodded, acknowledging the thank-you.

"You know what those fuckin' things are?"

Chris nodded. "They're called Baobhan Sith and Macdow controls them."

DTF Agent Mixon approached the vampire, and the incredulous Leonard Singer was catching the tail end of the conversation.

"Bob and what?" the stunned DTF chief said. His stomach felt like it was about ready to expel the churning dog. Acid bubbled up and stung the back of his throat.

"Baobhan Sith, they're uh, supernatural creatures. That's why bullets didn't hurt them."

Mix raised an eyebrow at the revelation.

"Whoa there, Blaze. Supernatural creatures. Shit. Bulletproof vests maybe," Singer said, not prepared to believe the detective, despite what he had just seen. There had to be another explanation.

"I told you . . ."

Singer interrupted. "Hold on. You're telling me that Colin Macdow controls some kind of monsters."

"That's exactly what I'm saying," Chris said, looking into the chief's eyes to reinforce the deadly earnest tone in his voice.

Agent Fortismo came out of the shadows. "The backup's on the way, Chief, I . . ."

Just then, the two creatures came charging out of the darkness again. With a deadly scream, Mary struck Singer with a tremendous kick to the head. The chief of the DTF fell to the ground, a dead man. His ear lay a few feet away. A chunk of hot dog sat on his distended tongue like an obedient pup.

Glynda struck Mix a glancing blow, knocking him unconscious. She would have stomped him to death except Chris Blaze slammed into her, sending her flying through the bars of the squirrel monkeys' cage. The little beasts chittered and fled the confines of the cage.

Fortismo pulled his pistol, but was too slow. Mary kicked him in the crotch, driving his testicles against the pubic bone, causing them to burst like water balloons. Fortismo blacked out from the sudden intense agony. The Baobhan Sith trampled him when he fell to the ground. The sounds of his shattering bones filled the air.

Finished with her dance of death, Mary joined her sister as Glynda wrenched free from the tangle of bars. The two women stood a few feet apart, eyes glaring at Chris with feral intensity. Blaze felt his own bloodlust rise up inside him and his face changed subtly into a mask of rage.

"C'mon, you bitches," he hissed through clenched fangs, his face twisting and popping as he began to change even more. His nose was a mere bump bordered by two holes. His eyes solid red, punched in the center by pitch black pupils. His blood red lips stretched over a mouthful of sharp teeth. He leapt at the closest creature, Mary, grabbing her by the throat and lifting her into the air. She kicked with a hoofed foot and caught him in the chest, driving him back. Chris howled in an inhuman bellow and charged her, slamming her back into the food shed, which crumpled under their force.

The monkeys in the zoo howled and rattled their cages at the violence. They wanted to escape. The animals knew that something profane was in their midst.

Recovering his senses, Mix opened his eyes and saw the frightening change in Blaze's appearance as the vampire battled the sisters. He staggered to his feet, fumbling with the heavy gold chain around his neck.

Glynda jumped impossibly high into the air and drove her feet down at Chris.

"Look out!" Mix shouted.

Chris dodged the blow and the Sith sank into the soft earth. Chris caught her in the face with a spinning punch. Her cheek exploded as it tore against her teeth.

Seeing Mixon, Mary leapt over Blaze and grabbed the stunned DTF agent. The speed of her attack caught him by surprise, but he was ready. Mix grabbed the charm around his neck and thrust it into her face. The Sith screamed and dropped Mixon to the ground.

"You!" Mary shouted as she recoiled in pain for a moment. She tried to attack again, but the power of the icon prevented her. She turned and shouted to her sister. "Glynda!"

The other Baobhan Sith looked away from Blaze and her eyes met those of her counterpart. They exchanged a fearful look and then the two Baobhan Sith took off into the darkness.

"Are you all right?" Chris said, running over to Mix, his countenance back to normal.

"Yeah, fine," he said, rising shakily to his feet. "What about you?"

"I'm cool."

"Your face doesn't hurt?" Mixon asked.

"My face?"

"Yeah, the way it changed I thought that it must hurt a little."

"Change my face? You must have been knocked silly from that kick."

"I don't think so."

Chris shrugged. "Who are you anyway?"

"I'm called Richard Mixon."

"Reggie's bartender buddy from San Miguel?"

Mix nodded. "Also an undercover DTF agent, but that's all over now."

"What do you mean?"

"You tell me how you can change your appearance."

"I can't change. You must've imagined . . ."

Mix interrupted. "Let's cut the shit, Chris. If we're going to fight the Baobhan Sith, let's be frank."

"What do you know about the Baobhan Sith?"

Mixon's face darkened. "I know that I must wipe them off the face of the earth."

"Why you?"

"Because," he paused, tucking his amulet back into his shirt, "I am Malcolm Stephenson, the Destroyer."

9

After scrubbing, Sue hurried into the emergency room. When she arrived, she saw the Cuban boy lying on the emergency-room table. He was pale and lifeless—his shirt stained with blood from a savage gash on his forehead. An auto accident had claimed the lives of his parents and he had lost a tremendous amount of blood from the wound to his head.

"Two units of whole blood and start him on IV," Sue commanded, hoping to save the boy. She began to check him for broken bones.

Dr. Don Argyll came into the room, as did Dr. Gary Charles. Charles went over to the table and felt the boy's pulse.

"What happened here?" Charles asked, in that deep resonant voice that exuded confidence.

"Traffic accident," Sue answered, as she continued checking the boy for broken limbs.

"I see. And the driver of the vehicle?"

"Both of the boy's parents were killed," Missy Davis, the paramedic who had rescued the boy, volunteered in a cheery voice. "No one knows he's here. We beat the other guys by twenty minutes."

A trace of a smile pressed across Dr. Charles's lips.

Sue saw that Argyll was smiling as well. She even felt a smile begin to crease her cheeks.

"Make sure you save him, Sue. We wouldn't want to lose such a fine lad," Charles said as he and Argyll left the emergency room.

"I'll do my best," Sue replied as she began to check for internal injuries.

Don Argyll stuck his head back through the double doors. "If the boy makes it, see that Myra knows about it. She'll have to prepare a special room for the guest of honor of this morning's services."

Sue smiled and went back to trying to save the boy's life so that they could take it from him later.

10

"Stephenson, the Destroyer?" Chris said. He had heard the name Stephenson mentioned by McNally several times, including tonight. "You're the one McNally was asking me about. I guess he and Macdow thought we were working together on the case."

"In a way we were." Mix said.

"So what's your story?"

"My real name is Malcolm Richard Stephenson. My mother remarried a man named Albert Mixon and I took his last name and my middle name so that Macdow wouldn't know about my heritage. The Scotsman thinks the last of the Stephenson clan is dead, and I want him to keep believing that. That's why I didn't tell your partner who I was—he might've been captured and could've told Macdow about me."

"You're the one that helped Reggie in San Miguel?"

"Yes, I kept an eye on him, hoping that the Baobhan Sith would attack."

"You used Reggie as bait?" Chris replied, not liking that notion.

"I couldn't have stopped him from investigating. I tried, but he was stubborn. So I kept an eye on him. That's why I went to Vergaza with him. And I'm glad I did, because one of them tried attacking us when we were on the road back from the village."

"Reg told me."

Stephenson continued. "I thought he might stop his investigation after that, but your partner was determined to check into Macdow, so I kept watch, and sure as hell one of the bitches attacked him when he was spying on the Scotsman."

"And you killed her?"

"Yes. That is my sworn duty," Malcolm said touching the amulet around his throat.

"I guess the obvious question is, why are the Stephensons sworn to destroy the Sith?"

Malcolm sighed. "You ready for a long story?"

"One of those kind that'll explain everything so we can live happily ever after?"

They could hear sirens in the distance.

Stephenson smiled. "Yeah. But we have to leave here before the police arrive."

"You mean you're just going to leave all this unexplained?" Chris said, sweeping his hand to indicate the carnage around them.

"No one from the DTF knows I'm here in Miami. Singer and I kept it a secret, so I can't be tied in. We can't afford to get caught up in this mess. We have to stop the Baobhan Sith. Besides, what could we say? You changed into a monster and I ran the supernatural creatures off with an amulet."

Chris touched his chin with an index finger. Stephenson was right. "Let's go. Oh shit, I didn't drive. I came with McNally."

Stephenson glanced over at the dead man. "Well, a dead man doesn't make the best driver. We'll take my car."

302

The two men hurried away from the slaughter, leaving the Miami Police Department to be sickened, shocked and confused when they arrived at the scene. The massacre would make national news the next morning, bringing in the FBI, but no one would ever solve the case.

Chris and Malcolm stopped in a dark bar called the Hideaway and sat in a corner booth as far away from the two customers sitting at the bar as they could get. Mix got up and ordered two beers at the bar so that they wouldn't be bothered. He grabbed the frosted mugs by their handles and carried the frothy brew back to the table. He sat, took a long draught, and began to tell his story.

"Many centuries ago, the Stephensons were the most powerful clan in all of Caledonia, which is now called Scotland. They controlled almost everything and were generally looked upon with favor by their workers. Our neighbors were the clan of Dow and they wanted our land. Several times we fought, but the Stephensons always won. Then James Dow, Dow the Black, killed the Priests of the Harvest and stole the Knowledge of the Banished Ones."

"Hold on. Priests of the Harvest?"

"Yes, the priests that prayed to the god of the Earth and Sky to make our crops grow. They were a religious sect not unlike the Druids."

"And this knowledge of the Banished Ones was like their Bible."

"No. The opposite. It contained spells and conjurations to summon the Banished Ones—monsters, for lack of a better word, held prisoner by the Earth Mother and the Father of the Sky and released by them only when their worshippers didn't please them. There was Truldeen, the god of pestilence. Killan, the god of draught. These Banished Ones were once worshipped by many followers. The Greeks knew them as the Gods

303

of Olympus as did the Romans. But they are all the same."

"So the Earth Mother and the Father of the Sky are who?"

"In Rome, they were a combination of their gods, but the Christians combined them into one Almighty God, and the Banished Ones were represented by Satan."

"So which Banished One created the Baobhan Sith and, while you're at it, how?"

"Dow sought the help of the Dark Mother of all the Banished Ones to help him conquer our clan. She was to possess the body of a human so that he could mate with her."

"Like Hera or Zeus were said to do in mythology?"

"Yes." Stephenson nodded. "Exactly."

Chris scratched his head.

Malcolm continued. "The Baobhan Sith are the children of Dow the Black and Maureen Andrews, the woman that allowed the Dark Mother into her body. For fifteen years, she gave birth to the Children, as the Baobhan Sith are known to their followers. They were born three at a time until she died, her body used up. There were forty-five of the Children born."

Malcolm took a sip of beer. He noticed Chris hadn't touched his drink, and Malcolm continued with the story.

"To repay the Dark Mother, Dow swore always to protect the children of their unholy union and to create a church and supply it with worshippers and humans to be sacrificed in her honor."

Unfortunately, the reference to the church didn't ring a bell with Chris.

Malcolm proceeded. "With this evil brood, Dow and his followers attacked my ancestors, almost wiping them out. They came at night, killing or capturing most of my people. The few Stephensons that survived fled into the lowlands vowing to destroy Dow and his monstrous family. Dow had won the land and power and reigned for ten years before the Stephensons and the now-enslaved clans sought vengeance. One of our number, Charles Stephenson, infiltrated the Macdow camp and read the Book of the Banished Ones, writing down the knowledge of the ways of destruction. Charles was discovered, but made it out of their camp with two swords buried in his back. He delivered the knowledge and we were ready to take back our land and end the evil. At the battle of Glenscarey, we succeeded in destroying most of the Baobhan Sith, but our own numbers were severely depleted. Only Angus Stephenson lived to carry on our name."

"So how did the others manage to get away?" Chris asked.

"Dow the Black was lucky. He and the remaining Sith, ten in number, were out on a hunting party when we attacked. They saw the battle and fled."

"So how did they know there were others?"

"Many years later, Angus Stephenson heard rumors of missing children and strange new churches with fanatic followers. Dow's name was mentioned, and Angus knew. He left Scotland and found out that Dow the Black and his brood had been travelling all over Europe spreading death wherever they went. They would enter a city, set up a church, and start to possess the minds of its populace, creating worshippers for the Dark Mother. Angus Stephenson hunted them, killing three of the creatures before my ancestor met his death at the hands of one called Mary, but not before passing on the secrets of killing the Sith to his two sons, John and Andrew."

Chris shook his head, started to say something, but closed his mouth and let Malcolm continue.

"A year later, Dow the Black died, but he, too, passed his legacy to his descendants, Thomas and

Dred. The sons of Dow, the Macdows—*Mac* means "son" in Scots—kept their father's vow to the Dark Mother and protected the Children. Like their father, they travelled in Europe and formed churches where they could. John and Andrew Stephenson remained in Scotland until both had heirs to pursue the Sith, in the event that they couldn't destroy all of them. After both brothers had male children, they went in pursuit of the Sith. I'll save you the rest of the family tree and bring you up to date on my part in this. My ancestors killed all but three."

"So your father passed on the burden to you?"

"No. Grandmother Stephenson didn't believe in the legacy and thought her husband, my grandfather, Tremaine, had lost his mind. Grandmother wanted to keep their son, my father, Stuart, away from his "insane" father so she took him to America while Grandfather was in Europe chasing the Sith. My father was raised in New York, went to college, and married my mother, Helen. True to the American way, my father made a fortune in the steel business and had time to father a child, me." Stephenson pointed to himself then continued his story.

"When my grandfather finally found Dad, he sent him letter after letter explaining to him the story of the clans of Dow and Stephenson, trying to convince him to do his sacred duty and destroy the Sith, but my dad would have none of it. Civilization had freed him from the old ways. He joined his mother in thinking that his father had gone crazy. Dad would not answer his letters. Grandfather died on a ship sailing to America—he was trying to convince Father to fulfil his obligation."

"So how did you get involved?"

"My father let his money go to his head. He divorced my mom and went away with his advertising manager, Libby. Dad just totally lost it. He didn't phone or call.

Left everything he had at home. He took nothing that tied him to our family. Not a clue as to where he'd gone. Mom and I moved from New York into the country. Two years after the divorce, when I was out of college, I went looking for my dad. I finally found out where he'd gone, but it didn't do me any good."

"Why's that?"

"My father had been murdered a year before I found out where he was. He was drained of blood, as was Libby." Stephenson shuddered at the memory. "The police had no clue as to who had done it."

"I'm sorry."

Stephenson gazed into the distance for a moment, then gathered himself.

"After the funeral I was going through my dad's things when I found the letters and realized what had happened. In that instant, I knew what my destiny was."

"And you took up the sword."

"Yes. I changed my name to Richard Mixon and tried to find the descendant of Dow the Black. I finally focused on the unlikely location of Central America. Colin Macdow was that man. I joined the DTF, convincing Chief Singer that I would be a valuable asset because I spoke excellent Spanish and was willing to infiltrate Macdow's camp. I got a job as a bartender in his hotel and started gathering what information I could. Two weeks later, Reggie showed up and you know the story from there."

"So what do we do now?" Chris said.

"For now I want to know about you, Chris. I know the Sith and I have never known a normal man to best them without the use of charms—and you are not a normal man. So what are you?"

Chris saw no need to conceal his affliction from Stephenson, who was quite familiar with the supernatural. He took a breath and started to tell his story.

Sue's shift ended and she felt herself being drawn toward the second floor chapel as if there was a rope tied to her waist. She walked toward the elevator that led to the second floor.

There was a crowd in front of the elevator waiting to take it to the second floor. When it arrived, the elevator popped open and the crowd squeezed in. Sue felt like a noodle in a can of Reggie's favorite food, Beefaroni, but she couldn't stop herself from entering. A hand, it didn't matter whose, for they were all one, pushed the button for the second floor. Up they went. The elevator opened and the crowd walked toward the chapel like cattle to the slaughter.

As they entered, Sue saw Argyll, hated him, and then sat next to him. He smiled. She smiled.

Inside the waiting room adjacent to the chapel, Macdow questioned Dr. Charles about the latest converts. He wanted to know their names so that he could address them when he gave the service that night. It always thrilled new members of the assembly to have the Father speak to them directly. It gave them a feeling that they belonged.

Charles held up three fingers dropping one each time he called out a name. "There's Ralph Halperin. Dr. Kelly BaBune. Dr. Sue Blaze."

Macdow grabbed the doctor by the arm. "Blaze? Did ye say Blaze?"

"Yes." Charles winced.

Macdow squeezed tighter. "Are ye sure tha's her name?"

"Yes, she started this week." He pried the Scotsman's fingers from his arm. Four white half moons indented his forearm from Macdow's fingernails. "Why?"

"I want ye to have someone check her file to see if she is married and the name of her husband."

"Why . . . ?"

"Dinna ask me questions. Do it!" Macdow glared at Charles with his green tiger eyes.

"But I know his name. It's Chris. He took her last night before she had a chance to complete the second night of the union of the congregation. We could hear snatches of their conversation."

"Chris Blaze?" Macdow roared. "Tha's the man that has been a thorn in my side since Vargas was taken!"

Charles tried to stammer a response, but was cut off by Macdow.

"Damn it, man. How could ye not know?"

"She never mentioned her husband to me or what he did."

"Did she not think aboat him? Could ye not see into her mind during the services?"

Charles sputtered an answer. "Sh-she had only attended once. She's not with us all the way yet."

"Damn it." Macdow growled. Had he known of this coincidence he could have stopped Blaze long ago.

"Shall we take her to the sixth floor?" Charles said, trying to please Macdow to make up for his failure.

"Nah now. She'll be one with the Sith soon enough. It does'na matter anyway, I have the Children bringing Blaze in tonight. McNally set it up. They should be here any moment. I told them we would be making an offering to them and the Dark Mother tonight."

"Good," Charles said, glad that he had not been reprimanded more harshly. He had been subjected to one session with the Baobhan Sith and didn't relish a second.

Still angry, Macdow flung his hand toward the door leading to the chapel. "Let's begin the service."

Charles motioned for Myra Lee to light the candles mounted on the three candelabras. She acknowledged him and started to complete the task.

The service began. The three bearers of the light

came out. Dr. Charles in his robe walked behind them. Macdow waited in the wings until announced by the chief of staff. He liked to create an aura of anticipation.

Dr. Charles began the services by intoning the litany of nativity which Sue found herself repeating as if she had been attending the services all her life.

Once that ritual was completed, Charles made an announcement.

"Fellow members of the congregation, I have wonderful news."

The group murmured with expectation.

Charles smiled and glanced over at Macdow who stared at him from the wings of the waiting room.

"The Father is here tonight and in the name of the Dark Mother, we will appease the Children." He motioned to the door on the other side of the altar and a couple of nurses came in with the young boy from the operating table. The boy was dressed in a robe of soft cotton. He looked around the room with a dull stare. Obviously he was confused. His wide brown eyes showed fear and bewilderment in equal amounts.

"And now I give you . . . ," Dr. Charles gestured grandly toward the door where Macdow would make his entrance, ". . . the Father."

Sue watched as the man from the elevator entered and stepped up onto the altar. He was dressed in a simple black cloth robe. His red hair shimmered in the light of the three candles. His pale blue eyes burned with the flame. The striking figure of Colin Macdow inspired awe and fear among the members of the congregation. He spoke, "Followers of the Baobhan Sith, I greet you with happiness in my heart." He clasped his hand over his chest. "We are so close to completin' our new home and with tha' completion we can begin our search for the Mother Host as told in the Prophecy of the Second Genesis."

Sue joined the applauding crowd.

Macdow stilled them with a wave of his hand. "I want to personally welcome the three newest members o' the congregation. If ye'd stand when I call your name. Ralph Halperin."

Halperin, a nurse, stood. His eyes caressed Macdow with worship.

The Scotsman nodded and motioned to the man to sit, which he did. He called out the second name. "Dr. Kelly BaBune."

The doctor stood and bowed his head to the Father. Macdow signalled him to return to his seat.

"And of course, Dr. Susan Blaze."

Sue rose up from the wooden seat and gazed at the stunning figure of Colin Macdow. Macdow met her adoring stare and smiled. He gallantly gestured to her to sit.

Dramatically, he raised his hands over his head. "Oh Clan o' Dow. Followers of the Baobhan Sith. Hunters of Stephenson. The Hunted of Stephenson. We will gi' our children this child as an offering to the Dark Mother." He pointed to the boy who had been laid on a table in front of the pulpit.

"An offering of our love for her love."

Suddenly, Sue realized that the boy was going to be sacrificed. In her mind, she knew that this realization should terrify and sicken her and yet part of her wanted to see it with morbid intensity bordering on lust.

No! her mind screamed. The vestiges of her real self forced themselves to be heard. *This is wrong. Wrong. I was sworn to help save lives, not take them.*

Kill.

I am a doctor.

Kill. Blood.

I want to save the boy.

Kill. Blood. Drink.

I want to save . . .

I want to . . .

311

I want to kill.

Kill.

Kill.

The crowd began the strange chant of the last night and she felt herself slipping under its influence. Each moment she heard the droning calls of "Baobhan Sith," she wanted more and more to see the sacrifice. And the more blood the better.

Macdow put his hands out to the crowd. "But we must wait." Macdow enjoyed increasing their ardor to a fevered pitch and then keeping them waiting until their zeal was insatiable. Such emotional brinkmanship helped further to indoctrinate them into the collective mind.

"The children are not here. They are on a mission to make the birthplace of the new generation safe from discovery. We must wait to give them our love."

Macdow took out a long curved pipe that looked like an ornate eel or a tongue and held it above the boy's chest. The twelve-year-old boy squirmed as four nurses held down his arms and legs as if they were administering a shot.

"The fountain of the red life must wait until they arrive before providing its bounty. Then we will drink to honor the joining. Drink to the search for the Mother Host."

The congregation stared at the stone tongue as if they could see the blood pool in the bowl shaped top. They were like a huge dog waiting for his supper. You could feel the hunger and anticipation. Macdow let them suffer.

Just then, Mary and Glynda appeared, out of the congregation's range of vision. Macdow saw them and realized something was wrong. He turned and whispered to Dr. Charles, "I must go."

Macdow smiled and put his hands up to still the murmuring crowd that had immediately sensed something was wrong. "I have to leave. Something's happened. We must wait for the offering until tomorrow's services. Dr. Charles, will you lead them in prayer?"

Charles nodded as Macdow brushed past him and made his way to the room that housed the Baobhan Sith.

12

"So that's why I haven't touched a drop of that beer," Chris said explaining the curse of the hunger to the pensive Malcolm Stephenson. "I only drink blood."

After he finished listening to Chris's story, Malcolm sat on the park bench and started to shake his head and smile.

"What the hell is so funny?" Chris wanted to know what could be so humorous in their dire circumstances.

"I was wondering why you were so quick to believe me about the Baobhan Sith. I've only told two other people in my whole life and they suggested I take up residence in the loony bin." He stopped laughing and his face grew grim. "They are also both very dead."

"Which is something I will be, if I don't leave now. I have to pick up my wife before the sun comes up." Chris got up and went outside. Stephenson followed.

"So that old myth is true then, just like the Sith," Malcolm said when he caught up to Chris.

"Yeah, afraid so."

Malcolm shook his head in awe of the supernatural and in pity for Chris. Then the intense face of the Baobhan Sith, Glynda, appeared briefly in his mind and he changed the subject to the necessity of a planning meeting. "Do you know where the port is?"

"Sure," Chris nodded. "I live about fifteen minutes from it."

"Great. I'm staying in a boat there. Meet me tomorrow night, slip 63, and I'll tell you everything you need to know about the Baobhan Sith. With your help, I know we'll get rid of them for all time."

"Okay, what time?"

"Let's say, eleven o'clock in the evening. I have some things to check up on during the day tomorrow. I have a lead on where Macdow has his headquarters. The place that has that information opens at ten. After I check it out, I want to be able to get plenty of rest. Now that Macdow knows I'm alive, he'll be on guard. I just hope he doesn't take off."

"I doubt he will," Chris said, unsure but optimistic. "Well, I've got to go."

"Eleven tomorrow night. Wait. You don't have a car."

"I don't have time to drive to my office and get it. I have to take a short cut," Chris pointed to the sky.

Stephenson didn't understand the reference until he saw Chris start to change. Malcolm watched the transformation with awe as Blaze shrank into a large bat about the size of a fruit bat. Malcolm had tangled with the Sith and knew that they had similar powers of metamorphosis, but he had never seen them transform. It was a spectacular and frightening sight. He watched the Blaze-bat disappear into the inky night and he smiled as he realized that he had just enlisted a strong ally to his cause. Perhaps they would end this evil for all time. He could only hope.

13

Colin Macdow went up to the sixth floor. He walked down the hall to the doors marked "private" and entered. Stepping into darkness, he lit a candle and walked toward the corner of the room where Mary and Glynda skulked in the shadows. He knew that something was wrong. They didn't dance as they usually did after a kill, but sat sullenly in the corner of the room. Macdow could see that Glynda's face had been damaged and was rapidly mending. Mary looked angry. He approached them.

"Wha' happened? You dinna get Blaze?"

Mary sat up. "We did as ye said and waited to see if Stephenson showed up to help Blaze. While we were lookin' we heard shoats and ran back to where McNally had Blaze."

Glynda interrupted her sister, she spoke with a slight slur as her cheek mended, "Singer and some o' his men had followed that fool McNally. They seemed to ha' known aboat him. Then the bastard, McNally, started firing a' them even though he and Manolo dinna have a chance to get away. We killed them so they could'na talk if they got captured and then we killed most of the others."

"And what aboat Blaze?"

"Nah the one called Blaze. He is of the Dark Side," Mary said, her eyes green fire.

"Of the Mother?" Colin exclaimed. "Blaze a Sith?"

"No, he was nah o' the children. But he ha' the hunger.

"Are ye sure?"

"Aye, sure," Glynda answered for both of them.

Colin put his finger to his chin in a contemplative gesture and sat back in the big wooden chair. "How do ye know?"

"He changed his face and he fought like Truldeen himself. But there's more. The other man. The drug agent that we dinna kill. He was kin to Stephenson the Destroyer."

"Stephenson!" Macdow said, with more confirmation in his voice than surprise. "I knew he was alive. He *is* the one tha's been helping the two detectives."

"Aye, he had the talisman of the Earth Mother."

"Stephenson!" Macdow repeated slamming a fist into his palm. "I thought we ha' killed the last of them."

"It was him. I swear it."

"I dinna doubt ye. It would explain everything."

"He killed Drucinda," Mary said confident that she was right. Only a Stephenson would know the abnormal location of the heart of the Baobhan Sith and to drive an oaken stake through that heart.

"Aye," Colin agreed. "And for that I will kill him myself." He clenched his fist.

Mary and Glynda smiled.

Macdow shook a finger at the two women. "And you're certain that this Blaze is one with the Dark Side?"

Both of the Baobhan Sith nodded, afraid of Macdow's wrath at their failure to capture or kill Chris.

But their master fooled them, as Colin's frown corrupted into an evil smile which bubbled into laughter, "Yes. Yes. The prophecy! It's finally happened. It could'na be more perfect. And she's right here."

"Who, Father?" Glynda asked, pleased that she had not been reprimanded for their failure.

"The perfect host for the Dark Mother," Macdow smiled evilly. "Dr. Susan Blaze."

14

Sue was amazed to discover that she was standing outside in the hospital parking lot. She didn't remember leaving the hospital or the services. Her mind was dull. She had a vague sense that she had missed out on something very rewarding, but couldn't remember what it was.

Dr. Argyll appeared beside her. "Wonderful service tonight, wasn't it?"

"Oh, yes," Sue said, although she could barely remember.

"It is a shame that the offering wasn't given. It's what really draws the congregation together. Don't you feel that way?"

"Yes," Sue said.

"I'm so glad you're becoming one of us."

"Me, too."

"Well, I will see you tomorrow."

"Yes."

Argyll left, and Sue started to walk to her car, although she hadn't driven. Suddenly a car pulled up and the door flew open. An angry face appeared in front of her.

"Damn it, Sue," Chris said, his voice hot with anger. "What are you doing wandering around out here?"

Sue looked up. Her face resembled that of a deer trapped in the headlights of an oncoming car. She stammered. "I, uh, was just tired of waiting inside. It was stuffy."

Chris shook his head in disbelief. "Stuffy? I told you to stay around people. Damn it! This Macdow is playing for keeps. Tonight I held my own against those Sith things and they still slaughtered six people. Two of them worked for their own boss."

Sue acted as though she were sickened by the news, but inside she was angry. *So Chris had been the reason why they hadn't experienced the offering?* His fight with the Children had prevented the Children from accepting the congregation's tribute to the Dark Mother and her Children.

"Get in." Chris was still hot. It was unlike Sue to be

so careless of her well-being. She was taking chances that were not only unnecessary but damned foolish. He put the car in drive and took off.

"What's wrong with you, Sue? Why are you acting so stupid about this. My God, they could've nabbed you from the parking lot and I might never see you again."

"I'm sorry, honey, I just, I don't know what's wrong with me lately. I'm not thinking clearly."

"Well, you damned sure better start," Chris said, trying to tone down his anger, but barely succeeding.

"I, uh, I will."

Chris pulled out of the parking lot and headed home. An indistinct itching began to skip through his system. He recognized the feeling and pressed the gas pedal to the floor. The sun would be coming up soon.

As Chris drove further away from the hospital, the events of the evening began to drift into Sue's subconscious mind. The congregation's influence retreated as the mechanism of secrecy began to take effect, so that Sue could function without drawing suspicion to Sisters of the Faith. The collective mind of the fold had planted in Sue's thought processes a mental command that prevented her from recalling any of the assembly's activities in her conscious mind until her indoctrination was complete. At the time of completion, all remnants of her personality would be submerged in her subconsciousness, where the knowledge of the fold of the Baobhan Sith now lurked. It would take one more night under the congregation's influence to complete her brainwashing and immerse all traces of Susan Blaze into the subliminal regions of her mind so that she no longer posed the threat of revealing the operation at Sisters of the Faith. The words of her husband came into focus.

"I'm worried about you Sue. You're acting, well, kinda weird."

Her mind cleared and she met his concerned gaze. "I'm fine. I've just been working a little too hard. I told you before, I have a lot of new responsibilities. My mind is so preoccupied. I mean if I make a mistake somebody might die."

"That somebody might be you if you aren't careful. I can't tell you enough how dangerous this situation is."

"I know. It's just that my job is very stressful."

"Well, if this is what we can expect from your new job, I wish you hadn't taken it," Chris said flatly.

"Sisters of the Faith is the best hospital I have ever worked at," Sue said, believing the lie that tumbled from her mouth.

"That may be so. But it sure is clouding your judgment on your personal well-being."

"I'm sorry." She smiled weakly.

"I just want you safe."

She kissed him and suddenly felt very afraid. But the fear vanished in the next moment. She sat back in the seat and closed her eyes.

Before she knew it, Chris was parking the car in their garage and they were getting out of the car.

"Come on. I need to get inside. The sun will be up any minute."

Sue got out and followed her husband into the house.

Chris took Sue in his arms. "Sue, I love you more than anything in the world. You've got to be more careful. The situation is even more dangerous than it was with Rakz. Macdow controls people and these Sith things. He can strike day or night."

"Okay, I'll be careful. Is Brand coming today?"

"He should be here any minute. I have to go. Be alert and don't do anything unless Brand is with you."

"I won't."

Chris kissed her and hurried into the dark room. He

undressed and got into bed just before the sun came up and sent him into the land of the dead.

Sue realized that she was hungry, so she went over to the refrigerator to get a bite to eat. In the back of the fridge, she saw the bottles of blood that she kept there for Chris. She stared at them and a snatch of the church service came back to her, then disappeared. She felt cold and realized that she had been standing with the door open for the past ten minutes. She went into the living room, sat in the dark and wondered if she was going crazy.

Chapter Ten

1

Malcolm Stephenson dragged his weary body down the wharf. He had spent the early morning and most of the afternoon going through the records of the building permits licensed in Dade county for the past three years. At about four o'clock, he'd found the one he was looking for and he left the county building to go to the Marina so that he could get some sleep. With the information he'd gathered, he knew that he and Chris had a long and dangerous night ahead.

Malcolm stepped off the pier and onto the deck of his thirty-foot wooden-hull boat. The boat was old and the engines didn't work, but Stephenson didn't use it for recreation, only as a place to stay. The boat was registered to another man so that Stephenson couldn't be traced there. He paid the owner the rent in cash one month ahead of time on the stipulation that he would remain anonymous. The owner had no problem with that arrangement since it included a clause that stated that he could evict the tenant immediately if he didn't make the payment on time. The DTF agency didn't even know that he was living there. They thought that he was staying at an apartment complex in Hollywood. He hoped that all his precautions would protect him, since Macdow now knew he was alive and in the city.

As he began to get undressed for a short nap, Malcolm couldn't shake the feeling that something awful was about to happen. He pulled his shirt over his head and tossed it into his laundry basket. He slipped out of his pants and into a pair of shorts then lay in the small single bed. He clasped his hands behind his head and closed his eyes to think.

Despite the good news that he now knew the location of Macdow's current lair of evil, the ominous sensation didn't leave him, but lingered like a vulture over roadkill. Malcolm just knew that something terrible was going to happen and there wasn't a thing he could do to stop it.

2

Sue stood in the darkness. The bird heavy in her hand. Slowly she raised it above her head. The black room was silent. Sue's arms trembled from the weight of the bird as she held it for a moment above her head.

"No," she said her voice soft and pathetic.

The glass shattered as Sue threw the heavy marble sculpture through the window of Chris's room. She watched as the sun's rays shot through the fragmented window pane, trapping Chris in their power. Chris lurched up shouting her name as he screamed and began to shrivel and crackle like a piece of meat dropped on the hot coals of a grill. His face blackened and cracked. His flesh began to smolder and flake off the bone. He reached out to his wife and croaked, "Help."

Sue saw the astonished, frightened expression on his face and felt herself laughing. She could hear others squealing with laughter as well, but when she looked around the room no one was there. The laughter was in her mind. She could hear the deep laugh of Dr. Charles and a high-pitched giggle that had to be young Dr. Argyll. Sue felt her stomach cinch up with convulsions as she continued to laugh and watch her husband die. The laughter slowly perverted into screams as her rebellious subconscious won out over the collective consciousness of the Sith for a moment and she realized what she had done. It was this screaming that had caused her to wake up. She looked around the room and saw that it was still afternoon. Chris was still in the sleep of death and wouldn't wake for another hour.

There was an abrupt rapping on her door. It startled Sue, and sent her heart rate even higher. The knocking was followed by a muffled voice shouting.

"You okay in there, Sue?" Ryan Brand said. Hearing her scream, he had rushed to the door, gun in hand.

Sue sat up in bed. "Oh, yes, just had a dream."

"Must've been a bad one."

Sue tried to maintain her composure. "I'm fine now. Sorry to have scared you."

"Wasn't scared, just ready."

"Thanks, Ryan."

"My job," he said, then walked back into the living room to clean his pistol.

Sue remained in bed, frightened for her husband's life. She sensed that the dream was a portent of the future, and she needed to warn Chris of the danger.

As she got up, the fateful dream began to fade quickly into the subliminal realm of her mind. She had one last thought before the mental mechanism of the

Baobhan Sith banished her memories of the dream into the nether regions of her brain. If she didn't tell her husband what was happening at the hospital, Chris Blaze would die.

3

Chris woke up with a start, his lungs filling with air. He immediately got dressed and hurried out the back passage and to the front of the house. He wanted to be sure nothing had happened to his wife during the day. She was a constant worry to him, especially with the way she'd been acting. He entered the house and saw Brand sitting on the couch watching the television. He nodded as Brand waved.

"Where's Sue?" Chris asked.

"I think she's getting dressed," the bald man said as he pointed to the bedroom.

"Everything okay today?"

"Not peep one."

"Good."

Chris looked over at the refrigerator, and his stomach ached for what was contained there.

"You can take off, Ryan," Chris said, his hunger burning in his gut.

"Sounds good," Brand said with a shrug. Boredom and he were constant companions that day and he wanted to end the friendship as soon as possible. The private eye got up and clicked off the television. He walked toward the door. Chris followed him outside to his car while they talked.

"So Sue was all right today?"

"Sure, slept most of it," Brand said with a casual wave of his meaty hand. "Had a bad dream, but that was it."

"Nothing else happened."

"Nah, quiet as a church mouse. Not peep one."

"Good. Well, have a good one," Chris said.

"Oh, I will. Got a date tonight," Brand said straightening an imaginary tie.

"Anybody I know?"

"You remember Lisa?" Brand said, making an hourglass shape with his hands.

"The redhead you used to date?"

"Yeah. We're trying to get back together."

Chris smiled. "Well, good luck."

"You do remember her then," Ryan said, referring to her bitchy attitude—a fault he could forgive because of her killer bod and sexual overdrive.

Chris smiled politely at the attempt at humor. He didn't feel like laughing.

"Want me tomorrow?" Brand said opening the door to his car.

"Yeah. Same time," Chris said leaning on the open door.

"Boy, if this job keeps up I'll be able to treat Lisa like the snob she is."

"I hope it doesn't." Chris said solemnly.

Ryan realized the joke was out of place. "Sorry, Chris. No harm meant."

"I know. I'll see you."

"Yeah."

Ryan Brand got in his car. Chris closed the door for him and waved good-bye. Brand tossed a salute and backed out of the driveway while Chris went back inside the house.

When he stepped into the foyer, he saw Sue standing by the refrigerator. She stared into the icebox lost in thought.

"Can't make up your mind?"

"Huh?"

"Dinner." He pointed into the refrigerator.

"Oh, yeah," she smiled and closed the door.

"So how are you?" Chris said, concerned about her behavior of the early morning.

"I feel great after getting a good day's sleep."

"Glad to hear that. You had a bad dream, Brand said."

"Dream? I don't think so."

Chris knitted his brow as Sue took a bottle of apple juice out of the refrigerator and went into the living room. She sat on the couch. She could see Chris open the fridge and grab a bottle of blood. He poured it into a thermos and started drinking it.

The phone rang, startling her.

"I'll get it," she said.

Sue got up and went to the phone.

"Hello?"

"Sue, this is Dr. Charles."

"Hello, Doctor."

"Sue, I have someone here that wants to talk to you. Is your husband there?"

"Yes."

"Don't answer questions with anything but a yes or a no. Understand?"

"Yes."

Sue heard a pause of silence as Dr. Charles handed the phone to the man.

"Sue, this is the Father."

A surge of excitement flowed through Sue's veins when she heard the Scottish accent of Colin Macdow. She felt honored to be speaking with the Father.

On the other end of the line, Macdow concentrated on controlling Sue's mind. She had been at the hospital

326

long enough for him to maintain control over her through his voice, but the command would only last about ten minutes before the built-in mind mechanism would shut down her thoughts about the Baobhan Sith. She had that much time to obtain the information he wanted her to get. Either he or Dr. Charles could draw out that knowledge once she got to the hospital that night.

"I wan' ye to listen. The Destroyer has taken your husband and tricked him into helping his cause. Did he tell ye aboat last night?"

"Yes," Sue said looking over at Chris who was watching her from the couch.

"Then ye know Stephenson has corrupted him against us. I want ye to find out where they are meeting so that we can stop the Destroyer from preventing the birth of the new generation. Will ye do this?"

"Yes."

"Good. Ye can tell us about the meeting when ye get to work. The Father loves you." Macdow hung up.

Sue smiled as she did the same.

"Who was that?" Chris asked.

"Dr. Charles."

"What'd he want?"

"That's what I wanted to talk to you about." She took his hand. "I'm sorry about the way I've been acting. I've just been really tired lately. As a matter of fact, I'm going in early today to get some blood tests. I think I may have anemia." She forced a laugh. "Now that sounds about right. A vampire whose wife is anemic. Have you been taking any sips while I'm asleep?"

"No," Chris said, warming to his wife's attempt at humor. This was more like the Sue he knew.

"Listen, I want you to stop worrying about me. If the

327

blood tests warrant it, I'll take some time off."

"You'd better."

Ask him about the battle last night. "So what was that you were telling me about last night? A fight or something. What happened?"

Chris explained to Sue about last night's confrontation with the Baobhan Sith and his introduction to Malcolm Stephenson. He also told her what Stephenson had told him about the legend of the Baobhan Sith.

"I'm meeting with Malcolm at Miami Marina at twelve tonight. He lives there on a boat."

"Don Johnson, Jr."

"Yeah," Chris laughed glad that Sue was acting normal again. "Anyway we're going to try and come up with a plan to stop these things. I want you to stay at work until I come get you. I don't want you alone for one minute."

"I'll be fine. You take care of business. I'll wait for you to come get me inside the hospital. I might even go to the service again. There's always a crowd there."

Chris smiled. "That'll work. Just don't get born again. We said we didn't want babies."

"You know I'll never be a mother. Besides that, if we did have kids they might have little fangs and it'd be hell to breast-feed them."

Chris kissed her. "I'm glad you're back to your old wise-ass self. I swear that some of Reggie Carver has rubbed off on you."

"I did notice a brown smudge the other day."

Chris laughed and then remembered that his partner was missing. His laughter died. "Damn, I wish that joker was here to fire a comeback at you."

"Still no luck finding him?"

"No. But McNally told me Reggie was alive and that they had him someplace in Miami. Stephenson says that he might find out the location today."

Sue felt a twinge in her gut. "Really?"

Chris nodded. "I hope he does—then we can end this thing."

"Yes," Sue said.

She had to get back to work and tell the Father of the meeting. She almost started to prod Chris in that direction when he rendered the attempt moot.

"Well, let's get going," Chris said. "I want you to get checked out thoroughly. Maybe you should take some time off if the tests are positive."

"I plan on it. I hate feeling this way."

"Not more than I do." He kissed her. He didn't notice that she flinched ever so slightly.

"Will you go into my room and get my jacket? The beige one. I want to eat a little something before we go."

"Sure."

Sue smiled as she watched her unsuspecting husband go back into the bedroom. Then she went into the kitchen to get something to eat. She knew she had done well. She had even managed to summon some of her sense of humor to allay his fears of her mental condition. The Father would be pleased. She didn't give any thought as to what would happen to her husband as a result of her information-gathering. The notion didn't even cross her mind.

Chris came out of the bedroom carrying her jacket.

"Thanks," she said, as she took it from him, slipped it under her arm and headed out the door. The information Chris had given her began to sink slowly into the mental abyss of her subconscious. By the time she got to the hospital she had no recollection of their conversation. But after meeting with Dr. Charles, she would recall all of it and set the wheels of death on an inexorable path toward Chris Blaze and Malcolm Stephenson.

4

As he unlocked the door of his office, Chris felt strong fingers grip his bicep.

"We need to talk to you, Mr. Blaze," the thin man in the shiny black polyester jacket said, as Blaze turned to face an FBI badge. The man was accompanied by a muscular black man with a solemn look on his face that emulated the movie screen's version of the stern FBI agent. The skinny white man spoke first.

"Carlson, FBI. This is Special Agent Mark Ahed."

"What can I do for you, Mr. Carlson?" Chris asked, knowing that they were investigating the incident at Monkey Jungle. He wondered how they got his name so fast.

"Where were you last night at around ten o'clock?"

"I was right here, why?"

"You got anybody that saw you?" Carlson's eyes narrowed into slits of doubt.

"No, my partner's out of town. I was working late on a missing-persons case."

"Do you know Mark McNally?" Mark Ahed said.

"We've met at the DTF headquarters. But just briefly. What's this all about?"

Carlson frowned and looked over at his partner and nodded.

"We need you to come with us, Mr. Blaze. My boss would like to talk to you," he said in a gravelly voice inconsistent with his thin frame. The voice had a put-on sound, as if he was forcing his voice down an octave or two. He jabbed a finger at Blaze, motioning for him to cooperate. Chris had worked with his type before in the department. Small and lean with a chip on the shoulder that would make Famous Amos envious. They were always trying to prove that they were tougher than they looked, even when such action was unnecessary. Jake Carlson was that kind of cop. He grabbed Chris by the arm.

Blaze shook him off. "Look, I'm . . ."

Ahed grabbed Chris's hand and forced it behind his back. Chris didn't resist. The spinning clicks of the handcuff signalled that the other cuff was secure.

"What the hell is this all about?"

"Mr. Blaze, you're wanted in connection with the murders of several DTF agents. We have reason to believe that you were in league with Mark McNally who was, as you probably know, a bad penny," Ahed said as he frisked Chris for weapons. "He gives Marks all over a bad name."

"You don't need these cuffs," Chris said, with a huff of disgusted weariness. He didn't have time for this delay.

"Just procedure," Ahed said. "We'll take them off later."

Blaze protested. "I have to be somewhere in an hour. It's a very important lead in a case I've been working on."

"Well, you're going to miss it," Carlson said in that same phony gruff voice he'd used before. He tucked his gun back into his shoulder holster.

Chris had to decide what he should do. Should he let these two FBI men take him down to their headquarters and wait for them to check up on his story? Or should he snap the cuffs and make his meeting with Malcolm? It was a meeting that he couldn't afford to miss.

"Am I under arrest?" he asked.

"No."

"Then why the cuffs?"

"Precaution. You are a suspect in a grisly multiple-murder case. You used to be a cop. Wouldn't you cuff you if you were me?" Carlson said, with a smug expression on his face.

Blaze nodded, tired of fighting the inevitable. He decided to let them take him down to the station. He figured that he could use his powers to get into the mind of his interrogator and tell him what to say. With an hour and a half left before his meeting with Malcolm Stephenson, he figured that he had time to extricate himself from the sticky situation without arousing undue suspicion. If he broke the cuffs and got away, he would become a man wanted by the FBI and only add to his troubles. And how could he explain snapping a pair of tempered steel handcuffs like they were twine?

"All right, let's go." Carlson said, after his partner finished the frisk.

The two FBI men led Chris out to their cruiser and helped him into the back seat. Ahed got in and started the car.

"Hit it, Mark," Carlson said, as he swung into the passenger's side by gripping the edge of the car's roof.

The agent pushed down the accelerator and they were off to their headquarters, where Special Agent Harley Givens waited to question Blaze.

5

Sue walked down the silent hall feeling good about herself. She had a buoyancy of step that revealed her sense of pride. The information that she had just given Dr. Charles would enable the Father to stop the Destroyer from causing trouble for the Children and would allow him to bring her husband into the congregation. Dr. Charles had told her that Chris would be captured and brought to the chapel to receive the indoctrination ritual so that he could become one with the Baobhan Sith. That news filled Sue's heart with happiness. Once Chris was a part of the church, they would be able to enjoy a loving and contented relationship again. She smiled, unable to contain her jubilation. Humming a tune that she'd heard on the radio on her way into work, she passed a couple of nurses on the way to the emergency room and merrily greeted them. They returned her salutation with knowing smiles on their faces.

Sue stopped and took a drink at the water fountain. Up ahead, she saw Macdow and Dr. Charles talking. She could tell that the Father was pleased. Colin saw her out of the corner of his eye—he turned and smiled.

Sue felt her heart jump at the attention given her by the most revered man in the congregation. She had a drip of water on her chin that she wiped off with the palm of her hand. A blush tinted her cheeks. Macdow's smile remained as he winked, and then walked with purpose away from Charles. She figured that he was on his way to the meeting between Chris and Stephenson—a conclusion that pleased her. Soon Stephenson would be dead and Chris would be a member of the fold. Life was wonderful.

6

This sucks, Blaze thought as he followed special

333

agents, Carlson and Ahed, down a long corridor that led to the interrogation room. He glanced at the clock on the wall and saw that a half hour was already eaten away from his time table. Agent Ahed opened the door and was greeted by a huge man about six-feet-six, and three hundred pounds of muscle. Harley Givens smiled at the black man whose sturdy six-one, two-forty frame was dwarfed by the giant.

"Good job, Mark," Harley said to the black man as he patted him on the shoulder. He gave a quick nod to Ahed's skinny partner who looked like a spindly sixth grader compared to Givens. "Carlson," he said tersely.

Chris got the feeling from the giant agent's use of Carlson's surname and the curt nod that there was a mutual dislike between the two men. And he was right. Carlson hated Givens simply because he was an awesome physical specimen, and Givens despised Carlson because he was always trying to be the tough guy even when the situation didn't warrant it.

"Hello, Mr. Blaze, sorry about the cuffs." He looked at Carlson with disdain and nodded to Ahed to remove them, which he did.

"Have a seat, Chris. Can I call ya Chris?" the giant agent said, as he twisted his moustache between Texas-sized fingers. Givens was a son of the Lone Star State— he'd served a hitch in the Texas Rangers before joining the Federal Bureau of Investigation.

"Sure," Chris said, liking the big agent immediately. He reminded Chris of Burly Fayer, the late private eye, whose name shared billing with them at their firm as a tribute to his courage in the Rakz case.

"Chris, I'll get straight to the point. Your name and Mark McNally's name were found on Len Singer's desk with the notation 'follow for meet the tenth.' You know what that means?"

"Well," Chris said as he stared deeply into the huge man's eyes and hoped that his plan would work. "I'll tell you."

"I ha' a job for us to do," Macdow said to the two Children. He had just received the news from Dr. Charles regarding the meeting between Chris and Malcolm. Sue Blaze had done well.

"A job?" Mary said smiling coyly. She knew what the Father meant.

"It's something I'm sure you're ginna love."

Glynda added her grin to that of her sister. They thirsted for the kill. Last night's failure to kill Blaze and Stephenson only served to fuel their bloodlust. They craved the hunt, loving the violence of the capture of their quarry and the sounds of bones breaking as the they stomped and ripped them apart. Fresh blood tainted with fear was the best-tasting kind.

For so long, they had been the hunted ones who had had to hide from the Destroyers. Decade upon decade, century upon century, the clan of Stephenson relentlessly hunted them down. The Sith spent their time hiding and feasting on victims provided by the Father and the congregation, but the victims were trussed and docile. There was no challenge, no sport. No thrill of the kill that they had enjoyed for so many years.

But then five years ago all that changed when Colin Macdow had killed the man they'd believed to be the last of the Stephensons. After his murder, they'd thought they'd finally achieved security.

For the past five years, they had been able to hunt

freely on special nights, stalking their victims and then taking them in an orgy of blood. But now it seemed that their freedom had been an illusion, as another Stephenson had been pursuing them all the time. Had they known that fact they would never have been so careless about their activities; Drucinda would still be alive and they would be in no danger of discovery.

But they could correct that mistaken assumption tonight. Tonight they could tear the heart of this young Stephenson's chest and suck it dry.

"Come wi' me," Macdow said, gesturing toward the door. "We ha' things to do."

The two women grinned, got up and followed the Father out the door and into the hallway.

8

Chris was pleased when he saw Malcolm standing under the lights of the dry dock's storage area. A gray trail of smoke curled from the cheroot clenched between Stephenson's teeth. Malcolm glanced at his watch as Blaze hustled to the tall man and stood beside him.

"Sorry I'm late, Malcolm. I had a little run-in with the Feds about that business last night. They found a note on Singer's desk about my meeting with McNally."

Malcolm shook his blond-haired head. "My turn to apologize. See, one of our guys, Joe Dustin, suddenly remembered a meeting between you and McNally, so we figured you were in this together. Then we got a call from the curator at Monkey Jungle to confirm that McNally was one of our boys and if it was safe to give him a key to open the place that night. I put two and two together and wrote the note to Singer."

"Thanks," Chris said sarcastically. The vampire PI hadn't known that his hypnoptic suggestions were short-term until Stephenson mentioned Joe Dustin's recollection of Blaze's meeting with McNally. He made a mental note not to forget the new information regarding his powers.

"So how'd you get out of it?" Malcolm asked, curious as to how Blaze got to the Marina as swiftly as he did. He knew how the FBI operated and it was not on the quick side.

"Well, I have this certain ability . . ." Chris explained how he had the power to hypnotize others.

Malcolm was impressed. "So you used telepathic powers on this agent Givens?"

A smiling Chris nodded. "I had him believing that I was undercover for the DTF and only Singer and one other agent knew about it. I told them that I was the one that left that note for Singer and I even had him call my number at home and pretend like he was talking to the other DTF agent who confirmed what I had said."

"I wish I could do that with informants."

Chris continued, "I had Givens so hooked that he almost made me believe that he was talking to someone. One of the other two agents in the room ate it up. But the other guy had a hard-on for Givens and kept butting in. I had Givens come down on him like bird shit at the beach."

Malcolm laughed. Chris was full of surprises, adding another unexpected asset in Stephenson's war chest against the Clan of Dow.

"The whole thing took a couple of hours, but Givens finally let me go."

Malcolm shook his head. "Damn. Can our luck get any worse?"

"Tell me about it," Chris replied, punctuating the sentence with a sigh.

"Well, I'm glad you're all right." Stephenson said, patting Chris on the shoulder. "I'd almost given up on you. I just came out here to wait. That boat was getting me claustrophobic."

Chris smiled. "So did everything work out today? Did you find out where this place of evil is?"

"I think so. I checked into all newly constructed buildings and their owners for the past three years. Macdow's pattern in the past has been to set up a new church and enlist the unlucky bastards that attend services as worshippers of the Dark Mother. He uses an ancient form of mind control to suck them in— probably similar to what you're able to do, only he works on a larger scale. As the number of people grows, so does the mind of the congregation. It becomes one giant brain so to speak. With each addition to the congregation, the mind grows in power and the time of indoctrination shortens. Each new member takes less time to become one with the Baobhan Sith."

"So there might be hundreds of followers by now?"

"Yes. First, this mind control affects the subconscious. At this point, you still have control of your actions outside of the church, where the collective mind isn't powerful, but you aren't consciously aware of what is happening at the church. You may dream about the Baobhan Sith and the events of the past involving them, the things in your subconscious, but when you're cognizant you can't remember anything about the Sith or the congregation. Then as you are more exposed to this giant mental force . . ."

"Jesus this is weird."

"Like a vampire detective."

338

"Touché."

Malcolm continued. "So the more you're exposed to this force, things begin to flip-flop. Your conscious mind is taken over by the Sith and your own personality is hidden in the subconscious so that the only time you can access it is through your dreams or hypnosis. Your waking moments belong to the cult of the Baobhan Sith. It's a damned insidious business."

"No shit. So what's the place you found?"

"I found a new building permit under the name of Sithco."

"Macdow's little joke," Chris said without humor.

"Yes. Anyway I discovered that he's a majority stockholder in Sisters of the Faith Hospital here in the city, and I believe that's where his latest congregation is forming. A hospital would be perfect because . . ."

"Wait a minute," Chris said, interrupting Malcolm. "Sisters of the Faith?"

"Yes, it's another one of Macdow's little jokes. He means the Baobhan Sith . . ."

Chris gasped. "Oh my God . . ."

"What? What is it?" Malcolm said, catching the alarm in Chris's tone.

Blaze rubbed his forehead as if it pained him. "No wonder she's been acting so strange."

"Who?"

"My wife."

Malcolm's eyes widened. "She works at Sisters of the Faith?"

"Yes, and I told her we were meeting here."

It was Stephenson's turn to be alarmed. His voice rose to a near shout. "Oh no! The Prophecy of the Second Genesis!"

"What?" The sudden declaration confused Chris.

"Do you and your wife have sex?"

339

"What?" Chris said—the incongruity of the question increased his confusion.

"Sex, damn it! Do you and your wife have sex. It's important."

"Yes, but . . ."

"Chris, the Book of the Banished Ones says that a woman of the dark side will give her body to the Dark Mother and then couple with the head of the clan in the century of twenty."

"And then?"

"And then she'll give birth to the Baobhan Sith three at a time until she is used up and dies."

Thoughtfully, Stephenson crushed his bottom lip between his fingers and thumb, then released it as he continued, "It all makes sense. The kidnapped people will be used as blood donors to supply the baby Sith with nourishment until they can hunt for themselves. A hospital's perfect for that."

"You're saying Sue will be the one they'll use to give birth to these monsters."

"Yes."

"So how do we fight these things?" Chris said unable to stifle the urgency in his voice.

"First, we'll need this."

Stephenson slipped an amulet with writing on it around Chris's neck.

"And then we need to take some of your . . ."

Suddenly, Stephenson's face exploded as the slug from a silenced .45 tore into his eye. He spun and fell to the ground, dead before he touched pavement. Chris reeled from the shock of three slugs that crashed into his ribs. He went down, but was quickly back on his feet.

Suddenly, the air was filled with shrieks as the Baobhan Sith, Glynda and Mary, came rushing out from behind a pallet of crates and attacked. Mary caught the stunned Blaze with a vicious kick that drove him slamming into the concrete wall of the warehouse. The impact left a series of cracks in the brick. Chris scrambled up and met the woman's charge with a hard punch to her face. The punch knocked her backward about six feet. She screeched, trying to damage Blaze's ears. Chris didn't hesitate but struck again before her screams had a chance to affect him. Driving his fists into her face and chest, he pummeled the creature with super speed. The dull smacks of his fists on her flesh defiled the quiet of the night with their nauseating rapidity.

But Blaze's attack would not last, as the other Sith, Glynda, caught him in the side just under his ribs with a sharp cloven hoof. Blaze reeled from the blow and spun away as the foot slashed at him again.

Mary's swollen bruised face rapidly mended as she disappeared in the shadows behind the warehouse to complete her healing and replenish her energy.

Glynda sought to maintain her advantage, but miscalculated on her lunge at Blaze. Chris stepped back, and, using her own force against her, he delivered a punishing fist to the back of her neck. A crisp snap sounded and the back of her head touched between her shoulder blades. She fell to the ground, paralyzed. With her neck bent in a U shape, her head touching her spine, she stared at Blaze with hatred in her emerald eyes. Her head snapped forward with a sickening crackle as the vertebrae began to knit together.

Chris heard rapid clopping footsteps behind him, turned to stop the charging Sith, but was too slow. Mary hit him square in the chest with unbelievable force, driving him into a stack of crates. He hit the collection squarely in the center and the heavy crates tumbled down on top of him in a rumbling mass of sound. Thousands of pounds of material fell onto the vampire's body, pinning him to the concrete floor.

"Shit!" Chris moaned. The weight of the boxes was pressing against his chest and legs. He couldn't move. No leverage. His superior strength was of little use under the avalanche of wood and steel. The only part of him that was exposed was his head. He couldn't get the load off him. It was too damned heavy. Chris looked up and saw a red-haired man standing over him.

"Mr. Blaze, we meet a' last. I'm Colin Macdow." He held a pistol in his hand. "Nice shot, don't ye think?" He motioned with his head toward the fallen Stephenson.

"What are you going to do with my wife?" Chris growled.

"Ah, she's ginna be the most honored woman in the congregation. I want to thank ye for your contribution."

"You bastard," Chris shouted struggling against the crushing force of the boxes.

Colin glanced over at the Children. Mary helped her sister to her cloven feet, while Glynda's neck continued to sound like crushed cellophane as it repaired. Mary picked up the dead Malcolm and tore his shirt off his body. She helped her sister to reach the man's chest. Glynda's tongue shot out of her mouth, stabbing into Stephenson's chest just under the nipple. She smiled as Mary squeezed the dead man and pumped a torrent of blood into the greedy mouth of her lampreylike tongue. The fresh blood would speed the healing.

"Leave some for the offering," Colin shouted. He laughed and looked down at the struggling detective.

"Not like the movies, eh, Mr. Blaze." He pointed at the dead Malcolm. "The fearless expert of the occult

342

does'na save the day and the hero does'na get the girl."

He shook his head as a look of disappointment touched his eyes. "I'd love to put a stake through your heart, but that would mean moving all these heavy boxes and we could'na do that. But I suppose the sun will ha' the same effect on you as it does on the Children."

Chris snarled as he tried to extricate himself. The boxes would not be moved.

The Scotsman tipped an imaginary hat. "I'll leave ye to it."

Macdow tucked the pistol into his holster and strolled over to the feasting girls. "Come on, lassics. Bring him along. We'll use his skin to make a robe for the Dark Mother. I'm sure she would love it."

9

Chris struggled to no avail as he attempted to lift the heavy boxes off him. Even with his supernatural strength, he could not budge the crates. They were simply too heavy. There was a small gap between them so that Chris could move his arms but he could get no leverage. Chris pressed against the weight of the boxes as he tried to relieve some of the pressure that was constricting him. He knew that the poundage of the crates couldn't kill him and yet their crushing force was enough to prevent him from escaping their trap.

The pulverizing weight of the boxes harkened his mind back to the time of his youth, when his father would hold him down while they wrestled and he was unable to get away. Chris felt the deep inner panic that had come over him at those times and it swept through him like a fire through a field of dried wheat. He struggled mightily against the boxes but they were simply too massive.

As he struggled to get away, Chris felt the inner clock in his body telling him that very soon the sun would be coming up, and with it would come his agonizing death. He had to get out of the situation.

He began to struggle even harder, using his considerable strength and power. His panic was driving him to attempt unprecedented feats. Slowly, the boxes began to shift, and Blaze felt he might escape the situation. He continued to mount his offensive of vampiric strength against the sheer weight and force that had pinned him to the cement floor.

The boxes creaked as they moved ever so slightly.

Just a little more power. He gritted his teeth and pushed.

The wood of the crates groaned against the force.

A little more.

Harder.

Harder.

Almost there.

Suddenly there was a loud snap like a gunshot, and the box that Chris was using as a lever shattered, sending the weight of the other boxes down upon Blaze and pinning him to the floor again. He tried to get free, but had spent too much energy. He was worn out. It was the end. There was nothing else to do but wait for the killing rays of the sun.

10

The congregation gasped when they heard the news come from the lips of the Father himself. The Prophecy of the Second Genesis had been fulfilled. One of their number was to be the Mother Host. All the women glanced at each other, each hoping that she would be the one chosen. A murmur swept through the crowd, as anticipation of the selection filled the atmosphere with electricity.

Colin Macdow stood on the altar smiling. Beside him stood Glynda, her tongue attached to the chest of the small boy cradled in her arms. She drank the warm blood from his body, an obscene parody of a mother breast-feeding her child. She needed the fresh blood to complete the mending process of her neck. Blaze's blow had been a severe one and had done considerable damage, and the Father had not let her take too much from the Destroyer.

Macdow rubbed the boy's hair and looked out to the group. "One of you will bring the new generation into the world, a new world of science and technology where men and women no longer believe in the powers of the Dark side. A world where we will be safe to raise the new Children." He gestured broadly, speading his arms out to signify the hospital. "We have a home where they will be safe until their time. We have the nursery where blood runs thick and plentiful and no child shall lack for food. And now we have the Mother Host."

The crowd hushed to a dead silence as Macdow lifted a palm toward Sue bidding her forward.

"Come, Susan Blaze. Come and join the Father."

Sue felt an exhilaration like none she had felt before. The crowd around her exploded with cheers. Argyll kissed her. Hands patted her on the back. Hugs. Kisses. Sue got up and floated on a wave of sound to the pulpit. At that moment all remnants of her own personality dissolved. She was to be the Mother Host of the Second Genesis and that was the most important thing that she could be. Nothing else mattered. Sue took her place at the side of Macdow who smiled gently and kissed her hand.

"And now I have another surprise. An offering to the Dark Mother that is the most loving gift we could give."

He motioned to Mary who was standing in the shadows of the waiting room. She smiled and carried in the body of the dead Stephenson. His ruined face stared at them through a lifeless opaque eye.

"I give you . . ." Macdow shouted as he raised his hands in a grand gesture . . . the last of the Destroyers."

The crowd gasped, then broke out in wild applause. People whooped and hollered, making the congregation sound like a rock-concert crowd appealing for an encore.

Macdow kissed Sue on the lips and offered her the sacrificial cup shaped like the tongue of a Sith. It was hollow, with one end round and sharp, the other tapered into a bowl. She took it and without hesitation plunged the sharp end into Malcolm's heart. The thrust made a scraping squishy thump as it separated ribs and struck the inert fist-sized muscle.

Macdow smiled and pushed Stephenson's chest to force what blood was left in him to pool in the bowl-like end of the sacrificial tool. He sipped from the bowl and then, with a drop of blood in the corner of his mouth, smiled and gestured to the congregation to get up.

"Come, taste the red life of the Destroyer. Enjoy. Soon we will begin to take our rightful place in the world." He licked the blood from the corner of his mouth like a lion after a kill.

As the congregation began to move up to the altar,

346

Macdow leaned over and whispered in Sue's ear. "Sue, we have much to do to get you ready to accept the Dark Mother. After the communion we will begin."

Sue nodded, dipping a fingertip in the blood to her last hope for salvation. As she tasted the cold blood, she completely forgot about Charles's promise that Chris would be captured and become one with the Baobhan Sith. The notion that they would live happily together as members of the church vanished. She could care less about the man whom she married. She was the Mother Host and that was all that mattered. Christopher Blaze, husband, lover and friend, no longer existed in Sue's mind. And soon the sun would see to it that he no longer existed at all.

11

Chris had thought that his vampiric powers would enable him to get out of almost any situation but this seemed not to be one of them. His powers were useless—his great strength ineffectual. The tingling in his body was telling him that the sun would come up at any minute and reduce him to a pile of charred ash. With grim irony, he thought of how his powers could alert him to his impending doom but could do nothing to extricate him from the crates.

And Chris started to laugh—great peals of laughter. It skittered across the cement floor, and reverberated against the sides of the warehouse. Laughter to the left of him. Laughter to the right of him. Laughter all over. It seemed to be the cackling of a madman with no hope, but this was not the laughter of a man trapped by hysteria and panic. This was the laughter of a man relieved.

What was I thinking?

My vampiric powers, of course.

He started to concentrate, and his form began to change. He grew smaller as his arms grew thin and a membranous tissue began to connect his side to his arm. His legs started to shrivel and the boxes shifted. Smaller and smaller he shrank, as a coat of fine brown hair rippled and covered his skin. His ears pointed and crawled to the top of his head. His nose sunk into his face spreading out to form a flat pug nose. The boxes creaked but did not fall.

When he finished changing into a bat, Chris was able to crawl out from under the boxes through gaps too small for a man. He scrabbled across the concrete floor on clawed feet and membranous winged hands, chirping like the bat he had become.

Freed from his dilemma, he felt a warm buzzing soaring through his veins and knew that he wasn't out of the woods yet. Blaze took off, flying with all the speed he could muster as he tried to beat the rising sun.

His wings displaced the air in small gusts. His body tingled with a thousand pinpricks as the sun began to lighten the sky.

Faster.

Got to get home.

Faster.

It's almost time.

A cock crowed in Chris's mind.

The sky lightened a bit more.

Got to make it.

Wings slapped the humid morning air.

He saw his home.

With moments to spare, he made it to the sanctity of his house. He changed back into a man as soon as he hit the fenced backyard. He didn't even have to concen-

348

trate, as his powers just gave out. He opened the back door and stepped into the bedroom. He slammed the door shut. A cascade of relief splashed over him. He had made it to safety.

Suddenly a thought struck him that dried up the downpour of relief like a greedy sponge.

Sue!

If Sue was a member of the congregation, then she was a threat to him! Immediately he regretted coming home instead of finding a safe place to rest that day. What could he do?

Blaze quickly surveyed the room, then grabbed the heavy dresser and started to put it in front of the door, but before he could make it, his body went limp as the sun came up. Chris collapsed into the sleep of the dead. Sue would be home soon.

Chapter Eleven

1

Earlier that morning, at around six-thirty, Sue had called Ryan Brand from the hospital and told him that she wouldn't be needing his services that day because she was working the dayshift. She didn't want him showing up at the house and not finding her there. Most certainly it would arouse his suspicion of foul play and send him on a search for her. She didn't want that, so she told him the lie and he complied without question.

After completing the call, Macdow had taken her into his private chambers in the hospital and anointed her with ancient oils and read incantations over her body that would begin to eradicate all goodness from her so that she could withstand the presence of pure evil in the spirit of the Dark Mother. If this purge of purity wasn't performed, Sue would go mad, for she would be unable to deal with the vile thoughts that the Dark Mother would conjure—thoughts no human should ever have to contemplate. She would complete the cleansing that night by taking the ancient drug made from the root of the plant called eye of the Devil, or Devil's root, which produced hallucinations. Macdow would guide her through the trip, conjuring vile images as he conducted a final test of her mental condition.

When she got home at around noon, she had no idea that Chris was asleep in his room. She hadn't given her husband a second thought, as she was exhausted and excited from spending the morning in preparation to receive the Dark Mother.

As she lay on the couch, she closed her weary eyes. Within moments, she was fast asleep. She slept for six hours before her subconscious tried to rescue her from her horrid predicament.

In her dream, Chris was alive and trying to pull her away from the evil clutches of the congregation. Hands snatched at her, pulling, tearing her arms with their sharp fingernails. Her husband had his arms around her waist but couldn't free her from the army of hands. He pulled and tugged but she couldn't be liberated. Out of the corner of her eye, she saw two obscure shapes approaching. She tried to turn her head to see them more closely, but couldn't, as a sausage-fingered hand latched onto her hair. She tried to scream, but a bloody thumb stabbed into her mouth and dug a nail into the roof of her mouth. With the implausibility of dreams, she felt the skin under his nail tickle her tongue. She wanted to puke.

Cloven footsteps thundered as the advancing shapes came back to Sue's attention. She tried to see them. A pair of fingers gouged her eyes, blurring her vision. The footsteps hammered in her ears as if they were stepping on her eardrums. A huge blur rushed past her. Chris screamed and Sue heard a rumble like thunder. She turned and saw Colin Macdow laughing at Chris, who was pinned under a heap of crates. Her husband struggled against the crushing force of the boxes, but couldn't move them. Sue felt warmth on the back of her neck like a hot breath. She turned, expecting one of the Baobhan Sith to be breathing on her. She gasped when she saw that the sun was up. She heard a high-pitched howl and then a sound like bacon frying. She whirled around and saw Chris start to blacken and crack.

When she woke up, she was in a daze. She grabbed a flashlight, hurried over to Chris's room, and opened the door. She smiled with relief when she saw him lying there on the floor. The fact that he wasn't in bed didn't even strike her as odd. She was just glad that he was . . .

He was . . .

What?

He was . . .

She rubbed her temples as an electric worm slithered and sparked in her head. The worm crept over the synapses to her brain cells, slowly and then shutting down those that were connected to her subconscious. Her mind sputtered as she tried to remember why she had come in the room. She looked down at the prostrate body of her husband and she didn't recognize him.

He was . . .

What?

He was . . .

Who was?

As Sue's subconscious shut down, the consciousness of the Sith mind slashed the remnants of the dream into fragments of disconnected thought. Pieces of Chris flew off in all directions. Fingers were disconnected from his hands—arms and legs from his torso. She was once again one with the Baobhan Sith.

And this time when Sue Blaze saw her husband Chris lying on the floor, she smiled for a different reason. She closed the door to the room and went to find a hammer and a stake of wood.

2

Colin Macdow slept well. His dreams were filled with screaming babies with lips stained bloody red. Tiny hoofed feet kicked off their wool blankets. All of the babies had bright green eyes and blond hair. A baby cooed and flapped black wings as it partially transformed by mistake. They would learn. In the dream the babes danced around a fire, burning in the chest cavity of Malcolm Stephenson. The Destroyer stared at the flames flickering above him and moaned in anguish. The logs of the fire were the bones of the detective, Blaze. His black partner hung upside down with a beer tap attached to his heart, providing refreshment to the guests at the dance. They filled skull cups with his blood and sipped daintily at the red fluid. He heard screams and turned to see Sue Blaze push another baby from her womb.

He woke up from the dream, feeling better than he had in years. Everything was as it should be. The Prophecy had been fulfilled and now once the Mother Host finished with her purification, Macdow would summon the spirit of the Dark Mother and begin the Second Genesis of the Baobhan Sith. No one could stop him now.

3

Sue stood over the inert form of her husband. In her hand she held a pointed wooden stake that had been propping up an orange tree in the backyard before becoming an instrument of murder. The sharpened point of the stake touched Chris's chest just over his heart. Voices screamed in her mind for her to drive the stake home with the hammer.

She held the hammer poised to strike, but she couldn't force herself to slam the heavy mallet down onto the head of the stake.

"No," she groaned as she struggled with every fiber of her being to stop the relentless cries in her head—they were shouting for her to murder her husband. The hammer rose upward.

From somewhere deep in her subconscious, the real Susan Blaze had risen from the dead and made her presence known. The collective mind was shocked by this resurrection, because they had never felt a love so strong, and had never lost control after a subject had been a member of the assembly for as long as Dr. Blaze. They realized that she was going to fight. Fight them for Chris's life.

"No, please," she cried.

The voices notched up another decibel level as they continued to screech to her. *Kill! Kill!*

The hammer rose again.

Kill!

"I love him," Sue shouted, trying to drown the voices in her head.

Kill him!

Sue felt the hammer rising up as if her arm had a mind of its own and was alive and out of her control. She watched it as it seemed to move by itself. She tried to stop its upward path but found that all she could do was watch it go.

"No, please." A hot tear spilled out and rolled down her cheek. The voices continued to chant inside her mind.

Kill!

Kill!

Fulfil your destiny as the Mother Host. Fulfil your destiny. You are the Mother Host of the Second Genesis!

354

Suddenly, a great weight lifted off Sue's mind as something inside her snapped. She felt lightheaded. Almost giddy. She smiled as she broke free from the influence affecting her consciousness. She looked down at her husband on the floor and her smile broadened.

She realized that they were right. What was this puny love compared to spawning an entire generation?

Kill him!

"Yes," she said happily as she raised the hammer above her head.

Chris's eyes opened just as Sue was swinging the hammer. Instantaneously, he reached up and stopped the hammer before it found the mark. He grabbed the stake from her hand and snapped it in two.

"What the hell are you doing?" he shouted, his voice thick with disbelief.

Sue turned and ran from the room. Chris got up and followed after his wife. He caught her and spun her around then screamed as she flashed the cross she had brought with her, just in case.

"Get back," she hissed, her face contorted in a mask of hatred.

"Sue, what's wrong with you? Put that thing away."

"Get back!" She shouted again, while taking a step toward Chris.

He drew back unable to do anything against the power of the cross. In those dreadful moments, Chris knew for sure that Sue was under the influence of the Baobhan Sith.

"Sue. No."

Realizing that she had failed, Sue grabbed her keys from the counter and took off, running into the night. The cross would only keep the vampire at bay not kill him. She needed to get to the Sisters of the Faith.

Chris tried to stop her but Sue thrust the cross at him

355

again. He recoiled from its power.

She got into their car and tore out of the driveway. She had to get to the hospital.

Chris changed into a bat and to reserve energy landed on the roof of the car, clutching the edge of it with his clawed hands. The wind whipped at him as Sue sped down the road toward the highway that led to the hospital.

When she got to the hospital, Sue got out of the car and ran into the front entrance. She had to tell the Father what had happened. She clutched the cross in her hand, expecting Chris to appear at any moment, but he had other plans.

Chris fluttered from the top of the car to the roof of the sixth floor of the building. He saw a man standing at a door leading into the hospital. Chris flew directly at the man, and then changed into human form in midair.

Stan Willem heard the beat of wings in the air, looked up and saw a man flying at him. He reached for the cross that Macdow had given him, but the flying man squashed him into the wall. Willem's world flashed white and then faded into darkness.

Chris hogtied Stan's arms and legs with the man's shirt and gagged him with another strip of material. Seeing the butt of a gun protruding from a shoulder holster strapped to the guard's chest, Blaze took it and stuck it in the waistband of his jeans. He moved Willem out of the path of the door.

The vampire grasped the knob and twisted. As he suspected, it was locked, so he reached into the man's pocket to retrieve the key. A sharp sensation burnt his fingers as he touched the cross in the man's pocket.

"Shhhit," Blaze hissed as he recognized the pain, withdrew his hand and tapped the man's pocket with the end of his shoe. He heard the jingle of keys against

356

the cross and knew that they would be of no use. He took the knob in hand and twisted it with all his power. The gears of the lock gnashed and then popped. Chris opened the door and stepped inside, finding himself at the top of a stairwell. He saw a door marked "off limits without hospital permission." He broke the lock on the door and stepped into an empty hallway. He had to find out where the hell Reggie was and find out fast. Now that the others knew about his vampirism he would need help from a human who was not affected by the cross. He looked up at the directionals for a clue as to the whereabouts of the blood donors. It was there, Malcolm had said that Carver was probably being held captive. As he read the list of locations, he saw a name on the directionals that could be one of Macdow's little jokes. The directional arrow beside the name pointed toward the east wing. It was there that Chris would find "The Nursery."

4

When Sue arrived at the hospital, the staff already knew of her failed attempt to kill her husband, and they took her directly to the Father. Colin Macdow realized that time was short. He knew he had to complete the purification as soon as Sue stepped into his room. He had already posted guards at all the entrances. He was figuring that the detective, Blaze, was probably on his way to the hospital. He instructed Sue to undress. After a couple of nurses anointed her with powerfully scented oils smelling vaguely of clove and beef tallow, Macdow gave Sue the ancient potion of Eye of the Devil and started her on the journey.

Sue reeled from the powerful effects of the elixir. It was a strong hallucinogenic. Colin Macdow acted as a malevolent Timothy Leary as he guided Sue on a trip into hell. The unspeakable visions that she witnessed were appalling and yet she felt a tingle in her sex from the pleasure of seeing them. Men penetrating sheep as they stabbed the poor creatures with sharpened sticks. Woman fondling and kissing each other as they castrated rows and rows of men stretched across racks. The women tossed bloody testicles into a pile, where little baby demons played with them. Other sights were too horrible to put into words. The smells were of sulfurous gas and putrifying flesh. The thick scent of blood. Stagnant waters laden with filth. It was the most dreadful place ever imagined; the world of the Dark Mother.

5

A steel hand struck Darrel Wako in the temple as he stepped out of the security door leading to the nursery. Chris caught the two bottles of blood that Wako had just drained from an unfortunate victim before they hit the ground along with the guard. He slipped off the top of one of them and drained it. He needed the energy. He kept the other bottle, setting it down beside the door. He had a suspicion he would need it.

Chris hauled the body of the nurse into an open storeroom. He grabbed one of the sheets from the shelf, rolled it and wrapped it around Wako's hands and feet, so as to secure him. He stripped a roll of white tape across the unconscious nurse's mouth. He hoped that the collective mind spoken of by Stephenson would not miss another one of its members.

Wako's assistant, Skip Alstern, heard the clatter and came out to investigate. In seconds, he joined his boss in the land of dreams and was resting in the closet, bound and gagged. They were the only two hospital staff members in the nursery, while all others prepared for the Trinity of Consummation.

Quickly Blaze entered the doors to the nursery. He had to find Carver.

6

Myra Lee helped Sue put on the light green gown that Macdow had given her to wear for the ceremony of the Possession. The former wife of Chris Blaze—divorced by a power greater than any justice of the peace—smiled as she ran her hands down the front of the gown, enjoying the softness of the fabric. Her stomach tingled in anticipation of the coming of the Dark Mother. She was ready. Very soon the Father would come to escort her to the chapel so that the congregation could summon the Dark Mother and she could take possession of the Mother Host. The mating would take place, and the seeds of the Baobhan Sith would take root in her womb and begin the new generation.

7

Reggie felt someone tugging on his arm and thought that the nurse had come back for another pint of his blood. It had been some time since they had taken any blood from him and he was beginning to regain some strength. But every time he started to recover, the nurse would appear to take another pint from him. He didn't know how many more of these pints he could give before he simply ran out of the will to live, and joined the others as mindless zombies. He felt the needle pierce his arm. He looked over, and through bleary eyes saw someone standing beside him. The lack of a white outfit on the body struck him with the force of a sledgehammer. He focused his eyes and saw Chris Blaze kneeling next to him draining his blood. *No, he wasn't draining him, he was . . .*

"Chris," he said weakly.

"Just lie there. I'm giving you a transfusion."

Chris let the blood flow back into Reggie's veins. He had learned the procedure during his time as a policeman, so that he could be of assistance to the paramedics. He had never had to use that knowledge until now.

The bottle drained quickly as Carver grinned at his partner. "Damn, it's good to see you."

"I hate to say it but you're a sight for sore eyes, too."

"Cliché, but appropriate. Do you mind?" Reggie said, cocking his head toward the bonds.

"Oh, shit. Sorry." Chris snapped Carver's nylon straps with his powerful hands. They broke with a loud pop.

"Man, that feels good."

Chris looked up and saw that the bottle was empty. He detached the needle from Reggie's vein. "We need to get out of here, Reg."

"What about the others?"

"We can't help them yet."

Chris helped Reggie stagger to his feet. Carver was weak from the loss of blood, but not as bad as Chris had thought he'd be. The transfusion would help. Good thing his captors kept him well fed so that he would produce healthy blood cells.

"Let's go."

Chris slipped his shoulder under Reggie's arm and propped him up. The two men hurried out of the room and started for the hallway.

"Where're we going?" Reggie said.

"To make plans. We're going to end all this tonight."

"I hope you're right."

"Here," Chris said, handing Reggie his pistol.

"Damn that feels good," Reggie said grasping the pistol in his hand. He went to tuck the gun into the waistband of his pants, but realized he was in a hospital gown. "Man, I need to get some clothes. I can't shoot vampire bitches with my ass hanging out the back of this gown."

"That gun will only work against the human side of the family."

"Family?"

"I've got a lot to tell you, Reggie. And I'll do it fast. Let's go in there."

Chris led Reggie into a dark room. Chris could barely see, even with his powers of vision. He saw what looked like a bed over in the middle of the room against the back wall. In the darkness, Carver was just a silhouette with two eyes and teeth.

"Damn, turn on the light," Reggie said, hating the dark, since he was unable to see anything.

"No. That might draw attention."

Reggie nodded dully. "Right. So tell me what's happening."

Blaze began to tell Reggie the story of the Baobhan Sith as related to him by the late Malcolm Stephenson. When he finished, he could hear the weariness in his partner's voice.

"Wait a sec," Reggie said scratching his head. "Sue's gonna let this Dark Mother bitch into her body so Macdow can make bacon and create more of those vampires with the horse feet?"

"Yeah, three at a time."

"Shit. So what the hell are we going to do?"

"That's a damned good question."

"I hope you got a damned good answer."

"I wish I did. Malcolm was about to tell me how to kill them when he was shot."

"Poor bastard."

Chris remembered Reggie's trip to California. "So what did this Kargosi guy tell you about the Sith?"

"Damn! That's right. I forgot all about that shit."

Quickly, Reggie recounted the information that the fat man had told him about the Sith, and they compared notes.

"A stake will kill them as well as the sun?" Chris asked, to confirm what Carver had said.

"That's what we figured. As for that 'vein of the dam' stuff, I dunno, maybe running water."

"Maybe."

"So what the hell are we gonna do? We can't let Sue get possessed by some monster."

"I know," Chris said grimly.

"Let's get out of here. I need to find something to wear."

Suddenly a side door to the room opened and a hiss filled the air. A low growl. A giggle. The patch of skin on Reggie's neck twitched as the door slammed shut. He turned toward the source of the sound and saw two pairs of green eyes blazing in the darkness of the room. He didn't know it, but he and Chris had stumbled into the room that safeguarded the Baobhan Sith.

"Go for the door, Reggie," Chris whispered.

"I can't see shit. You'll have to get it." Reggie cocked his pistol.

"So, Mr. Blaze," Mary said, as she saw the reverse image of Chris in the Sith's infrared vision. To their eyes in the darkness, Blaze looked black and Carver white. "Ye dinna die after all."

"But ye will tonight." Glynda added.

Chris hustled for the doorknob as Mary clopped across the room and grabbed him. But Blaze was too

362

fast. He flung open the door before she could stop him. The bright white light from the hallway spilled into the dark room.

Momentarily blinded, Mary stepped back but she quickly recovered. Chris took advantage of the brief opening and slammed a fist into her face. She flipped backward from the force of the blow, landed and slid a few feet on the floor.

Reggie ran toward the door as Glynda made her move for him. She remembered his part in the slaying of her sister and wanted revenge. If he hadn't been out there spying on them that night, Dru would still be alive. She hissed as she lunged for the black man, only to be met by a powerful body instead. Chris drove his forearm up under her chin, and lifted her two feet off the ground. She backed away and was joined by her sister. Chris covered Carver as he went out into the aisle and saw three men barreling down the hallway toward him. Carver popped off two shots. One slug took the kneecap off one of the men, spinning him like a top. The other missed, and went pinging against a steel cart.

While the injured man howled in pain, the other two men ducked into a room and pulled thier pistols.

"Oooh, my knee!" Terrence Morton screamed, as he clutched his injured leg.

"That lucky black bastard," Donald Kidd hissed to Ed Maise as the two huddled in the doorway. They had felt the danger in the collective mind and come running.

Reggie ducked back inside the door, bumping into Chris.

"Fancy meeting you here," he joked grimly.

"How many are out there?" Chris asked as a bullet splintered the door jamb.

"Three, but I put one of them down."

363

"Look out, Reg!" Chris shouted as he saw Mary flank him and go for the black detective. At the same time, Glynda went for the vampire private eye.

Carver tried to run, but was stopped by a powerful hand.

"Are ye going somewhere, black boy?" Mary said in a sweet voice.

Carver brought the pistol up and jammed it in her eye.

"See ya, bitch."

He pulled the trigger and Mary's head rocked back. She dropped Carver, who scampered away from her.

In the dim light from the hallway, Reggie could see that she was smiling. The grin sent chills up his spine.

"Ye shouldna have done that," she said, with a gooey mess sliding down her cheek. Without seeming to move, she was by Carver's side, grabbing the gun and wrenching it from his hand. She gleefully tossed it across the room.

Chris got lucky when Glynda tried to kick him with her cloven left foot. When she made her move, he went down on his knees and swept her right leg causing her to fall to the ground.

Carver was not so lucky.

With a swipe of her sharp nails, Mary tore Carver's gown then stuck out her tongue. Carver could see the sharp teeth that formed a circular mouth at the end of the dark red tongue. She imbedded the teeth in his chest over his heart. Carver screamed as he felt the teeth boring a hole into his flesh. "Chris! Jesus, help!"

"Noo!" Blaze shouted as he sped toward Mary slamming into her. Carver spun three hundred and sixty degrees in the air like Miami Dolphin, Nat Moore, did in that famous tackle they always showed on football specials. He landed on the hard floor, but was not badly hurt. Chris and Mary's momentum sent them crashing through the drywall.

Chris was up first, but then went down, as Mary's sister, Glynda, slammed him with a kick to the back. She'd come up behind him when she felt the men outside making a move toward the door.

The two men, Maise and Kidd, entered the room and started firing their pistols into the darkness. Reggie dove for cover behind the Sith's bed. Goosedown flew, as lead projectiles tore into the mattress. He saw his gun under the bed and crawled to get it.

On his back, Chris rolled out of the way as Glynda's hoof slammed against the floor. The Sith tried to strike again, but two shots slammed into her head. She howled from the pain and fell to the ground. A head shot was always painful. Reggie turned and fired at the two men at the door. The gun clicked. Empty.

They heard the clicks and smiled. They moved forward, firing as they did.

Mary was still trying to remove a splintered stud that had its nails embedded in her shoulder pinning her to the shattered wall. Chris flashed to his feet and grabbed Mary's arm. He tore her free, ripping the flesh of her shoulder as he swung her like a baseball bat into the two men who were firing at Carver. The force of the swat dislocated Maise's shoulder. The injured hit-man slammed into Kidd, whose pistol flew out of his hand.

"Ye damned bastard," Mary howled, as she grabbed the door jamb to stop another swing and tore a sharp piece of wood from it when Chris yanked her off and slammed her into the two men again. One of her hooves caught Kidd in the temple and his world crumbled into black dust. Maise's shoulder separated even further. In agony, he would present no further danger.

"Look out!" Reggie shouted as he saw the recovering Glynda go for his partner. Carver moved to stop her, hoping to slow her up so that Chris had time to prepare. He tired to tackle Glynda, but it was like tackling a couple of pistons of a ship's engine. She went right through him.

Chris released his grip on Mary, but was too late to meet her sister's onslaught. Glynda caught him and pinned his arms behind him. The fierce Sith held him, as her sister prepared to strike with the makeshift stake created when she'd ripped off the door jamb.

"Kill him, Mary," Glynda shouted, her skull snapping and popping as the bone mended. Grey bits and blood clung to her blonde hair. She held Blaze with a fury begot of pain.

Helpless, Reggie watched as Mary thrust the sharp wood toward Chris's heart. But Blaze was stronger then Glynda. He broke her hold and was able to avoid a thrust to his heart. The wood slammed into his throat, striking his carotid artery. The blood that Blaze had ingested earlier spurted from the wound. It slashed two red lines across Glynda's face. She howled, letting him go as the blood burned her flesh. Fearing the power of the red life, Mary backed away from the vampire and changed her target to the black man. But Carver had also been hit with the geyser of blood and she couldn't touch him. It was as if he had a impenetrable barrier around him.

The Children realized that they were momentarily defeated. Frustrated, they howled and then, to the horror of Blaze and Carver, took out that frustration on the two members of the congregation that had failed to help them. In a bloody show of strength, they tore the men's arms out of their sockets and gouged their eyes into bloody holes with stonelike fingertips. The savagery was short, and they soon disappeared down the hall dragging the men behind them. Mary crushed the head of the third man in the hallway with a stomp of her cloven foot and added him to their revitalizing diet.

"C'mon," Chris said, confused by the sudden stoppage of the assault. The wound on his neck mended as he spoke. "We need to find somewhere to regroup."

"Hold on a sec." Reggie said standing there half-naked in the torn gown. "I think I figured out what that clue about the vein of the dam meant."

"What do you think?"

"Well, when you were fighting that chick she stabbed you and your neck did an Old Faithful routine, your blood got on her sister and some of it got on me. It burned the shit out of her and when the other one tried to get to me, she couldn't. I think it's because of the blood. I think the vein of the dam is the vein of the *damned* as in 'damned to the life of the undead.' Remember? 'The vein of the damned will protect.'"

Yeah," Chris said smiling at the discovery of a new weapon. "Come to think of it the same thing happened to me when I fought the Sith at our office. She bloodied me and it must have touched her."

Chris's big grin was catching. Carver smiled broadly as well. "I think your blood will protect us from the Sith."

"Wait a minute. Remember the second part of the message Kargosi translated," Chris said urgently. "Bless the red life and the Sith will die?"

"Yes."

"This amulet Malcolm gave me before he died. It has writing on it and—what did he say before he was shot? 'We'll need this and' . . . What else?" He struggled to remember Stephenson's exact words. And then it came to him. "'We'll need this and some of your' . . . Your what?"

"Blood." Reggie said confidently. "He must have been going to say blood."

"My God," Chris said, smiling with realization born

of knowledge, "I think I have a plan."

"Well, let's hear it."

"First we need to find a couple of things we'll need. Some tubing, a couple of empty bottles, a syringe—and then we need to locate the chapel."

"Okay. Do you think we can find something for me to wear?"

Chris looked at the remnants of the gown. "I hope so. And then I'll tell you what I have in mind."

8

Macdow came into the room and kissed Sue lightly on the lips.

"You look beautiful," he said, pulling her close and kissing her again.

Sue smiled.

"Are you ready?"

Sue nodded, her face as blissful as the Madonna's.

At that moment, the two Children entered. Their dresses were stained with the blood of the ill-fated men of the congregation. Their faces told a story of failure.

"What happened to ye?" he said.

"We found Blaze in our room," Glynda said. "The black man was with him."

The reference to her husband didn't even raise Sue's eyebrow. She couldn't care less.

Macdow erupted. "We ha' guards posted with crosses at every entrance to the hospital. How could he get through to the sixth floor?"

"I dinna know," Mary said.

"So what did ye do when ye saw them?"

Mary recounted the confrontation to the Father, and she explained how Blaze's blood had been spilled and had its effect on them. She finished the story with a pained expression of her face. "Should we have stayed to fight?"

"Aye. The blood of the damned can protect, but it's only for a short time. Perhaps five minutes, and then the fresh air will kill the unholy taint that exists in his blood. It must be blessed for it to last, but they could'na have known that. It was just luck."

Mary looked at her sister. "We dinna know or we would have stayed on and killed them."

Glynda nodded.

Macdow shook his head. "It does'na matter now, we must get on wi' the ceremony. I will'na post guards on the outside of the chapel so that if and when they come, we'll trap Blaze inside with the power of the cross. Then you can kill him and his black friend and honor the Dark Mother with their heads."

The Sith smiled. "I wonder if they know about the length of time the blood will protect them?"

Macdow returned the nasty grin. "Let's hope not."

9

Reggie felt sick as he dabbed the blood of his vampire friend on his body. They had taken all of Blaze's blood, three pints worth, and now Carver was preparing himself in case the Sith attacked again before he had a chance to bless the blood. He also had to find the hospital's blood supply so that Chris could replenish his strength.

Finished with applying the mystical protection, Carver slipped on the surgical coveralls that he'd found in a storeroom. He held the amulet Chris had given him and read the strange words carved into its hard wooden face over the pints of blood. Although he guessed at the pronunciation of the old Scots language,

369

when he finished with the blessing, he'd noticed a slight darkening of the blood. Reggie thought it a good sign.

He looked across the doctor's office and saw Blaze sitting on the corner of the desk. The vampire appeared to be sick. He clutched his gut and bent over. He slapped the makeshift transfusion kit, sending it crashing off the big desk where they'd performed the blood withdrawal.

"Chris, you okay?"

Chris's chin almost touched his chest as he moaned with pain. The violence coursing through his veins boiled from his gut. Ripples of agony jarred him. His stomach felt like a volcano erupting inside his body. The pain was molten hot. He began to see visions of death and destruction. Hundreds of people dying as he flew through their midst tearing open veins and arteries with fang and claw. His victims screamed as he drained them dry. Blood splashed the screen in his mind. The carnage was atrocious. And it all felt so damned good.

"Chris, man, what's up?"

Suddenly, Chris looked up. His face was twisted into a mask of vampiric rage. His fangs dripped with saliva. His eyes were completely white.

"Mother fu- . . . Chris, man, chill."

Reggie knew immediately that they had made a big mistake in taking all of Blaze's blood. They had figured that they would need all the blood they could get, but had not considered the consequences. Now those consequences were staring Carver in the face with blank white eyes and sharp stakelike teeth.

"Chris, now be cool. It's me Reggie."

Blaze growled and sprang to his feet with uncanny agility.

"Chris," Reggie said, backpedalling and motioning with his hands for the haywire vampire to stay back. "Chris, don't do it. Fight it."

370

Blaze smiled, baring his fangs, and took a step forward.

This blood on me ain't working either, Carver thought dismally as Chris chuckled and took another step forward.

"Shit."

Blaze howled as a bolt of agony lanced his stomach. He leapt into the air and landed beside Carver. The vampire grabbed Reggie by the arms and lifted him off the ground.

"Chris, for God's sake!"

Chris smiled and bit deep into Reggie's neck.

"Oh shit!" Carver screamed as he heard Blaze sucking his blood. He tried to break the grip of the vampire, but his efforts were futile. He began to feel weak. Chris had lost control and was going to kill him.

"Help me! Chris, stop!"

Slowly the ache in the vampire's guts disappeared, replaced by a bliss he had never known. Chris was in rapture. Euphoria. The blood flowed hot and heavy into his aching veins. It tasted like the most luscious ambrosia in the world, a world colored red and wonderful.

Reggie groaned and whispered, "Please, stop."

Chris floated on the sea of blood. Calming. Beautiful. The satisfaction was indescribable.

"Chris, for God's sake, stop."

Blaze heard a weak voice in his mind. It sounded familiar, and he realized what he was doing. He pulled away, but when he saw the blood trickle from the wound, the delicious blood, he buried his fangs into Carver's neck again. The pleasure was just too great. He had to have more. He drank.

As the aching hunger vanished and utter fulfillment replaced it, the real world came back into focus. Blaze saw the diplomas hanging on the wall above the desk

371

blur then sharpen. The empty bottles of blood appeared opaque, then became crystal clear. He gazed around the room, confused for a moment. Then he discoverd the limp body of his best friend in his arms. Reggie Carver was dead.

10

The pews of the chapel were completely full. The entire congregation was in attendance. A sense of excitement swirled in the air like mist on the Scottish moors of Macdow's homeland. The air crackled with anticipation of the momentous event that awaited the congregation; the Trinity of Consummation, the three events that signalled the rebirth of the next generation of the Children: the Summoning of the Dark Mother, the Possession of the Mother Host and the coupling of the Father and the Dark Mother Incarnate. Once the Trinity was completed, the first of the Children would be born in three months. The short gestation period insured that many Sith would be born before the Mother Host died.

The lights dimmed, signalling the arrival of the Father and the Mother Host. The bearers of the three candelabras stepped through the side doors and led the way for Colin Macdow and Sue Blaze. The bearers were Dr. Gary Charles, Dr. Don Argyll and Myra Lee. The triumvirate surrounded the Father and his bride-to-be, bathing the couple in the orange glow of the multitude of candles. The Trinity was about to begin.

11

"Noooooo!" Chris bellowed as he cradled his dead

friend in his arms. "God, what have I done?"

He hugged the limp body of Reggie Carver and cried. Hot tears streamed down his cheeks. He hated himself for what he was and the terrible thing that his vampirism had caused.

He'd killed his best friend! Drained him dry.

Damn, I didn't stop to think. I knew that I shouldn't give in to the darker impulses and I didn't even consider what would happen. Now look what I did. Look!

He stared at the empty face of his partner. Carver's eyes were dull and his skin had a grey cast unlike the rich brown that it had once been. His mouth was slightly open, frozen in a plea for salvation.

Suddenly all the events of his recent past raced by Christopher Blaze and a dreadful understanding revealed itself. The evil face of Batiste Legendre, the man who had cursed him to this existence, loomed large in his mind's eye. He remembered the words of the curse that had made him a vampire and now he understood why Legendre had chosen to punish him with that particular hex. Nothing could be worse than what he had just done.

His mind flashed to his first meeting with the vampire. Yosekaat Rakz, who had tried to get him to drain another human being so that he could fathom the ecstasy. At that time he had resisted the temptation, instinctively understanding that such rapture had a price. But now! Oh God, *now* he had experienced that ecstasy. And yes it was the most wonderful thing he had ever known. But one hour of such bliss was not worth one second of the crushing despair that it had caused him.

His mind shifted as he saw the dabs of blood on Reggie's forehead and arms. The blood that was supposed to protect Carver from the creature of the dark side. He wondered why the blood hadn't protected Reggie? Was it because Chris was not the same as the Baobhan Sith?

The Baobhan Sith! His mind screamed, wrenching him from the past.

The Sith and Colin Macdow!

They had Sue!

Chris rocketed back to the present. His thoughts sped to his wife, who was in the grasp of Macdow and his brood. He saw her beautiful face. Sue! The woman he truly loved was in terrible danger. The sudden realization that Sue was about to take a step into the black world he had just visited, sent an electric bolt of panic through Blaze. He couldn't bear to lose her as well as his best friend. That shocking prospect triggered his rage, as all the events of the past moments overloaded his brain. All the things that Colin Macdow and his evil had caused, inflamed him into action. He had to save her!

Gently setting Carver's body down, he kissed him on the forehead. Blaze stood up, rushed to the door and yanked it off its hinges. His fury burned away all thoughts of the plan that he and Carver had devised. Only one thing was on his mind. He headed for the chapel to save his wife.

12

A cool supernatural breeze wafted through the chapel. It didn't move anyone's hair or clothing. It was intangible and yet everyone could feel it caress their skin with its cold touch. The Dark Mother was coming. A faint vision of her could be seen in the gleaming metal of the crest above the altar.

Colin Macdow stood at the altar and spread the sacred oil onto the naked body of Sue Blaze. He dipped

374

his fingers into the gallon vat and dabbed the oil on her sensually. She shuddered as he spread it onto her erect nipples.

The congregation watched, eyes open and mouths shut in awe. A stillness settled over them. You could hear a hair break in the silence.

A splintering crash erupted from the back of the chapel as the doors shattered into shards of wood. All eyes turned and the congregation saw Chris Blaze, eyes red fire, standing in the doorway.

Four men stood up and immediately attacked. The enraged vampire dispatched them with such speed it was as though they hadn't even moved. The only reminders of their assault were their broken bodies littering the pews.

"Sue!" Chris shouted in a voice so loud that those close to him had their eardrums shattered. Sue didn't move.

"Sue!"

Two women fell to the ground howling in pain from the decibel level of the cry.

Sue didn't respond.

Chris pointed at Macdow. "You bastard."

Macdow smiled and in seconds Chris was upon him. He had grabbed the Father by the throat, but he, himself, was seized by the two Baobhan Sith that were waiting in the shadows for him to appear. Mary and Glynda each grabbed one of his arms and twisted them free of the Father's throat.

Macdow's smile broadened as he pulled out the cross from his robe and wielded it against the vampire. "Ye should'na have come, Blaze. Ye canna stop us."

Chris snarled and tried to turn away from the cross, but Mary twisted his head toward the powerful icon.

Macdow helped the naked Sue get off the stone slab, and he handed the crucifix to her. She shoved it in her husband's face.

Chris recoiled, groaning at the potency of the cruifix. Suddenly, he remembered his plan and regretted not following through with it. His anger had made him careless . . . and most likely dead.

"Your wife tells me tha' a stake through your heart will kill you. I even understand tha' she tried to do it to you this afternoon. Pity she dinna finish ye then. But no matter . . ."

He motioned for Argyll to get the linen-wrapped package on the stone altar. The doctor did so, and unwrapped the parcel. It was a large mallet and a sharpened oak stake.

Chris's eyes widened. "Sue, for God's sake, it's me."

Sue smiled and slapped Chris in the cheek with the cross. His flesh sizzled, leaving a red imprint of the cruifix on his cheek. In that excruciating moment, he knew he was doomed.

Macdow pulled another cross out of his robe and handed it to Dr. Charles. The chief of staff held it toward Chris. The vampire felt his strength ebbing.

"Move him over to the altar," Macdow commanded.

Sue and Charles thrust the crosses into Chris's face and the Baobhan Sith began to maneuver him into position. He could do nothing to stop them.

As his wife and the man with the mole on his forehead drove him down onto the stone slab, Chris tried one last time to break through to his wife.

"Sue, help me. You can't do this. I love you."

Sue paused for a moment.

Chris thought he felt a change come over her. "Sue! I love you."

Sue looked at him, her eyes flashing recognition.

Chris whispered, "I love you."

His wife's mouth dropped open as if she suddenly realized what she was doing. She turned toward

Macdow, and then without warning, she stabbed the crucifix at her husband. She laughed.

The mocking laughter hurt Chris more than to gaze upon a thousand crosses as he understood that she was lost to him. His Sue was gone.

Macdow shook his head at the detective. "She's ours now."

He placed the stake over Chris's heart and held out the mallet to Sue. Killing her husband would be the final act in her removal of the good in her system.

Sue handed the cross to Don Argyll and took the mallet from the Father.

"Suc . . ." Chris said, knowing that he had lost.

Sue raised the heavy hammer over her head.

"No!" A voice shouted from the back of the chapel. All eyes turned toward its source.

In the shattered remnants of the doorway stood Reggie Carver.

Blaze shook off the shock of seeing his friend alive, and realized that he must not have drained him all the way. Perhaps in his state of total hunger, Chris's mind had tricked him.

"Chris!" Reggie shouted.

The diversion was all Blaze needed. He lashed out and kicked the cross out of Charles's hand while at the same time twisting his right arm from the grasp of the Baobhan Sith, Glynda. He rolled to his left, driving his fist into the side of Mary's head. She screamed and let go.

Chris turned and saw Carver slam into Dr. Argyll, knocking the cross out of his hand before he had a chance to use it on Blaze. The doctor's body careened into the dais, splashing the sacred oil all over him and Myra Lee, with whom he collided. The collision into Myra dislodged a couple of candles and one of them tumbled from the candlebra. Its flame touched the

377

volatile oil, igniting it quickly. Fire shot up Argyll's robe, obscuring his handsome face. He howled and spun into Myra Lee who also caught fire when the oil on her clothing ignited. Quickly both were engulfed in yellow-orange flames.

Carver turned from the blazing bodies of Argyll and Myra Lee. Their screams were appalling as they whirled about the altar trying to beat the flames out with their fiery hands. Reggie had wanted to set the wheels of the plan in motion another way, but now it was too late.

Abruptly, Carver was no longer there. Mary attacked Reggie, catching him from behind with a brutal kick that drove him off the altar and into the pews. Carver thought that Chris's blood would protect him, but it did nothing to stop the enraged Baobhan Sith.

As he landed in the crowd, a few of the assembly tried to grab him, but he broke away with ease. He leapt back onto the altar to confront Mary, a bad mistake. She met him in midleap and applied a crushing bear hug.

"Chris, help me!" Carver shouted with a grunt.

But his partner was in no position to help, as Macdow had managed to retrieve one of the crosses and had the vampire at bay once again. Glynda had Chris's arms pinned back. Sue picked up the stake and mallet.

Argyll spun around like a fiery top then crumpled to the ground, a flaming hulk of dead flesh. Rancid smoke filled the air. Myra Lee was already dead, burning like rubbish in a barrel.

Sue smiled when she saw that the two detectives had been stopped. Now she could take her place as the mother of the Second Genesis. She put the stake against Chris's chest.

Reggie coughed as the smoke from the burning

378

bodies filled the room. The heat toasted his skin. He looked up and prayed. It seemed that they had lost.

The congregation sat mesmerized by the struggle between the Dark Side and the Light.

Sue prepared to strike the killing blow, when the sprinkler system kicked on, due to the blazing bodies of Argyll and Myra Lee.

"Yes!" Reggie shouted as the water rained down. But his joy was short-lived when he saw that the water was clear. He'd failed to find the right pipes. They *had* lost!

Then he saw the liquid shift from clear to a pinkish color and he knew that he'd made the right choice. The bodies of Argyll and Mrya Lee sizzled as the water started to put out the fire that had killed them.

Suddenly, a terrible shouting shattered the air with its fury. Mary screeched in pain, and dropped Carver. She tried to run, but could only whirl in a circle as the rain pelted her. Her flesh began to melt.

Glynda released Blaze and began her own revolutions of death. She spun around so fast that pieces of her eroding skin flew off and slapped wetly against the faces of the mortified assembly.

Chris smiled as he realized that Reggie had completed the mission that they had devised. The black man had succeeded in getting the blessed vampire blood, the Blessed Red Life, into the sprinkler system of the chapel. And now it rained death down upon the Baobhan Sith.

Mary and Glynda had both stopped spinning and now stumbled around on the altar. Their flesh was oozing yellow blue gelatin. Mary's nose dropped off and landed on the floor with a splat. Glynda raised her arms, trying to stop the rain, but the tissue of her arm slithered down to her shoulders, collecting in a glob of slime. As the sprinklers continued their downpour of death on them, the slippery ooze slid off their bones.

Mary's eyes bubbled and exploded. She fell to the ground. Her sister fell on top of her and they melded into a sopping sludge.

Macdow howled with rage as he realized what had happened. All his plans were destroyed. There would be no Trinity of Consummation that night. No Second Genesis. No new generation of Children. And it was all because of Blaze and Craver.

"Ye fuckin' bastards!" Colin screamed as he thrust the cross into Chris's face.

Chris hissed and tried to shield his eyes, but was trapped by the stone table and had nowhere to go.

Macdow turned to get the stake to kill the interfering detective and saw Sue standing at the ready with the stake and the mallet. Macdow smiled.

"Kill him," the Father said, the evil grin twisting his handsome features.

Sue raised the stake and drove it home with the hammer.

Macdow's smile ripped open into a shriek as the stake pierced his chest and found his heart. Macdow stared at the stake for a moment and then toppled over the cross clenched in his hand. In the moment before death, he muttered a single word, "Come." Then he was still.

The death of the Baobhan Sith had freed Sue from the collective mind as, at the same time, it emancipated the congregation. The staff of the hospital began to come out of their stupor, and the chapel filled with screams as the people confronted the horrible scene. The moans of the injured were recognized and the medical staff's instincts took over as they began to tend the wounded people. Some of the staff hurried to call the police.

Chris took Sue in his arms and kissed her. "Thought I was a goner," he said smiling.

She returned his smile. "Don't you remember, the good guys always win." She kissed him with passion.

"Yeah, Blaze, we always win."

Chris and Sue turned at the same time and saw the grinning Reggie standing next to them.

"Reggie, man, I thought I killed you," Chris said clapping his friend on the shoulder. He was so happy to see his partner alive, he wanted to kiss him which he did.

"Hey, I'm not that kinda guy, Blaze."

"You're alive," Chris shouted.

"Of course, I'm alive. What do you mean?"

"I thought I drained you. Don't you remember?"

Reggie knitted his brow. "No, but . . ."

Carver's mouth fell open as he glanced up on the wall. He stared at the shiny metal crest of the Dark Mother above the altar.

"What is it, Reg?" Chris said as he turned and looked at the ornate crest. He saw the oddly shaped woman in the reflective metal.

"What's happening?" Sue cried. "Is the Dark Mother coming?"

Carver whispered, "Look at that shit."

Sue looked up and saw a distorted figure in the polished metal of the crest. It looked like a woman. Then she realized that it was a woman and that she knew her. The woman was Dr. Susan Blaze—she was the figure in the burnished metal shield. Then she realized that she was the only person reflected in the mirror. Neither Chris nor Reggie cast a reflection.

"Good God," she gasped.

"Reg," Chris said. "You're a . . ."

"I'm a vampire," Carver said with amazement touching his face. He felt his canines and confirmed the truth. "Holy shit, I am a mother humping Vampo-dick son of a bitch."

"Reggie, I'm sorry." the stunned Chris said. "God, I . . . I'm so sorry."

"A vampire," Reggie said, his voice thick with disbelief. "I am a vampire." He emphasized each word.

Sue touched Carver gently on the shoulder.

"Reg, I'm sorry," was all Chris could think of to say.

"Count Carver," Reggie said touching his teeth again. He was lost in the perfect shock of the moment. His whole life had changed in one brief instant of time. He would never see his face in a mirror again. A hunger would plague him for eternity. No longer would he feel the sun's warming rays against his skin. Reggie began to feel a strange tingling in his body. He wondered what was happening to him, when Chris answered his unspoken question.

"The sun will be up soon."

The stunned Carver turned to his partner. "Sun?"

"Yeah," Chris said, "We have to go home to my room. The sun can't touch us there."

"Your room, yeah," Reggie said dreamily. "We'll be roomies." He looked shell-shocked.

Chris turned to his wife. "Sue, stay here and make sure that everyone on the sixth floor is released and taken to a real hospital. There's about fifty or sixty or seventy people up there."

"I'll grab some people to help me. Take care, Reggie," she whispered as she touched his cheek.

"We need to get home," Chris said kissing his wife. "Come on, Reg."

As the disturbed fledgling vampire stumbled beside Blaze, he tapped his partner on the shoulder. "We're gonna be one helluva team, Blaze. Two bloodsuckers for the price of one." Carver's voice seemed disconnected from his body.

Blaze put his arm around Reggie. "Let's get you home."

382

Epilogue

Chris and Reggie woke up exactly at the moment that the sun disappeared from the horizon. It had been six weeks since they had solved the Vargas case. Diego Vargas was now San Miguel's new president and Maria was his first lady. Tomas Montoya was back to practicing law in Viera. The Sisters of the Faith Hospital was closed shortly after Sue's rescue from Colin Macdow. Carver had been transformed into one of the undead. Chris looked across the room and saw his partner. Reggie's face was contorted into a mask of rage. The black vampire hissed and clutched at Blaze with taloned fingers.

"Knock it off, Reggie," Chris said. "You can't scare me with that shit."

Carver's face relaxed back to normal. "You're no fun."

Blaze got out of bed and walked across the room. He tugged a pair of pants off the hanger and slipped them on. Carver was still in bed laughing but he suddenly changed into a bat and flew around the room. Blaze wished he had never bitten his detective partner.

As Carver flitted around the room, Chris could hear his partner's squeaking laugh. The man-bat buzzed the vampire's head and Blaze swatted at him. He opened the door and went into the living room.

Reggie changed back into human form. "Chris, where you going?"

"Away from you." Blaze said. "Man, once a joker always a joker, even when you die and come back as a vampire."

The black man laughed. "Save me a bottle of O-positive. You know it's my favorite."

Blaze smiled and shut the door on his best friend.

Life as a vampire was strange, but fun.